Also by Diane Jeffrey

Those Who Lie
He Will Find You
The Guilty Mother
The Silent Friend
The Couple at Causeway Cottage
The Crime Writer

Praise for Diane Jeffrey

'An engrossing, enthralling, intriguing thriller' **Liz Nugent**

'Compelling storytelling' ***Daily Mail***

'A thoughtful drama exploring an unlikely friendship'
John Marrs

'Bursts with suspense and intrigue with lots of thrilling twists'
Jane Corry

'Tense and twisty' **T. Orr Munro**

'A tense, gripping domestic noir that shows just how fast the dream of a new life can turn into your worst nightmare'
T.M. Logan

'Deliciously dark and suspenseful … A tour-de-force'
Alex Michaelides

'Pacy, twisty and full of shocks, all the way to the jaw-dropping finale' **S.E. Lynes**

'A scorchingly good thriller' **Lisa Hall**

'Brimming with tension, riddled with doubt and suspicion, insidious and compelling with a terrifying ending that had me catching my breath' **Sue Fortin**

'A thought-provoking and gripping read' **Roz Watkins**

'Heartbreaking and nuanced – with a clever twist but so much more than a thriller … beautifully written and gripping'
Catherine Cooper

'An addictive read' **Annabel Kantaria**

DIANE JEFFREY grew up in North Devon, in the United Kingdom. She now lives in Lyon, France with her husband and their three children, Labrador, cat and kitten.

Diane is an English teacher. When she's not working or writing, she likes swimming, running and reading. She loves chocolate, beer and holidays. Above all, she enjoys spending time with her family and friends.

Readers can follow Diane on X @dianefjeffrey or on Facebook /dianejeffreyauthor

A Mother Always Knows

DIANE JEFFREY

ONE PLACE. MANY STORIES

HQ
An imprint of HarperCollins*Publishers* Ltd
1 London Bridge Street
London SE1 9GF

www.harpercollins.co.uk

HarperCollins*Publishers*
Macken House, 39/40 Mayor Street Upper,
Dublin 1 D01 C9W8
This edition 2026

1

First published in Great Britain by HQ,
an imprint of HarperCollins*Publishers* Ltd 2026

Copyright © Diane Jeffrey 2026

Diane Jeffrey asserts the moral right to be identified as the author of this work.
A catalogue record for this book is available from the British Library.

ISBN: 9780008735609

This novel is entirely a work of fiction. The names, characters and incidents portrayed in it are the work of the author's imagination. Any resemblance to actual persons, living or dead, events or localities is entirely coincidental.

All rights reserved. No part of this publication may be reproduced, stored in a retrieval system, or transmitted, in any form or by any means, electronic, mechanical, photocopying, recording or otherwise, without the prior permission of the publishers.

Without limiting the exclusive rights of any author, contributor or the publisher of this publication, any unauthorized use of this publication to train generative artificial intelligence (AI) technologies is expressly prohibited. HarperCollins also exercise their rights under Article 4(3) of the Digital Single Market Directive 2019/790 and expressly reserve this publication from the text and data mining exception.

Printed and bound in the UK using 100% Renewable
Electricity by CPI Group (UK) Ltd

This book contains FSC™ certified paper and other controlled sources
to ensure responsible forest management.

For more information visit: www.harpercollins.co.uk/green

For Florent, my husband, my best friend, *mon amour.*
xxx

There is always another story, there is more than meets the eye.
—WH Auden, *Twelve Songs*, 'VIII'

A mother's love for her child is like nothing else in this world. It knows no law, no pity. It dares all things and crushes down remorselessly all that stands in its path.
—Agatha Christie, *The Last Séance*

Author's Note

A Mother Always Knows is a work of fiction and I have taken liberty with the North Devon geography to fit the needs of my story. There's no Holtleigh, Shallowcott or Brayworthy, although I hope that these made-up place names sound Devonian. South Lydacombe School is also a figment of my imagination. However, certain places, depicted in my novel, do indeed exist, for example, Barnstaple, Saunton Sands, South Molton and Lower Buryknoll Wood, although, as far as I know, no murder has ever been committed in these woods. Any likeness to any individual, Devonian or not, is purely coincidental.

Chapter 1

Carla

<u>NOW: SEPTEMBER 2024</u>

At first, the locals assume he has run away. With the exception of his mother, who has rung round everyone she knows, including me, no one seems overly concerned he has gone missing. His disappearance has been given only a fleeting mention in an online article for the *North Devon Echo Live* and has had no coverage at all, as far as I'm aware, on television. Even the police seem to be making only a token effort to determine his whereabouts. He's an adult, after all, having turned eighteen last October. Plus, he went AWOL only a few days ago. And locals never really expect anything sensational to happen in the small, remote town of Brayworthy, nestling on the edge of Exmoor, especially not during the month of August. Between you and me, I'm delighted he has disappeared and hope he doesn't show his face round here again any time soon.

All of this changes, of course, at the beginning of September, when a body is discovered.

Jo is the one who gives me the heads-up. My phone pings with her text as I'm doing the day's Quordle and drinking my first coffee of the morning. Joanne has been my best friend since school – the same school where my kids now go and she teaches mathematics: South Lydacombe. She's married to a police officer, which is, I suppose, how she was clued in before nearly everyone else.

I put down my cup and call her immediately. When she answers, I skip the formalities and get straight to the point. 'Do they know if it's … him?' I can't bring myself to say his name.

'No.' Jo knows who I mean. He's the reason she has texted me. 'I don't know any more than I told you in my message,' she says. 'A body has been discovered in the woods. The body of a male. Ian wouldn't say any more than that. He was on his way to the scene. I don't know if he actually knew any more than that when he rang me.'

'Who found it … him?'

'I don't know. A dog walker or a jogger, I imagine. I don't think the police were actively combing the area looking for him.'

'Which woods?'

'Lower Buryknoll Wood.'

'You have got to be kidding me. Is this some kind of sick joke?'

It takes Jo a few seconds to get it. 'Oh, I see,' she says when the penny drops. 'Joshua Knoll. Uncanny. It's probably just a coincidence. Listen, I've got to go. I've got a class at nine and I want to get in early. First day of the new school year and all that. Even after all these years, I get a bit nervous.'

'Sorry, Jo. I'm holding you up. Good luck! You'll smash it! You're the best teacher that school has.' It's sincere – I really believe it – but my voice sounds strained.

'Thanks. I'll do my best to keep you posted, Carla. Try not to worry. It might not even be him.'

'Jo, just one more—'

But she has ended the call before I can ask the most important question, although I doubt she knows the answer. Not yet anyway. *How did he die?* Jo's husband, Ian – DI Ian Rowland – is CID. *Criminal* Investigation Department. If he's in charge of this case, it doesn't look good.

I set down my mobile on the kitchen counter, having lost my enthusiasm for the word game I was playing before Jo's text was delivered. Sensing someone behind me, I jump and whirl round.

'Good morning, sweetie,' I say, as my daughter walks barefoot across the terracotta tiles to peck me on the cheek. How much of the conversation did she overhear? 'Did you sleep well?'

'Morning, Mum,' Iris says. 'Not too bad.'

I observe her as she puts two slices of bread into the toaster and flicks on the kettle to make herself a mug of green tea, her latest fad. She clearly doesn't know. She'll have checked her mobile, as she does every day now – first thing in the morning and last thing at night, and several times in between. She'll have scrolled through any new messages in her WhatsApp groups. She's looking for stuff that concerns her, not news of him, but she'd have seen it if there was anything.

The news will be out soon, though, and it will spread like wildfire, whether the body turns out to be his or not. I should warn her, in case. But what if it isn't him? She's been through enough. I don't want to panic her unnecessarily.

Before I can work out what to do, Olly saunters into the kitchen, looking scruffy in his school uniform, even though I washed and ironed his shirt and trousers and hung everything up in his wardrobe at the end of last term. The shirt is not tucked in, the trousers are creased and the knot in his tie, which hangs about halfway down his chest, could hardly be smaller or tighter. His blazer looks as if it has spent the summer holidays on the floor. It was his eighteenth birthday yesterday, but although he's tall and muscular, he still carries himself like a child: lanky and awkward, as if he hasn't quite grown into his body. He's grown out of his uniform, though. I bought the kids new shoes, but I should have bought Olly a new pair of trousers, too. He nods almost imperceptibly in my direction and sits down at the table.

'You need to lose the bedhead, bro,' Iris comments. She's right. His wiry, blond hair is standing to attention, as if he has just been electrocuted.

'Good morning to you, too,' Olly grumbles as he pours himself a bowl of cereal and adds milk from the carton, stopping just before it overflows.

Iris takes a seat opposite her brother at the large, wooden table and butters her toast. She chats to Olly about the teachers she has just found out she'll have for this school year. In the mornings, Olly's conversation is usually limited to monosyllabic words and grunts, but he's making an effort, for Iris's sake. She sounds cheerful and has painted on a smile, but I know she's dreading going back to school. She finished off the last school year studying from home, apart from one disastrous day when she plucked up the courage to go in to lessons. Going back properly and going in to school every day is a big leap for her.

Leaning against the worktop, I tune out their conversation and focus on the questions whirring through my mind. Should I tell Iris about the body in the woods? Is it Joshua Knoll? Assuming it is him, if he accidentally broke his neck falling into a ravine or something, it could be a good thing. Iris might finally be able to turn the page and move on to the next chapter of her life.

But what if his death wasn't an accident? What then?

I have to tell Iris. I'm not sure what effect Josh's death might have on her, but if he's dead, she needs to know. She needs to prepare herself. Just in case. Forewarned is forearmed. This may cause a major setback for her. If everyone is talking about Joshua – and they will be if it turns out to be his body – it will dredge up her ordeal all over again.

Just as I resolve to break the news to my children, chaos erupts in the kitchen. Cheddar, our golden retriever puppy, who was asleep in his basket, wakes up, gets overexcited when he sees Olly and Iris, and pees on the floor. Olly goes to load his dirty dishes into the dishwasher instead of leaving them on the table for once, but he drops his bowl, smashing it to pieces and splattering milk everywhere. Margo, my eleven-year-old stepdaughter, who ate breakfast long before the others, materializes in the doorway, on the verge of tears, ostensibly because she can't find her pencil case, but more likely because she's stressed about her first day in senior school. And my mobile blares out with an incoming call – no doubt from Daniel, my partner and Margo's dad. He has a demanding job – as a management consultant – and usually I'm supportive of his career, but I curse him under my breath for being away on business, on today of all days. And for calling at a bad time.

The bus stop is within walking distance, but by the time I've finished troubleshooting and clearing up the mess, we're running late. I bundle all three kids into the car and drive them to the school itself. We arrive seconds before the bell goes.

I need peace and quiet to work – I'm a fiction editor – but when I get home, it's dissonantly calm. I've been looking forward to the kids going back to school so that I can knuckle down and read the novel on which I've agreed to provide feedback for a structural edit. I haven't even started reading the book yet, but I can't wait to lose myself in the author's imaginary world and shut out reality. I'm supposed to email my report to the publisher who has outsourced the work to me in a few days' time. It's going to be tight. I usually work well under pressure and in the mornings. I make myself another coffee, then head for my study, Cheddar following me from room to room like a shadow.

But two hours later, I'm forced to admit defeat. I've read only the first three chapters. The caffeine has worked – my mind is racing – but I can't concentrate on the manuscript. My thoughts keep wandering to the body in the woods. Does this have anything to do with what happened to Iris? I decide to go for a walk and get some fresh air, clear my head that way, much to Cheddar's delight.

I walk briskly across the fields behind our cottage in the light breeze and timid sunshine. The view across Exmoor, which always takes my breath away, fails to act as a buffer for my thoughts, and my vivid imagination runs amok. I picture a wooded area, by a stream, swarming with uniformed officers and other professionals, and a blue forensic tent, perilously perched on an escarpment. I'm tempted to go home, put the dog in the car and drive the short distance to Buryknoll Wood. We could resume our walk there. But the woods are vast and even if I did locate the body, it would look suspicious if I suddenly showed up. Besides, the chances of me finding out any more information about the dead man, including his identity, are slim to non-existent. I expect the police have closed off all access to the woods anyway.

After a light lunch, I manage to read through five or six chapters of the book I'm supposed to be editing. It takes me far longer than usual because I have to reread paragraphs or even whole pages as I'm struggling to take anything in. Reluctantly, I call it a day. I can't afford to take a day off, not if I'm going to meet the deadline, but I can't do justice to this novel unless I give it my full attention.

I get the dinner ready before the kids come home. That way, I can help Margo if she's got any homework, and ask Iris and Olly all about their first day back. I'm not much of a cook – Daniel usually makes the meals – but I have a few tried and tested menus I can handle without messing up. I stream some opera music through the Bluetooth speaker from my phone – Maria Callas performing Beethoven's *Fidelio*. Olly and Iris hate opera, so I can't listen to it when they're home. I turn it up loud, hoping it will drown out my thoughts. Then I get out everything I need to make a shepherd's pie. That will do nicely for Olly, Iris and me. There's some leftover veggie lasagne for Margo, who stopped eating meat a few months ago to help save the planet. As a result, we all eat less meat and more fruit and veg, which has to be a good thing.

I rummage around in the drawer where we keep some of the utensils, but I can't find the knife I use to chop up the onions. We don't put the sharp knives in the dishwasher in case they rust – one of Daniel's many house rules – but I look in the dishwasher anyway. We sometimes bend or break the rules when he's away. I check the other drawers and pots on the worktop in case it has been put away in the wrong place. In the end, I take out a different knife – it's bigger and sharper. It slips as I cut into the onion and slices into my middle finger. It stings, and the pain, more than the music, is a welcome distraction.

When Iris and Margo burst noisily through the front door late that afternoon, I finally manage to consign the dead man to a corner of my mind, although he lies in wait there, threatening to leap up and ambush me at any moment.

It's nearly 10 p.m. when my mobile goes. The kids are all upstairs – I checked in on them a few minutes ago. Margo's asleep; Olly and Iris are in Olly's room, watching a Netflix series on Olly's laptop. My heartbeat quickens when I see the caller ID. This can't be good. Not at this hour. I swipe to take the call.

'Carla? Hi. I've got some news, but you have to swear not to tell anyone. I could get Ian into trouble.'

'I can't promise that, Jo. Not if it concerns my daughter.' Jo knows as well as I do that the second this call ends, I'll ring Ash.

'Then at least—'

'I'll be as discreet as possible.'

'OK. And you didn't hear this from me. Two things. Firstly, the man in the woods. He hasn't been formally identified yet, but—'

'It's him.'

'Yes.'

'And the second thing?'

She hesitates and I know it before she tells me. I take a deep breath and I hear her do the same. 'Carla, they're treating his death as suspicious,' Jo says.

'What does that mean?'

Jo spells it out. 'It means it looks like he was murdered.'

'I got that,' I mutter.

What I really meant was: what does that mean for us? For my family?

Chapter 2

Iris

THEN

The first time Joshua asked her out, she said no. Then he asked her again. And again. The third time he asked, she gave in.

'Third time lucky,' he said, a boyish, triumphant grin on his face.

She often wishes she could go back to that day and just stick with her original 'no'. Then none of what came afterwards would have happened.

Even now, she has no idea why he picked her. He was in the year above her and Olly at school. She didn't really know him, although he did cross-country, too. All the girls on the team were mad about him. She hadn't really clocked him, to be honest, even though he was cute and super fit. Perhaps that was part of the attraction for him. Like, maybe he saw her as a challenge or something.

It wasn't like he wore her down or anything. She just thought: well, why not? He seemed mature. He was certainly persistent. In

Iris's – admittedly limited – experience, most boys her age tried to stick their tongue down your throat at a party or else they sent one of their mates or their sister to sound you out if they fancied you, but he actually came up to her himself and asked her out. Three times. The first time he asked her to the cinema. The second time it was to the beach – he had his driving licence, which was pretty cool. And the third time, he had two tickets for Pink: *The Summer Carnival* in July. It was, like, three months away, but how could she say no to that? How could anyone say no to that? He spun this whole story about winning the tickets in a draw at his dad's golf club. She didn't believe a word of it. But she thought, the tickets must have been expensive, and if he'd splashed out on tickets in the hope she'd change her mind and go out with him, he must be really into her.

'You don't give up, do you?' she said.

'Not on you,' he replied glibly. It makes her gag when she thinks of it now, but she found it sweet back then.

It's only now she realizes he wasn't going to take no for an answer. It's only now she wonders if she should have called him out on the whole ticket thing. It didn't bother her then, but maybe it should have.

Things went fast from then on. Too fast. They immediately became exclusive, or 'tight' as Josh phrased it, which meant, as far as Iris could see, that not only did they not go out with anyone else, but that she hardly got to hang out with her friends either.

They'd been seeing each other for three months when school broke up for the summer. Throughout that period, Josh kept saying how badly he wanted her, but he also said he would wait until she was ready. She felt kinda pressured, though. The day before he went on holiday with his family to Greece, she had sex with him for the first time. At his place. In his bed. His parents were both at work and his brothers were out. He was gentle, but it hurt even so. At least it was over relatively quickly. Her first time, but not his.

He knotted the condom and threw it in the waste paper basket without getting out of bed. Then he got a little box out of a drawer in his nightstand and handed it to her, looking happy, maybe even smug. It was a necklace, or rather two necklaces. The pendants – a fox and a wolf – fitted together like two pieces of a jigsaw puzzle, the wolf's body curled around the fox. It was like his-and-her jewellery. Iris found them a bit tacky and instantly felt ungrateful for having that thought.

Josh took the fox necklace – on a silver chain – from her. She turned and held up her hair so he could put it around her neck and do up the clasp. The wolf pendant hung from a black leather lace and as she, in turn, put it around his neck and did up the clasp, he grinned. She swiped aside a thought in her head: would he have given her that present today if she hadn't had sex with him? She was sure he would have, but it felt a bit weird, almost like he was rewarding her.

'I'm going to miss you so much,' he said, as they both continued to lie under the bedcovers.

'Perhaps it will do us good to be apart for a couple of weeks.' She'd been thinking this a lot lately – she was looking forward to spending some time with her friends, but she'd spoken without filtering. 'You have to admit, we've been living in each other's pockets quite a lot.'

She was repeating her mum's phrase. Mum was right, but it was clearly the wrong thing to say. Josh's face darkened and he disentangled himself from her arms, rolled away from her and got out of bed.

'I don't know if we'll have the internet where we're staying,' he said, pulling on his boxers. 'You probably won't hear a word from me the whole time I'm away.'

He said this without so much as glancing in Iris's direction and it was like it was her fault. Or her punishment.

'I'll still be here when you get back,' Iris said, trying to soften the blow she'd apparently dealt him, although she didn't really get what it was that had pissed him off.

The day after Josh arrived in Greece, he posted some photos on Instagram and Snapchat. Photos of the beach and the hotel. In the comments, he'd written: *Clear seas and skies, hotel with great food and Wi-Fi. What more could a guy wish for?*

Iris messaged him – voice and text messages – several times. She sent him a DM on Instagram in case he didn't have any phone signal. She tried WhatsApp. But when he didn't write back, she stopped. His radio silence felt deliberate and hurtful, especially as he continued to post photos on Insta and Snap almost daily. She was convinced it was over between them. But the very day he came home, he rocked up to her house, laden with presents he'd bought her in Greece and at the duty free.

'Why didn't you reply to any of my messages?' she asked.

'I thought we weren't supposed to contact each other while I was away,' he answered, a bewildered look on his face. 'Wasn't it you who said something about not living in each other's pockets?'

He apologized profusely, swearing blind it had all been a big misunderstanding, promising to make it up to her. She was super relieved they were still together.

It seemed like such a small thing at the time, but with hindsight, she should have seen it for what it was: a red flag. It was to be the first of many. But it was already too late. She'd fallen in love with him.

Chapter 3

Carla

NOW

Ash is late, as usual. His inability to arrive on time for anything was one of the things that drove me mad when we were married. It still does, but I no longer feel I have the right to nag him about it. Sitting in the café where we've arranged to meet, I drum the fingers of one hand on the table and bite the nails of the other hand.

I would have gone straight round to Ash's house last night after Jo's phone call, but I'd downed two generous glasses of white wine after dinner. I texted him to ask if we could have lunch together today instead. I don't make a habit of eating out with my ex, although we often have lunch or dinner together – just the two of us or with one or both of our kids – at his place. He lives in the hamlet of Shallowcott, a five-minute drive from Holtleigh, where we live, but he works – as a bank manager – in Barnstaple, which is a good twelve miles away. I'm sure Ash senses something's up, even though I was careful not to say anything in my message that would alarm him.

When he finally shows up, a wave of relief instantly extinguishes the spark of annoyance that was flickering inside me. He strolls towards my table, his muscular body stuffed into a suit. I'm used to seeing him in casual clothes – jeans and a worn T-shirt of some defunct Seventies or Eighties rock band like Queen or Nirvana. He's in his fifties and he's still incredibly attractive, an older version of Olly. Ash might look uncomfortable in his work clothes, but he scrubs up well. I brush away this thought, feeling disloyal towards Daniel.

'You all right?' Ash asks, sliding onto the bench opposite mine. The concern in his voice brings a lump to my throat. I'm an emotional yo-yo today. I order myself to get a grip. 'How are the evil twins?'

Presumably, he means Oliver and Iris. Obviously, they're not evil. They're not twins, either, although they look very alike. They're both blond – naturally, at least; Iris has dyed her hair dark – and they're both blue-eyed, like Ash. Olly is the elder of the two. By almost eleven months. But they're in the same year at school, Olly having been born in September and Iris the following July. Ash and I didn't plan to have children that close together. I was breastfeeding Olly, for goodness' sake. Ash claims that's what drove the two of us apart, trying to bring up two babies at the same time. For me, the catalyst for our divorce had more to do with my husband shagging our next-door neighbour when Iris was only a few weeks old. We muddled through another five years, but the damage was irreparable.

Anyway, water under the bridge. We've both moved on since then. Ash has moved on so many times I struggle to keep track, and I moved in with Daniel six years ago. Ash and I might have failed in our marriage, but we consider our divorce to be successful. We are close, far closer than we ever were when we were together. I know I can count on him.

'Are you OK, Carla? You're not, are you?' He reaches across

the table and takes my hands in his. It's all I can do not to burst into tears. 'What's wrong?'

'Josh is dead,' I whisper. Ash's sapphire eyes widen. 'They've found his body in Lower Buryknoll Wood.'

'How appropriate,' he remarks wryly. 'How did he die? How did you find out?'

'Joanne told me.' I lean towards Ash and lower my voice. I don't want the people on the tables around us to overhear. 'Looks like he was killed.'

'Murdered, you mean?' Ash says this too loudly, but no one so much as glances in our direction.

I nod.

'Shit. How? When?'

I shrug. I can't seem to get any more words out.

'I'll ring Roly.' Ash looks around. The café is full now, not to mention noisy. 'I'll just pop outside.'

He gets to his feet and extracts his mobile from an inside pocket. He heads for the door, scrolling through his phone. Ash met Ian — Roly — at university. They were both at Birmingham. They hit it off straightaway, although they're poles apart. Ash is tall, burly and blond; Ian is short, skinny and dark-haired. Ash was born and brought up locally and has the North Devon burr to prove it; Ian grew up in Northern Ireland and speaks with a lilting brogue. Ash is athletic; Ian smokes his way through at least one pack a day. I could go on, but you get the picture. Anyway, Ian was Ash's best man at our wedding, which is where Jo met him. Ian, I mean. They got engaged a year later and married a year after that.

I watch my ex-husband through the café window, as he paces up and down in front of it, talking animatedly into his mobile and raking his hair with the fingers of his free hand. It's a nervous gesture and the familiarity of it tugs at one of my heartstrings. Olly has also picked up this mannerism, though Ash's hair bounces back into place, whereas Olly's remains sticking up.

When Ash comes back in, he's pale. He sits down and locks his eyes onto mine.

'So?'

'Roly wasn't well pleased that Jo has been bringing you up to speed. Josh's parents haven't even formally identified the body yet. They're doing that later today. It's a murder inquiry. Roly's home patch. He's the senior investigating officer.'

I know my ex-husband. I've known him for years. I can read his expressions and body language like a book. I know what he's thinking and feeling, as much from what he leaves unsaid as from what he says. And right now, I can tell he's stalling. 'Go on.'

He inhales a deep breath and lets it out slowly. 'Josh was stabbed.'

I gasp. 'Oh God. How awful.'

I'm not sorry Josh is dead and, I admit, several times over the past few months I've wanted to kill him and his parents myself, one after the other – throttle them with my bare hands or blast all three of them into the afterlife with a shotgun. But this is shocking. I can't imagine what it must be like to lose one of your children, and it must be even worse to lose a child in such a violent way. It's not something I would wish on anyone, no matter what they or their offspring had done.

'What else did Ian say?'

Ash breaks eye contact.

'Ash?'

'His body had started to … decompose, according to Roly. Tests will confirm it, but the police believe his body has been there for a few days.'

Ash's words escort me inside the forensic tent my imagination conjured up yesterday and I look down on the face of a dead teenager, barely recognizable as Joshua Knoll, his lips black, his face swollen. I blink rapidly to expel the grotesque image from my mind.

'Carla?'

Ash's voice jolts me back to the café. 'Sorry, Ash. What did you say?'

'Do you want me to take you home? What can I do? Will you try to eat something?'

I'm nauseous, and right now I can't imagine ever feeling hungry again. My mouth is dry, though, and I'm thirsty. 'I'd like some tea, please.'

Ash signals to the waitress, who bounces over to us. When her smile inverts to a frown, I realize that, without meaning to, I'm scowling at her. When she comes back with my tea, she fixes me with narrow eyes, smirking, and I wonder if she's spat in my cup.

It's one of those metal teapots with a spout that seems to have been deliberately designed to drip all over the place. Ash pours. He knows I don't put sugar or milk in my tea or coffee, but he opens a sachet of sugar, empties it into the cup and stirs it with a wooden stick. He gets up and fetches a handful of those cheap, unabsorbent paper napkins, then attempts to mop up the tea he has spilt.

'Shall I call Dandr— sorry, I mean Dan.' He pulls an apologetic face. 'Shall I call Dan for you?'

My partner's name is Daniel Duffy. Dan Duffy, to his mates. Ash calls him Dandruff. Which is ironic because Daniel's completely bald. Ash doesn't use the nickname in Daniel's presence, obviously – he calls him Dan, although they're certainly not mates – but Daniel knows. Unsurprisingly, my partner doesn't find my ex-husband's nickname for him amusing. He gets his own back, though. He insists on calling Ash by his first name – Quentin. Behind his back as well as to his face. Ash hates it. Daniel is the only person who calls him Quentin. Even Ash's mother calls him Ash.

'No, it's OK. He's away until the day after tomorrow. I haven't told him about any of this yet.'

'Why not?'

'He wasn't ...' I trail off. I was about to say Daniel wasn't as supportive as I'd have liked with everything Iris went through during the last school year, but I stop myself. That's not fair on Daniel. Iris isn't his daughter. She's Ash's. And Ash was an absolute rock. Neither Iris nor I would have got through any of that without him. Ash was dependable and available; he said and did all the right things. 'I'll tell him when he gets back,' I say. 'He'll be home the day after tomorrow.'

'I can drop in on my way home this evening if you like,' Ash offers. 'I'll bring a takeaway.'

'That would be nice. Thank you. Ash, Iris doesn't know yet either.'

Ash is silent for a few seconds. He strokes imaginary stubble on his chin, the way he always does when he's thinking something through. Then he says, 'She has to know, Carla. We could tell her together later, if you want.'

'OK.' I've finished my tea, and I'm fiddling with the stirrer.

'Don't worry. Everything will be all right. We'll be fine.'

I look up, into Ash's eyes, and something passes between us. I know Ash is thinking along the same lines as me. He's worried, too. He can't possibly know for sure that we'll be OK. A teenage boy has been murdered. The police will be looking for the killer.

And our daughter has motive. She'll be the main suspect.

Chapter 4

Ian

NOW

It was late when he got home last night and he has had to get up early. Again. It's only been a couple of days and already he's very short on sleep. He'll expect his team to put in the hours, too, until this case is solved. He has recently completed the final course on the Management of Serious Crime Development Programme and he has his sights set on a promotion to detective chief inspector in the not-too-distant future. This is his first case as senior investigating officer. He's desperate not to bollocks it up.

He manages a smile when Jo steps outside. She hands him a cup of coffee then wraps her dressing gown tightly around herself, shutting out the cool morning air. She doesn't have to get up for at least another hour. He assumes she has got up for him, although she has just gone back to school this week – he means, to work – after the summer holidays, and she's stressed about her own job, so perhaps she didn't sleep well either. She keeps him company while he has a smoke. She's been on at him to give it up, but she refrains, for once, from giving him the evil eye while he puffs away.

This morning, she doesn't ask for details about the case and he doesn't offer any. There are certain aspects of his job he's not supposed to discuss at home, but he has always told Jo far more than he should. She's smart, way smarter than he is, and she has helped him to come at an investigation from a different angle more than once. But for this particular investigation, he's going to have to be very careful what he tells his wife. He has hardly seen her, but he has rung her. He only gave her the bare facts, but it didn't take her long to pass on that info to her bestie. It could have been embarrassing for him. It could even have got him taken off the case. So, he's glad she doesn't probe. If he's working a case that gets under his skin, like this one, he has to compartmentalize, as Jo knows, which means not allowing work to bleed into his home life. Not that he's going to get a lot of home life for the foreseeable.

He's not going to be able to just switch off whenever he comes home to try and grab a few hours' kip either. The image of Josh's dead body will haunt him – day and night – until they've arrested the murderer. Ian deals with his fair share of domestic violence, drugs-related crimes, burglary, possession of weapons. He has seen quite a few dead bodies over the course of his career. Sure, he was used to seeing dead bodies even before he became a peeler – he grew up in Derry, near the Bogside, during the Troubles. He has become immune to some of what he comes across and hardened to most of the rest of it. You have to if you want to stay sane. But it never gets easier when a child is involved. (Technically, Joshua Knoll was an adult – just – but he was still a kid in Ian's eyes. His whole life ahead of him.)

When Ian was called out to the unexplained death the day before yesterday, he was told they were dealing with the body of a young male in his late teens / early twenties. He immediately thought of Joshua. Ian hadn't known Joshua Knoll well, but he'd seen him a few times at Ash's or at Carla's, back when Iris was dating him. Joshua had gone missing – the mother, Yvonne, had been making a big song and dance about it (by which Ian means she was hysterical), although the parents didn't actually report their son missing for three days. The subject had been assessed as low-risk. Joshua had stormed out of the house after a row with his father, Richard Knoll (they argued a lot, according to Yvonne), and it wasn't out of character for Josh to take off like this – he'd been known to sleep over at friends' houses before, sometimes for a couple of days, without checking in with his parents.

Richard supposed his son was cooling off somewhere and would eventually come home. Joshua had taken clothes with him and, it transpired, he'd used his credit card to buy food the day after he'd left. (Shame he hadn't taken his mobile. That would have made their job a lot easier.) He wasn't on medication. No mental health issues. (Carla would beg to differ on that one, for sure, but Ian's talking self-harm or suicide attempts, not narcissistic personality disorder, which is what Carla has unofficially diagnosed Joshua with.) The whole thing had only landed on Ian's desk the day before yesterday, ten days after the kid had been reported missing and nearly two weeks after he was last seen.

When Ian had arrived at the scene – a clearing in Buryknoll Wood – he was briefed by the officer in charge of the incident. He'd got suited and booted up, slapped on his mask and walked into the tent. He took one glance at the victim. He recognized him, despite the fact the kid had clearly been dead for several days and his face had taken on a greenish hue. He'd promptly run back out of the tent to boke up his breakfast. Not his finest hour. His colleagues would be taking the piss for some time yet, so they would. That was another requirement in this job. Besides the thick skin, you needed a good sense of humour, preferably gallows humour, the darker the better.

This morning kicks off with a team meeting. Ian has officers on house-to-house duties, although the nearest houses are a few miles from the part of the woods where Joshua's body was discovered. He has more officers scouring the woods beyond the immediate crime scene. And he has officers checking out CCTV, although that's a long shot. Even though the UK is one of the most surveilled countries in the world, North Devon has pretty sketchy coverage and the nearest CCTV is also several miles from Lower Buryknoll Wood.

One of their priorities right now is interviewing friends and relatives of the victim. Now they've identified the victim, they need to identify any possible suspects.

'It's important to use the evidence to make hypotheses,' Ian reminds his team. And himself. Not that they have much evidence. 'It's tempting to jump to conclusions and then twist the evidence to fit half-baked theories,' Ian continues. 'It's vital to keep an open mind and not develop tunnel vision.'

That said, initial gut feeling, Ian likes Richard for this. As anyone knows, when it comes to murder, the killer is usually known to the victim. And there was something a bit off about Richard from the get-go. Contrary to his wife, he didn't seem particularly worried about his son's disappearance. It would seem from the tent, food and sleeping bag they found at the crime scene that Joshua was camping in the woods. Presumably this is where he was cooling off from the row he'd had with his father. The forensic pathologist confirmed that the murder had been committed here – the body hadn't been discarded in this location after death – so it seemed safe to conclude that Joshua wasn't lured to the woods to be killed, but rather killed in the place he'd chosen as his hideout. Did Richard find him? Did he know where to look? Ian has gone easy on the fella so far, but he will need to talk to him again later today.

Talking to people who knew Joshua will also help them to build up a profile of the victim. Find out how the kid lived and they will probably find out how he died. Well, they know how he died, more or less – the pathologist will give him the gory details (he's going to see her straight after this meeting), but it's clear that Joshua was stabbed. *Why* he died is what he means. And *who* had motive.

Ian checks everyone knows what to do and ends the meeting. Then he sets off for the Royal Devon and Exeter Hospital in Wonford. It's a journey that should take him about five minutes, but instead takes him twenty. As he parks in the car park, he regrets coming. He could have sent Helena, his deputy SIO. Perhaps he should have. Leaning against the wall of the building, he smokes a cigarette before going inside. He hopes he's not going to make an eejit of himself again in the mortuary. If he barfs in here too, he'll never live it down. He doesn't usually feel quite so nauseous when he sees dead bodies, even decomposed ones. It's because he knows the victim, he supposes. Or, more likely, because Joshua wasn't much older than his daughter, Millie. He stubs out his cigarette and pops two cubes of chewing gum into his mouth. He spends a few seconds psyching himself up. He'll be wearing a mask and he'll breathe in through his mouth. That should do the trick.

He knows Lorraine Davies, the Home Office pathologist. She'll want to get down to the nitty-gritty as soon as they set foot in the post-mortem room. His stomach roils in trepidation. He and the CSI photographer follow her as she strides down the corridor. He practically has to skip to keep up with her. 'Any thoughts on time of death?' he asks.

'He's been dead for at least a week,' she says. 'The twenty-eighth or twenty-ninth of August is my best estimate. I can't narrow it down any more than that, I'm afraid.'

'Shit,' Ian mutters into his mask. It's a slightly delayed reaction because he has to do the mental arithmetic. If his calculations are correct, Joshua was reported missing two or three days before he was killed. Someone's head is going to roll. Thankfully, not his. When he inherited the misper case, Josh was already dead.

Ian listens while Lorraine talks him through the various

wounds (there are several of them), including the stab wound that would have proved fatal. Ian throws quick glances to where she points on the body and nods at the photographer to take close-ups. He feels the blood draining from his face.

'It's not all bad news,' Lorraine says brightly. Perhaps she has noticed his discomfort.

'Oh?' Ian says, perking up.

'We have collected some fibres and a hair. A *human* hair. A head hair. Found it right here.' She points to Joshua's bare sternum, just below his neck.

Lorraine looks almost triumphant, but Ian's bubble of hope bursts as quickly as it formed. A fingerprint (even a partial one) would be better, far better. Fibre analysis and hair analysis have limitations. Even if they get a match for the hair, it can't in itself provide absolute identification. And, further down the line, the presence of the defendant's hair on the victim can easily be explained away in court by any barrister worth their salt.

'Can we rule out crime scene contamination?' He sounds doubtful.

'That's not in *my* job description,' she says.

'Yeah, I know. I was thinking out loud. We found a footprint at the scene, you see,' he says. 'We've had torrential rain on three separate days over the past week and the print was perfectly preserved.'

He doesn't say any more. Lorraine will have grasped the subtext. The footprint can only have been made after it had stopped raining and therefore several days after the murder. He has already sent someone round to check out the shoes of the retired couple who discovered the body while out picking blackberries. No match. Which means that the crime scene was probably contaminated during initial response. In other words, the foot belonged to one of the officers. And now the hair. He'll have to find out if any of the first responders entered the crime scene without wearing protective clothing. Specifically, a hood.

A spark of irritation flares inside him. Why couldn't they be more careful? Then he remembers that he threw up inside the taped-off crime scene.

He reminds himself to keep an open mind. It's a long shot, but the hair might just lead them straight to the killer.

Chapter 5

Carla

NOW

Iris knows. Somehow, she has found out about Josh. I spot her through the window of my study and I can tell from her wan face, her lips pinched into a thin, straight line, and from the way she shuffles up the driveway towards the cottage, scuffing at the gravel with the toes of the new black leather shoes I bought her for going back to school. I wasn't expecting her for another hour and a half. She must have skipped cross-country training and caught the earlier bus home. Olly's not with her. It looks as if he's gone running. I leap up, head through the kitchen into the hallway and open the front door before Iris can reach it. Standing on the doorstep, I take her in my arms and rub her back, as if she were still a small child.

'Everything will be all right,' I say, finding no better words than the platitude Ash came out with only a few hours ago to comfort me. It didn't work on me and it won't convince Iris either.

I feel her stiffen. 'You knew!' she says into my chest. 'Why didn't you tell me?' Her voice is accusing and indignant. Gently but firmly, she pushes me away, then pushes past me into the house.

Minutes later, we're sitting opposite each other at the kitchen table. Judging from her red eyes and the vertical streaks of mascara on her cheeks, Iris has been crying. She's pale. I've made her some green tea and she cradles the mug in her hands, which are shaking slightly.

'How did you find out?' I ask. 'Does everyone at school know?'

'No.'

Not yet, I add silently to myself. It's only a matter of time before it's all anyone can talk about.

'Millie told me this afternoon at break. She overheard her parents talking about it on the phone,' Iris says. Amelia Rowland – Millie – is Joanne and Ian's daughter. She's in the same year as Iris and Olly at school. 'How did *you* know?'

'Jo.'

'You should've told me, Mum.' Her hands might be trembling, but her voice is steady.

'I know. I'm sorry. Dad's coming round this evening. We were going to fill you in then. How do you feel?'

'You sound like Melanie.' Iris rolls her eyes at me.

Melanie is Iris's counsellor. Iris still goes to see her regularly, at Ash's and my insistence, even though she says that the sessions aren't helping her and she doesn't want to talk about it anymore.

Iris shrugs. 'Relieved, happy, sad, angry,' she says. 'Mostly scared, I guess.'

I don't tell my daughter that I'm scared, too. Terrified, in fact. For her.

Margo is dyslexic and, three days a week, she is to have help with her homework after school – an hour with a learning support assistant employed by the school to tutor a small group of pupils with learning difficulties. Margo and Olly arrive home at the same time – Olly sweaty and muddy; Margo bright-eyed and unusually talkative.

'Where's Iris?' Olly asks without so much as a greeting. 'She didn't come running.'

'She's having a nap on the sofa.' As I say that, I marvel that she was able to fall asleep. I'd have expected Josh's death to prey on her mind too much for her to do that. But perhaps she just feels utterly exhausted by it all.

I watch Olly from the living room doorway as he tiptoes to the sofa and looks down at his sister. He has his back to me and I can't see the expression on his face. Once upon a time he might have shouted 'boo' in Iris's ear or drawn whiskers on her face or something. But we've all kept Iris wrapped in cotton wool since the beginning of last December and, instead, Olly takes the blanket from the back of the armchair and puts it over her, pulling it up to her chin and then tucking it around her. So, Olly knows about Joshua, too.

Olly goes upstairs to get showered and changed. Margo gives me an overly detailed account of her day. We usually snuggle up on the sofa to do her reading – we aim for at least two chapters a day – but because Iris is asleep, we sit down at the kitchen table. By the time Olly comes back downstairs, Margo and I have finished reading for this evening and Ash has arrived, armed with bags of curry. Olly lets him in and I wake up Iris.

Ash must have had time to pop home – he's ditched the suit and is wearing jeans and a faded R.E.M. T-shirt. And socks – Daniel doesn't allow anyone to wear shoes in the house, including our guests, especially Ash.

'I've got chicken tikka masala, biryani and beef vindaloo,' he says as I get out plates and cutlery.

He smells good – clearly, he's had time to take a shower, too. I notice he has also brought a bottle of white wine.

He turns to Margo and adds, 'Oh, and for you, young lady, saag paneer and aloo gobi.' She brightens and I throw Ash a grateful smile for remembering that my stepdaughter is a vegetarian. 'With lots of rice and naan for everyone, of course.'

There's so much food that there will be enough for us to heat up again tomorrow. The day after that, when Daniel comes home, I'll make the effort to cook another of the few meals I can master.

I send Margo into the living room to choose a film on Netflix. 'Find something that everyone will enjoy,' I say.

'I'll take in the popcorn,' she says, skipping off happily before I can change my mind.

We don't usually watch TV in the week when the kids are at school. In fact, it doesn't even happen that often at the weekends as Iris and Olly tend to beat a retreat upstairs in the evenings after dinner and I don't see them again until I poke my head round their bedroom doors to say goodnight.

Olly helps clear up without having to be asked. Another rare event. I remember him dropping his bowl yesterday morning, but I bite back a warning to be careful with the plates.

'Iris knows about Joshua,' I say to Ash.

'How are you feeling, Iris?' Ash asks. 'Are you all right?'

'Not you, too!' she replies, clearly trying to pretend it's no big deal and she's OK.

I must say, Iris is taking this better than I thought she would. But perhaps the shock hasn't kicked in yet. I leave her with her father in the kitchen and usher Olly into the living room, carrying the bottle of wine in one hand and my glass in the other. Ash has had one glass and I know he won't drink any more. He's a good driver, although a slightly overcautious one – he can be a bit heavy-footed on the brake. I've never known him to have bouts of road rage or to drink-drive.

'Does everyone in school know about Joshua?' I ask Olly, careful to keep my voice low so Margo doesn't hear.

'Dunno,' he says.

'Who told you?'

But he doesn't get to answer as Margo asks, 'Olly, can you hand me a bowl for the popcorn?' She points at the sideboard on which a handful of birthday cards still stand from Olly's eighteenth. Was that really only the day before yesterday? It seems like weeks ago.

He does as she asks. She has plopped down on the sofa and pats the seat to one side of her for Olly and to the other side for me. Iris and Ash join us in the living room.

'What film have you decided on, Maggot?' Olly asks, taking the bag of popcorn from Margo's hands and opening it.

'Don't call me that,' she says, but it's a half-hearted protest. Margo's big stepbrother can do no wrong in her eyes. '*Crazy, Stupid, Love*,' she says.

'Good choice.'

Margo beams.

Margo, Iris and I have watched the film before, but it makes us all laugh. I almost forget for a moment that Joshua has been murdered. Almost.

I remember, too late, that in the film Jessica takes nude photos of herself for Cal. Very awkward. And, far more importantly, potentially triggering. I glance at Iris and see that her jaw is set in a determined line. Olly chooses this moment to pass her the popcorn. If there's one good thing that has come out of this mess, it's how close the two of them have become. A few moments later, I hear Iris laugh, just a little, but it's enough for me to breathe normally again.

I notice that Ash has topped up my wine and, as I lean forwards to pick up the glass from the coffee table with one hand and grab a handful of popcorn with the other, my attention is drawn to the plaster on my finger.

Josh was stabbed. Those words come to me, in Ash's voice. When he told me that earlier, I didn't make the connection. But now ... I try to dismiss the suspicion that's corkscrewing its way into my head before it can twist in any deeper. No. What on earth am I thinking? There's no way. There's no connection. It's a coincidence. I mustn't go there.

But I can't shake the feeling that something about Iris's reaction to the news is a bit off. I thought she'd be grief-stricken. Or not grief-stricken, exactly, but definitely more upset. Instead, she hasn't shed a single tear since she arrived home and is now giggling in front of the TV. I suppose people react in different ways to shocking news like this.

It's no good. I have to double-check. 'Excuse me for a moment,' I say, getting to my feet. 'I need the loo.'

Ash and the kids are all glued to the TV and no one pays me any attention as I slip out of the living room into the kitchen. Olly's legs are crossed on the coffee table, barring my way, but he doesn't move as I clamber over them except to lean round me as I block the television screen from his view for a few seconds.

I open the drawer where the knife is kept – the one I wanted to use the other day to chop the onions. I start to take out the utensils one by one – garlic press, bottle opener, nut cracker …

And there it is. It must have been here all along. Somehow, I knew it would be. I'm not sure what possessed me. I make my way back to the living room and take my place on the sofa again, sandwiched between Margo and Iris. But try as I might, I can't get back into the film. I can't relax, even though the knife is in the drawer, where it should be, where it has always been. I heave a sigh, but my relief is tinged with unease.

Because if I doubted my daughter, even for a split second, how can I expect anyone else to believe she's innocent?

Chapter 6

Iris

THEN

After Josh came back from Greece, he made it up to her. He went running with her and went on and on about her technique, cadence and core exercises. He mansplained everything, but she didn't care. She followed his advice and he cheered her on at cross-country trials like she was competing in the Olympics or something. She smashed her best times. He showered her with attention and praise. He made her believe in herself, truly believe in herself. She was literally buzzing with all the attention he lavished on her. It was like he could see her. *Really* see her. And her potential.

'Dream big, babe,' he said – he liked to call her 'babe' or 'bae' – Before Anyone Else, obviously. 'You're the strongest and smartest person I know. You can do anything you set your mind to.'

He moulded her into a shinier version of herself. And not just in cross-country. Josh, who described himself as a maths geek, wasn't that clued in about art, literature or classical music – the things that made Iris tick. But he made an effort, read up on stuff that interested her. And little by little, he charmed – or maybe pushed – his way into every aspect of Iris's life. School, home, her head. He gave her pep talks before tests and compliments on her paintings and sketches, even her violin playing, although Josh himself wasn't at all musical. She flourished under the spotlight he projected just on her.

Despite their different interests, Josh was always going on about how similar they were. He'd say stuff like how Iris often said aloud what he was thinking; that she watched the same Netflix shows and films as he did; that she listened to his favourite bands too; that they both loved Thai food; that he had the same dream as her of one day backpacking around South America. So many coincidences. It sometimes made Iris feel like he was aping her. But, Josh? He said it just went to show they were made for each other. Iris was his soul mate.

Josh *loved* to talk in superlatives. She was the best thing that had ever happened to him and this was the happiest he'd ever been in his life. He told her he loved her. It seemed soon, too soon, but he repeated it so often – *loads* of times every single day – that she eventually said it back to him. It would have been super awkward if she hadn't. It was weird, though, because it was partly because he loved her so much that she was so attracted to him. No one had ever loved her that much. It was seriously intoxicating. But even back then, there were times when Iris thought it might be better if he loved her a bit less. She'd asked him if they could slow down when he came back from his holiday, but everything was speeding up. It was all moving too fast again, like they had to make up for lost time. She felt dizzy.

Another month or so passed. Afterwards, Iris would look back on it as their honeymoon period. It was intense, but fun, on the whole. Then came their first big row. Iris didn't really do social media that much. Well, it depends what you call a lot. Before, she probably spent, like, twenty minutes a day, half an hour max, a bit more at weekends – far less than her friends. Her screen time was higher than that, obviously – she often did her homework on her laptop and watched series on it, too. But she wasn't really into Snap and Insta. Once she was going out with Josh, they were texting so much during the day and sending voice messages to each other or FaceTiming in the evenings. So, her screen time deffo went up as a result, but, honestly, she hardly bothered with social media at all anymore. Every time she picked up her phone, Josh had left a message for her. It was sweet, but also a bit over the top.

But one day she posted this pic to Instagram of her with Olly. Biggest mistake ever. Their dad had taken the photo as they were playing badminton in the garden at his house one Saturday at the beginning of the Easter holidays. But then one of her classmates – a guy she didn't even know that well except for working with him on some English Lit assignment – liked the post and commented. Something totally harmless. She couldn't even remember what it was. Josh had a complete meltdown. He wanted her to delete the comment and block the classmate. When she refused, he went into full-on sulk mode for days. She texted him, telling him he had no need to be jealous and he could trust her. She could see from his read receipts that he'd seen her messages, but he completely ignored them. After a fortnight of his constant emails, text and voice messages, his silence was ear-piercing.

His behaviour reminded her of when he'd gone on holiday and hadn't answered her messages. He'd claimed then that it was due to a misunderstanding. This time it felt deliberate. Hurtful. He was ghosting her. In the end, she was so pissed off she wrote a message calling him babyish and telling him to grow the fuck up.

When he finally got in touch, the evening before they went back to school, he told her his aunt had died unexpectedly, it had been utter chaos at home and he hadn't had the time or headspace to find the words to reconcile with her. He referred to the incident as a 'petty argument', which, she supposed, it was.

She felt bad – she'd insulted him after all – and she was the one to apologize first. She vowed to herself to stay off social media from then on. That would avoid any further drama.

Josh never actually said sorry. Not in so many words. He just said he loved her so much it was only natural he should feel jealous. He was totally overwhelmed by his feelings for her; he'd never felt anything like this before. It was only much later that Iris realized 'sorry' didn't seem to be a word in Josh's active vocabulary. Instead, he'd say things like, 'My bad' or '*Mea culpa.*' Once he even went so far as a 'I'm sorry *if* I upset you.' But even though he never really apologized, he always made it up to her. He always made things better. For a while. Until the next time.

Iris wasn't entirely sure when the next time was. Was it the time they argued because he sent her forty-three text messages one day – he actually counted them – and she only wrote back to twelve of them? He sulked for a few days before the texting started up again. From then on, she tried to reply immediately to every one of his messages, but she noticed that *he* sometimes seemed to keep her dangling, waiting for an answer, although he promised it wasn't on purpose. Or was it the time they'd rowed after that awful family meal at Josh's place? Yvonne, Josh's mum had asked him to take his younger brothers to football practice, but Josh forgot. He blamed it on Iris. She can't even remember now how he made it out to be her fault. Iris actually felt like she had to apologize to Yvonne! Then Josh seemed to get a kick out of putting Iris down and correcting everything she said for the rest of the dinner. He made her feel like a complete idiot in front of his family. The row started in the car when he took her home afterwards. She started it. She was so mad at him. He drove way too fast around the bends and scared the shit out of her. Then he ghosted her for at least three days.

So that was the blueprint for their relationship. It was an on-again / off-again one. All or nothing. Iris spent a lot of the time they were together thinking she should get out of it for good, and all of the time they were apart pining for him like she was missing a piece of herself. Deep down, she could see she'd become completely dependent on him. But she continued to go round and round, up and down, like she was stuck on a rollercoaster ride and couldn't get off. She loved him. And the good times were sooooo good, they more than made up for the bad times. Highs and lows. Was this how drug addicts felt? You know it's bad for you, but you keep coming back for more because every now and then it makes you feel really, really good.

Chapter 7

Carla

NOW

Crooked Oak Cottage. No wonky trees in the garden, as you might expect if you're not from around here. It's named after the river, although Crooked Oak River does indeed take its name from a gnarled tree that has been leaning precariously for centuries. Ash and I did up this place when we moved back to North Devon from London. We were going back to our roots, but it was meant to be a new start. It was supposed to be a good move, in more ways than one. But we must have been mad taking on a major DIY project at a time when our marriage was shaky and our kids were so young. Things capsized fairly quickly between us. Final nail in the coffin and all that. We put Crooked Oak Cottage on the market, but to say it wasn't quite finished would be a massive understatement. It was barely inhabitable and completely unsellable. So, Ash left; the kids and I stayed. Ash and I got divorced, stopped arguing and, after a while, I continued renovating the cottage. Even though he no longer lived in it, Ash often gave me a hand. As well as fixing up the house, we were fixing our relationship, laying the foundations for a solid friendship.

Crooked Oak Cottage is my haven. I love being at home; I love working from home; I'm a homebody. I used to have a hectic job in London, working as a commissioning editor for one of the big five publishers. I had a long commute, worked long hours. I was a workaholic and I was good at my job, but I found it increasingly difficult to juggle my career with motherhood.

I'm still an editor, but I work freelance. I make a decent living. Although I miss my colleagues, I've never regretted moving away from London; I've never looked back. But today I feel lonely. Threatened. As if my world is slowly but irreversibly falling apart. I can't wait for Daniel to come home.

I decide to make headway on the edit I've been assigned. I've worked with this author before and I usually love her work. But the words make no sense to me and I can't get into it. The manuscript might as well have been written in Chinese. Or the font switched to Wingdings. After a while, I give up and make myself a bite to eat – a cheese and ham toastie with coleslaw, which I take through to the living room to eat in front of the lunchtime news.

Bloody Joshua. He's the main story on the regional news. I should have known. My fork, loaded with slaw, stops halfway to my mouth and I lower it to my plate, my appetite washed away, leaving nausea in its wake.

It's only a short news bulletin. They don't seem to know much. Either that or they're not revealing anything at this stage. Even so, I lean forwards on the sofa and hang on to the newscaster's every word.

'The death of a man whose body was found in woodland is being treated as suspicious, according to the police,' he says. 'The body was discovered by a couple who were picking blackberries in the woods. The man has been formally identified as eighteen-year-old Joshua Knoll, who was first reported missing more than a week ago. He is described as tall, blond and athletic, and he was wearing a navy-blue hoodie, jeans and trainers at the time of his death. Police would like to ask anyone who has any information to come forward.'

A photo of Josh appears on the screen, showing him from the waist up. It's at least a few months old because he's wearing his school blazer but finished his A levels in June. I stare at his handsome face, into his hazel eyes. He has been here, to Crooked Oak Cottage – inside my home – countless times. Always charming, ever polite, with a white, toothy grin affixed to his face, the same one he's wearing in the picture.

Daniel adored him. They'd bonded over a shared love of football, both fervent Arsenal fans. They'd drunk lager together as they watched matches on TV, sitting here on this very sofa. But although initially I'd been delighted to see Iris so happy and radiant, I soon became mistrustful of Josh. There was something about him that seemed off-kilter. I became convinced his courteousness was a veneer, and occasionally I caught a glimpse of what hid behind it. An expression that flashed across his face – blink, and you'd miss it. A throwaway remark that could have a disturbing undercurrent, depending on how you interpreted it. Or how he held his chin, tilted slightly upwards, in a way that hinted at a sense of entitlement. I couldn't put my finger on what it was about him that bothered me, but I couldn't muzzle the voice in my head warning me he was bad news.

'It's because you think he's not good enough for your daughter,' Daniel had said. 'No one will ever be good enough for our kids. I'll be the same when Margo starts dating.' He'd pulled a face. 'Oh God, it doesn't bear thinking about.'

But it wasn't that. Olly had had one girlfriend who lasted much longer than the others. Liv. I became very fond of her and I was genuinely gutted when they split up. I thought she was good for him. They went well together, Oliver and Olivia.

I never voiced my doubts about Josh to Iris. Perhaps I should have done.

Daniel has barely stepped into the house and closed the front door when it all spews out of my mouth. I don't even greet him properly – no hello, no kiss, nothing.

'Joshua Knoll has been found dead in the woods. The police seem to think he may have been murdered.'

'I know.' He sighs and gives me a peck on the lips.

He walks past me, pulling his cabin-sized suitcase, and then picks it up and heads up the stairs. At first, I think he's being dismissive. A little spark of irritation flickers inside me, but it fails to catch. His reaction should probably reassure me. If Daniel isn't worried, then perhaps I've been overthinking this. Maybe I'm being paranoid. Why would anyone suspect Iris? She and Josh split up nearly a year ago. And she's had nothing to do with him since he … well, for several months.

'Can we talk about this later?' he calls over his shoulder. 'Give me a chance to get unpacked?'

I see the look he throws me. It's not dismissiveness. It's evasiveness.

'What?' I demand. I race upstairs after him and follow him into our bedroom. He swings his case onto our bed. 'What, Daniel?' I'm standing with my hands on my hips and I suddenly see myself through his eyes. I drop my arms to my sides and dial my voice down a notch. 'How did you know? Did you hear it on the news?'

'No.' He plops down on the bed. 'I spoke to Richard Knoll a few minutes ago.'

I raise my eyebrows. 'I see,' I say, although I don't. Josh's father and Daniel used to be mates, but their friendship went south alongside Josh and Iris's relationship, or shortly afterwards. 'Did you … you didn't call him, did you?'

'No. I bumped into him. At the petrol station. Rich … er … Richard … well, he told me. About Josh.'

'OK.' I draw out the two syllables. Things are far from OK. It annoys me that Daniel has just called Josh's father by an abbreviation of his first name. It's too familiar, too friendly. Richard Knoll is not a friend anymore. Quite the opposite, in fact.

'Did he ... how was he?'

'How do you think, Carla?' he barks. 'He looked like a man whose life has just been turned upside down. He's lost his son, for Christ's sake.'

Daniel doesn't often snap at me. I must look taken aback because he reaches for my hand and pulls me closer to him.

'Sorry,' he says when I sit on the bed next to him. 'It's been a long day.'

'S'OK. That's not what I meant, though. I meant, how did he behave towards you?'

A wry smile. 'He was ... irate, shouting. Actually, I thought he was going to deck me.'

That's not good. The Knolls must already suspect Iris if Richard wanted to punch Daniel. I taste blood in my mouth and realize I've been biting my lip.

'What did he say?'

Daniel doesn't answer straightaway. I look at him, silently urging him to spit it out. At the same time, I want to take back my question or clap my hand over his mouth. I don't want to hear his answer.

'He demanded to know where Iris was on Wednesday the twenty-eighth and Thursday the twenty-ninth of August.'

Presumably Joshua went missing – or was murdered – on one of those days. My heart skips a beat or two, then starts up again, too fast. This confirms what I thought – the Knolls do suspect Iris – but it still hits me.

'What else did he say?'

'That Josh was stabbed—'

'Yes. Jo told me.'

'—several times.'

'Richard said Josh had been stabbed several times?'

'His exact words were "multiple stab wounds",' Daniel says.

Another blow, and this time it winds me. *Josh was stabbed several times.* I repeat Daniel's words in my head, over and over. And Richard's: *multiple stab wounds*.

I turn to look at Daniel, trying to work out what he's thinking. But his expression is impassive. I didn't know Josh had been stabbed more than once. Somehow, this makes it worse. More violent, if that's possible. It can't be self-defence; it can't be an accident. It suggests a frenzy. It smacks of pent-up hatred, vengeance.

I hear Iris's voice in my head. *I hate him, Mum. I wish he was dead.* How many times did she repeat those to sentences to me? After every nightmare, after every failed attempt to get her life back on track. I shut out her words.

The Knolls obviously believe Iris killed their son. How long before the police suspect her, too? Iris had every reason to get even with Josh. But I know my daughter. She's not capable of stabbing anyone. Not several times. Not at all.

Chapter 8

Ash

NOW

'Are you sure this is a good idea?' Ash asks, pacing up and down the living room of his house, his mobile pressed to his ear.

It's a bad idea. Carla must have known he wouldn't be happy about this. He doesn't know why she has rung to tell him.

'Ash, for the past year, we've been pushing Iris to go out more – to go out, full stop. You can't seriously want me to keep her in now she does have plans?'

Dandruff's there. Ash can tell. Carla's voice always sounds different over the phone when her partner is around – a harder edge and no affection. Ash suspects Dandruff doesn't like Carla talking to her ex-husband. He'd probably prefer it if they didn't get on.

'But Josh hasn't even been buried yet,' Ash argues.

'So?'

'Well, it doesn't look good, does it?'

'Would she look less guilty if she stayed at home?'

'That's not what I meant,' Ash lies. Carla will see through him, even over the phone. But he's pretty sure she's not thrilled about this either. They're usually on the same wavelength.

'This is Millie's eighteenth birthday party, Ash,' Carla continues. 'The girls have been planning this for weeks. Ian and Jo are staying in a hotel for the night so Millie can hold the party at home. There's no reason Iris should stop having fun just because Josh has … died.'

Stop having fun? When was the last time Iris had actually had fun? He doesn't voice his thoughts. This is precisely the point Carla is making. Iris finally wants to go out again. To socialize. They've been encouraging her to do just this. They can't turn around and say no now. And Iris is so happy that everything's all right between her and Millie again – she was really upset that Millie was avoiding her a few months ago. This will be good for Iris. Carla's right. As always.

'It just makes Iris seem a little uncaring, that's all,' Ash says. 'She's going to be out there celebrating while Josh is lying in a mortuary somewhere.'

'Uncaring? Why should she care, Ash? So, they went out together once upon a time? It's been over for almost a year and that kid almost single-handedly wrecked her life.'

Ash wants to point out that that was never proved. But what's the use? He knows as well as Carla that Josh was behind what happened. He doesn't want to get into an argument, especially when they're probably both thinking along the same lines. Carla would get the last word, as ever. So he bites back his retort.

'She's not staying over,' Carla says brightly.

Like that makes it look better. On the plus side, Iris won't get too drunk if she has to face one of her parents later. 'In that case, I'll pick her up, if you like, when the party's over,' he offers, half-hoping Carla has already roped Dandruff into doing it.

'Would you? That's very good of you, Ash.' He can hear the triumphant smile in her voice. So that's why she rang to tell him about the party. 'Daniel has just got home from his business trip. We appreciate it. I told her one o'clock at the latest.'

Great. It might be the weekend for some people, but he'll have to get up the next morning. He works on Saturdays. 'I'll be there,' he says, '1 a.m. on the dot.' He waits until Carla has ended the call before adding sarcastically, 'Could you not have given her a later curfew?'

Ash parks in the street where the Rowlands live shortly before midnight. He's careful to park a few metres away from the street-lamp, but in a space where he has a clear view of the house. He slumps down in his seat, feeling like a burglar casing out a house. He can hear the music from here, feel the vibrations of the bass. He doesn't envy the neighbours.

This is a stupid idea. You're being a bloody idiot. You need to get a life, Ash! No one – not even Carla – has ever dared to talk to Ash the way he talks to himself. What *is* he doing here? He had a bad feeling and couldn't spend another second sprawled on the sofa, binge-watching some mind-numbing series on Netflix and twiddling his thumbs. He contemplates driving home, but he'd check the time on his phone every other minute until it was late enough to come back and pick up Iris, so there's no point. He'll just sit here for the next hour or so.

Last year, when Olly and Liv were about to turn seventeen, Olly had asked Ash if he could hold a joint birthday party at Ash's place. Ash hadn't been keen. He'd heard all sorts of stories from his mates about disastrous parties – teenagers being sick all over the place, passing out from drinking too much alcohol, having sex in just about every free room in the house. A couple he and Carla knew had been called home from the restaurant because some drunk kid at a party at their house had fallen down the stairs and their son had had to call the ambulance. Against his better judgement, Ash had said yes. It was his son's birthday, after all.

To say Carla wasn't pleased would be putting it mildly. She

was as worried as Ash about all the things that could go wrong. In the end, Olly's girlfriend saved the day by suggesting a weekend trip to Disneyland Paris instead. Her parents had come up with the idea and they'd offered to take them. Olly was about to turn seventeen, but he wasn't too old for Mickey Mouse, it seemed. Ash and Carla had gladly shelled out the money for Olly's train and Eurostar tickets, a two-day ticket to the theme park and a hotel room for two nights at the Disneyland hotel.

Movement on the other side of the road snaps Ash back to the present.

'Shit!' he whispers to himself, slouching further into his seat as two teenage boys pass by on the pavement opposite.

They pause, looking directly at his car, and he thinks he has been rumbled. For a few seconds, he keeps still and low, but then he sneaks a peek. No, they haven't clocked him. They're no longer looking this way, but he can see their faces, illuminated by the dim street light. With a jolt, he realizes he knows them. His heart flounces about in his ribcage as he waits for them to cross the road and knock on his window or give him the finger or something. *Get a grip*, he tells himself. He'll say he has come to pick up Iris if they ask. Not that it's any of their business what he's doing here. What are *they* doing here? There's no way Millie would have invited them to her eighteenth. Or to her house at all, for that matter.

The two boys walk around the corner and sit on the low wall in front of the Rowlands' house. Both of them take something out of their pockets. Small objects. He squints, but he can't make out what they're doing from here. He wishes he'd brought a pair of binoculars and immediately feels ridiculous for having that thought. It's not like he's a private investigator. He has come here to make sure Iris is OK, not that it's really possible to check up on her through a closed front door. A flame from a lighter tells him what he wants to know. They're skinning up. He observes the kids as they roll their joint and smoke it.

The front door opens and a group of girls – four of them – come out. Millie is among them. The boys whirl round. Then they get up and walk toward the girls. Ash cracks open the window, but can't make out their conversation. He's ready to leap out of the car if there's any trouble, although Iris will no doubt be mortified if he does that. It looks as if the boys are offering the girls something. Cigarettes? Weed? Millie shakes her head. The girl to her right gives them the finger.

Both boys turn tail and walk away, down the driveway and through the gate. The older of the two boys drops the roach on the pavement and stamps on it. Then, finally, they piss off. Ash lets out a sigh of relief. He waits while the girls smoke their cigarettes. Do Jo and Roly know Millie smokes? He'd be surprised. Jo has been on at Roly for years to stop. She definitely wouldn't be happy about her daughter starting. Not that Ash would ever say anything to them. He's glad Iris and Olly don't smoke. As far as he knows. He suspects Olly smokes the odd joint, though. He's sneaked into the house – Ash's place, not Carla's – with bloodshot eyes, the giggles and the munchies after an evening out once or twice. Ash can hardly tell him off. He did the same thing when he was his son's age.

The girls finish their fags and stub them out. Unlike the boys, who left the roach of their joint in the street, they take their cigarette butts back into the house. The music blares out through the front door when Millie opens it, then suddenly becomes quieter and more muffled as the girls close it behind them.

Ash looks all around him. He's not aware that he's formed a plan until he catches himself executing it. He takes a sterile, plastic glove out of the small first-aid kit under the passenger's seat. He looks all around him and checks his mirrors before getting out of the car and darting across the road. He picks up the roach with his gloved hand, then races back to his car. The whole thing takes him less than a minute. Then he starts up the engine to drive home.

Chapter 9

Iris

THEN

After a while, the highs became fewer and further between. Perhaps this was normal in a long-term relationship, just like Josh said. Iris wouldn't know. She'd never been in one. Had Josh changed or had she just got to know him better? She got the impression there was a fake Josh and a real Josh, but she couldn't work out which was which. Was the real Josh the person who had shown her so much love in the beginning? The one who had showered her with praise and presents? Or was he showing his true nature when he sulked and put her down and fobbed her off and blamed her for stuff and called her names? Either way, would she ever get the perfect guy she'd known in the beginning back? The guy she'd fallen in love with? Would she ever experience something as great as that first high again?

They were together 'for better and for worse', Josh would say, like they'd taken actual wedding vows. Well, things had definitely got worse. At the start of their relationship, he'd been so caring. Maybe he didn't love her as much anymore. Perhaps these 'teething problems', Josh kept talking about, were as much her fault as his. Hell, maybe they were all her fault. She was probably the one who was fucking this up. She was the one who wasn't good enough for him. She would have to do better. He was going off her. She felt like the spotlight he used to shine on her had dimmed and everything she did suffered as a result, like she couldn't achieve anything without his attention. She didn't feel like running, or even playing the violin, without his encouragement, which he seemed to be withholding.

He wasn't big on support anymore either. Now, when Iris had a bad day, she couldn't turn to him for comfort because his day had always been worse. When things were going smoothly, something always went wrong – Josh had a problem at home / at school that he was struggling to deal with; someone (else) in his family died; he'd been wrongly accused by one of his teachers / parents / friends of doing something unthinkable; he had an injury and was depressed because he couldn't go running; one of his brothers / his mother was ill and it might be really serious. His dad was being a total dick and didn't understand him like Iris did. Josh seemed to thrive on drama.

Why did she put up with it for so long? Why the fuck didn't she dump him sooner? Iris still asks herself these questions now. At the time, she couldn't have answered that, but now, thanks to hindsight and therapy, she thinks she has worked out some of the answers.

One of the reasons she didn't break up with him was guilt. Josh would tell her how insecure he was and how she made him feel whole. Plus, he'd had a whole load of 'issues' before her – anxiety and insomnia and stuff. And he was terrified that his anxiety would return and he'd be really ill if they ever split up.

'You're the only good thing in my life,' he used to say. 'I don't know what I'd do without you.' He'd said it over and over again.

Iris also stayed because she didn't have many – any? – friends anymore. Other than Millie, she only ever hung out with Josh. What would she do without him? In a way, she needed Josh as much as he needed her.

She was also scared of what he might do to her if she did split up with him. Would he tell everyone in school her secrets? Or would he tell them lies about her? Would he get everyone to ignore her or be mean to her? He was that sort of person. Unforgiving.

And she loved him. Or thought she did. Despite everything. He'd hurt her so many times, but he was trying his hardest to do better.

There was never really any last straw. So it took a while, but Iris eventually came to the conclusion that their relationship had become toxic and no matter whose fault it was, this had to stop. She didn't feel like herself anymore, she didn't even like herself. It was like her identity was tied to his. She could barely remember who she was before she started going out with Josh, but she'd been happier back then than she was now; that much was certain.

The first time *she* dumped *him*, he sent her links to a bunch of songs and even a playlist he'd made on Spotify. He was, Iris guessed, using someone else's lyrics to express what he wanted to say. She didn't reply, but felt bad about it, like she'd sunk to his level now she was the one ignoring him. Then he sent her a really long email, listing all the reasons he loved her. It was really moving. It made her cry. Iris caved in and wrote back. And before she knew it, they were back together again. There followed another honeymoon period, but much shorter than the first. And then they were back on the rollercoaster.

The second time she tried to split up with Josh, he wrote her another email, begging her for one last chance and saying he couldn't live without her and he was having dark thoughts. Suicidal thoughts.

Iris had given him lots of last chances during their relationship. Also, she wasn't sure she totally believed him – she no longer believed a lot of what he said – but there was no way she could take that risk. What if Josh harmed himself? How could she think of ending the relationship if he was thinking of ending his life? If he decided he couldn't live without her, would she be able to live with herself?

She was trapped.

Chapter 10

Carla

NOW

I pride myself on being a rational person, but I'm a firm believer in my own form of karma. I used to be anyway. I like to think that if you do good deeds, then good things end up happening to you, whereas if you do something bad, you eventually get what's coming to you. Since what happened to Iris – my beautiful girl, who is generous and empathetic to a fault – I've become more cynical. Life is often unfair and it doesn't work that way. Tragic things happen to good people; bad people often come out on top. But now Josh has been murdered, I wonder if he has finally had his comeuppance.

I put this to Daniel as we get ready for bed that evening. It's later than usual because he got home so late. I was in no hurry to get to bed. I won't sleep well. I'm glad Iris has gone to the party – she deserves to have some fun after everything she went through, but I'll toss and turn until I hear Ash's car pull up and Iris coming through the front door.

Gently, Daniel takes me by the shoulders and turns me towards him. I'm wearing only my underwear and at first, I misinterpret the gesture. I'm about to say I've missed him but I'm really not in the mood tonight, but his expression is serious, not amorous, as he looks into my eyes. My words stick in my throat.

'Carla, Josh was eighteen years old. Whatever he did, he didn't deserve this. If he was behind what happened to Iris, he made a mistake.'

I feel betrayed because of Daniel's 'if'. I also feel really mean because he's right. Josh was only a kid. He didn't deserve to be stabbed to death. But Josh's 'mistake' ruined my daughter's life. It could easily have cost her *her* life. She was – understandably – withdrawn and depressed for months afterwards. She became paper-thin and gaunt, practically agoraphobic, and I was terrified she would harm herself.

'I know you're worried about Iris,' Daniel continues. 'But if she has nothing to do with this, she has nothing to be afraid of.'

There it is again. That 'if'. With that two-letter conjunction, Daniel has expressed a sliver of doubt about Josh's guilt as well as about Iris's innocence. Anger boils inside me and I push Daniel away.

'For Christ's sake, Daniel!' I shout, then lower my voice a notch. These walls are thick, but I don't want to risk waking up Margo and Olly even so. 'Just for once it would be nice to know you're on my side.'

I turn away from him, unhook my bra with one hand and grab my nightshirt with the other.

'I am on your side,' Daniel protests. 'Carla, darling, I've always been on your side. I'm sorry. I'm jet-lagged and that didn't come out the way I meant it.'

In bed, Daniel holds me and the tension eases from my shoulders a little as I inhale his clean, familiar smell. But long after he has fallen asleep, I lie awake, listening to his slow, regular breathing and staring blindly at the ceiling in the dark.

*

Sitting at the kitchen table, nursing my second coffee of the morning, I eyeball my laptop. I haven't found the willpower to lift the lid and boot it up yet. When I'm alone in the house, I often work in the kitchen, wheeling in my office chair from the adjoining study. It's lighter and warmer in here, for one thing, and the view is better – over rolling green fields, either side of the winding river Bray – although such beautiful scenery can sometimes be more distracting than inspiring. This morning, the rain is belting down and it's misty, so I can't blame my lack of concentration on the view. Nor can I take Cheddar out for a walk to clear my head.

I drain the dregs of my coffee, grimacing as it's now cold, and decide to do a bit of housework. It's always more motivating to knuckle down to some editing when the place is clean and tidy. Perhaps instead of clinging to a belief in karma, I should turn to Saint Expeditus. The patron saint, amongst other things, of those suffering from procrastination.

I clean the worktops and downstairs loo, dust the bookcases and shelves in the sitting room, hoover and wash the floors, Verdi's *Rigoletto* blaring out of my Bluetooth speaker. It's strangely therapeutic doing such mindless tasks, and I start to feel better.

When I've finished downstairs, I lug the vacuum and the bucket of soapy water upstairs and get to work in the bathrooms and bedrooms. Olly's room looks like a bombsite. There are crisp packets and mugs on the floor. With a groan, I throw the rubbish into his wastepaper basket and leave it at the top of the stairs to empty when I've finished up here. Next, I pick up his dirty clothes and stuff them into the overflowing laundry basket on the landing. I tidy his desk, make his bed and pull back the curtains. No matter how often I nag him to clear up after himself, he remains messy. He's an adult now, unlikely to change, I suppose. I sigh in defeat.

I hardly ever go into Iris's bedroom. She keeps her room

spotless. But as I pass the closed door, I pause. Iris's counsellor, Melanie, advised Iris to write a journal, to jot down her thoughts and feelings so they could work through them together in their sessions. I know Iris did this, at least at first – I bought her a Moleskine notebook to use as a diary and I saw her jotting things in it once or twice. Did she hold on to it? Is she still writing in it?

My heart trounces as a thought occurs to me. Could there be anything ... private in her diary? Something ambiguous that could be used against her if it – assuming it exists – found its way into the wrong hands?

Without thinking through what I'm about to do, I open the door and walk into the room. The contrast with Olly's room is remarkable. Everything in here is tidy and clean. It even smells fresh. How can you bring up two children the same way and have them turn out so differently? I rifle through the drawers of her desk. No diary. As I close the last drawer, I think I hear something and whirl round. Iris will never forgive me if she catches me in here. I'm doing this for her, but she'll see it as an invasion of her privacy. And she'd be right.

But it's my imagination. There's no one there. I carry on, peering under ornaments and into jewellery boxes and rummaging through the wicker basket containing her socks and undies. I look through the books on her bookcase. Every few seconds, I check over my shoulder, anxious in case someone should come through the door and find me here.

Nothing. I find nothing. After a few minutes, I sink onto the bed. A wave of guilt washes over me. I'm snooping, searching for something that's none of my business. I can't believe I'm doing this.

But I have to protect my daughter. That's what mothers do. My eyes are drawn to the drawer in her bedside table. Of course! If I wrote a diary, that's where I'd keep it. I move to the end of the bed and open the drawer. It's uncharacteristically messy and there's lots of stuff inside, so I tip the contents onto the floor and sit on the carpet, my back against the bedframe, to sift through everything. Paracetamol; earplugs; a box of rings; a box of condoms – I wince at that; no mother likes to think of her daughter having sex – receipts; shop loyalty cards; an anti-stress ball, which rolls under the bed. There's a small, velvety box and I open it to peek inside. It contains a necklace, which I recognize as a present from Josh. A fox pendant on a silver chain. It was part of a pair – Josh had the other one. Iris stopped wearing hers when they split up. She was irritated that he continued to wear his.

But there's no diary. Perhaps Iris is one step ahead of me. She may already have got rid of it. Or maybe I haven't looked in the right place.

With a sigh – a mixture of relief and frustration, I put everything back into the drawer, fit the drawer back into the bedside table and close it. Then I check the wardrobe. Under clothes, in pockets, even inside shoes and boots. At this point, I see how ludicrous I'm being. Thank God no one is at home to burst in on me. I'm not sure how I would explain this.

Standing up, I take Iris's navy-blue pyjamas – I don't know if they need a wash or not, but I'm about to put on a load of darks. I empty the laundry basket on the landing, separate the washing and wrap my arms around the bundle of dark clothes. I grab Olly's wastepaper basket on my way past and make it downstairs to the utility room without dropping so much as a sock.

As usual, I check all the pockets as I load the washing machine. There's always something that someone has forgotten – earbuds, bus pass, money, keys, you name it – even though I ask everyone to check before they put their dirty clothes in the laundry basket. I find a scrunched-up tissue in the pocket of Iris's jeans. Iris still has a bit hay fever, even though the pollen season should be more or less over by now, and she's a little snuffly at the moment.

But as my fingers close around it, I realize there's something wrapped inside it. Standing up straight, I open the tissue. I left the music on when I went upstairs and the third and final act of *Rigoletto* crescendos to its climactic end. A resounding silence follows, as I stare in disbelief at what I'm holding in my hands. It's a necklace. One of a pair. I've just put Iris's half – the fox on the silver chain – back into the drawer of her bedside table. This one – the wolf pendant on a leather lace – belonged to Josh.

But that's not all. My hand shakes as I examine the pendant. There's a brownish stain on it. It could be mistaken for rust if it wasn't for the tissue, which is unquestionably bloodstained.

My heart clenches as if it's being squeezed in a vice. Why does Iris have this? Is this … could this be Josh's blood? I drop the tissue to the floor. My mind goes into overdrive and I try to block the images my imagination conjures up: my daughter ripping the necklace from Josh's neck as he lies in the woods, bleeding out, with a knife sticking out of his body.

What do I do now? Ash. I need to talk to Ash. I slide my phone out of the back pocket of my jeans. My hand is still trembling as I bring up his number. My call goes straight to voicemail, Ash inviting me in his West Country accent to leave a message. I don't.

Instead, I toss the necklace into the pedal bin in the kitchen. I empty Olly's waste paper basket, too, covering the stained wolf pendant with crisp packets and banana skins. Then I go into the cloakroom and flush the bloody tissue down the toilet. A nosebleed. That's probably all it was.

A scenario unfolds in my head. Josh gave the necklace to Iris, perhaps he threw it at her, wanted nothing more to do with her. She meant to throw it out. With the bloody tissue. I prefer that to the version I came up with just now, in the utility room.

Am I doing the right thing? I came into Iris's room intending to get rid of her diary in case she'd written anything that could be misconstrued. I didn't consider that I might be destroying evidence. But I'm her mother. By definition, I'm hard-wired to shield my children from harm, even if that means covering for them. I didn't manage to protect my daughter when she needed me before. She has been through hell. I'm not going to let her down this time.

My mobile goes. It's Ash. I press the red button to decline the call. Then, head braced against the rain, I take out the rubbish bag. It's bin collection day tomorrow. It will be as if I'd never set foot in Iris's bedroom this morning, as if that necklace had never existed.

Chapter 11

Ian

NOW

'What's this, Ash?' Ian asks, although he can see through the plastic what it is.

'Look, the younger Knoll boys smoked a joint outside your house on the night of Millie's party and—'

'What were they doing outside my house? How do you know this?'

'I was on taxi duty. I picked Iris up that night. I saw them. They were sitting on your wall.'

'Oh.' Ian fiddles with his cigarette packet. *Quitting Will Improve Your Health* is written on it in big, bold, black letters. Jo's always nagging him to stop smoking. He thinks she's more interested in improving their finances than his health, though. Ian has given up more times than he can count.

'They were sitting on your wall, puffing away on a spliff. You know, Jonah and Jeremiah or whatever their names are. Their fingerprints will—'

'Jordan and Jasper Knoll.'

'Right. Jordan and Jasper. Both names beginning with J. Joshua, too. I bet the parents get confused all the time. The teachers, too.'

Ash gives a dry chuckle, but Ian doesn't join in. He has an inkling of where this is going and he doesn't like it. They're sitting at a wooden picnic table in the garden of The Grove, Ash's local, Ash nursing a pint and Ian drinking a coffee. He needs the caffeine fix. It's bloody cold out here, but there's no one else out here so at least they can talk without worrying that someone might overhear. And Ian can smoke. He lights up an Embassy.

Ian is shocked at Ash's appearance. Everything about Ash exudes desperation. His blue eyes are dimmed and underlined with tired, black bags; he's hunched over.

'Please,' Ash says. 'You said if I ever needed you …'

Ian hated thinking about it. He never talked about it. His darkest secret. His greatest shame. His biggest mistake. He'd known it would come back and bite him in the arse one day.

That day has come, apparently. Ian owes Ash, and Ash is calling in that favour. At least, that's what Ian thinks his best mate is doing.

He and Ash met at university – Birmingham – during freshers' week. They were in the same hall of residence. They hit it off straightaway, although, on the surface, they had little in common. They weren't even on the same course. Ian was from Derry; Ash was from Devon – Ash could hardly understand a word he said in his thick accent. They were like Little and Large, only a lot younger and even less funny. But their friendship was firmly cemented the night Ash saved Ian's skin.

He'd been stupid. Really stupid. He'd never been stocious, never even drunk alcohol before he came to university – Ian's father was an alcoholic until he drank himself into an early grave. Afterwards, his mam didn't keep a drop of alcohol in the house, not even wine to use in her cooking.

He thought he was relatively sober when he left the party, but it soon became clear to him that he couldn't hold his drink at all.

Ash had tonsilitis and was on antibiotics. He'd only drunk one pint at the party. He'd cycled to the party, which was off-campus at a student house, whereas Ian had driven out to Aston to buy some second-hand books he'd seen advertised that he thought would make good background reading for his criminology degree. He'd come to the party straight from Aston. He and Ash left at the same time and agreed to meet up back at their hall of residence.

It was dark and she was wearing dark clothes. She came from out of nowhere. Her dog ran across the road and she ran after it. Technically, it wasn't Ian's fault. He told himself that again and again over the weeks that followed, while the girl was lying in hospital with a broken leg, concussion and internal bleeding. But who was he kidding? Who knows if his reactions would have been quicker if he hadn't been blathered. He thought he must have been driving more or less at the speed limit, but he couldn't swear to it. What was he thinking? He wanted to go into the police force, for feck's sake! That wasn't going to happen if he had a criminal record! After a while, Ian couldn't even be sure if his version of events was accurate. Had he swerved? Had he been driving too fast? Recklessly? He didn't think so, but, again, he couldn't swear to it.

Ash arrived a few seconds later. He jumped off his bike and shouted orders at Ian.

'Get the triangle from your car and set it up! Hurry!'

She was breathing, but unconscious. Ash thought something might be broken so he said they couldn't put her in the recovery position. He'd worked last summer as a lifeguard at his local pool. He knew more first aid than Ian did.

Ian did what he was told. Then Ash left Ian watching over the girl, their coats wrapped around her, with strict instructions not to move her, to talk to her non-stop and to monitor her breathing. This was back in the day when very few people – and hardly any students – had mobiles, so Ash legged it to the nearest payphone, which, as luck would have it, wasn't that far away. He called 999.

Ash couldn't have been gone more than a few minutes, but it seemed like hours. It was late and no one else came by the whole time. When Ash got back, he said, 'The ambulance is on its way. I expect they'll send out a police car, too.'

'She ran out in the road, after her dog,' Ian said.

'How much have you had to drink?' Ash asked.

'Too much. Way too much.'

Neither of them spoke for a few seconds.

Then Ash said, 'Is your car insured for any driver?'

'Aye, it is.'

Everyone in the family had used Ian's car before he came away – his brother, his sister, his mam. Ian had worked summer and weekend jobs and paid for it, but he didn't really need it at uni and he'd been a buck eejit to insist on taking it. Plus, it would have been far easier to take the plane than the ferry to come over to the mainland in the first place.

'Ride my bike and meet me back at the hall,' Ash said.

Ash was willing to take the rap for Ian. Ash was breathalysed. He was under the limit. Ian would have failed the test.

Her name was Tracey, she was seventeen and she lived with her parents in a tiny terraced house about half a mile away from where Ian had run her over. She was taking A levels that year. Ash and Ian walked her dog two or three times a week for months, even after she got out of hospital and even after the cast finally came off her leg and she could do it herself, albeit with a pronounced limp.

Tracey couldn't remember the accident itself. Ash's insurance sorted out compensation. Ian was terrified Tracey's parents would sue Ash for dangerous driving; he was terrified his secret would come out in the end.

But as the weeks became months, he began to relax. Tracey and her parents had accepted Ash's version of events and there were no witnesses. No one who could tell them that, actually, Ian was the one driving. Drink-driving.

A truncated version of all this flashes through Ian's mind now, as he puffs on his cigarette and Ash looks at him imploringly.

'I just thought ... I didn't think,' Ash continues. 'I took a glove out of the first-aid kit under the passenger's seat and sprinted across the street and picked it up.'

'And what do you want me to do with it?'

'You know what I want you to do with it, Ian. I'm asking you as a friend.'

This is what Ash does. He protects those he loves like a loyal German shepherd. It's second nature to him. But Ian can't be part of this, even though Ash went above and beyond to save his skin. 'Och, Ash, mate, I could lose my job.'

Ian might not have this job if it wasn't for Ash, but although Ian has a feeling that Ash is thinking this, too, neither of them says it.

'Dammit, Roly, she's innocent!'

'Then she has nothing to fear.'

'She's my daughter. She's your goddaughter!'

Ash has raised his voice. He's usually so composed. The Ashfords have been under so much stress. Ian's afraid that's going to all start up again before it's really calmed down.

'Ash, I can't plant fake evidence,' he says. 'Not even for you. And we can't frame the kids of a family who have just lost their son.' Ian watches Ash's face fall. 'Even though their son was an evil bastard,' he adds, hoping that will cushion the blow.

'I don't want to frame them. Not as such. I just want there to be a clue that points away from Iris.' He emphasizes the word *away*.

'What makes you think there's a clue that points towards her?'

'Come on, Roly. She had a motive. You know that as well as I do. Better than I do. What makes people kill?'

Ian takes one last drag on his cigarette, then exhales the smoke through his nose and stubs out the fag in the ashtray. 'There are loads of reasons, Ash. Literally shitloads.'

'Nine times out of ten it's for money, love or revenge. Isn't that what they say?'

'In films and books, maybe. But this is real—'

'Promise me you won't come after Iris.'

'I can't promise you that. You know I can't promise you that. We'll have to go where the investigation takes us. We're going to have to talk to a whole load of kids who knew him, Iris included.'

'Jesus, Roly.' Ash rakes his fingers through his hair. 'This is such a mess. Can *you* talk to her? Don't let someone she doesn't know interrogate her, will you?'

'It won't be an interrogation, Ash. More like a wee chat. She doesn't have to come in to the police station or anything. Not unless we need a statement. But, yes, I can talk to her personally, if that makes you feel better. She's a minor. She'll need a parent present, so you can be there too.'

Ash nods.

'Look, for all we know, there's DNA on Knoll's body,' Ian says. 'Or on his clothes. We should find out soon enough.' Seeing Ash's blue eyes widen, Ian adds hastily, 'I didn't mean Iris's DNA. I meant the murderer's. I'll keep you posted. You know, unofficially. OK?' He's not sure why he promises this. He can't tell Ash anything. He's not even supposed to share anything with Jo.

Ash drains the rest of his pint. Ian has never seen him look so scared. Ash gets up to go. Ian stands, grabs Ash's arm, retains him.

'Hang on. I'll drop you home,' Ian says, although Ash's house is just a stone's throw from the pub.

Ash pulls away and walks off without saying goodbye.

Ian sits back down and smokes another cigarette. He's consumed with guilt. Guilt for smoking a fag when Jo so badly wants him to quit. Guilt for running over Tracey. He has his Catholic upbringing to thank for all the guilt. (The fact he's a lapsed Catholic only makes it worse.) Above all, he feels bad about not helping his best friends and his goddaughter more when they were having such a shit time. He tried to be there for them, but he wanted to do more than just show support. But cybercrime isn't his field.

Murder, now that *is* his field. This time he can do something. He's the fecking SIO on the case. But he can't possibly do what Ash has asked him to do. He'll feel bad about not doing it, though. It's a damned if you do, damned if you don't situation.

On the table, next to the ashtray, is the knotted glove containing the roach. Honestly, it's like the bloody thing is staring at him. He gets up and scissors over the bench. Then he pulls his keys out of his pocket, grabs the plastic glove and strides across the car park to his car.

Chapter 12

Carla

NOW

I've spent the morning so far procrastinating – something I'm a natural at, especially when I have a tight deadline – and I'm finally booting up my laptop when the doorbell goes. The noise impinging on my concentration makes me jump. Cheddar barks and leaps up from where he was sleeping on the rug. I swear under my breath. It must be a delivery, although I can't remember ordering anything online recently. It's gone midday, but I haven't had a shower yet and I'm still wearing my PJs and an old, shapeless cardigan over the top.

I zip up the cardie and push my feet into the slippers I kicked off under the desk, go through the sitting room into the hallway and open the front door. I'm surprised to see Ash. He's dressed smartly, so he's obviously come from work.

'I've brought lunch,' he says, thrusting two M&S salads, a loaf of fresh bread and a packet of Red Leicester into my arms. 'Can't stay long. I've got an appointment with a customer at two.'

Ash doesn't normally show up unannounced or uninvited. Or when the kids are out. And it's a long drive from Barnstaple – an hour's round trip – just to pop in for lunch. I look over my shoulder. I've had more work come in over the past couple of days and I really want to type up my editorial report and get it sent off today – before tomorrow's deadline. 'Your timing's bad, Ash.'

'Oh. Have you got someone ...?' He leaves the end of his sentence unsaid, his eyebrows shooting into circumflexes as he looks past me into the house. Then he frowns and blushes, no doubt hearing how that sounded.

'No, Ash. That's the sort of thing *you* ... Sorry. I was working. I haven't taken the time to get dressed yet.' My tummy rumbles and I realize how hungry I am. 'It's fine. Come in.' I step back and let him step inside. 'I'm just going to grab a shower. Make yourself at home.' I point towards the open door to the kitchen.

Ash is in a bit of a hurry, I'm hungry and I'm keen to find out why he's come, so I make sure my shower is a quick one. I don't bother to wash my hair, just scrape it back into a ponytail. I'm only gone a few minutes.

When I enter the kitchen, Ash is sitting at the table. His long legs are sticking out from under it. He hasn't taken off his shoes, forgetting, or perhaps flouting, one of Daniel's rules.

'I've always loved this room,' he muses, scanning it.

I described my dream kitchen to Ash long before we even bought Crooked Oak Cottage. A rustic country kitchen with a long wooden table. An Aga with large copper pans hanging above it and tantalizing smells emanating from a cast-iron casserole dish on the hob. Big windows, lots of light. Terracotta tiles on the floor. Warm, cosy, inviting. The heart of the house, where I pictured myself learning to cook all sorts of delicious meals for my family. Ash and I tiled the floor and put up the shelves and cupboards ourselves. It really is my dream kitchen, minus the copper pans. And the tempting aromas, at least, when I'm the one cooking. It was once our kitchen. Ash knows his way round it. He has laid the table for our lunch.

We eat in silence. It's a comfortable one, but I sense Ash has something to tell me and I'm not sure I want to hear it. He waits until we've finished eating and he has made coffee.

'I saw Joshua's two little brothers – Jordan and Jackson the other day—'

'Jordan and Jasper.'

'—smoking a joint.'

'Go on,' I say as he pauses. I have no idea where he's going with this.

'I think they're dealing drugs. Weed. They tried to flog some to Millie.'

'Really? Where was this? Have you told Ian?'

'It was in front of the Rowlands' house. On the night of the party. When I went to fetch Iris. The Knoll boys were sitting on the garden wall, skinning up. Yeah, Roly knows they were there. I didn't tell him they tried to sell Millie some weed, though. She didn't buy any, so it didn't seem important. Did you know she smoked?'

'What, marijuana?'

'No. Cigarettes.'

'Oh. No, I didn't. Why are you telling me this? Did you drive out all this way to share that with me?'

'No, no, I didn't.' Ash runs his fingers through his hair and looks away.

I know my ex-husband. There's something he's not telling me. But he has clammed up for now. He's probably been talking to Ian about Josh's death. Oh God. Maybe the police already suspect our daughter. But I when I put this to Ash, he shakes his head.

'Roly says they don't have any suspects yet,' he says.

I have to ask. 'Ash, do *you* think Iris had anything to do with … Josh's murder?' The words are barely audible as they leave my mouth. I shouldn't be asking myself that question, let alone Ash.

'How can you ask that?' Ash says.

He sounds shocked, which reassures me a little. Despite my best efforts, I haven't been doing a very good job of silencing the voice in my head that keeps reminding me that everything points to Iris. First, the knife. Then Iris's reactions when she came home from school that day – or rather, her lack of reaction. And the fact that no one wanted Joshua dead as much as Iris did. This can all be explained away. A) I was wrong about the knife – it was there all along. B) Iris was all cried out and utterly exhausted and in shock by the time she got home – understandably – so she didn't cry in front of me and she fell asleep. C) Just because she had a motive and had repeatedly wished Josh dead out loud to me doesn't mean she killed him.

But now there's the bloody tissue and the necklace. I've come up with an explanation for that, too, and I try to hold on to it, even as I wonder if I'm clutching at straws. But I'm finding it harder to convince myself this time. Even though I'm her mother. I know in my heart that Iris is not capable of such violence. But I also believe that anyone – *everyone* – is capable of murder if pushed hard enough. And Iris was certainly pushed.

'Do you?' I insist, meeting Ash's eyes.

'No! No, of course not,' he says. I believe him. Ash thinks Iris is incapable of doing anything wrong. She's a daddy's girl. She's his blind spot, just as Olly is mine. 'Listen, Carla, Joshua was probably killed by some grockle he had a run-in with. But you and I both know she's likely to come under suspicion at some point. At the very least, she's going to be questioned.'

'Did Ian tell you that?'

'Roly said they were talking to everyone who knew Josh well.'

I take a deep breath. I wasn't going to admit this to Ash, but he deserves to know. Iris is his daughter, too, after all. And she and I both need his support. Again. 'I found Josh's necklace. You know, the one with the wolf pendant.'

'Where?'

'Wrapped up in a tissue in the pocket of Iris's jeans.'

'When?'

'Just the other day.'

'All right. Well, he may have given it back to her shortly before he died,' Ash reasons. 'She resented him wearing it after their break-up, didn't she?'

'Ash, the tissue was covered in blood.' I can hear the panic in my voice. I don't need to explain my thinking to Ash. The bloody tissue suggests Iris got the necklace back after Josh's death, not shortly before it.

'So you think it's Josh's blood?' He sounds incredulous.

'I don't know what to think!' I sound hysterical now. I'm on the verge of tears.

'Carla, it's probably Iris's blood. I'm sure there's a perfectly reasonable explanation.' I can tell he believes what he's saying. I wish I believed him. 'Why don't you ask Iris?'

'I don't know if I can now. I should have asked her at the time, but I threw out the necklace.' I'm doing my best to get a grip, but a sob escapes. 'And the tissue,' I add.

I expect Ash to berate me for destroying something that might be evidence. But he doesn't. Instead, he takes a deep breath. I sense he's about to tell me something. Whatever it was he went to the trouble of driving out to Crooked Oak Cottage on his lunch break to share with me.

'I picked up the roach of the joint the two Knoll brothers smoked,' he says. 'I gave it to Roly to … for the crime scene … their fingerprints, you know … I just wanted something to send the investigation in a different direction. Away from Iris. I know it wasn't her, obviously, but I'm scared they'll come after her.' He looks embarrassed. 'I don't know what I was thinking.'

I do. I'm also terrified that Iris will come under suspicion. But now I've found the tissue, I'm starting to suspect her myself, whereas in Ash's head, there's not even a sliver of doubt about her innocence. As usual, though, when it comes to our offspring, Ash and I are working in tandem. I'm bent on destroying evidence and he's trying to plant it.

'Roly wasn't having it, of course,' Ash says when I don't say anything. 'Listen, I'll ask Iris about the necklace, OK?'

I nod mutely. I can't speak past the lump in my throat.

'Have you told Dandruff about it?' Ash asks. 'Sorry, I meant Dan.'

I shake my head.

'Good. Don't. Don't tell anyone else. About the necklace or the joint. Especially not Jo.'

Ash gets up, comes round to my side of the table and squeezes my shoulder. He's about to leave and I desperately want him to stay, having jettisoned any notions I had of getting any work done today.

'I'll ask Iris about the necklace,' I say, finally finding my tongue. I think it's better if it comes from me. She'll get mad if she discovers I talked to Ash about it before talking to her.

'OK,' he says. 'Keep me posted.'

'Ash, what if the police end up suspecting Iris?'

'We'll cross that bridge if we come to it, but we won't,' Ash says with a lot more confidence than he can possibly be feeling.

Chapter 13

Iris

<u>THEN</u>

Later, Iris found it ironic. She'd been sitting cross-legged on her bed, making notes on Deborah Tannen's theory of 'genderlects'. Basically, the idea that men and women learnt different ways of communicating through socialization. Or, in other words, that men and women could walk away from the same conversation with completely different interpretations of what had just been said.

She was really into the linguist's book, *You Just Don't Understand*, which Mr Lawton, her English teacher, had recommended as background reading, when her phone beeped with a text. She smiled, knowing it would be Josh.

Wanna see how you make me feel?
J x

She thought he'd just send her a selfie. He'd be grinning in it, showing off his perfect teeth, one of the perks of having an orthodontist for a father. She fired off a quick text in reply.

Sure x

Her phone pinged again, almost immediately. She was about to highlight an important bit in the book. But if she didn't reply straightaway, Josh might get salty, so she stopped reading, picked up the phone and looked at the screen. She gasped. Not what she'd been expecting at all. Girls and boys definitely didn't speak the same language. So, yes, ironic. A little disturbing, too. This wasn't a selfie that showed off Josh's perfectly aligned, white teeth. It was a dick pic, a zoomed-in close-up of Josh's hand on his erect penis.

At first, she felt a bit irritated. She was trying to study and she hadn't signed up for this. But somehow, she couldn't tear her eyes from the screen. If she was honest, she was feeling a bit turned on.

It didn't occur to her straightaway that he was expecting a similar reply. She was still staring at the photo when another message came in.

WTTP?

She dropped the phone on the bed, as if it had burnt her, squealing out loud. No! She deffo did NOT want to trade photos. She reached for her phone and typed out an answer. It took her a while to get the wording right – she wasn't going to send a nude selfie, but she didn't want him to sulk or ghost her. When she was satisfied, she added kisses and exclamation marks to keep him calm and sent the message.

Thx for the pic!!!

> Doing homework right now.
> Some other time, maybe.
> xxx

By which she meant no. No way.

But, predictably, that's not how Josh took it. She hadn't been clear enough or, more likely, he'd chosen to go with a different reading of what she'd written. He replied, saying he'd hold her to that. Then, over the next couple of weeks, he gradually dialled up the pressure, reminding her she owed him a nude pic and promising to delete it as soon as he'd seen it. She didn't need to be a prude. She had such a beautiful body. He loved her so much. He'd do anything for her. Didn't she trust him? Yada, yada, yada.

Eventually, he wore her down, but she was careful not to show her face in the photo. Nothing that gave away her identity. For several days, he was like the cat that got the cream. He was also particularly attentive and loving. He said and did all the right things. The perfect boyfriend.

She thought that would be the end of it. But, nope, it was just the beginning. Before she knew it, they'd moved on to videos. He sent one of himself in the shower, all lathered up and spending *way* too long soaping his genitals. She knew she'd be expected to return the favour, if you could call it that. Every time she sent a pic or a vid, she made him promise to delete it after viewing it.

Mrs Davis, the day matron at school had talked to them a few years ago about sexting and sextortion in PSHE – personal, social, health and economic education. Mrs Davis was clearly out of touch with reality as well as uncomfortable about standing in front of a group of prepubescent teens. She stared at the floor and went red every time she said words like 'sex' or 'nudity'. She reeled off definitions of words like grooming, catfishing, upskirting and fake porn. She repeatedly used terms such as 'illegal', 'without consent' and 'against the law'. She insisted on 'stranger danger' when communicating online.

There had only been one PSHE lesson on this, shortly before lockdown, a few years before Iris was even going out with Josh. Not that that was an excuse. Iris was aware of the dangers of sending nude photos and videos, but to begin with at least, it didn't really cross her mind that those dangers applied to her. She wasn't being taken in by a catfish; she was exchanging intimate pictures with her boyfriend. He'd seen her naked body IRL, so it wasn't like she was revealing anything he wasn't familiar with. And he said nice things about her body when she sent him pics, which made her feel good about herself. He made her feel beautiful. Plus, he was sending her photos and videos of himself, too. They trusted each other. He would never use her photos to blackmail her. He didn't need money – his parents were minted and Josh always had rolls of cash on him.

A nagging voice in Iris's head, that sounded creepily like Matron's, piped up every now and then to tell her she was being stupid and naïve. But Iris did her best to stifle it. She'd overheard Mum saying to Jo once that teenagers needed 'new and naughty', that becoming an adult was all about 'taking risks and pushing boundaries and having sex'. All her life, Iris had been a good girl. She'd done everything she'd been told – by parents and teachers alike. And since meeting Josh, she'd realized something. Her life had been boring before him. She'd been boring. And bored. Plain vanilla.

But, after a while, when things started to go tits up with Josh, Iris saw how dumb she'd been. When she finally dumped Josh for the third and last time, not long after his eighteenth birthday party, he texted non-stop. He would write things that Iris didn't know how to interpret. When she didn't react this time to 'I can't live without you', he tried a different tack.

> I can't stop looking at photos of you. I wouldn't want anyone else to see you like this. Ever.
> xxx

Was this a thinly veiled threat? Why did he say 'I wouldn't' instead of 'I don't'? Was she reading too much into it? But since she'd known him, Josh had alternated punishments with rewards. That was his nature. That was how he behaved. Was he going to punish her?

Iris thought about blocking Josh – his phone number, his email, his social media accounts. But that wouldn't make the problem go away. And it might be better if she got his messages. That way, if he was going to blackmail her, at least she'd receive the threat and know about it. From that day on, Iris lived with a knot in her stomach. It tightened whenever she was likely to encounter Josh – at school, at cross-country training or competitions.

But time passed and nothing happened. He didn't blackmail her. The messages kept coming. Sometimes the tone was angry; at others he was apologetic, nostalgic or even loving. His words were never threatening. After a while, he wrote less frequently and the knot in her stomach eased.

His punishment, when he did inflict it months later, was ruthless. And the fallout turned out to be worse than she could ever have imagined.

Chapter 14

Carla

NOW

It's a simple question, or so it seems to me, but it quickly morphs into a confrontation and I wish I'd let Ash handle this after all.

'What are you accusing me of, exactly?' Iris demands, her hands on her hips.

'I'm not accusing you of anything,' I say. 'I just want to know how you came to have Josh's necklace in your possession.'

'You think I killed him, don't you?'

'No.' It doesn't sound convincing, not to me anyway. I hope she doesn't notice. 'Iris, sit down and let's talk.'

Iris remains standing and starts pacing up and down the floor of her bedroom. She's stomping, but I don't think it has the desired effect with her socks on the thick carpet.

'You do! You think I killed him! That's why you've been checking up on me! You had no right to go through my things!' She's almost shouting.

'I only checked your pockets before I washed your clothes!'

My voice has ratcheted up a notch, too, and I force myself to lower the volume. 'The necklace was in the pocket of your jeans.'

'I'm not talking about my jeans,' she says. 'I'm talking about the drawer in my nightstand.' My mouth opens and closes again. How does she know I went through the drawer? It was a mess in there even before I tipped out her stuff. 'And don't bother to deny it,' Iris continues, 'I know you went through it. I found the anti-stress ball under the bed.'

Ah, now I remember the ball rolling under the bed when I tipped the stuff out. I must have forgotten to put it back in.

'What were you looking for? Where else did you look?' Iris demands.

I decide to answer the first of these questions and ignore the second one. I'm not about to fess up to rummaging through her wardrobe as well, but I can level with her about the diary. 'Iris, look, I'm worried about you. I'm worried the police might think you had something to do with Josh's death. I wanted to make sure there was nothing that might …' I'm about to say 'incriminate', but I catch myself.

Iris glares at me through narrowed eyes. I'm making a right hash of this.

'I know you started a diary,' I continue, 'when Melanie suggested you should write down your thoughts and feelings. I can only imagine how much you must have hated Josh after what he did to you and I thought maybe we should … I should …' I sigh. 'I thought it might be a good idea to get rid of it in case anything you wrote could be … misinterpreted.'

I can see Iris's expression softening. 'Oh,' she says, conveying something resembling forgiveness in that one syllable.

I try again. 'So are you going to tell me?'

'About the diary?'

Why do I always feel as if I'm talking at cross purposes with my teenage kids? Iris stops pacing and folds her arms across her chest. Hmmm. I'm not quite forgiven, then. I need to tread carefully. 'Well, I meant about the necklace, actually,' I say, 'but—'

'I mean, Josh knew I was pissed off at him for wearing that stupid his-and-her necklace.' She pauses, as if daring me to reprimand her for her language. I don't. I want to hear what she has to say. 'So he gave it back to me. Sort of like a peace offering, I s'pose. Like that could make everything better!'

'I see. When I found it, it was wrapped in a bloodstained tissue. Whose blood was it?'

'Mine!' Another hesitation. Is it my imagination or is she working out what to say? Weighing up her words? Coming up with a story? 'I cut my finger,' she continues. 'A paper cut. It hurt like hell and bled like mad. So I wrapped the tissue around my finger. I was going to chuck the necklace out, so I wrapped it in the tissue 'cause that was for the bin, too. Clearly, I forgot to throw it out.'

'Right, well, I threw it out, the tissue and the necklace, so it's gone now.' I pull on the door handle, ready to leave her room before she can tell me I had no right to discard her stuff.

'And I threw out the diary,' Iris says quietly.

I freeze for a split second, stunned by her admission, then I step out onto the landing and close her bedroom door behind me.

I've decided to attempt a new recipe from the Mary Berry cookbook Margo gave me last Christmas – sausage and red pepper hot pot. I need to get a few things from the supermarket. Sausages and red peppers, for a start. I ring Ash via speakerphone from the car. He's at work and I expect to get voicemail, so while the phone rings, I mentally prepare a message.

To my surprise, he answers my call on the third or fourth ring. 'Carla. Everything all right?' The rhotic sounds of his North Devon accent are really pronounced in that one, tiny question and the familiarity of his voice almost makes me smile.

'Yes, Ash, everything's fine. I just rang to say that I asked Iris about the wolf pendant and bloodstained tissue. You were right.

It was her blood.' I tell Ash what she told me.

'Ah, good. I told you there would be a reasonable explanation, didn't I?'

'Yes, you were right,' I repeat.

'Do you believe her?'

'Yes,' I say, but it comes a beat too late. Ash will know I'm lying.

The hot pot is simmering on the hob and I've taken Cheddar out for a walk despite the drizzle. I've also done a little bit of work. I'm feeling exhausted, but very pleased with myself, as I sit down with Margo in the living room to do her reading. I've made a mug of tea, which is steaming on the coffee table in front of me and Margo has pulled the blanket over our legs.

Just as Margo opens her book, the doorbell goes. I mutter a mild swear word under my breath, not loud enough for Margo to hear.

I open the door and find myself face to face with Yvonne Knoll, Joshua's mother. I was irritated when the doorbell went; now I'm furious. How dare this woman show up on my doorstep! She's not welcome here. It's still spitting, but there's no way I'm inviting her in.

She's quite a lot taller than me, so it gives me some satisfaction to look down on her from my raised position inside the house. I'm struck by her appearance. She looks thin and ill. She's overdressed – in a tweed skirt, blazer and heels – and she's wearing far too much make-up, as always, but her foundation and concealer fail to hide the dark rings under her eyes, the deep-red lipstick doesn't fill in the cracks in her dry lips and her blusher seems to highlight her gaunt cheeks. Her bleached teeth – no doubt courtesy of her orthodontist husband – are the only thing about her that remain polished. She looks so frail that I almost give in and allow her to step into the hallway, but then I think better of it. I don't want this woman anywhere near my family or inside my home.

'I shouldn't have come here,' she begins. She's right about that. 'I wanted to talk to you, you know, mother to mother. I ...' Her voice trails off, as if the motivation she'd had for coming here is now abandoning her. I'm not going to help her. I wait.

Her hair is wet and bedraggled now. A streak of black mascara has run down each of her cheeks. I can't tell if she's crying or if it's the rain. She looks absolutely terrible. She swipes at her face with her hand and I notice her chipped nails. She usually looks as if she's just stepped out of a beauty salon and has never done an hour's housework in her entire life. I feel myself thawing, ever so slightly – she cuts such a pathetic figure, you'd have to be heartless not to feel a bit sorry for her, but I'm not caving in. She can stay outside in the rain until she has said what she has come here to say.

'I know you went through a lot with Iris during the last school year,' she continues at length. 'I know how close you are to your daughter. So, perhaps you can understand a little the pain I'm going through right now. When a woman loses a child, well, there's no word for it, is there?'

I wonder if she means there's no word like 'widow' or 'widower' for someone who has lost their spouse or 'orphan' for someone who has lost a parent. Or does she mean her pain is indescribable? I don't ask. But I feel a sudden pang of guilt at the lack of compassion I'm showing her. She's a mother who has just lost her son.

'I want justice for my son, just as you wanted justice for your daughter,' she says. 'And I think perhaps I could have – *should* have – helped you get justice for Iris, even if it meant encouraging my son to admit he did something very wrong.'

At this, any pity I had for this woman evaporates. My hand clenches at my side as the anger boils up inside me like lava. The nerve of this woman! She has more or less admitted that Joshua was responsible for everything Iris has been through since last December and she thinks that I'm going to force a confession out of Iris for Josh's murder.

'I have no right to ask you to help me now, but you and Iris are the only people who can help me,' she pleads.

I'm not a violent person, but it takes every ounce of my willpower not to ram her perfect teeth down her throat. 'Yvonne, I think you should leave.'

'I want justice for Joshua.' Her voice has a harder edge to it now. I see my own fury mirrored in her eyes.

'And I want you to go. Don't you ever come here again. Don't come near me or my family. Do you understand?'

I try to close the door, but she pushes against it.

'A mother always knows,' she says. And with that parting shot, she turns on her high heels and teeters down the gravel driveway towards her car.

I slam the front door and swear, loudly this time, even though Margo is standing in the hallway. She jumps and Cheddar scuttles into the kitchen with a whine. Margo follows him.

I look up to see Iris standing at the top of the stairs. How much of that did she overhear? She turns and heads along the landing to her bedroom. Then she slams her door, too.

I sit on the stairs and concentrate on breathing in through my nose and out through my mouth. It takes several minutes before my heart rate and breathing slow down. And then a few more until I stop shaking.

Chapter 15

Ian

NOW

He's standing in the porch, sneaking a quick smoke, when he spots the trainers. He has come home for dinner this evening (Helena, his deputy SIO, insisted she had it all under control), and he was hoping to disconnect for a few hours. No hope of that now he's seen the shoes. His mind is firmly back on the case.

They haven't made much headway. They're still waiting on the forensics, even though he has nudged (well, harassed, if he's honest) the lab people, asking repeatedly for the samples to be fast-tracked. He's not optimistic about the results. The victim's body was found several days after death and it rained heavily on at least three of those days. For the moment, he doesn't have much to go on. This is his first case as SIO and he's feeling the pressure.

He'd always wanted to be a police officer. Secretly. It wasn't really something you could mention to your parents or your careers adviser at St Mary's Boys' School when you were from the Bogside. The Police Service of Northern Ireland has come a long way since its Royal Ulster Constabulary days and they're recruiting more Catholics, but in a place like Derry, that still carries visible, raw scars from the Troubles. You can't really get away from religion and politics. His family would never have approved. A copper on the mainland, however, didn't seem to carry the same stigma as a peeler in Northern Ireland. Or perhaps it did, but his mother was able to be vague about what he did for a living with him over here. (He'd once heard her tell an elderly neighbour that he worked in security.)

He has always felt like he needs to prove himself in his job, like he has to justify his career choice. To his mam. To himself. The murder of Joshua Knoll is both shocking and tragic, but it's also a good opportunity for Ian to make a name for himself, maybe even advance his career. In this neck of the woods, you only get murders once in a blue moon. He may not get another chance.

He keeps thinking he should step down, though. Or at the very least tell his manager he has an emotional involvement in the case. He has arranged with Ash and Carla to talk to Iris tomorrow. It's not really his job. Technically, it's probably against protocol. Two of his officers have been handling the interviews with Josh's family and friends, although Ian himself went to see Richard and Yvonne. Despite what Ash seems to think, Iris isn't a suspect, but she does have a motive and Ian has a feeling she might become one. And as Ian is Iris's godfather, there will be a clear conflict of interests. He'll be taken off the case.

He stubs out the fag on the side of a plant pot, tries to ignore the shoes, left neatly side by side on the doorstep, opens the front door and steps inside the house. He's greeted by raucous laughter from Millie's bedroom upstairs. It brings a smile to his face, albeit briefly. The girls are having fun. They deserve to. They've both been working so hard at school. Millie has set her sights high. She wants to get at least two A stars. And, according to Ash, Iris is getting excellent marks, despite missing so much of the last school year. He wonders if Iris knows he's calling round tomorrow morning to interview her.

He goes into the kitchen and makes himself a mug of tea. He's still clasping the mug in his hands, the tea long gone cold, when Jo finds him. His brain registers that she has spoken to him, but won't replay her words.

'Sorry, darling. I was miles away. What did you say?'

'I said, you smell of cig … Never mind. A penny for them?'

Ian sighs. 'It's the case.'

'You want to talk about it?'

'You know I can't.'

'That doesn't usually stop you,' Jo says.

He sighs again. 'If I talk to you, you can't go blabbing to Carla.' He looks at her sternly. He knows women talk. But it's not on this time, for obvious reasons.

'OK. I promise.'

'Ash came to me with the butt of a spliff. He'd wrapped it up in a plastic glove to preserve the fingerprints.'

'Whose fingerprints were on it?'

'The two younger Knoll boys smoked it outside our place on the night of Millie's party, according to Ash.'

'What were they doing at our place?' Jo has raised her voice.

Ian doesn't answer. He shakes his head and frowns, both almost imperceptible movements.

'Wrong question,' Jo says, as if reading his mind. 'What did Ash want you to do with the roach?'

'He wanted me to plant it as evidence to keep Iris out of the frame,' Ian says.

'No way!'

Ian is silent for a few seconds. He has never told Jo about Tracey. He tells his wife everything – well, most things – and he would have told her if it had ever come up. He'd intended to tell her when they first met, but the longer he put it off, the less it seemed to matter. Or maybe the more it seemed to matter. Until he reached a point where there was no way he could bring it up anymore. Too much time had passed.

This time she misinterprets his silence. 'Ian, you didn't do it, did you?'

'No, of course not.' He doesn't admit he went back and forth on that a bit. He has actually kept the roach. Just in case he goes back on it again. But he doesn't think he will. He can't plant evidence. He could lose his job. It's a bit late now anyway. Plus, it would take a lot more than a handful of Hail Marys and Our Fathers for him to ever forgive himself if he did something like that.

He's about to tell Jo about the shoe, but just then Millie and Iris burst in, looking for food.

'Don't eat too much,' Jo warns, as Millie takes a family-sized packet of crisps out of the cupboard. 'It'll be dinnertime in half an hour.'

'Are you staying for dinner, Iris?' Ian asks. 'You're welcome to if you'd like.' He catches the look Jo throws him, but pretends not to.

'Um ... better not,' Iris says as the girls head for the door. So, she knows he's arranged to question her.

'You making the meal, are you?' Jo says as soon as the girls are out of earshot.

'Well, I'll help if you like,' Ian says, which earns him another look. 'I'm a dab hand at setting the table.'

'I mean, I know Ash is your best mate, but he can't expect you to put your job on the line for him like that,' says Jo, picking up the conversation more or less from where they left off.

'Aye, I know.'

He sets the table and heads outside, ostensibly for another smoke. He feels Jo's disapproving eyes on his back as he slopes out of the kitchen. He has to check out that shoe.

He takes his packet of Embassy out of his shirt pocket and lights up a cigarette. He smokes it right down to the butt and stubs it out before he picks up one of her trainers. The left one.

It's a size six and a half. Vans. Old Skool. Maroon or Bordeaux or deep red or something, although the colour is irrelevant. Ian turns over Iris's trainer and looks at the sole. The shoe they're looking for has a distinctive tread pattern. The top and bottom have a criss-cross design and the middle looks like honeycomb. Just like this one. Shit! He examines the top of the shoe, but although it's a little dirty, there are no stains or anything like that. He replaces the trainer, lining it up next to the other one, leaving it exactly how he found it.

It's much later, long after Iris has gone home, when he tells Jo about it. They're getting ready for bed, although Ian doesn't think he'll be able to sleep. Too many thoughts vying for attention in his brain. Jo has been giving out at him for being elsewhere, not listening to a word she has been saying – the usual. And it just spills out.

'We found a footprint in the woods,' he begins, 'within metres of where Joshua Knoll was murdered.'

'Go on,' Jo says, sitting on the edge of the bed and giving him her full attention.

'Size six and a half.'

'Women's?'

'I think the shoes are unisex, but the size is more likely to suggest a woman's foot, yeah.' He gets straight to the point. 'Unless I'm very much mistaken, Iris's left shoe is a match for the print we found. We'd have to check the wear on the soles and so on, but—'

'What do you mean, it's a match?'

'Same size. Same make. Same model. Vans. Old Skool. They have a particular pattern on the soles.'

'Come with me,' Jo says.

He follows her downstairs and through the kitchen to the utility room. She picks up a pair of shoes. Vans. Old Skool.

'This make and model?' she says, thrusting a pair of blue trainers into his hands. 'These are Millie's, obviously, but every other girl in her and Iris's class must have a pair. Probably some of the boys, too. They all wear the latest trend, Ian. Last year, it was Nike Air Force One, a few years ago it was Converse in the summer and Uggs in the winter. Stop overthinking and come to bed. It's cold in here.'

Jo leaves the room, no doubt expecting him to follow her back upstairs. Looking at his daughter's shoes in his hands, Ian heaves a sigh of relief. Every other teenager has the same shoes. The footprint could be anyone's. His relief is short-lived. He looks at the label inside one of the shoes. These are also a six and a half. He reasons with himself. It's just a coincidence. For Millie as well as for Iris. He should take his wife's advice and go to bed. He needs to switch off.

But as he lies awake in the dark that night, staring at the red digits projected from the alarm clock onto the ceiling, he can't help going over what he hasn't told Jo. He hasn't told her that the footprint was left after the crime was committed. Probably a few days afterwards. After the rain. That it was found in an exposed area, a small clearing in the woods. Next to Joshua's body. That if the shoeprint had been left by Joshua's murderer when they'd killed him, it would have been washed away by the rain.

Ian knows the footprint means that someone was there *after* Josh died. At first, he thought it might have been left by one of the first responders. But now an image has planted itself in his mind. Someone standing over and looking down on the dead body. The print definitely wasn't left by the couple who found him. Both the man and woman wore Wellington boots to go out and pick blackberries.

But just because the footprint wasn't left there on the day of Josh's murder doesn't mean that it wasn't left by his murderer. Ian's theory is that, for whatever reason, the victim's murderer returned a few days later to the scene of the crime.

Chapter 16

Iris

THEN

It started off like a normal school day, nothing special. But by morning break something definitely felt off. Iris was sitting on a bench in the quad, soaking up some sun and chatting to Millie when she clocked a bunch of boys from the year above her staring and sniggering. She didn't think anything of it until two girls, coming out of the toilets in the building opposite, also pointed. One of them giggled behind her hand while the other threw back her head and cackled. Were they talking about her? Laughing at her? At Millie? At both of them? Perhaps she was just being paranoid. Iris didn't know any of the pupils, boys or girls.

Iris was in Year 12 at the time and South Lydacombe's stupid IT Acceptable Use Policy forbade pupils to use their mobiles during the day 'unless authorized by a member of staff, in class or in the library, for educational purposes'. Only students in Year 13 were allowed to go on their phones during break times 'in certain designated areas', like the common rooms and tuckshop.

Which basically meant that pretty much everyone in the year above Iris knew before Iris herself. It wasn't until lunchtime that Iris realized everyone was laughing at her and talking about her. But she still didn't have a clue what they were saying.

'What's going on?' Millie whispered as they sat down at the long wooden tables in the school dinner hall.

'Beats me,' Iris said.

So, there she was, in Geography, the first lesson of the afternoon, bored out of her mind, when she overheard the pupils behind her whisper her name. She wanted to whirl round and demand to know what everyone was saying about her. Instead, she strained her ears, tuning out Mr Steven's droning to try and eavesdrop on their conversation. She couldn't make out much, just the odd word here and there, but she did catch another name. Joshua Knoll.

She shivered, as if the temperature in the classroom had suddenly dropped several degrees. Had Josh started a malicious rumour about her? Or maybe it was his new girlfriend, Sasha Spencer-Lyles.

It was Megan Jessop who filled her in later that afternoon. Megan was the head girl *and* captain of the girls' school cross-country club, the school's golden girl. She was a year older than Iris – in Josh's class. Iris had had a history test in her last lesson and hadn't quite finished writing when the bell went. Mr Mason had allowed her an extra five minutes. The other girls were already in the changing rooms, getting changed into their running kit when Iris got there. The second Iris stepped inside, it was like someone had hit mute. She scanned the faces. Some of the girls were staring at her, their mouths open; others seemed to be concentrating on their shoelaces. At least they weren't laughing at her. But she could totally feel them judging her.

'Will someone tell me what's going on?' Iris's voice came out sounding like a whimper.

Megan approached Iris, took her by the elbow and led her

straight back out the door she'd just come through. 'I tried to find you earlier to tell you,' Megan said. 'I thought you'd know by now. I didn't think you'd come to training.'

Iris wished she'd just spit it out.

'Some students have been sharing a video of you on their group chats and social media,' Megan continued. 'Someone posted the video to my drama WhatsApp group this morning.'

'What sort of video?' But Iris already knew the answer.

'Come with me,' Megan said.

Iris's legs threatened to give way as she followed Megan round the corner of the building, where they were less likely to get caught using a mobile phone. Leaning against the wall, Megan took her mobile out of a pocket in her tracksuit top, brought up a post on WhatsApp and angled the screen towards Iris. Below the message: *Have you seen this?!* was a video. Iris didn't need to press play to know which one.

She turned away from Megan, bent over and threw up on the ground. Megan held Iris's hair back from her face with the hand that wasn't holding the phone, even though her hair was tied up.

When they were dating, Josh had coaxed her to make a video for him. He'd even given her specific instructions. He wanted to see her naked and touching herself. This video was supposed to be for his eyes only. He'd promised to delete it. Clearly, he hadn't kept his promise. Had he shared it deliberately?

'We should report this,' Megan said, magically producing a tissue from another pocket for Iris to wipe her mouth with. 'I'll come with you.'

Iris nodded. She had no intention of going to her cross-country training session now anyway. Josh would be there and she couldn't face him. Not today. Maybe not ever again. She didn't want to face anyone. Iris was rooted to the spot. Paralysed. Megan had to literally pull her along to find Mrs Hamilton, the deputy head pastoral.

Mrs Hamilton was in the staffroom. Iris was a little intimidated by her, to be honest. She had long black hair, angular features and a penchant for black clothes and she was, like, really bossy.

'Mrs Hamilton, would it be possible to speak to you privately about a very serious matter?' Megan said. Her intonation implied it wasn't a question. She had the right tone of voice – firm, mature, not too dramatic, even though she was a great actress if her performance in the school's production of *Les Mis* last year was anything to go by.

Mrs Hamilton suggested they should go to her office. Megan and Iris sat down on one side of the wide desk opposite Mrs Hamilton, who asked, 'Now, what seems to be the problem?'

It was Megan who spoke. Iris couldn't find any words and couldn't have spoken them anyway.

'Mrs Hamilton,' Megan said in her plummy voice, 'it has come to our attention that a video of Iris has been circulating today on group chats and social media around the students of South Lydacombe.'

Mrs Hamilton looked at Iris, who looked away. Iris fixed her gaze on a large print of Hokusai's *The Great Wave off Kanagawa* on the wall, but the picture blurred.

Without taking her eyes off Iris, Mrs Hamilton asked, 'What does this video show?'

Neither Iris nor Megan answered.

'Megan?' the deputy head pastoral prompted.

'Er … in the video, Iris is naked and she's … um …' It was the first time Iris had known Megan to be inarticulate. 'She's … masturbating … or, at least, pretending to,' Megan said.

'I see. And does the video show anyone else?'

'No, only Iris.'

Only Iris indeed. Only she could have been so stupid. What on earth possessed her to send that video to Josh? She'd been so blind. She'd loved him so much, or she'd thought she did. But if he'd really loved her, he wouldn't have put so much pressure on her to do it.

Oh God, Mrs Hamilton wasn't going to ask to see the video, was she? A knot in Iris's stomach tightened. She thought she might puke again. Looking around frantically, she located the waste paper bucket under the desk just in case.

Mrs Hamilton was quiet for a moment, then she leant forwards, resting her hands on the desk and clasping them together. 'Iris.' Her tone was kind. That was something. She waited for Iris to look at her before continuing. 'Did you make this video for someone?'

Iris nodded. So far, she hadn't said a single word. She still wasn't sure she could speak past the lump and bile in her throat.

'Can you tell me who you made it for?'

'J-J-Josh,' Iris managed.

'Josh?'

'Joshua Knoll,' Megan chipped in helpfully. 'Iris's ex-boyfriend.'

'So you sent Josh this video when you were dating, I assume?' Mrs Hamilton said.

Iris nodded again.

'Iris split up with him and he didn't take it well,' Megan said.

Mrs Hamilton ignored Megan. 'And did you send it to anyone else?' she asked Iris.

Iris shook her head. The tears came then, and in seconds, Iris's body was shaking with her sobs.

Megan inched her chair closer and put her arm around Iris's shoulders. Mrs Hamilton pushed a box of tissues across the desk. She must have been used to people crying in her office. She grabbed a notepad and took a pen out of a pot on her desk and jotted down some notes. Iris read what she'd written upside down. Iris's full name. And Josh's full name.

'OK, Iris, I want you to listen to me.' Was it Iris's imagination or did Mrs Hamilton sound slightly impatient? Iris made an effort to pull herself together. 'As you know, all students at South Lydacombe are required to sign the IT Acceptable Use Policy and it is strictly forbidden to distribute images and videos of someone without their permission, particularly when those images and videos can cause harm and distress. Anyone who has shared this video – *every*one who has shared the video – is in breach of the AUP. Those students will be subject to disciplinary action.'

Then it hit Iris. Megan hadn't told Mrs Hamilton that she herself had received the video. Or who had sent it to her. Iris had only glanced at Megan's phone. She hadn't seen the name of the sender. Someone in her drama group chat, Megan had said. Iris didn't do Amateur Dramatics. Megan wasn't in Iris's year. According to Megan, the video had been circulating on group chats *and* on social media. How many pupils had forwarded this video? People Iris probably didn't even know and who didn't know her or anything about her. Until now. The whole school must know by now. How long before students at the neighbouring schools saw the video, too? For all Iris knew, it was already doing the rounds.

Mrs Hamilton thanked and dismissed Megan, then turned back to Iris. 'I'm going to ring your parents and get them to come and pick you up. I don't think it's a good idea for you to take the bus home and Mr Brook will want to have a word with you and your parents before you go.'

Iris definitely didn't want to take the bus home. But her stomach lurched at the thought of her parents finding out about this.

Mrs Hamilton picked up her landline and punched in the number for Iris's mum's mobile. But it went straight to voicemail. The same for her dad, who was probably still at work.

Daniel answered, though. Mrs Hamilton hadn't put the call through the speaker, but the volume was up loud and Iris could hear Daniel's voice and make out what he was saying.

'Mr Duffy, this is Mrs Hamilton, the deputy head pastoral at South Lydacombe. I'm afraid there has been an incident at school—'

'We're aware of that, Mrs Hamilton,' Daniel interrupted. He sounded gruff. 'My partner left home twenty minutes ago to see the headmaster and pick up Oliver.'

Olly? What had happened to Olly?

Mrs Hamilton looked as bewildered as Iris felt. But Daniel ended the call before they could get any answers.

'Let's go and see the headmaster, shall we?' Mrs Hamilton said.

Iris trailed behind Mrs Hamilton down the corridor to Mr Brook's office.

'Not now,' came the bark from inside, when Mrs Hamilton knocked on the door. But she ignored the headmaster and opened the door.

'Ah, come in and take a seat,' Mr Brook said when he saw Iris and Mrs Hamilton.

Iris was astounded to see Mum and Olly, who was wearing his running kit, in the headmaster's office. What was going on? The headmaster filled in Mrs Hamilton in a few sentences. Iris listened, but it took her several minutes to compute the information. Olly had been suspended for a week for punching Josh at cross-country training. Mrs Davis, the matron, had called an ambulance as she suspected Josh's nose was broken. The headmaster already knew about Iris's video. He and Mrs Hamilton would take action first thing tomorrow morning.

Iris hung her head. She couldn't look anyone in the eye. This was all her fault. She'd caused trouble for her brother. She'd brought shame on her whole family. She wished the ground would open up and swallow her whole. She wanted to be someone else – anyone else – somewhere else.

She wanted to die.

Chapter 17

Ash

NOW

Iris only needs one adult present and Ash has had to rearrange a meeting and two appointments at work, but there's no way he'd leave Iris and Carla to go through this without him. They're doing this round at his place – Mayflower Farm. Carla thought it would give them more privacy than at Crooked Oak Cottage on a Saturday morning. Ash is secretly pleased he won't have to face Dandruff. He's not a bad bloke, but Ash doesn't like him. Perhaps it's an alpha male thing. Perhaps it's just because Ash resents Dandruff for living in Crooked Oak Cottage, which used to be *his* house, under the same roof as *his* kids. His dislike for the guy has grown over the past few months. Dan wasn't as supportive as he should have been with Iris. Carla didn't say so, not in so many words, and fair enough, Iris isn't Dan's daughter and Ash lives just up the road. But Carla is a great stepmother to Margo – the kid even calls her 'Mum' – whereas Dandruff failed to measure up as a stepfather. And as a partner. *Don't be judgey, Ash.*

He hears Carla's car pull into the driveway and watches out of the window as his ex-wife and their daughter make their way to his front door. He opens it before they can knock. Carla is dressed in smart casuals and she's wearing make-up. Most of the women in Ash's life – and there have been a few – get togged up on weekdays, but can't be arsed to make an effort at the weekends, unless he takes them out to dinner or something. But Carla is the other way round, probably because she works from home. She sits at her laptop, in pyjamas or jeans and a hoodie, and she sees more people at weekends than during the week. She doesn't need make-up anyway. She turned fifty at the beginning of the year – quietly, in the middle of all the chaos – and she's still the most beautiful woman he knows. With the possible exception of their daughter, who has also made an effort with her make-up and clothes. Everyone always said his daughter looked like him, but that was because of the blond hair. She's all Carla, really. Now Iris has cut her hair and dyed it dark, she resembles her mother more than ever. Standing next to each other, on his doorstep, both with anxious expressions on their faces, they make him think of a before-and-after advert.

They have time for coffee before Roly is due to arrive. Ash makes it in the kitchen and ushers them through to the living room. They'll be more comfortable in there than sitting up to the table in the kitchen. They're careful about what they say in front of Iris, although Ash doubts she's listening. She's barely looked up from her phone since she arrived. Ash's eyes flit from his daughter to his ex-wife. He sees half a dozen questions race across her face. He notices her hands trembling slightly, even before she drinks from the coffee cup she's cradling. She's leaning forwards in the armchair, her elbows on her knees.

'All right, Iris? Nothing to worry about,' Ash says, as much to reassure Carla as Iris, who looks like she couldn't care less.

'Yeah, I know. Routine. Mum said.'

Ash knows her nonchalance is an act. He doesn't remember

seeing her glued to the screen of her smartphone like this for a long, long time. And she's chewing gum so fast her jaws must ache. She's no doubt playing the role she thinks a typical teenager would play.

Ash is stressed, too. He thinks he's doing a better job of hiding it than Carla and Iris, but his mouth is dry despite the coffee and he can't sit still. Roly has insisted that this is an informal chat, nothing to worry about, and that Iris is not a suspect. But how long, realistically, before the police zero in on Iris?

When Roly arrives, he's not alone. Neither he nor the officer with him, who Roly introduces as Detective Constable Gail Ward, is wearing a uniform. Ash thinks this is standard, that CID get to wear plain clothes, but perhaps it's to put Iris at ease. What does he know? He leads them through the kitchen to the sitting room, where Carla has stood to greet them. Iris has remained seated on the sofa, but at least she has put away her phone.

'Hi, Carla. Hi, Iris,' Roly says, then introduces his DC again for their benefit.

Ash leaves the armchairs for Roly and his colleague, and sits back down on the sofa, next to Iris, who is sitting in the middle, bracketed by him and Carla.

Both Roly and DC Ward refuse Ash's offer of tea or coffee.

'Iris, you know why we're here?' Roly gets straight to the point.

She nods. 'To talk about Josh.'

'That's right. We've been talking to his family and friends and, basically, anyone who knew him. If we can build up a picture of him and how he lived, we might be able to find out more about how he died and ultimately arrest his killer.'

'OK.'

'Now, I know you were once close to Joshua, so you knew him well and that could help us. What can you tell us about him?'

'He was my boyfriend. We went out for, like, six months. He liked cross-country running; he was good at running. He was average at school. In the bottom sets. He flunked his A levels and didn't even get into his last-choice university.' Ash thinks his daughter sneers just a little as she says this. 'He decided to work – he was working in The Grove as a bartender – and then travel around South America when he'd saved up enough money.'

'Did he tell you that?'

'No. Someone else did. Josh and I haven't – hadn't – been in contact for a long time.'

'When was the last time you saw him?'

'The last time I saw him? I went back to school for a day at the end of the school year. Maybe, June? I didn't speak to him. I just sort of saw him from a distance and headed in the opposite direction.'

'OK. What about the last time you were in touch with him, when was that?' DC Ward asks.

'Right up until I blocked him on my phone. He would send messages. So I blocked him. Like, last November?'

DC Ward jots something down on a notepad. 'What sort of messages did he send you?'

'Usually short ones. Sometimes it was just a link to a song. He would be nice or horrid, depending on his mood, I guess.'

'Have you kept these messages?'

'No. I deleted everything when I blocked him.'

'And what about when you were going out, Iris? Was he nice or horrid when he was your boyfriend?'

'Both,' Iris says. Ash hears the quaver in his daughter's voice and sees Carla put her hand on Iris's knee. 'He could be really lovely, but also very nasty.'

'What did he do that was nasty?' DC Ward asks.

'He would ghost me when I didn't say what he wanted to hear. He would be full of praise one minute and then put me down the next.'

'He was manipulative and narcissistic,' Carla chips in. Everyone looks at her. 'Sorry,' she says, 'but he was.'

'Did Joshua have lots of friends, Iris? When you knew him, I mean,' Roly asks, ignoring Carla's outburst.

'He was popular at school, yeah.'

'Did he get on with everyone or were there pupils he didn't get on with?'

'I don't know. I wasn't in his year.'

'Why don't you ask Sasha Spencer-Lyles?' Carla asks. 'She's his girlfriend. I mean, she was his girlfriend at the time ... um ... when he died. She was in the same year as him when they were at school.'

'Thank you, Carla,' Roly says. 'We've been talking to everyone in Joshua's close circle.'

'I don't know about other pupils, but he didn't get on with his dad,' Iris offers, looking at Roly.

Ash notices Roly sit up straighter. 'Go on,' he says.

'His dad was strict, stricter with Josh than with his two younger brothers. They would argue a lot, even in front of me. And Josh would sort of punish him by holing up at a friend's house for a day or two without telling him where he was. He stayed over at our place once. I mean, not here – at Crooked Oak Cottage – because things got so bad with his dad.'

This was news to Ash. He hadn't known Carla had let Joshua Knoll stay over. He arches his eyebrows at Carla, but she seems to be deliberately avoiding eye contact.

'And what about his mum? Did he get on with her?' DC Ward asks.

'Yes. He was his mum's favourite son, I think. She treated him like a prince and gave him everything he wanted. Money, a car. I think she sort of made up for the way his dad treated him.'

'Didn't his mother worry when he hid at friends' houses?' DC Ward asks. 'Or did Joshua text his mum, but not his dad?'

'Yvonne had the Find My app on her phone. She always knew where Josh was. She bought the phone for Josh and that was the deal. So she wouldn't worry about him. He didn't mind. She didn't care where he was; she just liked to know he was OK, that's all.'

'OK, Iris, that's very helpful. We're almost done here,' Ian says.

'I just have one last question, if I may,' DC Ward says. 'Iris, you and Josh split up several months ago.'

'Yeah. A year ago, actually,' Iris says.

'Can you describe your feelings towards him in more recent weeks and months?' DC Ward asks.

Ash doesn't like this. Roly must have filled in DC Ward about what happened to Iris and he can see where she's heading with her question. Iris is still in therapy because of the damage Joshua caused her. She hates his guts. For all Ash knows, Iris is itching to dance on his grave. *Careful what you say, Iris.* He actually crosses his fingers behind his back, although he's not superstitious in the slightest.

Iris shrugs. 'I didn't feel anything for him. It was over between us a long time ago. I went back to school this year. I just want to forget what happened and move on.'

Good girl. Good answer. Ash doubts that Iris will ever forget what Josh did to her. But it would have made things a lot easier for her to get on with her life if he'd passed his A levels and moved away instead of getting a job locally.

'Can you think of anyone who might have wished him harm?'

She shrugs again. 'No.'

Ash hears her voice crack and turns to look at her. A single tear rolls down her cheek. He looks at Roly. A look that says, *that's enough now.* Roly has known Iris since she was about two days old. He's glad Roly himself has come to talk to Iris this morning and he gets that his friend is just doing his job. But he wants him to leave. Now.

Roly seems to read the message in Ash's eyes. 'Thank you. You've been very helpful, Iris,' he says again. 'We won't trouble you any more today.' He gets to his feet. DC Ward follows suit.

'I'll just use your loo if I may,' she says.

'I'll show you where it is,' Iris says and leads her out of the room.

'He wasn't a nice person, you know,' Carla says to Roly once she has left the room. Ash tries – in vain – to silence her with a small shake of his head. 'He was probably mean to someone else. He got what he deserved, Ian.'

'Carla, no one deserves to die the way he did, especially not so young. He was only a few weeks shy of his nineteenth birthday. I saw his body, you know. And it made me feel sick to my stomach. He wasn't much older than Millie – that's the thought that went through my mind. He wasn't much older than Iris. Jaysus, Carla. It could have been Olly. Joshua Knoll died a very violent death.'

Carla looks suitably sheepish. Ash sees her open her mouth to say something, but she closes it again as Iris comes back into the room.

'I'll see you out, Roly,' Ash says.

At the front door, as they wait for DC Ward, Roly turns to Ash and says, 'Look, mate. About what you asked me to do. I can't—'

'I shouldn't have asked,' Ash says, combing his fingers through his hair. 'Just forget it, yeah?'

'I can't plant evidence for you. I want to protect Iris. I do. I know her. I've known her all her life. I know she had nothing to do with this, Ash. But there's only so much I can do.'

'I understand.'

There's a silence, which Roly eventually breaks. 'I can't tell you anything about the investigation. You know that. I couldn't—'

'I said I understand.'

'I couldn't tell you if they found anything at the crime scene – a footprint, for example.' Roly has lowered his voice. 'Hypothetically speaking. Even if I wanted to.'

Ash tries to read his friend's face, but Roly is looking down, at the floor. Ash follows his gaze. Roly is staring at the floor, where Iris has kicked off her ankle boots. Dandruff has got her well trained.

'I understand,' Ash says once again. A wave of different emotions breaks over him: gratitude mixed with affection for his best friend as well as a stab of shame for the position he has put him in. 'We're quits,' he adds, but he thinks perhaps he owes Roly now.

DC Ward materializes in the hallway and she and Roly leave. Ash lets out a sigh of relief as he closes the front door behind them and leans against it. He can hear Iris and Carla in the living room, but before he goes to join them, he stands there for a moment, in the hallway, and, just as Roly did a minute ago, Ash stares at Iris's boots.

Chapter 18

Carla

NOW

Iris and I are still sitting on the sofa in Ash's living room. Iris has turned her attention back to her phone. I look over her shoulder. She's scrolling through clothes on Vinted. Perhaps that's what we need. Some retail therapy. I could take Iris shopping in town. On second thoughts, she's probably way too old for that now. She'll ask me to transfer some money into her bank account and buy stuff online without leaving the comfort of her bedroom. She looks up, maybe feeling my eyes on her, and gives me a tight smile. Some of the tension that had built up in my shoulders eases. I think the interview or the chat, or whatever you want to call it, went reasonably well and Iris doesn't seem too perturbed, which is the main thing.

But when Ash walks slowly back into the living room, the stunned look on his face tells me he has a different take on how things panned out.

'Iris, are you driving home?' I ask, nudging her gently. I drove over here. I thought it would be better for both Iris's and my nerves.

'Yeah, sure.'

'In that case, say goodbye to your dad and go and get set up. Do your checks, get your app ready, L plates on.'

'I know the drill, Mum.'

Iris is taking her test next week. She's a good driver – cautious and alert, like her dad. But I'm a bad passenger – nervous and mistrustful. The number of times I've bitten back a comment or pushed down hard on an imaginary brake pedal. And there have been more times when even a short drive has ended in a row. I went through the same thing with Olly. It was a huge relief when he passed his test. I'll be glad when Iris can drive on her own, too.

'What's wrong?' I ask Ash, as soon as Iris has left the room.

'Roly made a strange comment about a footprint at the scene of the crime. It was like he was speaking hypothetically, but he was looking at Iris's shoes in the hallway when he made it.'

'What did he say exactly?' I ask.

'He sort of apologized for not, you know, um … using the roach I gave him.' Ash clears his throat. 'Not in so many words, but that was the gist of—'

'Ash, what did he say *exactly*? I repeat.

'He said he couldn't tell me if they found anything at the crime scene, even if he wanted to. Like a footprint, for example.'

I let this percolate for a few seconds. 'Maybe he just spotted Iris's shoes on his way out and that's why he mentioned a footprint,' I suggest. 'Maybe he really was speaking hypothetically.'

'Hmm.' Ash isn't convinced.

'I'll talk to Iris about it, shall I?'

'Good idea.'

I say goodbye to Ash and head out to the car. Iris hasn't adjusted the mirrors or the seat and seems to have been waiting for me to get into the car to do all that. I'm about to make a comment, but think better of it. It will only start a fight and it's not as if we're in a hurry.

During the drive home, I try to work out what to say, but it's not easy combing through my thoughts with Taylor Swift blaring out of the speakers. I can't very well say that Ian let on there may have been a footprint at the scene of the crime and ask Iris if there's any chance it's hers. I can already see how this is going to play out, no matter how I broach the subject. Iris will round on me for not trusting her. She'll ask me the question I've been asking myself: what sort of mother thinks her daughter might be a murderer?

I still haven't come up with the right words when Iris parks in the driveway of Crooked Oak Cottage. I'm going to have to wing it, play it by ear. Iris takes off her seatbelt and is about to leap out of the car, but I put my hand on her arm to restrain her.

'Iris, I need to ask you about something,' I say.

'OK.' She sounds uncertain.

But just then Margo races out to the car to greet me, Cheddar in tow. I'm relieved, although I know it's only a temporary reprieve. I'm going to have to talk to Iris about this.

Once inside, I kick off my shoes in the hallway next to Iris's Chelsea boots. For all her bravado, acting as if she didn't care, she dressed up smartly today for her interview with Ian – linen trousers, a blouse and her leather boots.

I head for the kitchen, from where I can hear Daniel humming. He sings – and hums – so tunelessly that it's almost impossible to recognize the song, but I love hearing his off-key melodies. Daniel's wearing an apron and the novelty Yeti slippers that Margo insisted on getting him for Father's Day. My lips twitch in amusement in spite of the circumstances. 'I don't know what you're cooking,' I say, 'but it smells amazing.'

He beams at the compliment. My stomach rumbles loudly, making us both laugh.

'Veggie chilli,' Daniel says. 'Olivia's here. She's staying for lunch.'

I raise my eyebrows, but he has turned away from me, back to the stove. I walk over to him, wrap my arms around him and kiss him on the back of his neck. 'Are they back together?'

'Don't know,' Daniel says. 'I didn't ask.' He wriggles out of my embrace and turns to me with a wooden spoon. 'Have a taste.' He holds out the wooden spoon in one hand, cupping the other hand underneath in case some of the sauce spills.

I'm happy to do as I'm told. 'That's delicious,' I say sincerely. 'Does it need more salt?'

'Nope. It's perfect. It's every bit as good as it smells.'

'It'll be ready in five minutes. How did it go with Ian and Iris?'

'OK,' I say. 'No trick questions. Ian and his colleague just wanted as much background information as possible about Josh.'

The table is already set, so I have time to go and talk to Iris. I go upstairs and pause in front of Olly's bedroom door, which is ajar and through which music is escaping into the corridor. It's not his usual angry rap or hip-hop, but softer. Something similar to The Weeknd or Daft Punk. I try – and fail – to keep up with current trends. Give me Anna Netrebko or Plácido Domingo any day.

Olly was still in bed when Iris and I left for Ash's this morning. I only have a few minutes. I should really go and see Iris. But I don't. Instead, I raise my hand and knock gently on Olly's door. I tell myself it's because I want to avoid a clash with Iris just before lunch. But the truth is, I would like to avoid having this conversation altogether. I've told Ash I'll ask her about the footprint, so I'll have to do it at some point. Sooner rather than later. Just not right now.

'Come in,' Olly calls.

I open the door to find Olly, Liv and Iris, Liv and Olly lounging on his bed and Iris sitting on the office chair. Iris and Liv always got on so well, so I expect they've got some catching up to do. Iris pretty much avoided everyone after December of last year, so I doubt she kept in touch with Liv any more than she kept in touch with anyone else.

Olly has his arm around Liv and she's snuggling into him. It looks like they are back together, then. I'm pleased. I'm very fond of Olivia, but, more importantly, I don't think Olly has been truly happy since they broke up.

'No, don't get up,' I say, as Liv scoots towards the edge of the bed. 'I just wanted to say hi.'

She smiles. 'Hi, Carla,' she says. 'It's lovely to see you.'

It's odd, Josh never called me 'Carla'. I asked him to, more than once. Iris called Josh's parents by their first names. But, to Joshua, Ash and I were Mr and Mrs Ashford – I kept my married name to make things simpler for the kids. He called Daniel by his first name, though. I think Josh did it deliberately, to set some sort of boundary, or make a point. Although the statement he wanted to make was lost on me. Maybe he just wanted to keep his distance, but, again, I can't imagine why.

Olivia is absolutely beautiful. She has long dark-brown hair and grey-green eyes; a heart-shaped face and skin that has been untouched by acne.

I can tell from the expressions on Iris's and Olly's faces that I'm intruding, so I tell the three of them we're eating in a couple of minutes and leave the room.

Throughout lunch, Olly grins like a Cheshire cat. But as I study Olivia, I get the feeling there's something about her that's different. I can't quite put my finger on what it is. She's as attentive as she always was towards Olly, she's polite to me, she praises Daniel for the meal and she makes Margo laugh.

Maybe she isn't quite as chatty as she was before, but that's probably to be expected. She hasn't been part of Olly's life – or of our lives – for several months, and Olly was heartbroken when they split up, not that he ever blamed her for that. In fact, I don't know why they broke up. Olly was evasive and didn't want to talk about it when I asked back then. And poor Olly's problems were relegated to the background while we all dealt with Iris's problem.

I catch Olivia's eye and she smiles timidly. I'm reading too much into this. Liv probably just feels a little awkward around us after not seeing any of us for so long. Olly is clearly just as smitten with her as he was before. I hope she's on the same page as him. I don't want him to end up with his heart broken – again.

After the meal, Iris says she'll clear up. She's quite helpful around the house – if I ask. She'll vacuum downstairs or upstairs – it's best not to ask her to do both – or she'll walk the dog or listen to Margo read. I've learnt not to bother soliciting Olly's assistance. He always has something more urgent to do. But Iris doesn't often offer to help or do something helpful spontaneously.

Daniel makes coffees for him and me and we take them into the living room. I curl my legs under me on the sofa. Neither of us speaks for a few minutes as we sip our drinks. Perhaps, like me, Daniel is lost in his thoughts. I can't help thinking of all the things I should say. There's so much I haven't told Daniel, so much I probably should share with him. He doesn't know about the necklace; he doesn't know about the shoes. I want to confide in him. No, that's not quite true. I want to feel I can confide in him. But since everything blew up around Iris, I don't. Daniel is upright, principled and honest. He wouldn't approve of me throwing out the necklace or of Ian giving us a heads-up about the shoes, if that's what he has done.

I take the empty coffee cups into the kitchen. Iris has finished tidying up in here, but she's standing by the bin and appears to be pushing something down into it. She doesn't see me at first and when she does, she jumps. She stares at me, seemingly rooted to the spot, like a rabbit caught in headlights. Her face goes very red. Then, without a word, she turns on her heels and flees from the room.

I know before I look what I'm going to find. Iris has made an effort to bury them under some rubbish and a different image superimposes itself in my mind for a split second – the bloody tissue with the necklace inside that I also threw out and covered with rubbish. I roll up my sleeve and push bits of paper and some food aside with the tips of my fingers to uncover the shoes. Her burgundy Vans. I close the lid of the bin and almost on automatic pilot, I put the coffee cups into the dishwasher and put on an eco-cycle.

As I turn around, I feel my legs buckle and I grip the table for support. It feels as if the walls are closing in around me and the floor is pitching. A rush of blood fills my ears, but doesn't quite drown out the thoughts streaking through my head, questions to which I know the answers. Could it be a coincidence? Deep down, I know it can't be. That's just wishful thinking. Those trainers were relatively new. She loved them. There's no reason to throw them out. No *other* reason. How did Iris know about the footprint? When I asked her to go out to the car, she must have eavesdropped from the hallway on my discussion with Ash. That explains why she wasn't ready to drive away when I came out.

I stare out of the window at the crab apple tree, laden with fruit. It swims in and out of focus, then seems to tip and I get the disquieting impression that my world is tilting on its axis and won't ever be righted. Because there's not even a scintilla of doubt left in my mind. My daughter has committed murder. I could try to deny it, put it down to coincidence or misunderstanding. I could even tell myself that Iris threw out her shoes as a precaution when she heard there might have been a footprint at the crime scene. But what I can't explain away is that Iris has countless pairs of shoes, and yet she knew which ones to throw out. Earlier, when we went round to Ash's, Iris was wearing her ankle boots. But she has thrown out her Vans.

It takes me a few minutes to catch my breath and see straight. Then I go up to Iris's bedroom. I knock loudly on the door.

'No!' comes Iris's tearful voice from inside.

I open the door anyway, only a crack before it slams in my face, and when I try to push it open again, it won't budge.

'Iris?' No answer. 'Iris!'

'Go away!'

I can hear her sobbing and an invisible, icy hand squeezes my heart. I let my back slide down the door until I'm sitting on the floor, hugging my knees to my chest. I imagine Iris sitting against the door on the other side, a mirror image of me. And a silent tear rolls down my face.

Chapter 19

Iris

THEN

The headmaster, Mr Brook, had told Mum that the school would be looking into the incident. But whatever they were doing, it wasn't enough or fast enough for her parents' liking. So, following Ian's advice, they contacted the police. Mum and Dad both took her to the police station in Barnstaple, where she had to speak to two officers – PC Andrea Quinlan and PC Max Lynch.

PC Quinlan was this small, round-faced woman with light-brown eyes that made Iris think of weak tea. She was nice, right from the start. Her colleague, though? He was the total opposite. He was tall and thin; he had a long face and a long nose to match and these judgey blue eyes that bored into Iris. He gave her the ick.

The first time they went to the police station, Iris had to give a statement. Her face flamed as she went through it all. It was bad enough going over it all – *again* – in front of her parents, but in front of total strangers? It was so humiliating. PC Lynch just looked at her the whole time like it was all her fault. Luckily,

PC Quinlan was the one typing up her words and asking her questions.

When PC Quinlan had read the statement back to Iris and she'd signed it, the officer asked her if she would mind leaving her phone with them for a couple of days. She did mind, but it wasn't like she needed it. So she just shrugged and passed over her mobile. It wasn't like she had much choice.

Then PC Quinlan turned to Iris's mum and dad. 'You need to react quickly before the video spreads to more platforms,' she said. 'My advice would be to contact the Revenge Porn Helpline. They'll help you take it down.'

Her dad looked from one police officer to the other, then from Iris to her mum. 'Don't the police do that?' he asked. Iris could hear the disbelief in Dad's voice.

'I'm afraid not,' PC Quinlan said.

'For one thing, we don't have the resources for that sort of thing,' PC Lynch added bluntly, turning his nose up like he was being asked to pick up dog poo on his rounds.

'Well, what can you do?' Mum sounded as desperate as Iris felt.

PC Quinlan's sigh said it all. 'We'll do our best,' she promised, 'but, to be honest, the law is not on our side.'

'I don't understand,' Iris's mother said.

'The current law doesn't help us to help you,' PC Quinlan said. 'As it stands, for the Crown Prosecution Service to agree to prosecute, we'd need to be able to prove that this video was shared with intent to cause distress.'

'What other reason would he have had for sharing it?' Dad asked.

'It might simply have been to score lad points,' PC Lynch said with a shrug. 'You know, get kudos from his peers?'

'And that's OK? Are you saying that's *not* illegal?'

'There's been an extensive review and there's a chance the law will change very soon,' PC Quinlan said, 'but for the moment—'

'We could probably do more if Iris had been filmed without

her knowledge,' PC Lynch chimed in, 'but she filmed herself and then shared the video willingly.' He made a sweeping gesture with his hands, palms upwards, that Iris interpreted as: *What do you expect?*

'Not with the whole school!' Dad's face was crimson. 'She shared it with one person. Joshua Knoll is the one who shared it with everyone else. And that was without Iris's consent!'

'That will be hard to prove,' PC Lynch said unhelpfully. 'Joshua Knoll will deny it, say his phone was hacked, claim he's a victim, too. It's been a few days. He's had time to get rid of anything incriminating on his phone or computer.'

'What about the threat to share?' Mum had spent hours every evening, trawling through stuff on the internet. 'That's illegal now, isn't it?'

'Yes, you're right. That amendment came into effect recently,' PC Quinlan said to Mum, and to Iris, 'Did Joshua threaten to share the video?'

Iris thought about that text Josh had sent, ages ago, after they'd split up for the last time. The one where he'd said he couldn't stop looking at photos of her and wouldn't like anyone else to see her like that. His words were all vague and ambiguous. Classic Josh. He didn't even say they were nude photos he was looking at. 'Not really,' she mumbled, studying her hands.

'Iris is a minor,' PC Quinlan pointed out. 'Did Joshua send you intimate photos or videos, Iris?'

'Yes,' she said. 'When we were ... going out with each other.'

'Well, that's illegal,' PC Quinlan said. 'An adult can't send intimate pictures to someone who's underage.'

'He wasn't an adult at the time,' Mum pointed out.

'I deleted them,' Iris said. She'd deleted them from the Cloud as well.

'There will be a trace somewhere, I expect,' Dad said, patting her arm.

Iris certainly hoped not.

'Listen, here's what you can do. Firstly, contact the Revenge Porn Helpline. Ask them to help you take down the video. Secondly, start collecting your own evidence. Anything you can find.'

Iris glanced at Mum, whose eyes and mouth were wide open. Iris could tell what she was thinking. She wanted to know why it was up to them, and not the police, to collect evidence.

PC Lynch answered the question, even though no one had actually asked it. 'Apart from the fact we lack resources, as I mentioned, most police officers aren't trained in digital investigation techniques.' There wasn't even a hint of regret in his voice.

'That's true.' PC Quinlan's voice was more apologetic. 'We'll do our best, though,' she repeated. 'I promise.'

But she didn't say exactly what they would do.

Iris and her parents left the police station. Iris could tell Mum and Dad were as gutted as she was.

It wasn't until the next week that Mum suggested Iris should go online and find as much evidence as she could. 'Texts, emails, photos, anything,' Mum said.

The police had given Iris back her phone by then, but she still hadn't turned it on. She didn't mean to look. But it was everywhere. She had text messages, some from anonymous numbers. Pupils were discussing it in WhatsApp groups. Either they didn't realize she belonged to those groups or else they didn't give a shit. There were jokes, at her expense. Criticisms, levelled at her. Some pupils had written private messages to her via Instagram, calling her names. She didn't even know all of the pupils personally.

For, like, five minutes, Iris read one comment after the other. Then she completely lost it. She roared as she chucked her phone at the wall. It hit with a load crack. Curling up on the bed, she hugged her knees to her chest and buried her face; she started to cry and, moments later, she was sobbing uncontrollably. She squeezed her eyes tight shut, but she could still see the words.

She could even hear them in her head.

What the fuck was she thinking?
Why did she send it in the first place?
She's brought this on herself.
You slut!

There had been some more lurid remarks by some of the boys in her school, but the ones that scrolled behind her eyelids hit harder. The victim shaming. It hurt far more, not just because this was what other people thought of her, but also because this was what she thought of herself.

Mum burst into her room and sat on the bed beside her. She held her tightly and rocked her.

'It's my fault,' Iris sobbed. 'This is all my fault.'

'No, it's not,' Mum said firmly.

'It is! Everyone says so. I should never have … sent that v-video. I deserve … I deserve what has happened.'

'No, you don't,' Mum said. 'That's like telling a rape victim she shouldn't have worn a short skirt. This isn't your fault.'

Dad came by that evening to pick her up. Iris had asked to spend the weekend at his place. As much as anything else, it might give Mum, Olly and Margo a break. They were all exhausted from having to deal with the shitstorm she'd started. As for Daniel, he looked at her in the same way as PC Lynch had looked at her. Oh, he pretended to be on her side, especially in front of Mum. But Iris could tell he thought she'd screwed up. And she had. Big time.

Iris paused on the stairs, her bag slung over her shoulder. Daniel and Margo were in the kitchen and the door was closed. Olly was at a mate's house. Mum and Dad were talking in the hallway and hadn't seen her.

'The people at the Revenge Porn Helpline have been really helpful and I'm reporting the video every time I find it to get it deleted,' Dad was saying. 'But it's like a game of Whack-a-Mole. Every time it gets taken down on one website, it pops up on another.'

Iris gripped the handrail like she was about to fall down the stairs. Dad must be spending his spare time trawling through porn sites. He must hate her for this. She certainly hated herself for putting everyone through this.

'Oh, God, Ash, what are we going to do?'

'Just keep doing what we're doing, I guess. Damage control.'

'Perhaps we could get a lawyer?' Mum said.

'Yes, that's what I was thinking. I'll ask Roly if he can recommend someone.' Dad looked up and saw her. 'Hey, Gorgeous,' he said. 'Ready to roll?'

Iris tried to nod. She could barely put one foot in front of the other to go down the stairs.

'OK. Let's get out of here,' Dad said, giving her a hug as she reached the bottom step.

Iris nodded again. She wished they could get out of here and go far away. Not just up the road to Dad's place. She wanted to leave this place, leave this country and start over. Some place new where no one knew her. Somewhere she could feel normal. Invisible.

Chapter 20

Carla

NOW

I'm about to knock on Iris's bedroom door again when it opens from the inside. I take one look at her tear-streaked face and it's all I can do not to start crying again myself. Without a word, she stands back, holding the door for me to enter, and closes it behind me. We sit on her bed. Tentatively, I put my arm around her shoulders. She doesn't push me away. Instead, she huddles against me.

'Iris, you know I love you, right? I always will, no matter what.' Not a great opening gambit, but I haven't rehearsed this. Her head nods into my shoulder. 'But I can't help you unless you tell me the truth.' I don't add what I'm thinking. That I'm not sure how much I can help her even if she does tell me the truth.

I wait until she stops sobbing, but when she still doesn't offer an explanation, I say, 'Why did you throw your shoes out, Iris? Can you tell me?'

She sits up straighter. 'I heard what Ian said about the footprint,' she says.

'And did you have reason to believe the footprint was yours?'

'There's a ... a chance it might be.'

'Because you killed Josh?'

'No! God, Mum, no! I didn't kill him. You have to believe me.'

I'd like to believe Iris, but I'm not at all sure that I do. 'I believe you,' I say. It's at least two beats too late, but I don't think Iris notices. 'So, why do you think the footprint was yours?'

'I was there. I found him ... his body. In the woods. The day before those blackberry pickers.'

I let this sink in. It's plausible. Or clever. I turn slightly so I'm facing Iris and study her. Is she making this up? It's hard to tell. 'Were you looking for him?'

'No. Yes. I mean, not really. We used to go running there together. Yvonne was worried. She kept calling me to ask if I knew where he could be. I told her to ask Sasha, but Sasha isn't into cross-country running. She wouldn't know about the trails we used to run along in Buryknoll Wood. It's a great place to run, but since Josh ... since we broke up, I hadn't been back there.'

Iris's account is hesitant and she won't look me in the eye. 'But you weren't running the day you found him,' I say. It's not a question. She has thrown out her Vans, not her running trainers.

'No. I thought I'd walk Cheddar. I carried him most of the way, in the end. It was too far for him.'

'OK. Let me get this straight. You used to run in the woods with Josh. Since you split up, you hadn't run there, but when he went missing you thought he might be there, so you went looking for him. Is that right?'

'I wasn't really looking for him. I wasn't expecting to find him. I thought if ... I told myself ... Oh, it's dumb.'

'Tell me.'

'You know how when you, like, fall off a horse, you have to get back on, or when you do a bad dive, you have to climb up onto the diving board and do it again?'

'Yes.' I have no idea where Iris is going with this.

'So, there were things I didn't do, places I didn't go to. After Josh. I didn't dare. And when Yvonne rang, I sort of got the idea into my head that I had to return to Buryknoll Wood, to prove to myself I could do it.' Iris is shaking. Not just her hands, her whole body. 'At first, I was a bit worried Josh might be there, hiding in the woods or something ... maybe to avoid his dad. But then I thought there was no way ... he wouldn't be there, not with all the rain we'd had. He'd been missing for, like, maybe a week or so at that point. And I also thought, well, one day I might have to face him, too. Or at least go somewhere he might be. Like the pub.'

We used to go to The Grove as a family – Ash, me and the kids – for a meal now and then – it's just up the road from Mayflower Farm – Ash's place – but we haven't been there since Josh started working there. I think Ash and Ian continued to go there occasionally for a few pints, even though they risked running into him.

'OK. So you went for a walk in the woods and you found Josh.'

'Yes.' Iris begins to cry again. I tighten my grip around her shoulders and put my other hand on her knee. 'He was ... dead. I think he had been dead for some time. He smelt really bad and looked really ugly, like, sort of bruised and swollen.'

I wince at the image Iris's description has conjured up. 'Why didn't you call the police?' I ask. 'You could have rung Ian. Or me. Or Dad.'

'Because I thought everyone would think I'd killed him. I wanted him dead, Mum. I wished him dead so many times after what he did to me.'

I nod. 'I know, sweetie,' I say. I've wished him dead several times, too. 'Iris, have you told anyone about this?'

'No. No one. Only you.'

'So you didn't touch the body? You left it exactly as you found it?' It's only as this question leaves my mouth that I realize what's going through my head. Am I seriously considering not going to the police with this? We can't possibly keep this to ourselves.

'Yeah. No. I mean, I took the necklace.'

'What?' My heart stops. Then stutters as it starts up again. Shit! I'd forgotten all about the necklace.

'That pathetic his-and-her necklace. The wolf one. He was still wearing it. He had no right to wear it after we split up. I took it. I wanted to get rid of it.'

Did Iris leave a fingerprint on the body? Her DNA? If so, how will they find out it's hers? Can the police swab suspects for DNA even if they're minors? These questions streak through my mind. I can picture the words; I even visualize the question marks. My heart sinks.

'Mum?'

'So you did touch the body.'

'No! No, I was careful not to. I was really careful not to … you know …'

Evidently, she wasn't careful enough. She left a footprint at the crime scene.

Tears are coursing down Iris's cheeks now and she hides her face behind her hands. 'I used a tissue and pulled it. It came easily. I think the lace must have been a bit broken. I know I shouldn't have done it. I didn't think it through.'

It's all credible. On the surface. It's just that something doesn't add up. Iris has changed her story, but is this version any more truthful than the previous one? What's the matter with me? This is my daughter. But that's just it. I know my daughter. And I can tell when she's not being honest. She avoids eye contact, has been known to turn on the waterworks – although I think her tears are genuine in this instance – and hesitates as she tries to work out what to say next.

But it's more than that. Why don't I believe her?

'Mum?' Her voice is small, scared. It reminds me of when she was a little girl and needed reassurance that everything was going to be OK – after a nightmare, or when she was ill, or when she'd fallen out with Millie, as best friends are prone to do from time to time as they grow up.

'It will all be OK,' I say, although I don't believe that either. 'I'll talk to your dad, see what he thinks. In the meantime, don't repeat any of this to anyone. All right?'

She nods. And gives me a hug, which is uncharacteristic for Iris. She grew out of cuddles long ago, much to my disappointment. She's not as tactile as I am and she thinks I'm too 'touchy-feely'.

I kiss the top of her head and get up. I feel an almost irrepressible urge to go to Ash, to talk all this through with the one person I can confide in and who loves Iris as much as I do. He's the one who brought up the footprint in the first place and an irrational spike of anger rises in me because of this, as if he's the one who caused the problem.

But Daniel is waiting for me at the bottom of the stairs. 'What was all that about?'

I try to tease my face into an innocent expression. 'All what?'

'I heard Iris slamming her door and crying. You've been crying, too.' He reaches out with both hands and strokes my cheeks. I must have panda eyes. I put on make-up this morning, for once, before going to Ash's for the – what would you call it? Interview? Meeting?

I want more than anything to go to Ash. But I can't tell my partner I'm going round to my ex-husband's. For the second time today. And I should be able to confide in my partner. I sigh, and taking one of his hands in mine, I lead him into the kitchen, where I make sure both doors are closed before I talk to him. A watered-down version. But the truth. I owe him that much. He's my partner and Iris's stepfather. And I could really use his support. I sit at the table, but he remains standing.

'This morning, Ian let something slip as he was leaving. Something about a footprint in the woods, near ... um ... Joshua's Knoll's body.' I pause, trying to gauge Daniel's reaction so far and also work out what to say next.

'Go on.'

'Ash told me what Ian had said. I didn't know Iris had overheard our conversation until just now when I found her shoes in the bin.'

Daniel doesn't speak for a few seconds, but I can see by his expression that he has joined the dots. 'Let me get this straight,' he says. 'Iris was at the scene of the crime and she is covering up that fact up by getting rid of the evidence. Is that about the gist?'

Instantly, I regret telling him. I warned Iris not to say a word to anyone, and here I am, blatantly disregarding my own advice. His eyes bore into me and I feel like a naughty schoolgirl about to be reprimanded by a teacher. I try to stare him down.

'I hope you're going to go to the police with this, Carla.'

'I don't know what to do.' It comes out as a whine.

'Carla, you have to go to the police.'

That makes me prickly, Daniel telling me what to do. I want him to talk through my options with me. I need him to be on my side, no matter what I decide. 'If I go to the police, they might think she killed Joshua,' I point out.

'Don't you?'

My stomach nosedives at these words, barely audible as they leave Daniel's mouth, as if he has tried to filter them, but couldn't stop them slipping out. How can he think that, let alone say it out loud? I'm aware I'm being hypocritical.

'Listen, Daniel. Iris found Josh's body. She arrived on the scene after he was killed. Days afterwards. Her presence there might explain the footprint, but it doesn't point to the murderer. I don't want my daughter to suffer any more because of that … boy.' I shout the last sentence. So much for closing the kitchen doors so no one would hear us.

Daniel puts his hands on my shoulders and, for a split second, I just want him to hold me. But then I catch the look in his eyes.

'If you're not going to report this,' he says, 'I can't stay here.' He matches me for volume.

'What?'

'I can't allow Margo to be in the same house as someone who may have committed murder and someone else who is harbouring a criminal.'

He's deadly serious and I can't get my head round what he's saying.

'You don't really believe …' But I don't finish that sentence. Deep down, I still think Iris probably did this. And that's what Daniel believes too. 'Don't you think you're overreacting?' I try a different tack and lower my voice. 'What would you do if it was your daughter, Daniel?'

'She's not my daughter, though, is she?' he says, his face close to mine. I resist the urge to slap it. 'And I am thinking about my daughter. I'm trying to do what's right for her. Just like you are with Iris.'

And with those words, he stomps out of the room. I call after him, shout and cry, but then my anger and my voice abandon me, too. Defeated, I sink onto the chair and, my elbows on the table, I cradle my head in my hands.

Chapter 21

Iris

THEN

Revenge porn. That's what everyone at school was saying it was. Iris hadn't been into school since that day, three weeks ago. She hadn't been on social media either. But Millie came round every now and then and brought her up to speed. Millie probably gave her a watered-down version of the fallout. That suited Iris.

Millie also told her that the class teachers in registration had warned the pupils that anyone found to have shared inappropriate material would face disciplinary action. The headmaster and deputy head pastoral had banged on about it in assembly too, apparently. All the parents had been sent an email saying the same thing – Iris already knew this because both Mum and Dad had received it. Class teachers had been checking pupils' phones, but because of the warnings, Iris supposed anyone with half a brain would have deleted her video by now. Or stocked it in the Cloud or something.

Revenge porn. Two words that made sense, but at the same

time cast confusion over the whole thing. Iris had been bugged about that term since PC Quinlan had suggested contacting the Revenge Porn helpline. She'd put up with a lot of Josh's shit. What had she done that made him hate her so much? That had made him want to seek revenge? But even as those questions writhed around in her head, she sort of got it. Josh had taken their break-up badly. She used to think he was way out of her league and knew this was also his thinking. He felt he was too good for her. Entitled. And so he was really pissed when *she* dumped *him*. Josh held grudges. He was a vengeful person. So that was why. A more puzzling question was why now? They'd split up, like, weeks ago. Two months ago, actually. Was it a case of serving a dish cold? Or was there more to it?

Mum had made an appointment with a counsellor Jo knew personally. Iris didn't want to go. She didn't want to talk about what had happened. She was deliberately staying off school and staying off social media and doing her best to bury her head in the sand. But her parents insisted.

'How did it go?' Mum asked as they drove home from her first session.

'Fine,' Iris said.

Iris hadn't been much more talkative in her session with the counsellor, Melanie, to be honest. She'd just sat there feeling sick, stupid and sad. And above all, ashamed. So she'd left the talking up to Melanie, who said a couple of things that made Iris sit up and listen.

The first thing was that abuse was more *insidious* when it was psychological rather than physical. Iris thought she knew the meaning of that word, but she'd google it when she got home, just to check. It wasn't really the word 'insidious' that got her, though. It was the word 'abuse'. Had Josh been abusing her while she was actually going out with him? Or had that only come afterwards? She needed to think about that.

The other thing was about revenge porn. 'I tend to avoid the term "revenge porn",' the counsellor said gently. 'I think it puts too much emphasis on why the perpetrator did what he did and not enough emphasis on the harm it causes the victim-survivor on the receiving end of it. The focus has to be on you.' Iris could see the logic in that. 'In addition,' Melanie continued, 'not all perpetrators are motivated by revenge, or not solely by revenge, anyway.'

There was a lot to work through in all of that. Terms that Iris needed to get her head round if she was going to be able to process it. Josh was a 'perpetrator'. She was a 'victim-survivor'. Or she would be if she got through this. Privately, she had her doubts about her ability – or even her will – to do that.

'What do you call it then?' Iris asked.

'Personally, I prefer the term "image-based sexual abuse",' Melanie said, 'but it's a bit of a mouthful. 'Or "intimate-image abuse". But we can call it whatever you like.'

Iris nodded. She could relate to Melanie's expressions more than to the term 'revenge porn', even if she thought Josh was mainly motivated by revenge. Plus, if Josh was taking revenge, it made it sound like she'd done something wrong, like she'd wronged him somehow. Also, Iris didn't like to think of the video of her as 'porn'. Technically, it probably was pornographic, but that hadn't been her intention. And she hadn't given her consent for the video to be shared for other people to ogle at.

'Cyber sexual abuse,' Iris said. She thought she'd heard or read that somewhere before. It was also a bit of a mouthful, but that was exactly what she was going through. She felt as if she'd been sexually abused. She felt dirty, she was hurting, she'd been exploited without her consent. Dehumanized. Humiliated. Exposed. Yeah, that was what she wanted to call it.

Iris could avoid all the pupils at South Lydacombe, apart from Millie, of course, but there was no getting away from the problem. For one thing, she couldn't stop thinking about the video. Plus, the whole issue had infected her home life, too. Olly, who had gone back after his week's suspension, had to face the mess Iris had left in her wake. He dragged his heels in the mornings and came home at the end of the day unhappy and angry. Iris imagined pupils whispering things about her without caring much if he heard or not. In her absence, he'd be their scapegoat.

Iris also overheard an argument between Mum and Daniel. She couldn't help eavesdropping. It wasn't hard. They were shouting.

'How can she have been so stupid?' Daniel yelled.

Iris asked herself that same question many times a day.

'Hey! That's not fair! She didn't know Joshua was going to disseminate the video. You should be asking why he shared something private with the whole school, not why my daughter shared an intimate video with her boyfriend.'

'It's not just with the school, though, is it? I received it via a messaging app from a concerned co-worker. Everyone at work knows about it. It's all over social media, too. It has racked up thousands of views, apparently. It's so embarrassing, Carla.'

Iris's stomach flipped. Thousands of views? The video had gone viral. Everyone she knew must have watched it. As well as a whole load of people she didn't know. She cringed with mortification.

'If your bloody co-worker had truly been concerned, they might have told you about it, but they certainly wouldn't have sent it to you,' Mum hissed. 'What they did was illegal.'

'And what Iris did wasn't?'

'For fuck's sake, Daniel! Iris has done nothing wrong. It's not about what she did. It's about what happened to her!'

Did Mum really believe that? Iris couldn't be sure. Her mum always stuck up for her and Olly when Daniel criticized them for something. Iris hardly ever heard her swear, though. And certainly not the F-word. Daniel and Mum were probably arguing about this a lot – the same argument, or variants of it, over and over again – just being more discreet about it most of the time.

Iris spent as much time as possible at Dad's. He was really supportive and he didn't judge her or give her the impression her stupidity had impacted his life, too. At Mayflower Farm – Dad's place – she didn't have to listen to that dreadful opera singing Mum played all the time. And, more importantly, she didn't have to feel Daniel's judging eyes on her or look at him and wonder if he'd watched the video when his colleague sent it to him. But she was alone during the day, whereas at Crooked Oak Cottage, Mum worked from home, which provided a comforting presence.

Mum wanted her to go back to school after Christmas. Iris knew she'd have to face the music one day, but she wasn't ready yet. And although she hoped things would calm down over the holidays, she wasn't optimistic.

'The longer you put it off, the harder it will be,' Mum said.

She was probably right. Iris felt lonely, like a recluse, whether she stayed at Mum's or Dad's. She only went out for walks with Mum and for her sessions with Melanie. She'd become really isolated. Melanie was right, too. Josh hadn't been motivated solely by revenge. Iris remembered how he'd cut her off from her friends when they'd been dating. He'd wanted her all to himself. Now he couldn't have her. But he could still see to it that no one else could. He could make sure she was *ostracized* – another of Melanie's words. Even though they'd split up ages ago, he was still able to degrade her. No, this wasn't just about revenge. It was about control. Josh was still pulling the strings, still dictating her emotions.

It was like he could still read her thoughts after all this time, because just when she was thinking this, he sent her a text. She'd blocked his number, like, a month ago, but it came in anonymously, with a six-digit code instead of a contact number. No doubt about it, though – it was from Josh.

It wasn't me. Someone must have got hold of the vid in my phone. Maybe they even sent it from my phone. I turned the page a long time ago and I have a new gf now. I don't wish you any harm, only the best.
J x

For a split second, she almost believed him. Then she snapped round. She might have believed his lies when they were dating. But that was over. This denial, this refusal to take responsibility for what he'd done, was gaslighting.

Iris showed the text message to Dad.

'"I don't wish you any harm" my arse. He's trying to cover all the bases, the little bastard,' Dad commented. 'PC Quinlan said we have to be able to prove not only that Josh disclosed the video, but also that he intended to cause the victim – *you* – distress.'

'Yeah,' Iris said.

'Roly said the same thing. We can't prosecute unless we can prove that intent to cause distress. Although he did say cybercrime wasn't his domain,' Dad added.

Iris wasn't convinced this was cybercrime. She'd looked it up. Unless you considered her video to be child pornography. Whatever. Even if Ian wasn't an expert on this, Iris knew Dad had been talking to him about what had happened. Not because Ian was a police officer, but because her dad needed his best friend's advice.

But it was the first time anyone had mentioned the possibility of *prosecuting* out loud to her. This was obviously why the police had told them to gather their own evidence, but the idea itself – the process of prosecuting Josh and everything that would entail – hadn't really sunk in. She hadn't thought it through until now. Iris couldn't face her classmates; she could barely bring herself to utter two sentences in therapy. There was no way she could face up to a court case. Anyway, Josh would deny sharing the video, just as he'd denied it in his text. She wouldn't stand a chance of winning. Iris just wanted it all to go away.

But maybe this would never completely go away.

Chapter 22

Carla

NOW

I'm sitting on the stool at the kitchen island at Jo's. Ian is working late, on the murder investigation, so Jo and I are having a girlie Friday evening in. We've got the house to ourselves – Millie is with Iris at my place and Olly is at Liv's. Margo, presumably, is with Daniel. I haven't heard from him since he moved out last weekend.

Wine and a film. That's the plan. To take our minds off things. God knows I need to think about something other than the mess my life has become and I'm grateful to Jo for the idea. I suspect one of the reasons Jo suggested it, though, is so she can show off her shiny new kitchen. I slowly scan the room, taking in all the unfamiliar details. I once knew Jo's kitchen almost as well as my own, but now it's unrecognizable. She and Ian had kitchen fitters in – neither of them is into DIY – and Jo couldn't wait to show it off. I have to admit, it's a massive improvement on the old one – with its brown cupboards and avocado green wall tiles, it always made me feel as if I'd time-travelled back to the Seventies. Now it's had a make-over, the kitchen is white and glossy, the cupboards all have an opening mechanism, so you push rather than pull to open the doors, and the polished concrete floor completes the modern vibe.

Jo's new kitchen is beautiful and I'm glad she's happy with it, but I'm not jealous. Ash and I chose and fitted the kitchen at Crooked Oak Cottage. In fact, we did up the entire house. Margo's bedroom was our last joint venture, though. We did that room up six years ago, when Daniel and I decided that he and Margo would move in. It's a poky room, barely big enough to be a bedroom – I used to store all sorts of junk in it before its transformation. But Ash helped me make it into a lovely bedroom for Margo, despite the lack of space.

It occurs to me that I haven't done any DIY since then, unless you count fixing the leaky tap in the utility room or giving the upstairs hallway a fresh lick of paint. One of the bathrooms has been in desperate need of a facelift for some time, but it's not the sort of job I can manage on my own, and Daniel has always claimed to be terrible at anything manual.

Jo takes a bottle of Chablis out of the fridge – also new and bigger – and opens it with some difficulty. I'd offer to help, but I buy screw tops precisely because I can't handle a corkscrew, although I was a dab hand at removing the metal caps from beer bottles with my teeth back when I was at uni. Jo pours generous amounts of wine into two oversize glasses, hoists herself onto a stool at the kitchen island and slides one of the glasses towards me.

'Cheers,' I say, raising my glass to chink with hers.

'Cheers,' Jo says.

I take a big gulp of the wine and look at Jo. Her blonde hair is scraped back into a high ponytail and her brown eyes lock onto mine. She's made up beautifully, but hasn't quite succeeded in concealing the dark bags under her eyes – she works so hard, not just at her lessons, but at all the extra-curricular activities she's involved in at the school, and she's always exhausted come the end of the week.

'So,' she says, 'how are you holding up?'

I'm not sure whether Jo is referring to the situation with Daniel or the one with Iris. I'm clinging to the hope that Daniel will come back, preferably after apologizing profusely, and that this is just a temporary glitch in our relationship. I tell Jo this, and shrug as if it's no big deal. I'm a bit worried that if I talk about it too much, I'll end up bawling my eyes out. I make out that it's all due to a stupid argument. I can't tell her the real reason Daniel has moved out – that he thinks Iris is a murderer.

As for the murder investigation itself, I don't know how much Ian has told Jo – knowing him, everything. He and Jo have always discussed his work and hers. He once joked that it's actually Jo who solves the crimes, not him. She must know that Ian and his colleague have talked to Iris. Perhaps she knows they found a footprint at the scene of the crime, but I'm not going to tell her I found Iris's shoes in the bin. I haven't told Ash yet, but I will. If I tell Jo, though, it will get back to Ian.

But Jo is my best friend, so I'm used to confiding in her. 'I'm terrified that Iris will end up a suspect in this ... murder case,' I admit. I find it hard, even now, to spit out the word 'murder'. It's something you hear about on the news or read about in crime fiction, not something that happens this close to home. 'I just think she must be the obvious suspect after what Joshua Knoll did to her.'

'Hmm. She has motive,' Jo agrees.

'Not helpful, Jo,' I say.

'Sorry. I doubt Iris was his only enemy, though.'

Ah, that's more like the sort of thing I want to hear. Does Jo know something I don't? 'What makes you say that?' I ask.

'Well, Ian is keen to talk to Joshua's latest girlfriend, Sasha Spencer-Lyles, but the family seem to be stonewalling the police's requests for an interview with her.'

'Can they do that?'

'Not indefinitely, no. This is a murder inquiry and Sasha knew the victim well.' Jo pauses to take a sip of her wine. I take another gulp of mine. 'I don't know why the family are trying to wriggle out of talking to the police,' she continues. 'It strikes me as a bit suspicious.'

'Do you know Sasha?'

'I did. I taught her last year. Bright kid. I know her mother, too. Not well, but well enough to say hello to, you know. Saw her on Tuesday evening, actually, at my Zumba class. She's a bit up herself, but she's all right. Friendly.'

Jo gets up and fetches a packet of olives and some dips from the fridge, and two small bowls, a packet of Twiglets and a packet of crisps. It takes her two attempts to find the right cupboard for the snacks.

'Don't know my way around my own kitchen anymore,' she grumbles. We both laugh. She goes to top up my wine. I'd told myself I'd only have one drink, and I put up a reluctant objection, covering my glass with my hand. 'Ian will drop you home when he gets in,' Jo says.

I don't need any more persuading than that. The alcohol is taking effect and some of the tautness has eased from my shoulders. I can easily cycle over to pick up my car tomorrow.

'Come on, let's take this through to the living room. You can choose the movie.'

We sink into the sofa and wrap the throws around ourselves. But rather than deciding on a film, we continue to talk.

'So, in other news – sort of – the headmaster has postponed the official reopening of the sports centre,' Jo says. 'Indefinitely.'

'Oh.' Why's Jo telling me this? I honestly couldn't give a toss. I've got other things on my mind. And what does she mean, 'sort of'? 'Why's that, then?' I ask, trying to inject a modicum of interest into my voice.

She doesn't answer and I sense an awkwardness now. Jo regrets bringing this up.

'Jo? What's going on?' I still don't get why she has mentioned this, but she now has my undivided attention.

'The headmaster had invited Richard Knoll to come to the school for the reopening of the sports centre at the beginning of the school year. They'd organized basketball matches and a fencing tournament and so on for the occasion.'

At the sound of his name, my fingers curl into fists. 'You make him sound like the guest of honour.'

'I mean, he was, in a way.'

'Why?'

'The Knolls pour money into that school, you know,' Jo continues. 'Have done for generations of Knolls – Richard's father, grandfather and great-grandfather were all pupils there, along with God only knows how many of their brothers, long before the school accepted girls.' She pauses just long enough to pop an olive into her mouth. 'Last year, Richard Knoll paid for the refurbishment of the sports hall as well as for a whole load of sports equipment. The centre reopened at the beginning of the month, for the start of the new school year, but Brook wanted to mark the event formally. I think he was pretty sure when he came up with the idea that the video wasn't going to come back and bite him in the arse. And he goes to great lengths to keep the school's benefactors buttered up.'

I don't know what to say to that, so I say nothing. But all of a sudden, the school's attitude to Iris's ordeal seems clearer. The headmaster promised to take immediate action when Iris's video was first diffused. He harped on and on about the school's strict IT Acceptable Use Policy and he promised me that anyone found in breach of that policy would be punished. But the weeks went by and nothing happened. The pupils, including Joshua, were all forewarned and had time to delete anything incriminating from their phones. No one was disciplined. No one except Olly, who broke Josh's nose. My fists are clenched so tightly now that my nails dig into my palms.

Iris is at South Lydacombe on a full scholarship and Olly on a bursary. Ash and I would have struggled to cover full fees for both of them. We never respond to the numerous requests for donations. Ash, Daniel and I all volunteer every year to help out with the school fête and I practically run the annual Book Fair, but it's clearly a poxy contribution in comparison with the Knoll family's philanthropy. No wonder the school didn't do more to help Iris.

'There's something that will make you even madder.' Jo encroaches on my thoughts. 'But I think I should tell you before you hear it from someone else.'

I unclench my fists, pick up my wine glass from the coffee table and take a slug. 'Go on,' I say.

'South Lydacombe is organizing a vigil for Joshua next week.'

Several swear words run through my mind and one or two escape under my breath.

'There will be candles, a minute of silence, solemn music, pupils can share their memories of Joshua, and so on.'

'But he's not even a pupil at the school anymore.'

'Yeah, I know. But his brothers are – Jordan and Jasper.'

'I know their bloody names,' I growl. 'Oh, God. Sorry, Jo. Thanks for letting me know.'

She puts her hand on my knee. 'I get it,' she says. 'The school are doing so much for him when they did so little for Iris.' She really does get it.

'Christ, they're making him out to be not only a victim, but also a bloody martyr. It's as though all his sins have been washed away now he's dead. He'll forever be remembered as the poor kid who was stabbed to death in the woods instead of the utter bastard who ruined Iris's life.' I glance at Jo, but my outburst doesn't appear to have shocked her.

'D'you know what?' she says. 'In a few months' time, maybe even in a few weeks' time, no one will remember him at all. This will all blow over.'

'I hope you're right,' I say. I'll hold on to Jo's thought. I'll be able to relax once this has all died down and everything has gone back to normal.

For a minute, Jo and I just sit there and munch on snacks. Then I pick up the remote controls from the coffee table. A film will lend me some essential escapism, if only for a couple of hours. And Jo doesn't want to sit here all evening talking about Joshua Knoll any more than I do. Poor Jo has provided a shoulder to cry on since the day I was summoned to the headmaster's office to pick up Olly and ended up having to take Iris home, too.

But just then, we hear the front door open and Ian's voice bellow from the hallway, 'Jo, you there?'

'In the living room,' she calls.

He storms into the room, clearly annoyed about something. 'Those fecking Knolls,' he starts, then stops as he sees me. 'Ah, I'm sorry,' he says, his voice notched down a few decibels, 'I forgot it was your girlie night in. Hi, Carla. How are you doing?'

'Good, thanks, Ian.' I slur my speech noticeably in just those three words.

Jo jumps in before I can ask Ian how he is. 'What have they done now?' she says.

Ian looks from Carla to me, no doubt trying to weigh up what he can and can't say in front of me. 'They're offering a substantial reward for anyone who can give information leading to the arrest of Josh's murderer.'

My stomach plummets at the same time as a wave of nausea rises to my throat.

'We advised them against it,' Ian continues, 'but Richard Knoll went to the *North Devon Echo* – it's already been posted to their website and it will be in print in this week's paper edition. And it will be broadcast on ITV News West Country, too.'

'How much?' Jo asks.

'Fifty grand,' Ian says. I splutter on my wine. 'It's already causing us a real headache. Crank calls, mediums offering their services. It'll only get worse. It means we're using up valuable police resources, wasting time, dealing with a whole load of nonsense and checking out fake information. But we have to do it in the unlikely event that one honest witness rings in with a useful lead.'

My nausea abates a little. The offer of a reward isn't necessarily a bad thing. It might send the police on a wild goose chase. I feel selfish for having that thought – I should feel sorry for Ian. But I welcome any red herrings the public can throw into the mix because they may help keep the suspicion off Iris.

Chapter 23

Ian

NOW

Ian knows he shouldn't pay too much attention to his hunches. Senior investigating officers are supposed to apply the 'ABC principle', where the 'A' stands for 'assume nothing'. Besides, his gut feeling, as he knows from experience, is often incorrect. But although it seems more likely the footprint was made by a first responder, he's still convinced it was made by the murderer. The offending shoe was a unisex trainer, so theoretically it could belong to a man or a woman. If it was a man, though, he has rather small feet. Could they be dealing with a young killer? A child or teenager? Or are they looking at a female murderer?

Ian knows the killer couldn't possibly be his goddaughter any more than it could be his own daughter. But he should never have said what he said to Ash about the footprint. Seriously, what was he thinking? He's on his first case as SIO and already he's making a balls-up of it.

His frustration is compounded by the fact he has several

members of his team (far too many, in fact) following up supposed tip-offs they've received over the phone in response to the Knolls' promise of a reward. Nothing useful will come out of all these calls, Ian would bet his boots on it. So far, the information they've been given has all turned out to be false and they've received God knows how many different descriptions of dodgy-looking individuals lurking in the vicinity of Lower Buryknoll Wood. One woman has denounced her husband and another has suggested they should check out her father-in-law's alibi. Ian could wring Richard Knoll's neck. He should be charged with causing wasteful employment of the police.

He's sitting in his office at the Devon and Cornwall Police Headquarters, in Middlemoor, a suburb of Exeter. It's a recent, state-of-the-art building with lots of glass windows. He's looking out of one them as he thinks about his best friend, his goddaughter and his career. In that order. Sighing, he turns back to his computer screen. Before he allowed his mind to roam, he was reading through statements and transcripts relating to the case.

An email lands in his inbox with a ding. The forensic results. Ian opens it straightaway and spends the next few minutes reading through the report. Then he leans back in his swivel chair, locking the fingers of his hands together behind his head, and thinks of Edmond Locard.

According to Locard's Exchange Principle, the culprit inevitably leaves something at the scene of the crime as well as taking something away from it. Locard was a French criminologist and he came up with this theory a hundred years ago, but police officers still bear it in mind today. Every contact leaves a trace. In the Major Incident Room this morning, Ian reminded his team of that very concept.

Unfortunately, Joshua Knoll's murderer was either careful not to leave anything at the scene of the crime and on the victim's body, or most (all?) of what they did leave was washed away in the rain.

But the hair that was left on the victim, the one Lorraine Davies, the Home Office pathologist found on Joshua Knoll's sternum, has grabbed his attention. Ian asked the lab to extract DNA. It was clutching at straws, if he's honest. They had nothing else to go on. The hair definitely didn't belong to the victim. And there's only a slim chance it belonged to the murderer. After all, the hair could have been transferred to Joshua's body, especially to that part of his sternum, which his hoodie left exposed, by anyone he came into contact with. *Every contact leaves a trace.*

Ian studies the report again. The hair had no follicle, which, as Ian knows, makes DNA extraction difficult, although not impossible, and some mitochondrial DNA markers have indeed been successfully extracted from the shaft of the hair. So, they have a partial DNA profile. But no matches in the database.

The microscopic analysis alone, however, has coughed up quite a bit of information. About the hair itself (length, diameter, colour) and about the person whose head it came from (sex, race, approximate age). Ian unclasps his hands and rereads the paragraph in question. The hair is 30.3 cm long; 101 microns in diameter; dark brown, almost black in colour. It belonged to a female, Caucasian, aged between fifteen and twenty-five. Ian closes his eyes. But the info that really stands out and that Ian can't unsee, even with his eyes squeezed shut, is that the hair came from the head of a blonde. A young blonde who dyed her hair dark brown.

Hearing a voice, Ian snaps his eyes open. DC Ward is standing at the open door to Ian's office. He always leaves it open, unless he mustn't be disturbed. 'Sorry. Miles away. What did you say?'

'The Spencer-Lyles are here. Sasha and her parents. Both of them. Without a solicitor.' She raises her eyebrows. 'Don't know how you wangled that, but well done, sir.'

He has given up trying to get DC Ward to call him Ian when they're not in front of a member of the public or a suspect. He's on first-name terms with every member of his investigative team in private except for DC Ward, which means he can't very well call her by her first name (Gail) either. So he doesn't call her anything, not to her face. In his head, he calls her DC Ward.

'Coming,' he says. 'Go on ahead.'

He wangled this interview by using his wife, but he's not going to admit that to DC Ward. He's not proud of it. They absolutely have to talk to Sasha Spencer-Lyles (what a mouthful!), who was Joshua Knoll's girlfriend right up until he died. But Sasha's parents have been damn uncooperative. Because Sasha's still only seventeen (she was a year ahead at school, apparently), they need to talk to her in the presence of an appropriate adult. When Joshua died, Sasha was at university, so they had to wait for her to come home. First Mrs Spencer-Lyles claimed her daughter was in no fit state to talk to the police. Then Mr Spencer-Lyles insisted he wanted a 'lawyer' present. Ian's officers insisted how urgent the matter was, but Sasha's parents wouldn't budge.

'I've got a good mind to charge them with perverting the course of justice,' Ian had complained to Jo over breakfast earlier that week.

'They're probably just worried that suspicion will fall on their daughter,' Jo had reasoned. 'They're nice people.'

'How do you know them?'

'Sasha did maths A level. She's a bright kid. She was in my class. I still see Sandra Spencer-Lyles at my Zumba class.'

'Isn't your Zumba class this evening?'

'Yes,' Jo said warily.

'I don't suppose you could …' Ian didn't finish his sentence. This was far from professional. He wasn't supposed to tell his wife all this, let alone ask her to intervene.

'Leave it with me,' Jo said, with a sigh, then muttered something inaudible under her breath. Ian didn't ask her to repeat it.

So here they are. Like Ash with Iris, Mr Spencer-Lyles insisted that he wanted Sasha to talk to Ian. As the SIO, Ian wouldn't normally conduct a preliminary interview with a friend or relative of the victim's. And he would have preferred Sasha to be interviewed at the Spencer-Lyles' home, where she would undoubtedly have felt more relaxed. Never mind. He has requisitioned one of the small rooms where they usually carry out more informal interviews. It has sofas that look more comfortable than they are, but it's bright and airy and hopefully not too daunting. There are some glasses and a jug of water on the coffee table.

DC Ward does the introductions.

'So, Sasha,' Ian begins, 'I'm sure you know why you're here.' He then proceeds to spout more or less verbatim the same spiel he used on Iris about building up a picture of how Joshua Knoll lived in the hope that they can work out more about how he died and eventually arrest the person responsible for his death. 'Anything you can tell us about Joshua would be helpful. Let's start with how you knew him and how long you've known him, shall we?'

Sasha looks at both her parents before replying. 'He was in my year at school. I've known him for years, but he'd only been my boyfriend for nine months or so when he … um … died.' Her voice wavers a little.

Ian does a discreet calculation on his fingers. Since last November, then. If he remembers correctly, Iris put an end to her relationship with Joshua last October, a couple of weeks after his eighteenth birthday. He didn't hang around before replacing her.

Sasha goes on to give a description of Joshua's likes and dislikes, talents and inabilities, which adds nothing new to the mix. Ian and his subordinate let her talk. DC Ward scribbles notes on a pad. Ian tries to sneak a peep, but he can't decipher the tiny, spidery letters, although that might be due more to his eyesight (does he need varifocals?) than to DC Ward's handwriting.

DC Ward looks up and asks the next two or three questions. Ian is happy to hand her the reins. He's struggling to concentrate on this interview.

Iris is naturally fair-haired, like Ash. Lately, she has been dyeing her hair more or less black. Ever since she went to her grandmother's house in the Lake District a few months ago to get away from it all for a while. She came back looking like someone else entirely, which, Ian supposes, was the point of her transformation.

'And how well did you get on with Joshua?' DC Ward's question trespasses on Ian's thoughts.

A stifled sob escapes from Sasha's mouth and a rogue tear rolls down her cheek. She swipes at it angrily.

'Have a sip of water, Sasha.' DC Ward pours from the jug. 'Take your time. We understand how difficult this is for you, but it's important for us to get to know the real Joshua. And we think you knew him well, so we really need to hear everything you can tell us.'

Ian catches the look Sasha throws her mother. Mrs Spencer-Lyles nods and Sasha turns back to DC Ward.

'He could be mean,' Sasha says, quietly. 'I was hoping to get away from him when I went to university, but he was ... what's the word? ... persistent.' She takes another sip of water.

'Joshua was controlling,' Mr Spencer-Lyles interjects. 'He would provoke arguments and then sulk until Sasha apologized. He isolated her from her friends and even from her mother and me. He wanted to micromanage every single detail of Sasha's life.'

Sounds like Joshua treated Sasha in much the same way as he treated Iris. Everything Ian learns about Joshua Knoll makes him think the kid was a nasty piece of work. Carla's label of a manipulative narcissist was dead on. No wonder Sasha's parents didn't want her to talk to the police. She has as much motive as Iris.

'I see,' DC Ward says to Mr Spencer-Lyles, and to Sasha, 'Did he make you do things you didn't want to do?'

'I didn't send him any nudes, if that's what you mean,' Sasha says. 'He wanted me to and when I refused, it made him really mad. He said I would do it if I loved him. He called me frigid.'

'He asked you to send him pictures of you naked?'

'Yeah. But I didn't do it. I mean, I saw what happened to Iris.'

'You think that was Josh's doing?'

'I dunno. But I expect that's where they came from. Iris must have sent the video to Josh. It probably was him, but I believed him when he said it wasn't. At the time.'

Ian clears his throat. This isn't about Iris's video. They're in danger of veering off track. 'Did anything else make him mad with you?' he asks.

'Yeah. Well, someone else. Mr Tomlinson. My physics teacher.'

Tomlinson. That rings a bell. Ian's fairly sure he's Millie's physics teacher, too.

'Why did Mr Tomlinson make Joshua mad?' DC Ward has taken over again, which suits Ian. His mind is still elsewhere. On the forensic report.

'Josh was insanely jealous of him,' Sasha says, rolling her eyes.

'Mr Tomlinson was a new, young teacher at South Lydacombe School. I think he was on his induction programme,' Mrs Spencer-Lyles says. 'He developed a bit of a crush on Sasha.'

'You think? A crush?' Clearly, her husband doesn't quite agree. 'The man was obsessed. He was stalking her, for God's sake, following her around and whatnot.'

'Stalking her?' That snaps Ian's focus back to the task at hand. He sits up straighter in his seat.

'Yes. He followed her on social media and sent her private messages,' Mr Spencer-Lyles says. 'He offered her a lift a few times after school.'

Ian doesn't like the sound of this. He'd like to get Jo's opinion of her colleague, although it would be unprofessional of him to ask her. That wouldn't have stopped him in the past, but he can't risk it getting back to Carla and Ash.

'These are serious allegations, Mr Spencer-Lyles,' DC Ward says. 'Did you report this to the police?'

'Well, no. It was near the end of the school year when we found out and we had other things to deal with at the time.'

'We thought it would just go away when Sasha went to university,' Mrs Spencer-Lyles adds. 'But Sasha kept screenshots of the messages, didn't you, Sasha?'

'You might want to consider making a …'

Ian's thoughts meander back to the hair. It's Iris's. It has to be. But she said she'd had nothing to do with him for months. Is there any way her hair could have been on Joshua's hoodie from when they were dating? If he hadn't worn it since back then, maybe? But no, Iris was still blonde back then. Plus the fact that some DNA markers were extracted suggests the hair wasn't degraded by age and was shed relatively recently.

Ian's going to have to go and see his manager. He can't keep his suspicions to himself and carry on as normal. Damn it! Ash was right all along. Iris is going to end up as their main suspect. She has motive; she has the right shoes and the right-size feet; and in all likelihood, she left a hair from her head on the victim's body. Each of those things alone would mean virtually nothing. But together, it looks suspicious. Way too suspicious to ignore.

He tries to tune back in to the conversation, but it has become white noise with only the odd word here and there that Ian recognizes. *Argument … jealous … love … threaten.* Ian only realizes DC Ward has wrapped it up when she and the Spencer-Lyles stand up. Ian also gets to his feet, a step behind everyone else. His hands are clammy and he wipes them discreetly on his trousers before shaking Mr Spencer-Lyle's outstretched hand.

'I'll walk you out,' DC Ward says to the Spencer-Lyles, holding her arm out towards the door. 'Are you all right, sir?' she whispers over her shoulder.

He manages a nod and a tight smile. 'Good work,' he says.

Christ, his mouth is dry. He walks along the corridor and into the men's toilets, where he splashes water on his face and drinks from the tap. His pale reflection stares at him from the mirror accusingly.

He comes out of the bogs feeling no better than when he went in, and heads along the corridor again. This time he stops at the last office on the right. He runs his fingers over the name plaque on the door. Detective Superintendent Nathan Hall. Ian looks up to his superior officer – literally (the guy is six foot three) and figuratively – Det Supt Hall has been mentoring and supervising Ian for ages, long before he was made the SIO of this case.

Ian hesitates for a few seconds, thinking again of his best friend, his goddaughter, his family, his career. He's going to let everyone down. He's overwhelmed with guilt and regret. But he has no choice. Taking a deep breath, he knocks on the detective superintendent's door.

Chapter 24

Iris

THEN

When everyone else went back to school after the Christmas holidays, Iris stayed off for two more weeks, holing up either at her mum's or at her dad's. Iris's parents had been in touch with both the headmaster, Mr Brook, and the deputy head pastoral, Mrs Hamilton, on a regular basis and, although her parents didn't seem satisfied with what the school was doing about the situation Iris found herself in, they'd all agreed that she'd be going back to school the following Monday. Iris was dreading it.

She'd kept up to date with her schoolwork. It was a welcome distraction. She caught up on the lessons she was missing and sent in her homework via the school's Intranet portal. Most of her teachers had written to her directly and sent her feedback on her work.

Iris had steered clear of social media since that time she was supposed to look for evidence and had stumbled on those insulting messages. She'd deleted the WhatsApp groups, blocked the phone numbers of people who had sent offensive texts, deactivated her social media accounts and she hadn't opened her emails. Until now, apart from that, she'd mainly had support from everyone around her – her parents, the staff at school, Olly and Melanie. Even Daniel had been supportive to her face. So she wasn't exactly prepared for her first day back.

It all kicked off at registration. Millie sat next to her, but then sort of inched her chair a bit further away, pretending she wanted to talk to the girl at the desk next to theirs. Then the boys sitting at the desk behind Iris and Millie's started to stage-whisper. It was obvious they meant for her to hear them.

'She's dumb, but she's hot. I wouldn't kick her out of bed,' said Christian Pollard. He was this really geeky kid, with horn-rimmed glasses.

'I'd like to bend her over and take her from behind,' Rupert Mead chimed in. Rupert was the smallest boy in the year. Most of the girls were taller than him, too.

All the pupils within earshot of Christian and Rupert tittered.

Tears sprang to Iris's eyes. She wanted to turn round and glare at them, but stayed eyes front. No way would she give them the satisfaction.

At break, Iris and Millie went together to the toilets, but when Iris came out, Millie had already gone. A toilet flushed and a pupil came out of the cubicle. The girl wasn't in the same year or the same house and Iris didn't know her name. Iris gave her a tight smile in the mirror as they stood side by side washing their hands.

The girl frowned at Iris's reflection. 'Slag,' she said without breaking eye contact, then she turned and walked away.

Iris went back into the toilet cubicle, bolted the door, sat on the lid of the loo and cried. She sometimes fantasized about what superpower she would like if she was a Marvel heroine. The ability to make herself invisible. That would be awesome. She could sit in on all her classes, but no one would know she was there. When the bell went, she gave herself a stern talking-to. She couldn't make herself invisible, but she could do the next best thing: keep a low profile. Keep her hand down. Try not to attract attention. So she got up and went to her English class. It was her favourite subject and Mr Lawton was her favourite teacher.

She was the last to arrive and everything went dead silent when she walked into the classroom. Everyone turned to gape at her. Killian Morrow looked her up and down and licked his lips like he was imagining her naked. Iris froze. Had he watched her video? Had they all seen it?

The seat next to Millie – Iris's place – was already taken. There was a free seat next to a kid called Tom Fischer. Tom was *really* popular. He usually sat next to Emiliano, the Italian exchange student. Millie had a huge crush on Emiliano. As did a whole load of other girls in their school. Emiliano was clearly absent today. Iris looked around. Nope, no other free seats.

'Hurry up and sit down, Iris,' Mr Lawton said, not unkindly.

She walked over to Tom's desk. He removed his bag from the chair as she pulled it out to sit down. She got her books and pencil case out. Iris was fighting to hold it together, but a tear rolled down her face and plopped onto the cover of Daphne du Maurier's *Rebecca*. Tom bent down and rummaged for something in his bag. When he straightened up, he slid a pocket packet of tissues across the desk.

She looked at him, surprised. 'Thanks,' she muttered, taking out a tissue.

'For what it's worth, I think your ex is a wanker,' he whispered. 'He deserves to be expelled for what he did.'

That surprised Iris even more. 'Thanks,' she muttered again.

'Tom, stop talking, please,' Mr Lawton called. 'Unless there's something you'd like to share with all of us?'

'No, sir,' Tom replied.

'A video, maybe?' Killian Morrow suggested. It wasn't loud enough for Mr Lawton to hear, but Iris caught it. Clearly, a few of her classmates did too – there were giggles and snorts. Killian was such a dick. Iris knew this. But it hurt even so.

Ignore them, Tom scribbled on a piece of rough paper as soon as Mr Lawton had turned his back.

Iris nodded. But it was impossible to ignore the reactions of her fellow pupils. Tom was the only one on her side. He thought Josh should be expelled. She hoped he would be. Then she wouldn't have to face him. She was terrified of bumping into him. She was fairly sure she'd spotted him earlier – at break. It was from a distance, but the sight of him still made a pain shoot through her tummy.

So far, Josh hadn't even been suspended. Mum was furious about this. She kept saying Josh would get what he deserved in the end. Mum believed in karma. What goes around comes around and stuff like that. She often said you got what you had coming to you. Iris wasn't so sure. After all, what had she done to deserve this? And her family, too. None of them had done anything wrong and yet they were all affected. Even Margo, who didn't understand what had happened, but who suffered from all the stress it was causing.

Iris didn't take in any of the lesson. She used to be one of the most active students in this class, but she didn't put up her hand once. Mr Lawton didn't ask her any questions either, thank God.

He kept her back after the lesson, though. 'How are you holding up?' he asked.

'OK,' Iris lied.

'Did Tom say something nasty to you?'

'No, sir. He was being kind.' Iris didn't add what she was thinking. That Tom was the only pupil who had showed her any compassion all day. This included Millie, who was supposed to be her best friend.

By lunchtime, Iris had had more than she could take. She couldn't concentrate in her lessons anyway. So what was the point? She should never have agreed to come back to school. She hid in the loos for the second time that day and rang her mum. She was crying – again! – down the phone and couldn't get the words out.

'Go and see Mrs Hamilton,' Mum said, 'and tell her I'm on my way to pick you up and take you home.'

Mrs Hamilton and Mr Brook waited with Iris in Mr Brook's office. When Mum got there, they told her that Iris should take as long as necessary.

'Iris's teachers have told me that her latest marks are good, not quite as good as usual, but still perfectly satisfactory,' Mr Brook said. 'Iris can continue to catch up on her lessons and send in her homework and we'll see how she's coping in a few weeks' time.'

Iris was *so* relieved she could stay at home, even if it was only a stopgap. She'd have to go back to school properly one day.

'Maybe we should get her away from here,' she overheard Mum saying to Dad on the phone that evening as they discussed her failed attempt to go back to school.

Did she mean move away? Did Iris want that? She had no friends here anymore. Even Millie was keeping her distance. Perhaps it would do her good to start over, somewhere no one knew who she was, somewhere no one had seen the video. The glimmer of hope she felt was quickly replaced by a pang of guilt. Even if Mum could work anywhere, Daniel would never agree to uproot Margo and come with them. And it wasn't fair on Olly. And Iris couldn't move away with Dad. He had a good job here and he couldn't move away from Olly and Mum because of her.

But it turned out to be another temporary solution. They meant get her away for a fortnight, not permanently. A change of scenery. They were sending her to her grandmother's house in Cumbria. Granny Ashford had Wi-Fi and Iris could just as easily do her schoolwork there.

Granny Ashford was eighty-one and lived out in the sticks in the Lake District. The nearest village was Hawkshead, a pretty village, but also tiny and kinda dead. Iris felt as isolated there as she had at home. Her gran, who was actually quite lively for her age, did her best to cheer Iris up, taking her for walks and to visit nearby tourist attractions – those that were open despite the off-season. Iris had already visited them when she was a bit younger. They ate variations of a ploughman's lunch at one in the afternoon and cooked together in the evenings. A couple of times, they went for a pub meal.

The first time Iris deliberately made herself vomit it was because she felt so sick after the first pub meal. She'd never done it before and it took several attempts. She pushed her forefinger and middle finger further and further down the back of her throat and retched until it worked. Afterwards, she did it every evening after dinner. Iris had already lost weight – she hadn't stood on the scales to check, but she could see she'd got skinny. It was because she'd had no appetite since she'd become a local porn star. Now, even though she was worried she'd lose more weight, she couldn't break what was becoming a nightly habit.

After a few nights, her gran noticed. She made Iris promise she'd stop making herself sick. Iris tried. She really did. One evening, her gran ambushed her as she came out of the bathroom after throwing up her meal.

'I'm going to have to phone your mum and dad, Iris,' she said.

Her parents decided to drive up that weekend to take her back to Crooked Oak Cottage, where Mum could keep an eye on her.

Iris got up the next day before her gran. She left a note to say she'd gone for a walk and would be back soon. She walked, like, two miles to the nearest hairdresser's. She'd been careful to stay off socials, but she'd looked up online how to donate her hair to make a wig for a young 'princess' with cancer, then she'd rung the salon about it. She was supposed to call back and make an appointment, not just show up, but she thought she'd have more time.

The salon was over some grockle shop and you had to go up these dodgy metal steps that looked like a fire escape to get to it. It was called *A Cut Above*. Iris thought *Curl up and Dye* would be more apt for how she felt right now.

She had to wait for half an hour and it was the trainee who cut and dyed her hair. Afterwards, Iris stared at herself in the mirror. Her long, blonde hair was totally gone. In its place was a short, dark bob. Iris was thrilled with the transformation. She looked completely different. She was unrecognizable, even to herself.

Chapter 25

Ash

NOW

Carla has something on her mind, Ash can tell. She's sitting next to him, in the passenger's seat, biting her lower lip and picking at the skin around her thumb. She's unusually quiet. Iris, who's in the back – she didn't want to drive – isn't particularly talkative either, but he puts that down to her driving test. They're on their way to the driving centre. He took the morning off work and offered to take Iris in to Barnstaple. He thought he'd better show willing – Carla often complains, quite rightly, that she's expected to do all the taxiing around simply because she works at home and is on hand – but when he arrived at Crooked Oak Cottage, only a few minutes late, she announced she was coming too.

'Feeling confident, honey?' he asks, to break the silence, looking at Iris in the rear-view mirror. He can't think of anything better to say.

'Hmm,' comes the reply, which Ash doesn't know how to decode.

They drop off Iris and wish her luck.

'I'm going into town afterwards,' she says. 'I want to buy some clothes. Either to celebrate or commiserate, whatever.'

'You'll smash it, Iris,' Ash says.

'I'm not sure "smash" is the right word,' Carla says seriously, which makes Ash and Iris laugh.

'I'll slay it,' Iris amends for Ash. He laughs a little more at this, but he sees Carla shudder at Iris's choice of words.

'Give us a ring afterwards and we'll come and pick you up,' Ash says. 'Take your time.'

Ash wants to go to a car dealership. He's spotted a second-hand Renault Twingo that would be perfect for Iris if she passes her test. Manual, petrol, forty-five thousand miles on the clock, five and a half grand, powder blue – Iris will love it. It would be an early eighteenth birthday present. When Olly passed his driving test earlier this year, Ash bought a car, too, also as an early eighteenth birthday present, with the money left to him by his father when he died a few years ago. It was intended for the kids' studies, but Ash has that covered. Just about. As long as they don't both do more than three years in further education. Olly totalled his car – a second-hand Civic Honda – within a month, weeks before he actually turned eighteen. Took a bend way too fast and ended up overturned – and unhurt, fortunately – in the ditch. Ash decided not to bail him out of that one. Since then, Carla has driven Olly wherever he needs to go, although it looks like Olivia might now take on that role. Ash has promised to buy Iris a car on one condition – that she puts up 'P' plates for a few months so that other road users will take her inexperience into consideration. He insisted for Olly, too. Not that it did much good. Ash is very safety-conscious when it comes to cars. Has been ever since Roly ran over Tracey.

When Ash suggests going to see the car together, Carla is unenthusiastic. 'You'll jinx it,' she says. 'Wait until she's taken the test.'

He's never known Carla to be superstitious, although she believes in her own form of karma – what goes around comes around, or some such nonsense. But she's got a point. *Don't jump the gun, Ash.*

'You're right,' he concedes. 'Bad idea.'

He suggests going for a coffee, but Carla's response is lukewarm.

'Well, what do you want to do?' he asks. He can tell she wants to talk to him.

'Let's go for a walk,' she says.

It's a blustery day, not one he would have chosen for a stroll. Plus, he's not wearing the right shoes. Or clothes. Once he has taken Carla and Iris home, he has to come back into Barnstaple and go in to the office. But he dutifully parks his car near the Old Bridge, and they start out along the Tarka Trail, following the river Taw upstream, towards Rock Park. It's an easy, flat walk, along a footpath. Ash's feet will kill him after this, but his expensive brogues should remain unscathed.

'Come on,' he says to Carla after a few minutes. 'Out with it.'

His phone beeps in his pocket. He barely hears it over the wind. It can't be Iris, not yet, and if it was someone at the bank, they would call him, but he pulls out his mobile and looks at the screen. He can feel Carla's suspicious gaze on him as he reads the text.

'Work,' he says by way of an explanation, firing off a quick reply.

She'll know he's lying. She can read him like a book. She'll assume it's a woman. Once a cheat, and all that. Ash made one mistake – admittedly, a monumental one – years ago and Carla has branded him a womanizer and a cheat for the rest of his life. She's right to be mad at him – he wrecked everything – but the words 'monogamous' and 'commitment' no longer scare him, as they once did when he was stupid and immature. Quite the opposite. He wants nothing more than to settle down. He just can't seem to find the right woman. He can't help but compare them all to Carla, and none of them comes close.

'It's about the shoes,' Carla begins as he activates the silent mode on his mobile and slides it back into his pocket.

He looks down at his brogues, frowning. Did he mention that thought out loud before?

'Iris's shoes,' Carla clarifies, impatience seeping into her voice.

'Oh.' And then he gets it. 'Oh, I see. What about them?'

'She threw them out. She must have overheard our conversation. I found her Vans in the kitchen bin.'

'A precaution, maybe?'

'Ash, she wasn't wearing her Vans that day at your place when Ian and his colleague came round. She was wearing her Chelsea boots. How did she know which shoes to throw out? Ian didn't specifically mention which make of shoe, did he? You didn't mention a make when you told me.'

'No, he didn't. I didn't. Good point. Did you ask her about it?'

'Yes.' Carla pushes her sleek, dark hair out of her face, but the wind blows it back. 'She got really upset and then changed her story. She's now saying she was at the scene of the crime, but Josh was already dead. He'd been dead a few days, according to Iris.'

That throws him. 'Really? She said that?' He thinks for a moment. 'Well, we've got nothing to worry about then.' He turns to face Carla. This is not what she expected him to say – he can tell by the look she gives him. 'What I mean is, if it *was* her footprint in the woods, that explains it.'

'I suppose so, but—'

'You think she did it, don't you?' he says. 'You think she killed Josh.'

She doesn't answer, which Ash takes as a yes. He sighs. Carla has often said that Iris can do no wrong in his eyes, but how can she seriously believe their daughter is capable of murder?

They've reached the entrance to the park. There are a few people, wearing high-vis jackets or running clothes milling around, and Ash realizes there was a parkrun here this morning.

Ash has only ever done one – in the Lake District one summer on holiday with the kids. Iris and Olly persuaded him to do the Whinlatter Forest parkrun, without telling him how hilly it was. His legs were sore for a couple of days afterwards. The stunning view over Derwentwater, though, almost made up for it. Ash keeps fit – he goes to the gym and the swimming pool regularly, hikes and goes mountain biking – but he's not much of a runner. Perhaps one of these days he'll do another parkrun even so.

'Daniel has left me,' Carla says, jolting him back to the present.

'What? Why?'

'Basically, he said he couldn't allow his daughter to live in the same house as Iris and me. He thinks Iris is a murderer and that I'm "harbouring a criminal".' Carla does the air quotes with her fingers.

Ash swears under his breath. He's annoyed at Carla. She's obviously told Dandruff something that she should have kept a secret. About the shoes or the necklace. Or both. But his irritation is nothing compared to the fury he feels towards Dan himself. Christ, the man needs to grow a pair and zip up the man suit. He should be looking after Carla and Iris, looking out for them, not running away. The bastard.

'I'm more upset about losing Margo, to tell you the truth,' Carla says.

'Jesus. What a mess.' He wants to reach out and put his arm around Carla, to comfort her, but he's worried she might misinterpret his gesture. 'Where has he gone?'

'To his mum's in Brayworthy, I imagine.'

Ash had forgotten Dandruff's mother lived in Brayworthy. It's a ten-minute drive from Shallowcott, the hamlet in which he lives. The Knolls also live in Brayworthy, in what has to be the biggest house in the village, perched on top of the hill. Unbidden, an image of the place enters his head now. He used to drop off Iris there sometimes.

'What are we going to do?' Carla asks him. She sounds desperate.

'Not much we can do,' Ash says. He stops walking, takes Carla by the shoulders and turns her so that she's facing him. 'Iris didn't do this. So there will be nothing to prove she did. And if they find anything of hers at the crime scene, well, the fact she was there explains how it got there.'

'Are you going to tell Ian?'

Ash thinks about that. He's seeing Roly later. At The Grove. That's what the text message was about. Ash didn't tell Carla because he's worried. Why does Roly want to see him? They often meet up at the pub for a swift pint or two, especially at weekends, so he doesn't really need a reason. But he senses Roly has something he needs to get off his chest. Is he about to arrest Iris? Or bring her in for questioning? Or is that a euphemism for the same thing? Perhaps Roly just wants to meet up for a pint between mates and Ash is reading a subtext into the message that isn't there.

'No,' he says eventually, as much to himself as to Carla. 'No, I don't think so. We'll only tell Roly if it becomes necessary.' He's looking ahead, at the obelisk, but out of the corner of his eyes he sees Carla nod. 'And, Carla? You can't tell anyone.' *Anyone else*. He doesn't criticize her for telling Dandruff whatever it is she has told him. He just hopes the prick will keep his mouth shut. 'Perhaps we should go back,' he says.

He ponders his words. He wishes they really could go back. Back in time. Change the course of events. Alter the outcome. Make sure Iris never went out with Joshua in the first place and save her from everything that happened afterwards and anything that might still happen because this particular chain of events was put into motion.

Carla is looking out over the water at a brown-feathered, long-billed wader. A curlew, perhaps. It's standing by the water's edge, puffing out its chest and looking self-important. He pulls out his phone and checks it discreetly while she's distracted. Ian has to confirm a time for this evening. Ash has received a text message, but it's from Iris, not Roly. He reads it and smiles, his trepidation dissipating slightly for a moment.

'She's passed,' he says to Carla. 'Let's go and see that car.'

Chapter 26

Ian

NOW

'Sorry, mate. I was held up at work. Want another?'

Ian looks up. He has been so lost in thought he's almost surprised to see Ash standing there. He eyes the two empty pint glasses on the table in front of him in disbelief, too. He's been in a complete daze.

'Yeah, go on, then,' Ian replies, as Ash picks up the empties. 'I'll get a taxi home afterwards.'

As Ash makes his way to the bar, Ian replays the conversation he had with Detective Superintendent Nathan Hall. Has he done the right thing? Could he have done this any differently? Entering his superior's office felt a lot like crossing the Rubicon. The point of no return. He didn't really have a choice, though, did he?

He decides to pop outside for a cigarette. He ends up smoking two, lighting the second one with the embers of the first. He's officially a chain smoker. Then he pockets his pack of Embassy, making a mental note to buy another packet from the machine before he leaves. He's running low. Strange that you can't smoke in pubs anymore (soon you might not even be allowed to smoke in pub gardens, if the Health Secretary gets his way), but you can still buy smokes in Ash's local. Ian doesn't know if that's the case everywhere. The only pub he ever goes to is The Grove.

When Ian steps back inside the pub, Ash is sitting at the table, looking both worried and impatient. Ian feels no qualms about making him wait. Ash was late, as usual, and Ian had to wait for him, so. He's mad at Ash, but not because he was late – Ian's used to Ash's tardiness. (Ash turned up late at the church for his own wedding, for Christ's sake. Carla and Ian were the only people not panicking. The bride and the best man. They knew he'd get there eventually.) No, his irascibility is irrational, as if Ash himself is responsible for putting Ian in the position he found himself in.

Ian takes the seat opposite Ash that he vacated a few minutes ago. He decides to get straight to the point. 'Listen, I have to tell you something.' Not very original, but this is the opening sentence he has plumped for. He tried to run through the whole speech in his head before Ash got here, but he didn't get beyond this bit.

'I seem to be everyone's confidant today,' Ash comments wryly.

When Ash doesn't elaborate, Ian hazards a guess. 'Carla?'

'Yeah. She ... er ... Dandruff's left her.'

'Oh,' Ian says. What else is there to say? 'Och, he's not good enough for her anyway.' That's the only thing he can think of. It's corny, but he happens to believe it. He steers the conversation back on track. 'So, as I was saying, er ... this is in total confidence, you understand, between you and me.' Ian points to Ash and then at himself as he says this, raising his eyebrows in expectation of some sort of assurance or promise that Ash will keep this to himself.

'You got it,' Ash says.

That will have to do, Ian supposes. 'We found a hair on the vict ... Joshua's body.' He notices Ash straighten in his seat. He ploughs on before Ash can interrupt him. 'It came from the head of a young, blonde woman, who dyes her hair black.' Ian pauses to let that sink in.

'I see. You don't think it's Iris's hair, do you?'

'I don't know what to think, to be honest.'

'If it is hers, could it have been on Josh's clothing or on a piece of furniture or something for a while and then transferred to his body? Is that possible?'

Ian is about to tell Ash they got a partial DNA profile from the hair, which means it was probably shed fairly recently. But he catches himself on. He can't keep giving Ash information about the investigation. He could point out that Iris only started dyeing her hair after the video went viral, when she no longer frequented Josh's place, but he drops it. 'Aye, anything's possible,' he says instead.

Ash looks thoughtful, as if debating whether to say something. He appears to decide against it and takes a few gulps of his lager.

'I ... er ... I went to see my manager,' Ian says. 'My superior. It got to the point where I felt I had to.' He watches as the blood drains from Ash's face and realizes what his friend is thinking. 'Oh, no. Not to denounce Iris or anything like that,' he adds hastily. 'I've stepped down as senior investigating officer.' Ash's eyebrows knit together into a stitch. 'I've been removed from the inquiry,' Ian clarifies. 'Due to personal involvement.'

'Because of Iris?'

'Well, that wasn't the reason I gave. I told the superintendent I'd known the victim and my wife had taught many of the teenagers we're currently interviewing, some of whom were friends with my daughter, and I felt there might be a conflict of interest. They tend not to take any risks with that sort of thing nowadays.'

'I don't know what to say, Roly,' Ash says. 'I'm so sorry.'

Ian didn't tell the super he didn't think he was doing his job properly, with integrity, and he doesn't tell Ash this now either. In Ian's mind, it boiled down to a simple choice: his friendship with Ash or his career. A no-brainer. Anyway, his career's not over. He may get another chance one day, although a murder case is a once-in-a-blue-moon thing, especially out here in the sticks.

'Thank you, Roly,' Ash says. Unless Ian's mistaken, Ash has teared up.

'Sure, it's no bother. No bother at all.' He drains his pint and waves the glass in Ash's face. 'One more for the road?'

'Why not? I'll get these.'

It's Ian's round, but he lets Ash get the pints in and goes outside for another smoke.

He's standing in front of his house, about to smoke his last cigarette of the evening, when Jo opens the door and hands him his phone.

'I answered it,' she says. 'Thought it might be important.'

'Hello?' he says into the mobile.

'Good evening, sir. It's Gail.'

Gail? He pulls the phone away from his ear and looks at the screen. His brain gets there at the same time as he reads the caller ID. DC Ward. 'Ah, good evening, er … Gail.'

'Sir, I know you've stepped down as SIO, but I thought you'd like to know we've made an arrest.'

Ian's heart skips several beats, then races as if to make up for it. Have they arrested Iris? 'Who?' he manages.

'Harry Tomlinson, sir.'

Ian is so relieved he can't place the suspect, even though the name rings a bell. Clearly, he has drunk too much, although it was – what? – four pints. He's such a lightweight. 'Who?' he asks again.

'Harry Tomlinson, Sir. The physics teacher at South Lydacombe School?'

'Ah, yes. The newly qualified teacher who was stalking Sasha Spencer-Lyles.'

'I think the correct term now is "early career teacher", sir.

The Spencer-Lyles made a formal complaint against him. We found scrapbooks with photos of underage girls – mostly his pupils – clearly taken without their knowledge and a sort of diary in which he wrote down his thoughts and fantasies. Some of it shows unequivocally how envious he was of Joshua Knoll.'

Ian's brain has gone into overdrive. 'Where did you find this?'

'Under the mattress of all places, would you believe it?'

'Did you have a section 8 PACE warrant?'

'No, his girlfriend recently kicked him out because she'd found out about his obsession with Sasha Spencer-Lyles. She allowed us to search her house. That's where we found the scrapbook, diary and photos.'

'Great work, er ... Gail. Well done!'

Ian thanks her for letting him know and ends the call. He smiles to himself, briefly. He's genuinely pleased to hear the progress his colleagues have made on the case. And it looks as though Iris is off the hook. At the same time, it also looks as though he didn't need to step down from the case after all.

Sighing, he opens his pack of Embassy. 'Shit!' he says. He forgot to buy another packet at the pub and he's down to his last fag. His lucky cigarette. When he opens a fresh pack, he always takes out one of the cigarettes and pushes it back into the pack upside down. He smokes this one last, making a wish before he lights up. (Nothing too unrealistic. No point in wasting his wish on world peace or a lifelong supply of Black Bush. He usually wishes for something for Millie or Jo or himself.)

Someone once told him this tradition of the upside-down lucky cigarette had something to do with the brand Lucky Strikes and American soldiers during the Second World War. He tries now – and fails – to remember the details. Jo often jokes that perhaps his last cigarette, if it really is lucky, isn't the one that will kill him. It wasn't even funny the first time.

His head is all over the place. It's the lager. He knows the investigation is crouching in a recess of his mind, ready to pounce on him. He'll have to sift through his thoughts at some stage. The case, the arrest, his removal from it.

He puts the cigarette in his mouth with one hand and crunches up the empty packet in the other. What should he wish for? That Iris will be OK? That *he*'ll be OK – perhaps he could wish for a juicy murder case further down the line so he can have another shot at being an SIO? He hasn't told Jo yet that he's been taken off the inquiry. He went to see Superintendent Hall two days ago. He has told his best mate, but he still hasn't told his wife, even though he usually tells her everything. He sighs. He'll do it in a minute when he goes inside.

He lights up. He knows what to wish for. That they've got the right man in custody. Because something about this doesn't sit right with him. He should know better by now than to trust his intuition, but Ian can't shake the feeling that Harry Tomlinson isn't Joshua Knoll's murderer.

Chapter 27

Carla

NOW

Brayworthy is four or five miles away from Holtleigh. It's a much larger village with two churches – three, if you count the ruined one – playing fields, where they hold the occasional cricket match, and a village hall big enough to hold parties, albeit rather lame ones, if the events I've attended there are anything to go by.

My mobile rings a couple of times as I'm on my way home from running some errands, but it's inside my handbag and hasn't connected to the car speaker for some reason, so I ignore it for now. I see the sign informing me I'm entering the village of Brayworthy and telling me to drive carefully. I haven't seen my partner or my stepdaughter for a week now. It feels like much longer. I miss them. I'm being drawn to them like metal to a magnet. It's not the same at home without them, without Margo's incessant chatter and Daniel's tuneless humming. I've exhausted the repertoire of edible meals I can concoct. Ash has threatened to buy me an air fryer and Olly has offered to pick up a takeaway this evening, if I lend him my car. That says it all.

A thought jabs me, demanding attention. If Daniel and I split up, would I get to see Margo? I call her my stepdaughter and think of her as my daughter, but technically she's not either. Daniel has repeatedly asked me to marry him, but I don't want to get married again. I don't think my marital track record is promising, for a start, and also the logistics of it all scares me. When I divorced Ash, I chose not to go back to my maiden name. I thought that keeping Ash's name would make things easier for Olly and Iris. If I married Daniel, he would expect me to take his name. Carla Duffy. Then I'd have the same surname as my stepdaughter, but a different surname to my son and daughter. Unless I double-barrelled it: Ashford-Duffy. Or Duffy-Ashford. But then I'd have a sort of compound of my husbands, not my own name at all. I know, I know, it's a pathetic reason not to get married, but it gives me a headache just thinking about it.

It hasn't been a problem until now, not being married to Daniel. But I'd have no right to see Margo if Daniel left me for good, no claims whatsoever to custody. And what would it do to her, poor baby? She's already lost one mother – to cancer.

Her voice echoes in my head as Daniel practically dragged her out to his car that day.

'Mummeeeee,' she'd screamed. Over and over. She was crying and so was I, although I was trying not to, doing my best to reassure her it would all be OK.

The narrow country lane meanders up the hill, past chocolate-box cottages with thatched roofs and fields. I slow as I approach the Knolls' house – Hilltop House – which is, unsurprisingly, right at the top, set back from the road. Hilltop House is massive. I know because I've been in it, had the guided tour. There's both a sitting room and a den. The bedrooms have en-suite bathrooms – all five of them – and those at the back of the house have stunning views over Lower Buryknoll Wood, Exmoor and beyond – as far as the Bristol Channel, a thick blue brushstroke underlining the horizon. Yvonne and Richard have an office each. Oh, and Richard has a man cave in the basement, next to his wine cellar. They even have a boot room. I'm not kidding. Yvonne and I don't share the same ideas when it comes to home décor. She goes for thick floor-to-ceiling drapes, shag pile carpets and old, dusty rugs, dark antique furniture, a chandelier in the hallway, William Morris wallpaper, hideous portraits of long-dead ancestors, that sort of thing. I like bright, airy and practical; wooden floors and tiles; warm colours; painted walls; photos and magnets on the fridge.

The gate is open. There's a white banner hanging across the front door. It has large black capital letters on it, but I can't make out the words from here. The curtains are drawn in one of the windows on the first floor. Yvonne and Richard's bedroom? It's the middle of the afternoon. I picture Yvonne in bed, popping one Diazepam after another to ease the pain, refusing to face reality for a little longer. I know she's living every mother's worst nightmare right now and I can't help but feel sorry for her. But as I pull up against the pavement opposite, the front door opens and she comes out. If I drive away, I'll attract attention to myself, so instead I slouch down in my seat, feeling very self-conscious. What am I doing here? I was on my way to see Daniel and Margo. I've made a detour.

After a second or two, I sit up a little, just enough to steal a peep at Yvonne. She's wearing a short skirt and a smart checked jacket. The obligatory high heels – I've never seen her wear normal shoes. Her back must give her gyp. Last time I saw her, standing on my doorstep, she looked bedraggled. Broken. I can't see her clearly from here, but she seems to be standing straighter, walking more purposefully. She strides towards her Range Rover parked in the driveway. I can't help thinking that, a bit like her shoes, an SUV is a very impractical choice of car round here, where you can't always squeeze past a car coming the other way along these country roads. I watch as she opens the door, folds herself into the car, closes the door and pulls out of her driveway. I slouch again, holding my breath, as though I might give myself away if she hears me as much as sees me. She drives right past me without registering me and I only start breathing again when she rounds the bend and disappears from view.

I do a U-turn in the road and as I swing the car round to the Knolls' side of the street, I can make out the wording on the banner. JUSTICE FOR JOSH. I stop the car for a moment and scan the house and its front garden. I wonder if there were journalists in front of the house, standing on the lawn, trampling on the flower beds, hounding the family for interviews. Locals were curious about this case – not at first, when Josh went missing at the end of the summer – but after his body was found, it became a story. Murders don't happen often in this neck of the woods – oops, bad choice of words – so it made for good headlines. I remember one of those headlines, from the *North Devon Echo* – STABBING SHOCKS SLEEPY VILLAGE. It made me picture the inhabitants of Brayworthy walking around with their hands outstretched like zombies or somnambulists, completely unaware of any danger. It was as if it took a brutal murder to wake them up. Briefly, parents were afraid for their children, fearing that the murderer might strike again.

But it seems to me that the interest in the case dwindled rapidly and life soon resumed as normal. Perhaps the death of an eighteen-year-old boy isn't deemed newsworthy enough. I imagine the banner, like the reward the Knolls are offering, is part of an ongoing effort on their part to keep people talking about Josh's murder. The Knolls have no doubt been dealing with their problems since his death, as we have been dealing with ours. A lot of fallout for everyone concerned.

I drive to the bottom of the hill, and pull up in front of Mrs Duffy's house. Daniel's mother has always been perfectly civil to me, but she and I have never been close, not the way Ash's mum and I are. Mrs Duffy has never even invited me to call her by her first name.

Ash once joked about this. 'You wouldn't either,' he'd said, 'if your name was Fanny.'

My mother-in-law's name is actually Theophania, which arguably isn't much better. Her mother was Greek. But her father called her 'Fanny', apparently. Needless to say, Ash found his own quip hilarious. I laughed, too, when he made it, feeling treacherous towards Daniel at the same time. Thinking about this now, I manage a small smile, but it's accompanied by a pang of guilt.

My mother-in-law's house is a small, slightly run-down, perfectly symmetrical cottage, in the dip of a valley, next to a stream. It doesn't get much sun and as Mrs Duffy feels the cold, she keeps the radiators on full blast. We come here sometimes for Sunday lunch – like Daniel, my mother-in-law's a great cook – and when we do, I wear a T-shirt in all seasons and weather. It's Sunday today. And almost lunchtime. Perhaps they're gearing up to eat their Sunday roast. Without me. Will I be welcome here again one day?

There's no room in Mrs Duffy's driveway for one vehicle, let alone two. I've parked behind her car in the road, but I can't see Daniel's car anywhere. Did I get it wrong? Has Daniel gone somewhere else? Where would he go?

I get out of my car and walk up the short pathway to the front door. Nearly everyone I know has a doorbell – the Knolls even have one of those video doorbells – but my mother-in-law has a stainless-steel door knocker in the shape of a hand. I'm about to lift it and rap on the door, but I decide to go home and text Daniel instead. I berate myself for bottling out, but I can't face Daniel just yet. Clearly, he's not here anyway.

But just then, my mother-in-law opens the front door and envelops me in her arms. She's not one for displays of affection and I instantly realize something is wrong. She gushes something into my shoulder. I can't make it out, but she sounds distressed.

'Mrs Duffy, what on earth's the matter?' I say.

'Is Margo with you?'

'No. I thought she'd be with you.' I gently disengage myself from her embrace. 'What's going on?'

I turn my head as I hear a car pull up on the road behind me. It's Daniel. He gets out of the car and rushes towards me. Something in the way he does this alarms me. His face is pallid, his body sagging as he runs, as if his legs are struggling to keep him upright. And then my heart somersaults. Margo is not with him.

He stops beside me, seemingly puffed out, even after the four or five metres he has run from the car to the front door.

'Where's Margo?' My voice is about an octave higher than it should be.

'I don't know,' he says, leaning forwards, his hands on his thighs, as he tries to catch his breath. 'I've been trying … to call you.' I remember my mobile ringing a couple of times from inside my handbag while I was driving. 'I thought she might be with you … I hoped—'

My mother-in-law cuts him off. 'Margo has been missing since yesterday evening,' she tells me.

Chapter 28

Iris

THEN

Before long, Iris came to think of herself as two separate people: the Iris before and the Iris after. The person she had become had issues. She couldn't walk into a room or meet new people without wondering if they'd seen the video. Sometimes she knew they had seen it because of the way they looked at her. She hated the way they looked at her; she hated the way she looked, even though her appearance was different now she'd had her hair cut and dyed; she hated her body; she hated herself. She had zero self-confidence. She had come up with this alternative backstory for herself. She was ready to lie if a stranger ever asked her things like what school she went to or where she lived.

Her vid had gone viral at the beginning of December 2023. By the end of the next month – the beginning of the new year – the law regarding the sharing of intimate photos and videos changed, just as PC Quinlan had predicted.

Mum got all excited about this. She showed Iris what she'd

found on her phone as they sat on the sofa, drinking tea, one Saturday morning. 'Look, Iris! You no longer have to prove that the images were shared with the intent to cause distress. That means we can prosecute no matter what his motives were. It also says sentencing will be stronger. And, get this, it's considered a serious offence if—'

'Darling, I think the law would have had to be passed *before* Iris's video was shared for it to count.'

Mum looked like she was going to cry. Trust Daniel.

He was right, of course. PC Quinlan confirmed it. 'But the good news is, it means that not only has the law changed, mentalities are changing, too,' she said when Mum dragged Iris along to the police station for what must have been, like, the fifth time. 'We might have a better chance of a successful prosecution even though Iris's video was shared before the new law came into effect.'

Iris had been thinking about something, a lot, ever since Mum and Dad started encouraging her to find any online evidence she hadn't deleted. But she hadn't dared tell Mum. Or even Dad. Mum wanted Joshua charged, prosecuted, imprisoned, hanged, drawn and quartered. Iris, too, wanted him dead. Or, at the very least, punished. But she didn't want to have to attend court. A court case would make everything worse. It would dredge everything back up. She'd have to go through it all again, relive everything. Would the jurors have to view her video in court? Or view it again if they'd already seen it? Oh my God, she might even have to watch them watching it. Would Iris be named in the newspapers? On TV? Probably. She'd be even more infamous than she already was. Anyone who hadn't seen her video would go online and find it. The new law guaranteed anonymity. The old one didn't. Although she *was* a minor, so who knew? Whatever. Iris just wanted it all to stop.

After she came home from Gran's, Iris spent weeks thinking about different ways of ending it. Her life, that is. Taking pills would be her best bet. But Iris wasn't good at swallowing tablets – never had been. They got stuck in her throat and made her cough and choke. Plus, the nearest chemist was quite far away. How many times would she have to go to avoid suspicion? And was she seriously considering trying to kill herself by drinking bottles of strawberry-flavoured Calpol or dozens of effervescent tablets dissolved in water? Would that even work?

Mum seemed to sense she was depressed and was clearly on a self-appointed suicide watch. She barely let Iris out of her sight; she kept telling her it would all be OK, eventually. She repeated it several times a day, like a mantra. Iris wasn't so sure, but she wanted to believe her. Then again, Mum also said Josh would get what he deserved, which Iris thought was bullshit.

Every time Mum brought up the subject, Iris tried to tell her she thought a trial would make everything worse.

'Nonsense, sweetie,' Mum said. 'You're not the one on trial. We'll get justice. You'll see.'

In the end, Iris told Dad. She just blurted it out. 'I don't want to go to court. I can't go through this again. I want to withdraw my statement.'

Dad took one look at her, squeezed her hand and said, 'OK.'

He rang Mum and then he took Iris to the police station in Barnstaple. She'd be glad to see the back of this place. PC Quinlan wasn't available, but her gangly sidekick was. Iris would be glad to see the back of him, too.

Dad explained the situation, that Iris wanted to withdraw her statement to avoid having to face a court case.

'I don't think that will be necessary,' PC Lynch said. He was poking the inside of his ear with his little finger, which was just *gross*. 'The CPS has decided not to prosecute. We simply don't have enough evidence.'

Mum and Dad had a row about it when they got back from the police station. Right there, in the hallway of Crooked Oak Cottage, in front of Daniel. Iris could hear them shouting from her bedroom and crept down the stairs to catch the tail end of it.

'It's not fair. We can't let Josh get away with this. We need to fight!' Mum had screamed. 'You said you'd get a lawyer. Did you do that? We could still bring a civil lawsuit against Joshua, get copyright of the videos. That would be a start. But we have to do *something*!'

'I understand how helpless and angry you feel, Carla. I do, too.' Dad's voice was raised now. 'But that's not what Iris wants. She doesn't want to fight. She wants to forget about all of this.'

'That's what she thinks now. But—'

'She won't change her mind, Carla.' Dad was really shouting now. Iris cringed. He never shouted. 'If we did find more evidence and got a lawyer and the CPS agreed to prosecute – and that's a lot of ifs – we'd be forcing Iris to go through this … this traumatic ordeal all over again in court. It could take months. Months when she could be healing. She needs to put all this behind her.'

Mum and Dad didn't often argue. She supposed they must have argued before they got divorced, but she didn't remember that. Dad usually let Mum win any minor disagreement and Iris had never witnessed any major ones. She'd never seen Mum back down before now either. Mum didn't tell Dad he was right or anything. She just harrumphed, about-turned and stomped off. Daniel was still hovering around, a smug expression on his face. Iris wondered if Dad felt like punching it. Mum's partner could be nice, but he could also be a total dick. He was insanely jealous of Dad.

Iris felt bad about causing trouble. *Again*. She went back to her bedroom and stayed there, wishing she could travel in time, forwards or backwards, it didn't matter which. Time travel would be a great superpower to have. She could go back and do things differently, never go out with Josh in the first place. Or fast-forward in her life to a time when this was all behind her.

Mum came up after a while and knocked on the door.

'Go away,' Iris said. Either she didn't say it loudly enough or

Mum chose to ignore her, because she came in.

'I'm sorry, sweetie,' Mum said. 'I shouldn't have pushed so hard. I just hate the idea of him getting away with it. But I hate the fact that you're suffering more. So if you're sure this is what you want—'

'It is.'

'All right.'

'Anyway, he won't get away with it. You said yourself he'd get what he deserved. Right?'

'Let's hope so, sweetie.' Mum spoke without much conviction.

Iris let Mum sit on the bed and hold her. Some of the tension left Iris's shoulders after a minute or two and the knot in her stomach loosened a notch.

When Daniel came home that evening, Iris was listening to Margo read in the kitchen and Mum was making dinner – she was trying out a new recipe and, so far, judging from Mum's sighs, it wasn't going well. Olly hadn't come in yet from cross-country training.

Daniel had his briefcase in one hand and the local paper under the other arm.

'Sorry to be the bringer of bad news,' he said. 'Go and have your shower, Margo.'

He took over making the meal while Iris and Mum, sitting side by side at the kitchen table, pored over the newspaper. The headline said it all really: MY SON HAS BEEN FALSELY ACCUSED OF SHARING INTIMATE IMAGES. But Iris read every word of the article anyway. Words and phrases jumped out at her, as if highlighted: 'first ever girlfriend', 'wild allegations', 'devastating impact on his mental health', 'hung out to dry'.

Joshua and his mother Yvonne were both named in the piece. Iris's name didn't appear, which was something, but everyone would know who Mrs Knoll was referring to. Iris felt sick.

'She's playing the victim card!' Mum spat out. 'How could she? We'll sue her for defamation.'

'No!' Iris screamed and raced upstairs. Mum still didn't get it, did she?

The same scene as earlier played out again. Mum knocking, Iris telling her to go away, Mum apologizing. It was like that ancient comedy Mum had insisted they all watched that time: *Groundhog Day*.

Every day was like Groundhog Day now for Iris. She got up, did her homework, went for a walk with Mum, tried to eat something, made herself sick whenever she could escape her mother's beady eye for a few minutes, watched a mindless film on TV, then went to bed. Then sleep, or try to, eat, vomit, repeat. How much longer could she take this?

Chapter 29

Ian

NOW

He has got nicotine patches. And nicotine gum. He hasn't tried out either yet, but at least he's showing willing. Surely buying the patches and the gum goes some way to cancelling out the entire pack of fags he has already puffed his way through today. Yeah, right. Who's he kidding? And it's only mid-afternoon. Probably just as well you can no longer light up in the workplace or he'd have smoked even more. In July 2007 it became illegal. Back then, Ian was only on about ten a day. Now he's closer to forty. Two whole packets. Jo's right. It's costing them a fortune for him to kill himself.

He could do with a smoke now as he observes the Harry Tomlinson interview. No doubt about it, Tomlinson is a sick prick. His diary entries attest to his obvious fetish for young female students in general and his obsession with Sasha Spencer-Lyles in particular. He also had a whole load of child pornography on his computer. He was Millie's physics teacher, too – Ian checked with Millie and Jo. Tomlinson won't be teaching physics to her or any other youngsters again, which is a relief. If he does go down for Josh's murder, he won't last a week in prison. They hate kiddie fiddlers inside.

Strictly speaking, Ian shouldn't be here, listening in from the viewing quarters. The superintendent is standing next to him, behind the one-way glass, eyeballing him from time to time, no doubt to remind Ian that he has work to do and that this is not his case anymore. It's Helena's. DI Helena Baker. His deputy SIO when he was in charge. Helena is dogged in her pursuit of the truth and justice. She never seems to be tired, never gets emotional and she's super-efficient. She's got a rep as a bit of a ballbreaker, but she wouldn't be where she is now if she wasn't. She's the same rank as he is, but she's at least four or five years his junior. He can't fault her or DC Gail Ward, who are conducting the interview. They're doing everything by the book.

Helena is flicking through some photocopied pages. 'Mr Tomlinson,' she says. 'According to your diary, you had a three-month relationship with a fifteen-year-old, which ended six months ago. You refer to her as "R" in your diary. Can you tell me who "R" is?'

Tomlinson just looks at her. Ian has to admit, he's a good-looking bastard. Tall (his legs barely fit under the table), muscular (with an unnecessarily tight T-shirt, no doubt to showcase his biceps and triceps), blond with a spiky goatee that Ian imagines is a failed attempt to look a little older than he is (twenty-five). Creepy, though. It's the electric blue eyes. The stare. The silence. Ian can't see Tomlinson's feet. He wonders what size they are. You never know, they might be disproportionately small for his height and build.

'What does "R" stand for, Mr Tomlinson?' Helena repeats.

Tomlinson is not ruffled in the slightest, or at least that's the impression he gives. Ian suspects it's an act. A mask that will drop eventually. The soulless interview room, with its furniture bolted to the floor and lack of natural light, was purposefully designed to make suspects crack.

Millie told Ian that a lot of girls at South Lydacombe had a crush on Mr Tomlinson. Ian supposes the pervert tried to use that to his advantage. He couldn't get Sasha Spencer-Lyles to fall under his spell, though. Not that she made a much better choice with Joshua Knoll.

Just when Ian wonders if Tomlinson is going to answer at all, he says, 'I didn't write that diary. My *ex*-girlfriend is stitching me up.' He emphasizes the 'ex'.

Helena riffles through more pages. 'I have some homework here,' she says, 'that you marked for Sasha Spencer-Lyles. You gave her a glowing comment and an excellent mark.'

'So?' Tomlinson says. 'She's a good student.'

He might not be able to see where Helena is going with this, but Ian can.

'So, I'm no expert, but the handwriting looks very similar to the scrawl in the diary. What do you think, DC Ward?'

'The same, I'd say,' Gail agrees. 'Almost illegible.'

'I mean, we could get handwriting experts to confirm you wrote the diary or you could save us some time here,' Helena continues.

'Notch up some Brownie points,' Gail chimes in.

'Or are you going to pretend your *ex*-girlfriend marked your pupils' homework, too?'

'It's pure fantasy,' Tomlinson says. 'There is no "R". I made her up. All right?'

Tomlinson is clearly a natural-born liar, but Ian is inclined to believe him on this. His bullshit detector was flashing madly when, at Helena's request, he read the diary to share his thoughts with her. (Helena was obviously just being nice. Ian knows she made up her own mind about it before she pretended to ask for his opinion.)

'It's a badly written young teacher / submissive schoolgirl

fantasy,' Ian had said. He didn't add that Tomlinson had probably penned it as a quick, one-handed read. Ian was glad he was holding photocopies of the diary and not the original.

'Well, quite,' Helena had agreed.

Ian hasn't been able to get that song by The Police out of his head since.

'So you did write the diary?' Gail asks now.

'So what? There's no crime in that, is there? There's no crime in indulging in sexual fantasies, is there?' He glances at the duty solicitor, as if to check that. The solicitor gives an almost imperceptible shake of his head, which Ian doesn't know how to interpret. Tomlinson doesn't seem to know either. His eyebrows have formed a deep groove when he turns back to glare at Gail and Helena.

'I'd like to read an extract from your diary out loud, if I may,' Helena says to Tomlinson. 'It says here: "I can't get Sasha out of my head. I'm sure she knows it. She's a prick-tease. Always wearing make-up and smelling good, her school skirt hitched up way above her knees, flicking her shiny hair when she realizes I'm looking at her. What she's doing with Joshua Knoll is beyond me. She needs a real man. I'd show her what a real man is. I doubt she's a virgin, unfortunately, but I could show her how a real man fucks. I just need to get Knoll out of the picture." Mr Tomlinson, would you please explain to DC Ward and me how you planned to get Joshua Knoll "out of the picture", as you phrase it in your diary?'

'I didn't ... I'd forgotten ... I don't know what you're implying ...' Until now, Tomlinson has been unfazed. But now he's clearly rattled. Well done, Helena! Tomlinson glances at his solicitor. 'No comment,' he mutters, lowering his head.

'It's an unfortunate choice of words, given the circumstances, wouldn't you agree, Mr Tomlinson?' Helena says.

'An uncanny coincidence that you wanted Joshua Knoll out of the way and a few months later, he was found dead,' Gail says. 'Do you know Buryknoll Wood very well, Mr Tomlinson?'

Tomlinson pales. 'I go for a wander in the woods sometimes, but I had nothing to do with that kid's murder,' he protests. He looks from one police officer to the other. 'You have to believe me!'

'Mr Tomlinson, do you remember where you were on Wednesday the twenty-eighth and Thursday the twenty-ninth of August?'

There is a knock at the door of the viewing quarters.

'Come in!' Superintendent Hall barks.

A uniformed officer enters. 'Ah, DI Rowland,' she says.

Ian recognizes her as one of the front counter staff, but has no idea what her name is, which strikes him as elitist and wrong, seeing as she knows who he is.

'Sorry to disturb you, sir,' she says, 'but there's a lady downstairs who is very distraught. She insists on talking to you.'

'Did she say what about?'

'Her daughter has gone missing.'

'OK. On my way.' He follows her out of the room. 'Did she give her name?' Ian asks as the officer holds the door to the staircase open for him, thinking he should have asked the officer for her own name. He steals a very discreet glance at her chest now he's close enough to read her name tag. She's Moody, apparently. Easy enough to remember. 'How come she has asked for me?'

'She says she's a friend, Sir. Her name's Carla Ashford.'

Carla? Oh, God, no. Iris? Missing? Ian races down the flight of stairs to the ground floor as if the building is on fire.

He sees her as soon as he bursts through the doors. She's pacing up and down the wooden floor in the large entrance to the police headquarters. As he rushes towards her, he clocks Daniel Duffy sitting on a plastic chair and does a double take. What's he doing here? Where's Ash?

It takes only a split second for the penny to drop. *Margo* is missing. Ian feels a flicker of relief it's not Iris, followed by a stab of shame.

He leads the way back upstairs, to his office. Carla should have called 999. She has leapfrogged the first responders by coming to him. They would have come out from Barnstaple. Instead, she has come to him in Exeter. Carla must mistrust the police; he gets that. She thinks the police failed Iris. He should really send Carla through the correct channels. But he can't let her down. He was of no use to the Ashfords when they needed him and he'll never forgive himself for that.

Carla leaves the talking to Daniel. Ian takes notes.

'She's been gone since yesterday evening. She didn't come home last night. She went to her friend's house – Ellie. But Ellie told me this morning when I went to pick up Margo that Margo had left early to go to Carla's. She—'

'Sorry, to go to Carla's?' But as soon as the words leave his mouth, Ian remembers Ash telling him Dandruff had left Carla and taken Margo with him. 'Where were you staying?'

Ian looks up from his notes and sees Daniel blush. It starts off like a red rash around his neck, spreading upwards, until even the top of his bald head is bright pink. In other circumstances, Ian would find this amusing.

'At my mother's house in Brayworthy. Margo wanted to walk—'

'Brayworthy,' Ian repeats, deadly serious, cutting Daniel off mid-flow. 'And does Margo's friend Ellie also live in Brayworthy?'

'Yes.'

'OK. Go on.'

'Well, she never arrived at Crooked Oak Cottage, obviously. And she's not answering her phone.'

'It must be switched off,' Carla says. Ian is struck by her pallor. 'I have the Find My app on my phone. Margo's last location is showing as Coombe Farm in Brayworthy – that's where Ellie lives – at five twenty-two yesterday evening.'

Daniel reaches out and takes Carla's hand. Of the two of them, he's holding it together better than she is, at least on the surface, and yet he's Margo's father; Carla is her stepmother. Ian remembers Ash saying that Carla considers Margo to be her daughter, whereas Daniel is very much Iris's stepfather.

He closes down that train of thought. Something is niggling Ian and that's not it. As he asks for more details and jots down Daniel's answers, he tries to put his finger on what it is. 'So Ellie's address is Coombe Farm, Brayworthy. Was Margo there for a sleepover?'

'Yes, that's right,' Daniel says.

'She's been taken, Ian,' Carla says. Her voice trembles with panic.

'We don't know that,' Daniel says. Ian thinks he detects a tear in his eye. 'Let's not jump to conclusions.'

'What's Ellie's surname?' Ian continues. They need to act fast, whether Margo has been taken or not. She's been out all night and may not have eaten or drunk anything since yesterday afternoon.

'Beare.' Daniel, perhaps reading upside down, spells it for Ian, who has written it down as 'Beer.'

'When did Margo leave Ellie's house?'

'At half past five, according to the Beares. Margo told them she was going back to her grandmother's. It's really only round the corner and it was still light. They offered to walk her back, but she refused.'

'And when did you realize Margo had gone missing?'

'When I showed up this morning. It was about 10 a.m. Ellie admitted she was covering for Margo and said Margo had deliberately set out yesterday evening to walk to Holtleigh from Brayworthy.'

Brayworthy. That's what's bothering him. Daniel's mother and Margo's friend aren't the only people who live in Brayworthy. The Knoll family live in that massive house at the top of the hill. Hilltop House, that's it. Not a very imaginative name, but it does what it says on the tin, he supposes.

His mind drifts down the corridor to the interview room

where Harry Tomlinson is being questioned in connection with Joshua's murder. A thought entwines itself around his brain and his stomach fizzes in fear.

Tomlinson spent last night in police custody, here, at the Devon and Cornwall Police Headquarters in Middlemoor, in a holding cell. He can't have taken Margo, if she has indeed been taken. But is there any way Joshua's murder and Margo's disappearance could be linked?

Chapter 30

Carla

NOW

Daniel has gone over everything at least three times in the car on the way to the Devon and Cornwall police headquarters, but I'm still horrified as I listen to what he tells Ian. Not that there's much to tell him. We have no idea where Margo is. I can't wrap my head around it. She has been missing since yesterday evening. She's only eleven. My stomach keeps constricting in fear and I'm struggling to get enough air into my lungs. Questions hare around my head. Has she spent the night outside? I shudder. It's October. Recently, the weather has been mild in the daytime, but it's cool at night. Is she alone? Is she hurt? Where is she?

I've checked my phone over and over and turned the volume right up, as loud as it will go. As I pull my mobile out of my handbag to check it once more, it rings. I jump and almost drop it.

'It's Iris,' I say.

Iris has the answer to one of the questions I've been asking myself. The most important one. Margo has been taken to the

North Devon District Hospital, in Barnstaple.

I leap to my feet and Daniel follows suit. We promise to keep Ian updated and race downstairs and out to the car. It takes us several minutes to even get onto the link road. I would have gone the other way, through Crediton and then along the A377, but I manage to hold back my remark. Daniel's driving, not me, and there's probably not much in it – either way it will take us well over an hour to get to Barnstaple.

Olly texts to say Ash is taking Iris and him to the hospital. That makes me feel a little better. They'll get there before us. I ring the hospital and speak first to a receptionist, then to a nurse on the children's ward.

'How is she? What happened? Is she hurt?' It comes out in a frantic rush.

'We don't really know what happened,' the nurse says. 'We're running tests.'

That's far too inconclusive for my liking and I'm about to demand more information, but the nurse offers to take the phone to Margo.

'Yes! Yes, please,' I say. I put the call through the speaker so Dan can hear Margo, too.

Seconds later, Margo squeals down the phone. 'Mummy!'

Tears course down my face, but I try to keep them out of my voice. 'Margo, honey, Daddy and I are on our way. Olly and Iris will be with you any minute now. Are you OK? What happened?'

'I don't know, Mummy. I feel sick and dizzy and tired.'

'Sick and dizzy?' Daniel's almost shouting. His knuckles are white as he grips the steering wheel. 'Are you hurt?'

'My head hurts, Daddy.'

I open my mouth, about to ask Margo if it's a headache or if she has received a blow to the head, but Daniel places a hand on my knee.

'Get some rest, Margo,' he says. I can tell by his face he's forcing himself to sound a lot calmer than he feels.

I take his cue. 'If you go to sleep, we'll be there when you wake up,' I add.

'Hurry,' she says.

I grimace. If Daniel drives any faster, we'll be in serious danger of not getting there at all. Or of ending up on hospital wards ourselves.

The nurse comes back on the line to say Margo must rest now. 'She's in good hands,' she tells us. 'You can take your time.' She asks me if Margo has any allergies or illnesses and says she'll give her some paracetamol for her headache. She needs a little more information about Margo's general health and so on. I dutifully answer her questions instead of butting in with my own.

It takes us an hour and a quarter to get there and they are the longest minutes of my life. In that time, every possible scenario runs through my head. Margo fainted, fell and banged her head. Then someone found her and took her to hospital this morning. Margo got lost on the way to Holtleigh and has been wandering around all night. She is dehydrated and has a headache. The rest of the scenarios are darker and even more disturbing and I do my best to block them out.

Ash is waiting for us in the foyer of the Ladywell Unit, where the children's ward is located. He's wearing an old Pink Floyd T-shirt that was once black, but has been grey for years. It's his DIY T-shirt and it has holes in it and paint stains on it. He has clearly dropped whatever he was doing and raced here with Olly and Iris.

'She's in the Caroline Thorpe ward – the children's ward, on level two,' he says, pointing towards the lifts.

'Cheers, Quentin,' Daniel says and rushes in the direction Ash is indicating. Briefly, I'm annoyed. Even now, with his daughter lying in a hospital bed, my partner persists on calling my ex-husband by a name he knows full well Ash despises. But my irritation evaporates instantly. It's automatic. A habit. It's nothing.

I start to follow Daniel, but Ash grabs my arm and restrains me. I snatch my arm free and whirl round to face him, annoyed with him now, but then I see the look on his face.

'I'll catch you up,' I call after Daniel, and to Ash: 'What is it? Tell me!'

He gets straight to the point. 'Yvonne Knoll brought Margo in. She was still here when I arrived with Olly and Iris.'

'What? How?' My brain is working overtime, trying to fill in the blanks. The Knolls live in Brayworthy, where my mother-in-law lives. And Margo's friend Ellie. 'Did Yvonne find Margo?'

Ash nods. 'They have some sort of annexe, next to the main house, apparently, that they use as an Airbnb rental.'

'Yes. A summerhouse.' I remember Yvonne pointing it out to me through one of the upstairs windows as she gave me her grand tour of Hilltop House. 'Are you saying Margo was in the summerhouse at the Knolls' place?' Ash nods again. 'What on earth was she doing in there?'

'According to Yvonne, she found Margo in there late this morning. She said she was very surprised. Margo didn't seem well, so she drove her to hospital and then rang Iris. That's all I know.'

Late this morning? Margo must have been inside the house when I was sitting in my car outside looking in, before driving to Mrs Duffy's house.

I look into Ash's eyes. 'There's something you're not telling me,' I say.

'No, there's not, I promise. But I'm pretty sure there's something she didn't tell me.'

I swear under my breath, an insult directed at Yvonne, as Ash takes my arm again and leads me to the lifts. Whatever happened to Margo, it wasn't one of the scenarios my overactive imagination conjured up on the way here in the car.

Ash accompanies me to the children's ward on level two.

'Thank you, Ash,' I say, as we reach the heavy swing doors.

'No problem. You all right?'

'Yeah, I've got this from here,' I say so he doesn't feel he has to hang around and wait. 'I'll keep you posted.' I stand on tiptoe to give him a quick peck on the cheek, but he pulls me into a hug. I close my eyes and hug him back. The familiar scent of him calms me for a second or two before I snap back to reality. 'Thanks again,' I mumble into his shoulder, then I break away and push open the doors into the children's ward.

I hear Daniel as I walk briskly along the corridor and follow the sound of his voice. Margo is awake. Someone has raised the head section of the bed and she tries to smile when she catches sight of me approaching, but it looks more like a grimace. Olly is holding one of her hands and Iris, on the opposite side of the bed, is holding the other.

I find a spare chair at the empty hospital bed opposite Margo's and carry it over, putting it down next to Iris's. She inches her chair closer to Margo's head to make more room for me.

Margo's not alone in the ward, there are three other kids, but only one of them has someone – her mother, perhaps – with her. I glance at my watch. It's almost 3 p.m. and well within visiting hours, according to the sign I saw on the swing doors into the ward, but there are now four of us crowded around Margo's bed. I don't know if there's a limit on the number of visitors a patient can have.

'What do you mean, you can't remember?' Daniel asks Margo, as I sit down. The apprehension in his tone is almost palpable.

Margo's face crumples, as if she's being scolded. 'I'm sorry, Daddy. I don't remember.' Her speech is a little slurred. 'I wanted to ring, but I forgot to take my charger to Ellie's. The battery in my mobile was dead.'

That explains why I couldn't locate Margo with the Find My app.

'It's OK, darling,' Daniel says. 'No one is angry with you.'

'Hi, honey,' I say to Margo, bending over to give her a peck on the cheek. 'How are you feeling?'

She gives a long sigh, as if she's fed up with answering this question. 'A bit better. Still dizzy. My arms and legs are heavy.'

Daniel fills me in. 'She can't remember much of last night.'

'Well,' I say gently, 'let's start with what you do remember. You were at Ellie's house and you left – is that right?'

Margo nods.

'And you left to come home, is that right?'

'I missed you.' She sounds apologetic.

'Aw, sweetie, I missed you, too. I'm here now. I'm just trying to work out where you were. You went the wrong way, you see. To get to Crooked Oak Cottage, you needed to leave the village and take the road alongside the river, but this morning, Mrs Knoll found you in her summerhouse.'

Daniel throws me a sharp look. He's about to say something, but I give him a quick shake of my head.

'The Knolls' place is in the other direction,' I continue. 'You go into the village and then up the big hill.'

'They said I could use one of their bikes. It would be quicker.'

'Who did, honey? Who said you could use their bicycle?'

'Jordan and Jasper.'

I clasp my hands together on my lap. Little pieces of the puzzle are falling into place, but not the main pieces. I still can't see the whole picture. But I should have known those boys had something to do with it when Ash mentioned Yvonne.

'OK, so you went with them to their house to get the bike. Is that it?'

'I was thirsty. But they said not to tell you.'

'Not to tell us what, Margo? Don't worry. You're not in any trouble. You must tell us everything you remember. What didn't they want you to say?'

Margo's eyelids close, as if they're too heavy to keep open, and for a few seconds, I think she's gone back to sleep. But then, without opening her eyes, she says, 'It was Red Bull.'

'They gave you Red Bull to drink?'

But this time she doesn't answer. Is it possible she had a can of drink with Jordan and Jasper Knoll, then fell asleep in the summerhouse? Maybe the boys left her there and Yvonne found her this morning. It sounds like a reasonable explanation, a harmless one, but the knot in my stomach has tightened, not loosened. There's more to it than that, I'm sure of it.

Iris leans towards me, puts her hand on my arm and says into my ear, 'Mum, you should get her blood tested for roofies.'

'What?' I glance at Daniel, but he doesn't appear to be listening in on our whispered conversation. He has worry etched all over his face.

'Rohypnol. It's a drug.'

Panic wraps itself around my throat, threatening to cut off my air supply. Rohypnol. The date-rape drug. 'I know what it is, Iris,' I say, 'but Margo's only eleven.'

'Mum, someone I know was given Rohypnol,' she says. 'There's a lot of it around, even out where we live in the middle of nowhere. I just think maybe we should check.'

Iris is right. I don't know all the symptoms or side effects, but I do know amnesia is on the list. And I'm almost certain lethargy is on there, too. And headaches. Oh, God. Do I need to ask for Margo to be examined for sexual assault, too?

I beckon to Iris to come with me to find a nurse or a doctor. I'm hoping someone will allay my fears. We find a nurse, who looks rushed off her feet. I ask if we can speak to the ward sister.

The ward sister turns out to be a young man and I realize I have no idea what the male equivalent is, to my shame. Head nurse? Nursing officer?

'We usually do a urine test, not a blood test,' he says. 'Flunitrazepam is detectable for longer in the urine than in the blood.'

'We should wake Margo up,' Iris says, chewing her lower lip. 'We can't wait for her to wake up. It might be too late.'

I know what she's thinking. The drug doesn't stay in the

system for long. The head nurse fetches me a plastic pot and asks if I need help.

'My elder daughter will help me,' I say and Iris nods.

'Have you ... Should we ... How would we go about checking for signs of sexual assault?' I ask him.

His eyes widen slightly. Am I overreacting? Imagining evil where there isn't any? He disappears again and comes back this time with a hospital gown and a large transparent bag.

'If you believe there's a possibility that she has been sexually assaulted, we will need to call the police and get them to come to the hospital with a rape kit.'

Oh, God. I can't put Margo through that. I can only imagine how invasive that would be. Not to mention painful and traumatic. And probably unnecessary. Iris slips her arm through mine.

The nurse must see the look on my face. 'Why don't you ask her a few questions when you take her to the toilet?' he says. 'If you think we need to check for sexual assault, we'll take it from there. As a precaution, remove her clothes carefully, especially her underwear, and put them in the plastic bag. And be careful, you know, not to destroy any potential evidence, for example, when she wipes herself after she has weed into the container.'

I tell Daniel the nurse has asked for a urine test.

'What? Now that she's sleeping?' he asks. 'Is it urgent?'

'Apparently,' I say.

I look at Olly, silently willing him to help me out. As if reading my mind, he leaps to his feet and suggests to Daniel that they should go and get a cup of tea.

Iris and I have difficulty waking up Margo and I have to carry her to the toilet. She's a dead weight in my arms. It's a team effort to get the urine sample. When I ask, Margo assures me nothing hurts down there and everything feels normal. A huge wave of relief breaks over me. Whatever has happened to Margo, she hasn't been sexually assaulted. I bag up her clothes anyway and Iris and I get an uncooperative, sleepy Margo into the hospital gown, then I carry her back to bed while Iris takes the urine sample to the head nurse.

Olly and Daniel come back with Ash, much to my surprise.

'Quen ... Ash was waiting in the café,' Daniel says, hooking a thumb over his shoulder towards Ash, who is standing behind him.

I catch a smirk on Ash's face. I can read my ex-husband like a book. His expression says, *there's a first time for everything*. It almost makes me smile, despite the circumstances.

He looks from Daniel to me. 'I thought maybe I could take Olly and Iris home,' he says.

'Good idea,' I say, glancing at Margo. She's sound asleep again.

Iris opens her mouth as if to protest, but then she closes it again. She seems to realize, as Ash does, that Daniel and I need some time alone.

Olly bends over and kisses Margo on the forehead. 'Get well soon, Maggot,' he whispers.

Daniel and I sit in silence, side by side, for a while after Ash, Iris and Olly have left. I'm the one who breaks it. I tell Daniel about the urine test, but I present it in such a way that it sounds as if it's just a precaution.

'That family has a lot to answer for.' His voice drips with venom. 'I'll bloody kill those boys if they so much as laid a finger on Margo.'

'I don't think she's been hurt or harmed at all,' I say.

'I'd like to come back home,' he says. His head is lowered and he avoids making eye contact. 'Margo would like that, too. She misses you all. She needs you, Carla.'

I'm not sure if he's asking for my permission – it is, after all, my house. Well, mine and Ash's, actually. Or is he simply telling me he's coming home? I don't say anything and he takes my hand, gives it a squeeze.

'*I* miss you, too,' he says, his voice scarcely audible.

It sounds like an afterthought. Can we be a team again? Or

are we only united in our growing hatred of the Knoll family? Would Daniel come back if it wasn't for Margo? Now something bad might have happened to his daughter, he finally gets why I'm so protective of mine. Is that his way of thinking? I sigh. If it wasn't for Margo, would I take him back? We were a team, once, Daniel and I. A reconstituted family. It was working until Iris's trials and tribulations. They tested our relationship to the limit and drove a wedge between us.

Margo has lived with me as long as she lived with her real mum. Margo's memories of her mother are faded and fragmented. I love Margo as if she were my own daughter and she thinks of me as her mummy. She even calls me 'Mummy'. But there's a gap between Daniel and Iris. And between Daniel and Olly. It used to be invisible, but now it's a yawning, unfillable hole. Perhaps it's because my kids were older when I met Daniel. Margo was only five. Or maybe it's because I'm the only mum Margo has now, but Iris and Olly have Ash.

Daniel lets go of my hand and puts his arm around me. Leaning in to him, I allow myself to hope we can get through this, get back to normal. He rubs my shoulder.

'Do you think it's connected?' he asks so quietly I only just catch it.

'What?'

'I mean, what happened to Iris and whatever happened to Margo. Both times the Knolls were involved. Could it be connected somehow?'

'I don't see how it can be,' I reply.

But now Daniel has planted that seed in my head, I know it will take root and grow.

Chapter 31

Ash

NOW

Ash thinks it unlikely Margo will be coming home from hospital this evening, so Olly and Iris decide to stay the night at Ash's place. They stop at Crooked Oak Cottage on the way to pick up Cheddar. Ash has some meals in the freezer they can choose from – he often batch-cooks and freezes half. They'll eat in front of the television. He never suggests sitting up to the table for meals when his kids come round, although they don't tell Carla that. Ash knows that TV dinners are a rare occasion at Crooked Oak Cottage, even at weekends, and never when Dandruff is home. Ash does have a table in the kitchen, somewhere, under stacks of clutter and post and laundry that he never seems to get round to tidying away or filing or ironing.

The house in Shallowcott has never seemed as much like home to him as Crooked Oak Cottage once did. It's called Mayflower Farm, although Ash has no idea why. If it was ever a farm, it wasn't for livestock, dairy or crops – it only has a small garden, no land as such. And although the Pilgrims set sail from Devon, it was from Plymouth, a good eighty miles away. Unless the 'mayflower' bit refers to plants that blossom in the spring, but Ash has never managed to grow anything other than weeds in the garden, in May or in any other month of the year. He was going to rechristen the place, call it something ordinary like The Lodge or The Barn or The Vicarage, but none of the names he could come up with suited the place any better than Mayflower Farm. Roly gave Ash's house the moniker 'the Mayflower', which Ash thinks makes it sound like a pub, but it has stuck.

It feels more like a home when his kids are here, and he hopes they feel at home. Olly and Iris each have their own bedroom, although there's no en-suite bathroom or view over Exmoor, as there is in the cottage at Holtleigh. There's only one bathroom, but there are two loos.

The place needs a woman's touch, really, although Ash wouldn't dare say that out loud in case it's sexist. He has had a few relationships since Carla – well, OK, numerous flings since Carla; it's been a long time, after all, and he's not a monk – but there has been no one he has been tempted to move in with, at his house in Shallowcott or anywhere else. Not that he would ever move too far away from his kids. He's not a commitment-phobe. He's just hard to please and rather stuck in his ways. He likes having his own place; he doesn't mind his own company.

He glances at the kids now. The girls – Iris and Liv, who came round to join them – insisted on watching *Strictly Come Dancing* on BBC iPlayer and Olly only put up a cursory protest. They all want Chris and Dianne to win. Ash is no *Strictly* fan, but he's astounded at what Chris has achieved and the example he's setting for everyone, disabled and able-bodied people alike. Margo loves this show, too, apparently. She usually watches it with Carla and Iris.

His mind strays to Margo, Carla and Dandruff. He hopes Margo will be all right. He hopes Dandruff and Carla will be all right, too. Maybe what has happened to Margo will bring them closer together again. He wants Carla to be happy, even if it's with Dandruff. Ash can tell Iris is thinking about Margo, too. She's sitting in the armchair, her legs curled up under her, but her shoulders are tense and she bites her lower lip from time to time. Olly, who is sandwiched on the sofa between him and Liv, seems to be making an effort, perhaps for Liv's sake, but his sighs punctuate Ash's own thoughts.

He has no idea what's wrong with Margo. Iris says she had a headache, she was so tired she couldn't stand up by herself and she couldn't remember what had happened. Ash is no doctor, but it sounds as if Margo was drunk. Or drugged.

And how does Yvonne factor into the equation? That woman wasn't telling him everything, Ash would bet on it. He strokes his chin pensively. Ten to one what she was keeping from him had something to do with her bloody sons. Jordan and Jasper. He can't help thinking they're cut from the same cloth as Josh was. And Yvonne is protecting them, just as she protected Josh.

Out of the corner of his eye, Ash sees Olly place his hand on Liv's knee. Liv flinches and Olly removes his hand. That surprises Ash. The two of them were very touchy-feely before, practically glued to one another. Now they're back together, they seem to be far less tactile. Then Liv takes Olly's hand and Ash wonders if he was just imagining an awkwardness. They're all a bit tense this evening. But then it occurs to him that he hasn't heard Liv laugh since she's been back in his son's life. She had such an infectious laugh. He remembers her cracking up whenever she tried to recount an amusing anecdote, so that everyone ended up laughing not at the punchline, but because Olivia herself was laughing. He vaguely recalls Carla saying Liv had changed. He hadn't attached much importance to her remark at the time. But Carla's right. *Carla's always right, Ash.*

His phone pings with a text. It's Carla to say they're keeping Margo in overnight for observation and until they get the results of her blood and urine tests. Just as he'd thought. Carla's going to stay with her and sleep on the chair next to her bed. Ash can't see Carla getting much sleep. He texts back to say Olly, Iris and Cheddar are staying with him at Mayflower Farm.

When the show's over, Olivia gets ready to leave. She has come in her own car, so Ash doesn't have to run her home. Iris helps Ash clear up the dinner things while Olly accompanies Liv outside to see her off.

'What's the matter with Liv?' Ash probes.

Iris, who is loading glasses into the dishwasher, looks at him sharply. 'What do you mean?'

'I mean, she's so serious. And quiet. She was joyful and full of life before. Is she OK?'

Iris doesn't answer straightaway. 'No,' she says at length. 'She's not OK.'

'What's wrong with her?' Ash asks. 'Is she ill?'

'No.'

Christ, it's like pulling teeth. 'Well, what is it, then?'

'It's not my story to tell, Dad,' Iris says.

She closes the dishwasher and heads upstairs to her room. It's none of Ash's business, but his curiosity is piqued. And he's a bit worried. So, when he finds himself alone with Olly, both of them side by side on the sofa in the sitting room in front of the TV again, he tries to sound out his son instead.

'Is everything all right with Liv?' he asks. 'She seems a bit … sad? Is everything OK between the two of you?'

'Why do you ask?'

'She just doesn't seem … herself,' Ash says.

'No, she's not.' Olly hesitates, perhaps unsure whether to confide in Ash or not. 'She was … assaulted,' he finally says.

'What do you mean, "assaulted"? Physically? Did someone hit her? Was she mugged?'

'No, nothing like that. Not physically, no.'

Not physically. So, she was either assaulted verbally or sexually.

He remembers Liv flinching when Olly touched her leg earlier. Oh, God. 'Olly, was Liv sexually assaulted?'

'I don't know if she would want me to tell you. Or Mum.'

'I won't say anything, Olly,' Ash promises. He doesn't need to say he'll tell Carla. That's a given. The kids know he and Carla tell each other pretty much everything. 'Is there something I can do? Do her parents know?'

'No, there's nothing you can do. Fuck, there's nothing even *I* can do.' Ash doesn't scold him for his language, although he has never heard Olly swear like that before. He notices tears well up in Olly's eyes. 'And, yes, her parents know.'

'Will she prosecute? Has she prosecuted?'

'No. There's no point.' Ash doesn't push this. Iris didn't want to prosecute Josh and he gets that. It was too much for her to go through the first time. She couldn't have gone through it again. He imagines it's similar for Liv. 'Who was it? Was it someone she knew?'

Olly shrugs. 'Just some guy at a party.'

Ash gets the feeling he's only being given part of the story. Something doesn't quite add up. What isn't he seeing? Olly opens his mouth, presumably to say something, but instead a sob escapes. Ash pulls Olly towards him and wraps his arms around him. Olly is an adult, almost as tall as he is and certainly as muscular. An image appears, a memory sputtering to life. Olly, tears coursing silently down his cheeks, as he sat on the bathroom floor at Crooked Oak Cottage, leaning against the radiator with his arm around Iris. Was that the last time he saw his son cry? It's a bad memory, a terrifying one, and Ash banishes it from his mind.

Olly pushes Ash away and seems to pull himself together. His face is wet and his nose is running. Ash digs a tissue out of his pocket – he has no idea if it's clean, but it will have to do – and hands it to Olly, who won't meet his eye.

'If there's anything I can do, Olly, anything at all, please tell me.'

Olly nods into his chest. 'You've done enough,' he says.

Ash doesn't know what his son means by that. Does Olly mean Ash's prying has made him cry? But it didn't sound sarcastic. Ash lets it go. 'Do you want something to drink?' Ash asks. 'A cup of tea? A beer?'

'Yeah, a beer would be good, Dad. Thanks.'

Ash fetches two bottles of lager and a bottle opener. Olly selects an action film on Netflix and they watch it together. But Ash can't follow the plot. He can't concentrate on the film at all. He thinks of Liv and he thinks of Iris. And he thinks of Olly, who had to deal first with the fallout of what Iris went through and who is now doing his best to help Liv get back on her feet.

When he and Carla moved to North Devon, it was partly for a fresh start, but it was also because they wanted to bring up Olly and Iris somewhere safe. It seemed idyllic when the kids were small – the countryside, fresh air, not far from the ocean. They live out in the sticks, away from the big dangers of the city, but trouble has found them here. Ash can't help thinking that he hasn't done a great job of keeping his family safe.

Chapter 32

Iris

THEN

So, things went from bad to worse, after Iris came home from Gran's house in the Lake District. She didn't go out, except to go from Crooked Oak Cottage in Holtleigh to Mayflower Farm in Shallowcott – from her mum's place to her dad's place – or with Mum to walk on Exmoor, along routes where there was zero chance of her bumping into anyone, let alone anyone she knew. Millie had blanked Iris that day at school, but outside of it, she acted like nothing was wrong. She came round every now and then until Iris asked her not to. Millie went on and on about school and Iris couldn't deal with it. Plus, Millie was probably only coming round out of pity, or because Jo and Ian sent her. It certainly wasn't for the good company. Iris's world was shrinking. She had hardly any contact with anyone in it, besides her family and her counsellor and her driving instructor. That suited her, but at the same time, she couldn't go on with things that way.

She had a knot in her stomach and a foul taste in her mouth

and they just wouldn't go away. Her hands shook a lot and she'd bitten her nails to the quick and started on the skin around her thumbs. She tried to do breathing exercises, like Mum suggested, but it was a total waste of time and effort. She was tired. All. The. Time. But when she tried to sleep, she lay awake, her heart pounding. Either that or she slipped into a light, fitful sleep complete with nightmares. She had two recurring dreams. In one of them Josh tried to suffocate her; in the other he threatened to kill her with a knife. She always woke up before he could do either, marinating in a pool of her own sweat, which was just gross. And pretty fucking scary. Iris would wake up, screaming, and Mum would come rushing into her bedroom to smother her with hugs and rub her back like she was a baby.

'I hate him, Mum!' Iris would sob into Mum's pyjama top. 'I wish he was dead!'

Melanie said she had to talk to herself in her head and think positive thoughts. 'Go easy on yourself. Keep telling yourself you're lovely, you didn't deserve this and it's not your fault,' she said.

But Iris didn't believe a word of any of the nice things she tried to make herself think. Her inner voice always piped up, drowning out those thoughts and firing words like 'worthless', 'slut', and 'stupid'. Victim-shaming. Self-blaming.

She couldn't see a way forwards. Dad spent God knows how long every single day trying to get the video taken down from various websites. It was going to follow her all her life, wherever she went. How could she ever trust anyone again? No other guy would ever want to be her boyfriend. She had no friends and no one would ever want to be her friend again either. Any prospective employers were going to find the video as soon as they did an online background check. She was totally screwed. Forever.

It got so Iris didn't even want to get up in the morning and wished she could go to sleep and not wake up. It took every ounce of her energy to get up, take a shower and put on some clothes. She could no longer concentrate on her schoolwork. The suicide thoughts she'd toyed with before now invaded her mind. She thought about killing herself non-stop. She was in a really dark place. In pain. Suicide seemed like the only way out. It would be better for everyone if she wasn't around. She'd caused no end of trouble and her family were all suffering. The problem would only go away if Iris herself did. Mum and Dad would take it badly, but they were bound to feel a bit relieved, too. No one else would miss her.

She remembered Josh's supposed suicidal thoughts and how he'd implied he was considering taking his own life. And here she was, actually planning to take hers. Ooh, the irony! How would Josh have done it? Jumped off a cliff, maybe. Exhaust fumes in his mother's SUV? But Iris was sure now that it had only been an idle threat, one of the many manipulative ways he'd used to bind her to him.

They'd talked about suicide once. He said it was the coward's way out. She thought you had to be really brave to do something so drastic, and, above all, really desperate. She was desperate now. But maybe Josh had been right. She felt like a coward.

She googled how to slit her wrists. Lots of hits for suicide helplines, but once she scrolled past all that, she found some useful tips. *One: use a sharp knife.* The one in the kitchen drawer that Mum chopped vegetables with would do the job. *Two: right-handers, use your left hand to cut your right wrist first. The tendons will be damaged, so you'll need as much strength as possible to cut into the other wrist.* That made sense. *Three: slit along the wrist, not across it.* She mimed the gesture along her arm. *Four: take a hot bath and some painkillers.* She'd take some of Daniel's anti-coagulants, too, so the bleeding didn't stop.

She planned it for the evening of Margo's parents–teachers meeting. Margo, Daniel and Mum would be out for a few hours. Olly had cross-country training, so he'd be back at some point, but he wouldn't disturb her if she locked herself in the main bathroom. He had an en-suite bathroom, the lucky git. She'd scored the room with the best view, though. Margo could have it when she was gone.

She'd written the note the day before. That way she wouldn't waste time on the evening itself. She didn't have much to say. Sorry, mainly. She was so sorry for uprooting their lives. Next, how much she loved them. Mum, Dad, Olly and Margo. She decided not to put Daniel's name. He was her stepdad, sort of, but he wasn't family. Not really. And finally, not to blame themselves. This was all her fault, not theirs.

Before leaving for the meeting, Mum and Margo came to her bedroom, where Iris was pretending to do her homework, to say goodbye. Iris held them too tightly and for too long.

'Are you all right?' Mum asked. 'I can stay if you don't want to be alone. Daniel can go.'

'No, no, it's fine,' Iris said, panicking. She needed to act normal.

She listened out for the front door closing behind the three of them and then heard Daniel's car roar into life outside. The noises galvanized her into action.

She ran a bath with hot water, as hot as she thought she could stand. But instead of getting into it, she crumpled to the floor. She couldn't say how long she sat, naked on the bathroom rug, holding the knife in her hand and shivering. The whole room was clouded with steam and her eyes were clouded with tears. Was she too much of a coward to take the coward's way out?

She didn't know Olly had come home until he hammered on the bathroom door. She wondered if he'd heard her crying or if Mum had texted to ask him to keep an eye on her. She didn't find out until afterwards that he'd found the note she'd written.

'Go away!' she shouted.

'Let me in!' he yelled back.

You could unlock the bathroom door from the outside with a coin in the lock, which had come in handy once when Margo got stuck in there and couldn't turn the lock herself from the inside. When Olly went quiet, Iris thought he'd left her, but then she heard the lock turn. When he burst in, she felt a strange mixture of shame and relief. Without a word, he took the knife from her hand, wrapped her in a towel, warm from where it had been hanging on the radiator. Then he took her dressing gown from the hook on the back of the door and helped her into it, like she was a child. He knelt down next to her and held her in his arms as she sobbed.

'It will be OK, Iris,' Olly said, over and over. 'I'll ring Dad.' His voice wavered and cracked, but he held it together. For her sake, perhaps.

But then she heard him sniff and felt his body tremble. Iris knew without looking at his face that Olly was crying, not loud sobbing like her, but quietly. She felt bad about upsetting him.

It took Dad about half an hour to reach Crooked Oak Cottage. Iris and Olly were still in the bathroom, their backs against the radiator, Olly's arm around Iris's shoulders. Dad barged into the bathroom. He was wearing his suit and had obviously come straight from work. He'd let himself in and came upstairs to the bathroom without even taking off his shoes. Daniel would not have been impressed. Weird how her mind came up with things like that at a time like this.

The next few weeks went by in a bit of a blur. Iris was pretty much wrapped in cotton wool. She was prescribed new medication, she had more appointments with Melanie, everyone watched Iris like a kettle of hawks around the clock, a team suicide watch. Mum didn't get much work done during the day. Olly moved his mattress into Iris's room and slept on the floor, so there was someone on call for her at night. Iris couldn't have made another attempt on her own life if she'd wanted to. She was never alone.

She didn't want to, though. Not anymore. She still didn't want to fight; she definitely didn't want to face a court case. But she didn't want to be a victim all her life. She needed to turn this around somehow.

It took some time, a lot of time. Dad was still finding her video and reporting it after seven months. It was like trying to put out wildfire with a water pistol. But the fire would die down eventually. Even if it left embers. Iris had to get back in control of her life. She needed to start by actually getting a life.

It was her birthday in July. Her seventeenth. It should have been a big deal, but there was no way Iris was going to celebrate it. She woke up feeling depressed about having to get up at all. But Dad had bought the best present ever. He handed her this big cardboard box, which seemed to be wiggling. The lid of the box wasn't taped down and it wasn't wrapped and Dad said she had to put it on the floor and open it quickly. She did. Inside was the cutest puppy. Iris squealed.

'He's a golden retriever,' Dad said.

'What's his name?'

Dad shrugged. 'You can name him.'

'Where did you get him?'

'I found an advert on the internet. I got him from this family in Somerset. Near Cheddar Gorge.'

'Cheddar. That's a good name for a dog,' Iris said. 'Don't you think?'

'It's an excellent name,' Dad agreed. 'He's exactly the right colour.'

'Does Mum know about this? Is she OK with it?'

'Yes. And so is Dandruff.'

'I bet he took some persuading.' Iris rolled her eyes.

'You can say that again. Anyway, there are some conditions if you want to keep him.'

'Anything! Go on!'

'One: you are responsible for him. You have to look after him, take him for walks whatever the weather and remember to feed him, brush him and wash him.' That sounded easy enough. 'And two: you have to go to puppy training classes. I've enrolled you in the Kennel Club in South Molton.'

Ah. Now that was harder. That meant actually facing people. People who may have seen her video. Iris hesitated, but only for a few seconds. She had to get back on the horse or the diving board or whatever. She had to start somewhere. This was as good a place as any. She wouldn't be completely alone. She'd be with her dog. 'OK,' she said. 'I can do that.'

And just like that she felt she was taking control of her life again. Baby steps, maybe, but she could do this.

Chapter 33

Carla

NOW

Margo is kept in hospital overnight, but the following day, after the doctor has done his rounds, Daniel and I are allowed to take her home.

Her tests have come back negative. No traces of flunitrazepam or any other benzodiazepine. But I'm not convinced. I go to find the head nurse – or 'ward brother', as I've taken to calling him in my head – and bombard him with questions.

'How long does it take for Rohypnol to become undetectable?'

'It depends. It varies from person to person and according to the quantity consumed,' he says.

'Do Margo's negative test results mean she definitely wasn't given any Rohypnol?'

'It's possible, despite the negative test results, that Margo did swallow some Rohypnol. The test results just show that there was none in her system when we checked for it. She's young, so she has a high metabolism, and if she had only a small dose, she would eliminate it fairly quickly.

'Will she suffer from any lasting side effects?'

'If we assume she swallowed a small amount of the drug, she may have a slight stomach ache or headache for a day or two, but she probably won't have any adverse effects at all. Was there anything else?' His tone is patient, but he looks harried.

'No. I'll let you get on. Thank you.'

I remember when I got pregnant with Iris. Ash and I would have preferred to have a little more time with Olly before another baby came along, and I was breastfeeding Olly at the time, so my second pregnancy was a bit of a shock-slash-surprise. I *knew* I was pregnant, but the test was negative. Ash was relieved; I was so disappointed. I'd been so sure. But a few days later, I took another test. This time, it was positive and we were both delighted, although that's beside the point. The point is, I'd taken the first test too soon.

Margo's urine test results remind me of this. A negative pregnancy test doesn't necessarily mean you're not pregnant. Margo's negative drugs test doesn't necessarily mean she wasn't drugged. I wince at the double negatives in my head and rephrase. *Margo may still have been drugged.* But it doesn't sound any better. In Margo's case, the test was too late rather than too early. I know she was drugged, just as I knew I was pregnant.

Daniel drives Margo and me home, back to Crooked Oak Cottage. It's spitting and the windscreen wipers are on too fast. They squeak back and forth. Margo chats to him non-stop from the back seat – it hasn't taken her long to bounce back to her usual self – and Daniel sounds upbeat when he can crowbar a word in. But I can tell he's upset by the way his jaw is set.

Their conversation doesn't need my input and I'm left alone with my thoughts. I glance over my shoulder at Margo and smile at her. She grins back, sending a mixture of relief and guilt through me. Relief that she's OK, that she's coming home. Guilt because I've failed my stepdaughter in much the same way as I failed my daughter. What should I have said to protect her? I've told her not to talk to strangers, not to trust anyone she doesn't know, but Jordan and Jasper aren't strangers and sometimes the people we know best are the least trustworthy. So, what should I have said? *Stay away from the Knoll boys.* With hindsight, that's the advice I wish I'd given both Margo and Iris.

It all comes back to the Knolls. Again. A thought strikes me and as soon as it enters my head, I know I won't be able to get it out. Did Yvonne know that Jordan and Jasper had spiked the Red Bull drink they gave Margo? Did Yvonne find Margo in that summerhouse and then deliberately keep her for as long as possible at Hilltop House, playing for time, until the drugs were likely to be out of her system? A growl erupts from my throat, which I quickly convert to a cough so as not to alarm Daniel or Margo.

Once we get home, we make Margo comfortable on the sofa. Iris tucks the throw around her and Olly fusses over her. Daniel fetches drinks and biscuits for everyone from the kitchen. My face is hurting from stretching my lips upwards. It probably looks more like a rictus than the smile I'm trying for anyway. I can't relax.

Daniel doesn't look relaxed either. I watch him as he studies Iris. He seems awkward around her. He speaks when she speaks to him, but with sardonic answers. Perhaps it's my imagination. He probably still wonders if she had something to do with Joshua's death and I can't really blame him for that. After all, I'm sure my daughter had something to do with it. But if that's what's going through his head, he'll have to let it go and be firmly on our side now he's home.

'I need to pop out,' I tell Daniel.

He raises his eyebrows, but his tone is gentle. 'What, now? Where are you going?'

I give him a kiss and answer a different question. 'I won't be more than an hour,' I say.

His eyebrows invert, almost joining above the bridge of his nose. I repeat my promise not to be gone long and hightail it out of there before he can ask any more questions and I have to lie in reply.

It's getting full in the driveway now with Iris's car, too. With her permission, I take her car – the powder blue Twingo – as it's parked behind mine. On the short drive to Hilltop House, I try to work out what I want to say to Yvonne, but it's still raining and I'm concentrating really hard. If I prang or scratch Iris's car, she'll be livid. She loves her wheels. Anyway, I don't have anything to say. I just want to hear Yvonne's version of events. I'll have to make a superhuman effort to be polite because if I get there and start shouting or bandying around accusations, she'll clam up and slam the door in my face.

The gate is open. I park where I stopped the other day, across the road from the house, and force myself to walk rather than storm up the driveway. It's only as I press on the 'smart' doorbell and look shiftily into the eye of the camera that it occurs to me she might not be in. Her car is in the drive, though, so I may be in luck.

But Richard answers the door.

'Hi,' I say, hearing the timidity in my own voice in that one syllable. I clear my throat. 'Is Yvonne there, please?'

He barely turns his head, maintaining eye contact with me, and yells his wife's name.

She takes her time to come to the door. When she sees it's me, she puts a hand on her husband's arm and says calmly, 'Thanks, Rich. I've got this.'

Richard looks relieved at being dismissed and, without so much as a goodbye or a nod in my direction, he disappears back inside.

Yvonne fixes me with hard, hazel eyes that remind me of Josh's. She's dressed smartly and wearing high heels. Does she wear them even when she's at home or was she expecting me? A sudden image bursts into my head. Yvonne, standing on my doorstep weeks ago, a diminutive version of her former self, wearing so much make-up it looked as if she'd applied war paint, and yet looking anything but fierce.

Today, in her high heels and from her elevated position inside the house, she towers over me and looks almost magisterial, threatening. I feel small. I'm the one who has come to her house demanding answers, just as she came to mine. I didn't give her the answers she wanted and I realize now she won't tell me what I need to know. A reverse image. The tables are turned. I wish I'd brought Daniel with me. In fact, I wish I hadn't come at all.

'Come in,' she says, stepping back and holding the front door wide open.

I try not to show my surprise and, for only the second time since I've known Yvonne, I step over the threshold, into her home. She lets me lead the way, but points towards the door into the living room. I remember last time, we all slipped off our shoes at the door. Force of habit. I deliberately keep mine on this time, even though it's wet outside and her immaculate living room has a cream carpet.

She waves her hand towards the sofa. Obediently, I sit. Yvonne chooses an armchair, which gives her a couple of inches on me. Again, I feel at a disadvantage. I grapple for my words. Yvonne looks at me, a mixture of anticipation and impatience in her expression. Does she expect me to thank her for taking Margo to hospital? I'm certainly not about to do that.

'I'm hoping you can help me understand how Margo came to be in your summerhouse overnight,' I begin. It sounds a little accusatory, although I'm aiming for something between firm and neutral.

'I found her there yesterday. It must have been early afternoon,' Yvonne says. 'She was sleepy and she complained of a headache. I tried to get hold of Iris – I don't have your number, I'm afraid – and when I couldn't get through, I took Margo straight to hospital. Then I did manage to get hold of Iris. I had no idea that Margo had spent the night in the summerhouse. This is news to me.'

She clutches her heart a little too theatrically, but I have to hand it to her – she's good. She did ring Iris. That much is true – that's how Iris knew that Margo was at the North Devon District Hospital. But I don't buy the rest of what Yvonne has spouted for a second.

'Margo came to your house with Jordan and Jasper on the Saturday evening. She was staying at her grandmother's, here, in Brayworthy. Your boys offered to lend her a bike to cycle home to Holtleigh.'

'I didn't know that,' Yvonne says, her eyes wide, but the warble in her voice belies her words. 'Tell you what, I'll give them a shout and we'll see if we can get to the bottom of this.' She stretches her thin lips into a fake smile, revealing red lipstick stuck to her otherwise white incisors.

She leaves the room for a moment and I hear her shout for the boys from the bottom of the stairs. They both come immediately. I sometimes have to call Olly and Iris several times to come downstairs. Have Jordan and Jasper been briefed?

She sashays back into the room, her sons following. They remain standing while she sits back down in her armchair. 'Mrs Ashford would like to know what you can tell us about Margo. Do you know how she came to be in our summerhouse last weekend?'

The boys both study the floor.

'Margo had to spend the night in hospital,' I add. 'She was tested for drugs.' I keep my eyes on Yvonne, but she doesn't flinch, which seems to confirm my suspicions.

'Jordan? Jasper?' Yvonne's tone is harsher than before.

'We offered to lend her a bike to cycle to Holtleigh,' one of them says. I have no idea which one.

'She was thirsty. We gave her a can of soda.'

'Did you spike her drink?' I ask.

'What?'

'Spike?'

'Did you put anything in her drink?' I demand. 'Specifically, Rohypnol? The date-rape drug?'

'Now, hang on a second,' Yvonne says. 'I don't know what you're implying, but—'

'I want to know if your boys spiked Margo's drink. It's a simple question, Yvonne.'

'Did she have any trace of drugs in her system?' Yvonne asks.

'Well, no, but it doesn't mean—'

'In that case, perhaps you should leave.' Her voice is as cold as her gaze. Yvonne gets to her feet, clearly expecting me to follow suit. I remain seated.

'I want to know if your boys spiked my daughter's drink.'

'Jordan, Jasper, did you put anything – anything at all – in Margo's drink?'

'No,' they reply in unison.

They both sound and look completely unconvincing. One is still staring at the floor; the other is practically hopping from one foot to the other, as if he's desperate to go to the toilet.

'So, how did she end up spending the night in the summerhouse?' I ask.

'Dunno,' one of them says. The other shrugs.

'Where was she when you left her?' I continue my interrogation, as Yvonne eyeballs me, her arms folded across her chest.

One of the boys looks to his mother, as if she has the answer. She gives an almost imperceptible nod in his direction, a discreet prompt.

'She was in the summerhouse.'

'She was tired,' the other one chimes in.

'We told her to close the door when she left,' the first one says, his gaze lowered again.

'I'm really sorry that Margo was ill, Mrs Ashford.'

'We hope she feels better soon.'

It's all I can do not to roll my eyes. I want to throttle the truth out of the pair of them, get them to say something other than the lines Yvonne has scripted for them in this pathetic, badly rehearsed farce. But I'm not going to get any closer to the truth here.

'Could it have been something she ate at her grandmother's house, do you think?' Yvonne asks.

This is a battle I cannot win. When Yvonne came to my house, we left things at a standoff. A deadlock. But, here, on her home turf, she has the upper hand.

I stand up, suddenly desperate to get away from Hilltop House, and all the lies contained within its walls. Yvonne follows me as, without a word, I head for the front door and yank it open. Leaving her to close it, I march out to my car, get in and start it up. Before I drive off, I take one last look at Yvonne, still standing in the doorway of her home, staring after me. I despise that woman, and yet a thought occurs to me and disturbs me. I like to think I'm nothing like this bitch, but we have something in common, she and I. We'd both do anything to defend our offspring. Indeed, we have both done everything in our power to protect our respective children. She has covered for all three of her sons and lied for them, just as I have covered for Iris and lied for her. Yvonne and I are not that dissimilar after all. I wonder, as I drive home, if she has had the same thought.

Chapter 34

Ian

<u>NOW</u>

Something is clearly wrong. Very wrong. Ian can see that as soon as he arrives at the Devon and Cornwall Police Headquarters in Middlemoor. There are police officers (uniformed and in plain clothes) all over the place (apparently milling around and gaping rather than doing anything important), an ambulance in the car park, a handful of paramedics running with a stretcher and someone on that stretcher. Shit! Ian hopes it isn't one of his colleagues. He parks, leaps out of his car and tries to get a better look. But all he can see as he passes the open back doors of the ambulance is the paramedics inside performing CPR on the patient. No pulse, then. Whoever is lying on that stretcher, they're in pretty bad shape. He's got a feeling he picked a bad day to give up smoking.

He rushes into the building and fires questions like bullets at Moody, the officer sitting at the front desk. 'What's going on? Who has taken ill? What's happened?'

'Good morning, sir,' she says pointedly. 'A bloke we were holding in custody was found dead in his cell this morning.'

'What was his name?'

She shakes her head. 'I don't know. Sorry, sir.'

Ian remembers just in time to thank her before darting off. He takes the stairs two at a time and has to pause at the top for what seems like several minutes to catch his breath.

Ian finds DC Ward in the staff area making herself a coffee. 'Good morning, Gail,' he says. He's not sure if Moody was picking him up on his manners (or lack of manners) before, but point taken if she was. 'What the fuck is going on?'

Gail turns to face him and he gets it from her expression.

'Bollocks! Not Harry Bloody Tomlinson.'

''Fraid so, Ian, sir.'

'Fuck. Suicide?'

'No, sir. The custody officer found him lying on his cell floor this morning. He appeared to be sleeping—'

'On the floor?'

Gail ignores him. 'But he was completely unresponsive. The custody officer thought Tomlinson was "pissing around" – his words, sir.' She does the corresponding air quotes. 'Then he realized Tomlinson wasn't breathing. Tomlinson's skin was still warm, so the officer raised the alarm and initiated CPR.'

'Damn it! The paramedics were still trying to revive him when they got him into the ambulance,' Ian says. 'Perhaps there's hope.'

Gail shrugs, as if to say, *no sad loss, sir.*

'So what was it? Epilepsy?'

Gail shrugs again. 'He didn't mention any physical health problems when we brought him in and he wasn't on medication for anything.'

'Well, maybe that'll get us off the hook. If he had a health problem he didn't reveal. Or didn't even know about. There will be an inquiry. An ombudsman.'

'He hasn't been declared dead yet, sir.'

'For God's sake, Gail. Call me "Ian", will you?' He sighs. 'Sorry. I'm irritable. I'm trying to come off the fags.'

'Good idea, *Ian*. And I'll take irritable over smelly any day.' And with that parting shot, she turns and struts out of the staffroom, coffee in hand.

Hmm. He deserved that, he supposes.

He heads for his office and tries to concentrate on his work. Tomlinson isn't his problem. He has a mountain of paperwork. Boring, but not stressful. But he can't banish Tomlinson from his mind.

His personal phone pings with a text from Carla, asking him to ring her when he gets a chance. He feels his eyebrows pull into a frown. Carla texted the other day to say Margo was home from hospital. What does she want? She usually only calls Jo.

He calls Carla back immediately.

Once they've got through the hello-and-how-are-you bit, she gets to the point. 'Ian, I'm ringing because Margo had some symptoms that the doctors and nurses at the hospital couldn't really explain,' she says. 'She was lethargic and dizzy, she complained of a headache and she couldn't remember much of what had happened after she'd was given a can of Red Bull.'

Ian's detective brain kicks in. 'Could it have been spiked? Who gave her the can of Red Bull?'

He hears her exhale slowly. 'That's what I believe happened, yes.'

'Who gave her the can of Red Bull?' he repeats.

'You'll never guess,' she says, her voice dripping with irony. 'Jordan and Jasper Knoll.'

'You're shitting me.'

'I wish I was.'

Carla tells him Margo's urine test at the hospital was negative. She also tells him about storming round to demand answers from Yvonne Knoll and her sons and getting nowhere. 'They were clearly lying through their perfect teeth, all of them,' she says.

'Carla, I believe you; I really do. I honestly wouldn't put anything past those boys or that family. But if you're ringing me for advice, I'm afraid I don't have any for you. It's your word against theirs. From the outside looking in, to a stranger, it sounds like Yvonne did you a favour, taking your stepdaughter to hospital because she seemed unwell.'

'I understand,' Carla says. He can hear her voice crack down the phone. 'Thank you for your time, Ian. I'm sorry to disturb you at work.'

'I'm sorry I can't be of more help, Carla. I really am.' Ian has a feeling he has said these exact words to her at least once before.

Ian told Ash about Tomlinson's arrest and it was mentioned in the local news, although the suspect's name wasn't divulged, so Carla obviously knows about it. For a split second, Ian wishes he could fill her in on the latest to cheer her up or at least take her mind off Margo, but apart from the fact it would be wholly inappropriate and unprofessional, Tomlinson might still be alive. The chances are slim, granted, but stranger things have happened. And Ian's not actually sure Tomlinson's death (*if* he's dead) is good news for the Ashfords. If Tomlinson's guilty, then his death is very bad timing. One thing's for sure, it would have been far better if they'd managed to wring a confession out of him (even a false one) before he collapsed on the floor of his cell.

After his conversation with Carla, it's even harder to get back to his tedious administrative forms. At one point, Ian realizes he has been sitting, staring into space and smoking his pen, for at least five minutes.

His mind oscillates between Iris and Margo on the one hand and Tomlinson on the other. The more Ian thinks about it, the more convinced he is there's a link between what happened to Iris and what happened to Margo. But Tomlinson can't be it.

What Ian would like to know is where the Knolls fit into all this. Jordan and Jasper were smoking and trying to deal cannabis in front of his house, according to Ash. And now Carla thinks they spiked Margo's drink with Rohypnol. There's more to it. Ian's sure of it.

Gail materializes at the open door to his office. 'Thought you might like a coffee, Ian,' she says, holding up a steaming cup in each hand.

Jo warned him to avoid coffee because it makes him want to smoke even more. Cigarettes and coffee, they go together. Can't have one without the other. But, sure, he's going to have the same problem with beer. You can't give up coffee, beer and cigarettes on the same day. 'You saint,' he says.

Gail enters his office, sits opposite him and slides the coffee towards him, weaving the cup around the mounds of papers strewn across his desk.

'I'm not just the bearer of gifts; I'm also the bearer of news.'

He takes a sip of his coffee. 'Good or bad?'

'Jury's still out on that one.'

'Go on,' Ian says. 'Hit me with it.'

'Tomlinson was declared DOA when they got to the hospital.'

'No surprise there, I suppose. What the hell happened?'

'Don't know. There will be a post-mortem, obviously.'

'Let's hope they find something – some underlying health condition – so we can't be blamed for his demise,' Ian says.

For a few seconds, they sip their coffee in silence. Then Ian asks Gail the question he's asking himself. 'So what happens now?'

'Beats me,' she says.

What does happen now? Is that it? Case closed? End of story? That would be good news for the Ashfords. He pictures the headline in the *North Devon Echo*: PRIME SUSPECT IN JOSHUA KNOLL'S MURDER CASE DIES IN POLICE CUSTODY. But Ian doesn't believe this is the end. Not by a long shot.

Chapter 35

Iris

THEN

Iris would look back on events, like the Pink concert or Josh's eighteenth birthday party or Millie's end-of-term party or the local round of the Cross-Country Schools' Cup. She could remember she and Josh weren't on speaking terms for these occasions. But, for the life of her, she couldn't remember why. It was like there was like there was a loose connection in her brain. Was there something wrong with her? Was she too young to get early onset dementia?

She got totally paranoid about her memory. It had become unreliable. Even when she and Josh were together, her memory seemed untrustworthy, especially when they made up after their rows. Her interpretation of what had happened was often so different from Josh's version of events. Like she'd misremembered it all. Then, once they'd split up, there were things Iris realized she'd completely forgotten. Things that Josh had tried to sweep under the carpet that she'd simply erased from her mind.

Trauma-induced memory loss, Melanie called it.

But the memories started to resurface. Gradually and in fragments; hazy and unpleasant. She'd hear a song or smell something – food or a perfume – or someone would say something, and she'd be reminded of something she'd conveniently forgotten while they were in a relationship. Iris wrote down all the memories so she wouldn't forget them again.

A lot of what Iris remembered was petty, so childish that to begin with, she thought she must be reading things into the situation that weren't there. She recalled one Saturday, for example, when she'd had too much homework to hang out with Josh and he didn't reply to any of her messages all weekend. She'd been convinced he was ignoring her, punishing her, until the Monday morning at school, when he told her he'd dropped his phone in the toilet and had to dry it out in a bowl of rice.

Then there was the time Mum had taken her all the way to the cinema in Barnstaple the day after she'd defended one of Josh's little brothers – jokingly – against Josh's jibes. Josh was supposed to meet her there. She waited for over an hour – the film was well underway – but Josh was a no-show. He was supposed to drive her home. She had to ring Mum to come back and pick her up. Josh – when she finally managed to get hold of him – told her she'd got the wrong day.

Josh had a great excuse or plausible explanation every time. He was so convincing that Iris ended up doubting herself. But she always gave him the benefit of the doubt. It was only when Iris considered all the recollections together, instead of individually, that she began to see clearly. She began to see through him. Things that were obscure before suddenly seemed obvious in hindsight.

What made her finally doubt him instead of herself was the image she had of him in her head. When she'd defended his brothers. When she'd told him on FaceTime she had too much homework. And on so many other occasions. Always the same expression. His eyes refusing to meet hers, his lips pursed in a thin line, his jaw set in a determined look. Like he was struggling to keep calm and hide the anger festering inside him like an infected wound. Like he was thinking: *you'll pay for that.*

After Josh died, the memories resurfaced more quickly and more clearly. They burst into Iris's head, assaulting her, when she least expected it – when she was reading a book or taking a shower or watching TV or eating dinner. Some of these memories were more serious, more traumatic. Like the time he threw a glass at her in the kitchen at Hilltop House. He missed – afterwards, he said he'd missed deliberately – but the glass shattered against the wall behind her and a tiny shard embedded itself in her neck, just below her ear. Or like the time he'd belittled her music tastes in front of his schoolfriends, saying she was an intellectual who only liked classical music and rolling his eyes.

'It was a joke,' he insisted later. 'My mates laughed, didn't they? Oh, babe. You shouldn't be so sensitive. You should learn to take a joke. You need to chill.'

It hadn't been funny; it had been humiliating and hurtful, but Iris resolved to chill.

She remembered good things, too, but viewed them through a different lens now that he was gone, so that the past came to mean something completely different in the present. Like all the gifts he bought her. T-shirts she didn't really like, and that were too small, but that she wore to make him happy. Or that damn necklace he gave her after she had sex with him for the first time. Or like all the attention he would lavish on her or the text messages, the way he would blow up her phone with texts and voice messages when she was busy or with her family. She'd thought the gifts and the attention were loving at the time, sweet, even if it was over the top. She thought it showed he cared about her and was thinking about her. But after they split up, she wondered how much of it was manipulative. And after his death, she wondered if Josh had ever acted innocently or lovingly, or if every single thing he'd ever done had been calculated.

Iris thought Josh's death might bring some relief. Josh could no longer hurt her – or anyone else. She expected some form of closure, but it didn't come. She'd seen his dead body, but he was very much alive in her head, in every memory that came back to her. She could still hear his voice. He haunted her, night and day.

'How do you feel?' Melanie had asked during their first session after he'd been killed.

Iris suppressed a laugh. It was, like, such a cliché, a therapist asking that question. She didn't know what to say.

'It's normal to feel happy, or even euphoric, after the death of an abuser,' Melanie continued. 'On the other hand, maybe you feel sad. Perhaps you're grieving. After all, Josh showed you his best sides before you saw the worst in him. It's completely normal if you feel sad, too.'

Iris shrugged. She didn't feel happy or sad. She didn't really know what she felt about Josh's death. A bit shocked. Sort of numb. Guilty. And scared. But she didn't want to talk about it.

It wasn't just memories that came flooding back after Josh's death. Iris's self-confidence began to return, too. She hadn't realized he'd chipped away at her confidence until she had none left. She came to think of him as a predator. He'd sucked all the goodness out of her, like a vampire sucking blood to survive. She'd become weak and he'd become strong. Now he was gone, she felt gradually stronger, like the worst was finally behind her.

Sometime after he died, Iris played the violin for the first time in ages. Uplifting songs. Some Lindsey Stirling covers. She hit a lot of wrong notes, but it felt good. Why hadn't she played for so long? She could hardly blame that on Josh. He wasn't musical; he liked hip-hop, rap, some rock, but he was tone-deaf. She'd been playing the violin since she was little. She'd taken Grade 8 and got a distinction way before she knew him. But he'd come to school concerts that she played in, listened, rapt, to her practising and eventually it was like she needed his validation to perform.

Iris also went for a run. Across Exmoor. It was exhilarating.

Liberating. Running was another activity she'd stopped doing. She didn't really know why. Maybe because she associated running with him; it was something she'd done with him. And, like the violin, Josh had become so involved with her running that she was lost without his input. She would never run again in Lower Buryknoll Wood, that was for sure; she'd probably never set foot in those woods again. But she vowed to start running regularly again. And she would play the violin again, too. She might not be able to set up the website now Josh was dead, but she could take up the hobbies she'd dropped. The things she was passionate about. The things that made her who she was.

The day she passed her driving test, Iris bumped into Sasha Spencer-Lyles. It was in town, in the high street. They could have just smiled, or even ignored each other, and carried on walking, but Sasha stopped, so Iris felt she had to. For a couple of seconds, Iris stood there while Sasha stared at the ground. Awkward.

Iris and Sasha had only talked, like, once. It was before Josh had leaked that video of her. Iris thought about that as she stood there, hoping she didn't look impatient while she waited for Sasha to speak, or hit her, or something.

'What are you looking at?' Sasha had said. Not a promising opening gambit, in Iris's opinion.

They'd been standing side by side at the sinks in the toilets at school, Iris washing her hands, Sasha fixing her already immaculate hair.

'Sorry,' Iris had mumbled, but she'd held Sasha's gaze in the mirror. And when Sasha's expression had softened, Iris had added, 'Be careful, Sasha. He's not what he seems. He's ... he can be—'

'You're just jealous,' Sasha had said and stomped out of the ladies' loos, ahead of Iris, closing the door on her instead of allowing her through, too.

Was Iris jealous? she'd wondered. Sasha and Josh were sickeningly lovey-dovey and it had reminded Iris of how it was in the beginning, when she and Josh were in love and she couldn't get enough of him and he'd wanted to spend the rest of his life with her. So, yeah, if she was honest with herself, at the time, she had probably been a bit jealous. Mostly, though, she'd just been relieved that Josh's attention was focused on someone else. But she hadn't wanted him to hurt Sasha or anything. Iris didn't know Sasha well, but she seemed nice enough, even though she'd just closed the door in her face.

It was Iris who spoke first the second time, when Sasha still hadn't uttered a word several seconds later. 'Are you all right?' Iris asked.

Sasha looked up and into Iris's eyes. 'Yeah. No. I don't know,' she said. 'You?'

'Same, I guess. A bit worried they'll think it was me.'

'I know, right? I had to give a statement to the police this morning and all the time I was thinking, what if they suspect me?'

'I'm sure they won't. Weren't you at uni at the time?'

'Yeah. In lectures or tutorials, probably. Or at home with my housemates. Should have a shitload of alibis either way.' She gave a dry chuckle. 'I owe you an apology.'

'What for?'

'That day in the bogs at school. You tried to warn me. I didn't listen.'

'It's OK.'

'It's really not,' Sasha said. 'I told Josh and I shouldn't have.'

'What did you tell Josh?'

'That you tried to warn me about him.'

'Oh. It's fine, really.'

'That's very big of you,' Sasha said. 'I felt guilty about that for, like, months.'

They went their separate ways then. They didn't have anything more to say to each other. But Iris stopped dead a few metres further along the high street. Sasha's words echoed in her head. *I told Josh and I shouldn't have. I felt guilty about that for, like, months.* Duh! Light bulb moment. Of course! Sasha told Josh that Iris had tried to warn her about him. Iris's video went viral … it must have been, what? A week later? Two weeks later? That was Iris's punishment for trying to give his new girlfriend the heads-up. The revenge porn. Sasha must have wondered if Josh was behind it, but Josh would have denied it. As Iris knows only too well, Josh can be convincing when he lies. Sasha was probably in way too deep by then, under his spell, too in love.

Iris should have known. Foresight. That would be such a cool superpower to have. Far better than invisibility or time travel. The ability to foresee – to *predict* – what would happen. If only she had known.

Chapter 36

Ash

<u>NOW</u>

The first Ash hears of it is on Heart North Devon radio. It's the main news story. He's driving home from work, brain-dead after a bad night's sleep followed by a tedious day of meetings, conference calls, emails and an unusually high number of complaints from irate customers, and he nearly ploughs into the back of the car in front of him when he hears the newsreader's opening sentence:

'The man arrested in connection with the murder of eighteen-year-old Joshua Knoll has died in police custody.'

Ash turns up the volume and listens attentively to the rest of the bulletin, making an effort to concentrate on the road at the same time.

'Harry Tomlinson, an early career teacher at South Lydacombe, an independent secondary school on the edge of Exmoor, was found dead in his cell this morning,' the presenter continues. 'He is thought to have had a previously undetected heart condition.'

The newsreader goes on to recap the circumstances of Joshua's murder, but there's no more about Tomlinson himself. Ash turns off the radio. He's reeling, his mind spinning with questions. What does this mean for them? For Iris? Is this good or bad news? Ash feels only a tiny pang of guilt for instantly thinking of his own family without considering the impact of this young man's untimely death on his loved ones. Roly had told him that Tomlinson was a 'shady hallion' and a 'bad article'. Ash had got the gist.

He tries to think it through. It would have been far better if he'd been convicted – or if he'd at least confessed – before his heart packed in. Ash doesn't believe Tomlinson killed Joshua Knoll for a second, but perhaps now everyone will assume he did. In which case, with a bit of luck, Tomlinson can take the fall and this whole nightmare will finally be over for Iris, even if the real killer remains at large.

He looks at the dashboard clock. He'd like to call Carla, but she'll be busy right now with the kids and Dandruff. Ash refuses to refer to them as Carla's family, even in his own head, because he feels that he himself is part of Carla's family. *You had your chance, Ash. You blew it.* Anyway, Carla needs to patch things up with Dandruff, which means Ash needs to take a step back, give them some space.

So instead of calling Carla, he makes a slight detour to call in at Roly's, although he's not sure if Roly will be home yet.

As luck would have it, Roly is outside, leaning against the front door, vaping. Ash parks the car and strides up the driveway.

'A step in the right direction, right?' Roly says, waving the e-cigarette at Ash as he approaches.

'Why didn't you tell me?'

'That I was quitting fags?'

'No, you moron! That Tomlinson had kicked the bucket.'

'Check your phone much, do you?'

'Not while I'm working, no.'

Ash has two phones – one for work; one for friends and family. Carla and the kids are the only people who have both numbers. Ash has never been into social media or played games like Candy Crush. His phone has never been glued to his hand. He spends far too much time as it is in front of a computer screen at work; he doesn't feel like downgrading to a phone screen at the end of the day. He spends a lot of time with his laptop in the evenings as well, checking for Iris's video. He pulls his personal mobile out of the inside pocket of his jacket. A missed call and a text from Roly. Same from Carla. He glances at one text, then the other – both about Tomlinson, predictably – clicks off the silent mode and pockets the phone. He'll text Carla later and tell her to call him when she's free.

'Is what they're saying true?' Ash asks. 'That he died in his cell.'

'Yes. The post-mortem confirmed it. Dilated cardiomyopathy.'

'What's that in layman's terms?' Ash asks.

'Some sort of disease of the heart muscle, apparently.'

'So, what happens next?'

'There will be an inquiry.'

That's not what Ash meant. He meant what happened next for his family. For Iris. 'Oh, God. I hadn't thought about that. You won't get into any trouble, will you?'

'Not me, personally, no. But I think we're all in the clear on this one. Tomlinson didn't declare any health problems. No one could have foreseen he might, you know, die.'

'Don't suppose he confessed with his dying breath, did he?' There's no hope whatsoever in Ash's voice.

'Sorry, mate.'

'So what happens now?'

Roly shrugs and vapes at the same time. It looks comical and Ash might have laughed if they'd been talking about something more trivial.

'Dunno,' Roly says. 'It's not my case anymore, as you know. I hope this is the end of it and that things will go back to normal.'

Ash isn't sure he knows what normal looks like anymore. 'You think he was guilty?'

'Honestly? No, I don't. He was a waste of good air, though. He might not have been a killer, but he was definitely a paedo. Not the sort of bloke you want teaching your daughter.'

'Oh, God, that's right. He was Millie's physics teacher, wasn't he? What did she think about him?'

'She thought he was creepy as fuck, although she didn't put it quite like that. Plus, Tomlinson admitted to going for a wander in the woods from time to time. And he vented his strong dislike for Joshua Knoll in his diary. Fancy a cold one?'

'Do you even need to ask?'

Ash follows Roly inside and into the kitchen. It turns out Roly hasn't stocked any beer in his fridge or even bought any lager to stock it with. Something to do with giving up cigarettes, although Ash doesn't get what that has to do with beer. So instead of swigging lager out of a bottle, as they would usually do, they each pour a can of IPA into a glass and add ice cubes.

Ash takes a gulp. 'So, more of a lukewarm one, then,' he comments, grimacing. The Rowlands' swanky new kitchen is so white he hardly dares to set his glass down in case it leaves a stain or he knocks it over. 'No one else at home?'

'Millie's at a friend's and Jo's at her Zumba class. Some peace and quiet for a bit.'

Ash has far more peace and quiet than he would like. It's one of the things he loves when he pops in at Crooked Oak Cottage – the noise. It's not noisy, it's just comforting. Homely. Carla's music – Ash isn't a fan of opera, but he thinks it could grow on him when he hears it there; Iris and Olly's banter or bickering, depending on their moods; Margo's non-stop chatter. Although Dandruff's discordant humming, not so much.

'Listen, mate, there's something else I haven't told you. It's about Dandruff.'

Not so much speak of the devil as think of the devil. Was Roly reading his mind? 'Go on.'

'Well, he rang me the other day, ostensibly to thank me for my help when Margo went missing, although I didn't actually do anything.'

When Roly pauses, Ash prompts him. 'So, what did he really want?'

'He said he wanted to talk to me about the case … the Joshua Knoll case. He said he didn't want to cause any trouble. He implied he might have some information.' Ash splutters on his IPA. 'He was beating around the bush.'

'Like you're doing now.'

'Right. Sorry. He mentioned Iris and some shoes that ended up in the bin. I told him he wasn't making any sense. In the end, he just asked me to forget he'd called. I didn't get a chance to tell him I wasn't on the case anymore.'

Was Dandruff going to dob Iris in? That's what it sounds like. He knew Carla had confided in Dandruff about something. So it was the shoes, then. Dandruff probably didn't realize that Roly was the one who had told him about the trainers. Was Dandruff really going to pass on information to Roly? After Carla accepted to take him back? The two-faced snake! Ash could confront him about it, but Dandruff would deny it. He didn't actually say anything in the end, by the sound of it, anyway. Ash has always thought that Carla was way too good for Dandruff; this is the first time he has considered Dandruff to actually be bad for her.

'What did you say to him?'

'I told him we'd made a breakthrough in the case, but made out I was telling him in confidence. My colleagues were interviewing your man Tomlinson at the time, but it was going to be in the news anyway.'

'Thanks, Roly. You did the right thing.'

'And what are you going to do?'

Ash thinks about this for a moment. 'Not a lot,' he admits, feeling helpless, 'but I'll keep a close eye on him. Give him a warning, if I get the chance.'

What else can he do? He wants Carla to be happy. Dandruff has moved back in to Crooked Oak Cottage. If he was thinking of telling Roly about the shoes, he has thought better of it. Ash is going to have to give him the benefit of the doubt. Even if there's no doubt at all in Ash's mind.

He has drunk as much of the IPA as he can bear, so he decides to make a move. 'Thanks for the chat and the beer,' he says, handing Roly the glass and getting to his feet. 'Thanks for everything, Roly.'

When he gets home, Ash puts on a wash and some alternative rock, then showers and changes into jeans and a sweatshirt. Despite the music, it seems quieter than ever at Mayflower Farm. He fires off a text to Carla, goes into the kitchen and opens the fridge. He pulls out some leftovers – peri-peri chicken – which he heats up in the microwave.

When he has finished eating, he checks for Iris's video on the web, but today, for the first time, he doesn't find it. His fingers intertwined, he leans back in his office chair and smiles. It's all dying down. At last. With a bit of luck, Roly's right. Things will soon go back to normal.

Ash is dozing off on the sofa in front of a documentary about Captain Tom and his family when Carla rings. He sits up and grabs his phone, suddenly wide awake.

'Hey,' she says when he answers. That one syllable alone is enough to make his heart skip a beat.

They talk about Tomlinson's death. Carla heard about it from Jo.

'How's Iris?' Ash asks.

'She hasn't said much,' Carla replies. 'I think, like us, she doesn't really know what to make of this ... development.'

'Dand ... Dan ... iel there, is he?' As much as Ash hates to think of Dandruff there, in *his* house, he doesn't want Carla to be alone to process all of this.

'Yes, he's reading with Margo.'

Ash can hear the smile in her voice, but he doesn't know if it's because he called her partner by his name or because her partner has come back home. Ash hopes Dandruff had his tail between his legs, but he wouldn't dream of saying this.

'And how's Margo?'

'OK. Good of you to ask. Incredibly resilient, kids, aren't they?'

He senses she's keeping something from him. 'Go on,' he prompts her. 'Out with it.'

'I had Margo tested for Rohypnol at the hospital, you know, the date-rape drug?'

'Seriously? Why—?'

'Anyway, the tests came back negative. But I think Yvonne knows more than she's letting on.'

'I got that impression, too. At the hospital.'

'Yes. You said. I think her sons – Jordan and Jasper – drugged Margo, and Yvonne kept Margo at Hilltop House for as long as possible in the hope that the drug would wear off and be eliminated from her system.'

'Was Margo … did she …?' Ash can't finish his sentence. *Christ, Ash. Make an effort. Try and be more articulate.*

But, as usual, Carla has read his mind. 'No. No signs of sexual abuse,' she says. 'I think those two budding juvenile delinquents must just have wanted to have a laugh. Or to see what the drug did. God only knows how they got hold of it.'

'What made you think Margo was drugged in the first place?' His tone has no hint of incredulity. If Carla's convinced Margo was drugged, then she was. Ash doesn't question her judgement for a moment.

'Well, Margo was lethargic, dizzy, complained of a headache, couldn't remember what had happened. Actually, Iris was the one who suggested it. She said there was a lot of Rohypnol about, even out here in the middle of nowhere. She also said one of her friends had been drugged.'

'One of her friends? Is that what she said?'

'Yes, I think so … No, hang on. Iris said it happened to someone she knew.'

His heart sputters as Carla's words replay in his head. *Iris said it happened to someone she knew.* And then Ash recalls Olly's words, from the conversation they had the last time his son stayed over, here at Mayflower Farm. *Just some guy at a party.*

'Ash? Ash? Are you still there?'

'Yes, sorry, Carla. I'm still here.'

'What's going on?'

'I think I might …' Ash pauses, runs the fingers of his free hand through his hair. Has he put two and two together and made five? 'I'm not sure, but I may know who Iris meant.'

Chapter 37

Carla

NOW

Ash suggests we should talk to Iris about it together, but we don't want her to feel cornered or ambushed. I'm not entirely sure it's any of our business, to tell you the truth. So, in the end, we decide that I'll broach the subject when the opportunity arises and when Iris and I are alone.

I think I may have my chance at the weekend. I moot the idea of going for a walk as the sun is out and Iris wants to take Cheddar to the ocean. Our dog loves swimming in the river and Iris wants to introduce him to the beach – at Saunton Sands. It's a bit of a trek, twenty-odd miles from Holtleigh – but I think Iris also fancies the drive. At least there won't be any holiday traffic at this time of year. No one else is interested in going, so the two of us get ready.

Iris's car, though, starts to play up before we get anywhere near the beach. It judders going up a hill and at first, I put it down to Iris's lack of experience as a driver.

'Put your foot down,' I say, as it slows practically to a halt.

'I am,' she growls.

I'm reminded of all the times we argued when Iris was a learner driver and I was in the passenger seat. She wasn't good at taking advice and, looking back, I realize I gave far too much of it. On top of that, I was a terribly nervous passenger, even though Iris has always been cautious and confident at the wheel. We were often at loggerheads. Ash did the whole accompanied driving thing much better than I did.

I tell myself not to criticize Iris. But she stalls the car.

'Do you want me to drive?' I regret the words – and the remonstrative tone – as soon as the sentence flies out of my mouth.

'Knock yourself out,' Iris says, pulling up the handbrake, flinging off her seatbelt and leaping out of the car.

We're in the middle of the road, but I intercept my criticism this time. We change seats. I berate myself for messing up what I wanted to be a lovely mother-daughter day. I was hoping for some quality time together. I also intended to ask Iris about the Rohypnol, probing gently so that she wouldn't shut me out. But that looks out of the question now.

On the next hill, the car shudders and slows, even as I press the accelerator to the floor. When it stalls this time, it confirms there's a problem with the car, not with Iris's driving.

'What do you think?' I say, turning to her. 'Should we go back and get my car instead?'

'Whatever,' Iris mumbles. Then she amends her answer. 'If you go back, we may as well stay at home.'

'Oh, Iris. I'm sorry,' I say.

I start the car. It seems to fare better now that the road has evened out, but there are a few hills to go before I get to the beach. I visualize the route ahead of me, all the way to the beach. The steepest hills are behind us. I should really turn back and head home, but I want to keep going. I'm not ready to admit defeat, even though the car is threatening to do just that. And

I haven't lost hope that Iris might come round, that she might confide in me about the incident she referred to involving the date-rape drug.

Iris said someone she knew had been drugged. Ash is right. It has to be Olivia. As soon as he shared his suspicions with me, it made sense. Liv's aloofness. The way she seems to have lost her sparkle. According to Ash, Olly said – or at least intimated – that Liv had been sexually assaulted at a party. Did Olly mean she was raped? And, if so, was she drugged and raped?

It doesn't bear thinking about. And perhaps Iris won't want to think about it. She may well refuse to tell me anything. That's OK. As long as she knows she can come to me if she needs to. I'm not sure if she trusts me to do my very best for her. After all, my best was nowhere near good enough last time.

When the video of Iris went viral, I realized just how hard it is to protect our children in today's world. Our kids have to navigate their way through many of the same dangers as we did – puberty, sexuality and sexual identity, eating disorders, substance abuse, addiction, peer pressure, academic pressure, social pressure, depression, anxiety. But these issues seem to have been elevated to a much higher level. And the internet has played a role in that as well as throwing new issues into the mix for good measure – social media, social isolation, cyberbullying, technology addiction, fake news.

Our parents warned us not to talk to strangers, to look both ways before crossing the road, to talk to an adult if we were bullied at school. They talked to us about the birds and the bees. They gave us the tools we needed to work our way through life, avoiding most of the potholes. How can we, as adults and as parents, do this in turn for our children? How can we warn them about their use of smartphones when we ourselves didn't have them growing up? Both Olly and Iris are Gen Z kids. By definition, Zoomers have grown up with social media and the internet. My children know far more about digital technology than I do. How can anything I say be credible? We didn't have the date-rape drug when I was growing up either. Yet another problem our children's generation has to deal with. It's not tools I need to be giving my kids; it's weapons. And it's not potholes they need to avoid; it's craters.

I steal a glance at my daughter. She has put on sunglasses and has twisted round in her seat so that her back is turned to me and she's looking out of the window on her side. She shows no signs of thawing yet.

We go through Braunton, technically a village, although it's more like a town in size. Another two and a half miles to go. We turn left at the traffic lights and exit the village, onto the coastal road. As we round a bend and the long, sandy beach comes into view, I start to relax. Nearly there now. Iris's car makes it all the way without shuddering or stalling again. I park in the Saunton Sands car park and Iris gets Cheddar out of the boot.

I scrape my hair back from my face and tie it up with a scrunchie from around my wrist as the wind propels us along the beach. It must be around low tide – the sea is a long way out and, in silence, we head towards it.

When the kids were little, Ash and I used to bring them here. We'd picnic and take them for a paddle. Even in July and August, when North Devon is bursting with holidaymakers, you can find a quiet spot somewhere along the three-and-a-half-mile stretch of golden sand.

I've come here several times in more recent years, of course, when Olly and Iris were still kids, with Daniel and Margo. We'd usually come during the summer, when colourful beach huts are lined up against the dunes, holidaymakers and locals alike queue in their swimming costumes for Mr Whippys at the ice-cream vans, the beach is dotted with sunbathers and windbreakers, and the sea is manned by lifeguards. But we've come once or twice during the off-season, on days like today, for walks along the beach, from Baggy Point towards Crow Point, generally turning back long before we reach it. It's been a while, though. We haven't come to the beach at all this year, I realize now.

I breathe the brackish air deep into my lungs, and look all around me at the stunning panoramic views. There's only a smattering of dog walkers along the beach and a handful of surfers braving the cold water. I'm struck by the expanse of the beach at low tide with so few people around. I've been spending far too much time in my own head – either worrying about my family or lost in fictional worlds for my job. I feel as if I'm reconnecting with nature.

Iris turns to me, grinning. I take this to mean that she's feeling the same thing and that, hopefully, I'm forgiven.

'Thanks for this, Iris,' I say. 'It was a great idea to come here.'
'You can thank me if Ringo gets us back home again,' she says.
'Ringo?'
'Yeah, my car. Olly's idea.'
'It was Olly's idea to name your car Ringo?'
'No, he just said I should give it a name. I chose Ringo.'
'As in Ringo the Twingo?'
'Exactly,' Iris says and grins again.

We both laugh uproariously. I'm not sure when I last heard Iris laugh like this. I laugh so much my tummy hurts. It's not even that funny. But it's as if I can finally release months and months of tension. Harry Tomlinson is dead and I'm starting to believe this is the end of our problems, the end of everything we've been through, especially Iris.

We've reached the water's edge. Cheddar isn't impressed at first. He tentatively dips a paw into the water, then shakes his whole leg feverishly, looking disgusted. Iris takes off her shoes and socks and coaxes him into the water, but he gets spooked by a wave and runs out again. After a few minutes, though, he starts to enjoy himself and seems astounded to realize he can swim.

After our walk, we decide to get a coffee before heading back home. The café at the top of the beach is closed, so we go to the Saunton Sands Hotel. It's a posh, four-star hotel and I feel very underdressed. Cheddar isn't allowed inside, so we sit at an outdoor table on the terrasse, which overlooks the beach. We're sheltered from the wind and sitting in the sun, which suits us perfectly. Cheddar, exhausted from the excitement of his first outing to the beach, instantly falls asleep at Iris's feet.

As we sip our coffees, I have second thoughts about asking Iris about Olivia. I don't want to ruin what is turning out to be a lovely day. But it's now or never.

'Iris, I wonder if I could ask you about something. Just say if it's none of my business, OK? I don't want to make you feel uncomfortable or stick my nose—'

'Mum, you can cut out the preamble,' Iris says. 'Get to the point?'

'Right. Well, it's about the Rohypnol. And, er, Olivia. I—'

'How did you know I was talking about Olivia?'

I don't tell her I didn't know for sure. 'Olly said something to your dad. He said she was sexually assaulted by some guy at a party.'

'Yeah. She was drugged and raped.'

'Do you want to tell me what happened?'

'Not really, Mum.' Iris sighs and turns away from me, shielding her eyes from the low sun and looking at the ocean. Then she pulls down her sunglasses, which were holding her hair back.

'OK. That's fine. I'm just concerned, you know? I don't know how best to protect you, how to protect Margo. I think you were right about Margo, by the way.'

I probably shouldn't have said that – Iris has had enough problems of her own to deal with and I don't want to burden her with more – but it gets her attention. Her head snaps back and her eyes lock onto mine.

'What do you mean?'

I have to tell her now. 'I'm convinced Jordan and Jasper spiked Margo's drink the night she spent at Hilltop House. It might sound stupid, or paranoid, and perhaps it is, but—'

'Nah. That makes sense.'

'—they were trying to sell pot outside Millie's house on the night of her eighteenth birthday party as well. It doesn't mean they push all sorts of drugs, but—'

'How on earth do you know that?'

'Your dad saw them when he went to pick you up that night. Anyway, I went round to Yvonne's and demanded answers.'

'Did you get any?'

'No. I think Yvonne deliberately kept Margo at Hilltop House until the drugs were out of her system before taking her to hospital. I think she would have brought her home instead of going to the hospital if she'd managed to get hold of you the first time she rang. Or perhaps when Margo regained consciousness, Yvonne got really worried that there might be something seriously wrong with her and decided to play it safe by taking her to A&E, I don't know. But I'm convinced those boys drugged Margo.'

'What makes you so sure?'

Am I sure? I could be wrong about all this. But as I list everything, I'm more convinced than ever. 'A few things. Margo's symptoms – the memory loss, in particular – and the fact that Jordan and Jasper gave her a can of Red Bull, which is pretty much the last thing she remembers. It's an energy drink. It shouldn't have knocked her out.'

I look at Iris. She has a strange expression on her face. I wait for her to say something, but she doesn't.

'You don't believe me, do you?' I ask. As much as I'd like for none of this to be true, for Margo not to have been drugged, it's really important to me for some reason that my daughter believes me.

'Oh, yes, I do,' Iris says. 'I believe every word of what you've just said.'

The words hang in the air between us for a few seconds. I can almost picture the sentence Iris has just spoken as I try to read between the lines. I pick up Iris's earlier line now – *that makes sense*. She didn't find my theory illogical, far from it.

'It was at Josh's eighteenth birthday party,' she says.

It sounds like the beginning of an account, a secret. I've confided in Iris and now she's ready to confide in me. I hold my breath.

'Olivia was drugged,' Iris continues. 'Josh and I had had a row. I mean, maybe not a row, but he'd upset me. I went for a walk to clear my head. Olly came with me. He tried to calm me down.'

Her voice cracks and I notice her eyes are shiny, tears threatening to spill down her cheeks. I want to reach out and put my hand on hers, but I don't dare to move in case she clams up.

'When we got back, we couldn't find Liv,' Iris continues. 'Someone said she was really drunk. Someone else said she could barely stand up. But Olly said she hadn't been drunk when we left and we hadn't been gone that long.'

Iris pauses. A cloud passes over the sun and it instantly feels cold. I shiver, although I'm not sure if it's because of the cold or because I can sense what's coming next. Iris pushes her sunglasses back up onto the top of her head.

'We found her eventually,' Iris says. Tears roll down her face now and she swipes at them and sniffs. 'She was barely conscious, Mum. She could barely talk. Charlie – one of Olly's mates – had driven to the party, so we took her to hospital.'

I keep quiet, immobile, afraid of jolting Iris into silence if I so much as breathe.

'They got the police in. At the hospital, I mean,' Iris says. 'Olivia was tested for the date-rape drug. It was positive. The police brought a rape kit with them, so they got evidence of the rape itself, but not the identification of … the … the rapist.'

Oh, God. Poor Liv. No wonder Iris suggested checking Margo for Rohypnol. She must have been reliving that evening with Liv, when they had to take her to the hospital.

And then my heart clenches. Because the connection between

the two incidents is suddenly blindingly obvious. But before I can say anything, Iris continues.

'Liv has no idea who drugged her and no idea who raped her. She was so ashamed and frightened she didn't even want to tell her parents at first. She just wanted to forget all about it. She didn't want to, you know, press charges, or whatever.'

I know Iris can relate to that. My daughter wanted to forget what had happened to her. She didn't want to prosecute Josh. She couldn't go through a court case. I didn't listen to her. I insisted until Ash told me to back off. I wanted justice. Justice for my daughter. But Justice has different faces; she wears different masks.

'Iris,' I say gently, 'what happened to Liv and what happened to Margo ...' Iris nods. She knows what I'm going to say next. 'It was at Hilltop House. Both times.'

'Yeah,' she says. 'In the actual summerhouse both times, too.'

I scowl, unsure what to make of that coincidence. Is it a coincidence?

'Josh ... he ... er ... supplied the drugs,' Iris says, making me wonder if I asked my question aloud. 'I only found that out afterwards. A long time afterwards. But he was selling drugs. Marijuana, Rohypnol, ecstasy.'

I swear to God, if that kid hadn't already been killed, I would kill him myself.

'But, Iris,' I say, 'this means that other people might have had motive. Someone else might have wanted Josh dead.' I was so sure Iris was guilty and now that I'm considering my daughter might be innocent after all, a feeling of shame bowls into me. 'Why didn't you tell your dad and me about this at the time? Why didn't you tell us Josh had been dealing drugs?'

Iris looks out towards the sea again, studiously avoiding eye contact. I follow her gaze. The water has crept several metres nearer to the shoreline than before. The sun is dipping into the ocean, its reflection a single orange brushstroke across the dark water. It's getting late. And cold. We should get going. I wait a few seconds longer in case Iris says something, but she has clammed up, as if she realizes she has said too much. As if she has given something away. But I get the feeling she hasn't told me everything.

Chapter 38

Iris

NOW

In the days just before Josh's eighteenth birthday party, Josh and Iris weren't really talking to each other. She can't remember exactly why now. She may not even have known at the time what she said or did to upset him. Sometimes he'd get salty and she'd realize she'd offended him or pissed him off or whatever, but she'd go over everything in her head – replay their conversations, reread their text exchanges and listen again to their voice messages – and for the life of her, she just couldn't work out where his mood had come from. She'd tread carefully – on eggshells – and hope it would blow over if she was, like, super nice. If she was lucky, Josh would eventually snap out of it and his period of sulking or ghosting her would come to an abrupt end. He would pretend nothing had happened, which always made Iris wonder if she was imagining things. At other times, he'd be low-key annoyed to begin with, his anger simmering for a while under the surface, scarcely visible like a dormant volcano, until he eventually erupted.

So, right, this was one of those times where Josh had been acting weird and Iris didn't know why. She'd bought him an awesome present ages ago and had been looking forward to seeing the look on his face when he opened it. But now she wasn't even sure she wanted to go to his fucking party.

On the day itself, hours before it was due to kick off, Josh sent Iris a text message. Honestly, it creeped her out the way he seemed to be able to read her mind sometimes.

**Can't wait for tonight. Come round early, Babe?
J x**

It was like there was nothing wrong. Was Josh just going to act like everything was fine between them? He was *really* good at sweeping everything under the carpet. Iris still wasn't sure whether she wanted to go. She needed to think about it, talk it over with Millie. When Iris didn't reply immediately to Josh's text, he called her. She tried to put her foot down. She said it wasn't OK to ignore her one minute and be all over her like a rash the next. But Josh always knew the right buttons to push, the right things to say when he wanted his own way and she couldn't stay mad for long. He needed her to help make his eighteenth awesome. How could he celebrate without his girlfriend by his side? He'd been busy lately and hadn't realized she'd been feeling neglected, blah, blah, blah.

When she got to Hilltop House, she gave him the present she'd bought for him. Josh was, like, really into Lego and she'd found The Milky Way Galaxy artwork on Vinted a few weeks ago. The seller assured her all the pieces were there. Even second-hand, it had cost her a fortune, but it was the perfect gift.

Josh opened the present and thanked her, but he was nowhere near as enthusiastic about it as she'd thought he would be. She'd put a lot of thought into what to buy him and spent a lot of money. His indifference hurt.

Things went from bad to worse. Once everyone else showed up, he started flirting – and then dancing – with Sasha Spencer-Lyles, like Iris was completely invisible.

Iris didn't want to make a scene, so she shut herself in the downstairs loo. She sat on the closed lid of the toilet, in floods of tears, pulling at the loo roll and using it to blow her nose and dab under her eyes, where the mascara must have run. She was desperately trying to get a grip. Her dad wasn't due to pick her up for another five hours. Millie was chatting up Emiliano, the Italian exchange student. Iris didn't want to disturb her. Olly was here somewhere, but he would be with Liv and their friends.

Someone hammered on the door.

'Oi! You gonna be much longer?' A male voice. 'I need to take a slash.'

'Coming,' Iris said. She stood up, opened the lid of the loo to throw in the balled-up toilet paper and flushed.

She stumbled out of the patio doors. It had been a warm day, but it was cool this evening, as if the weather was slowly shifting now that they were officially into autumn. It was still light, though. She'd go for a walk. That would kill some time. And the fresh air might help clear her head. Someone must have told Olly she was in a bit of a state. He caught up with her before she got to the end of the driveway. It sounded childish, even to Iris, when she told her brother what was wrong.

But Olly didn't look at her like she was being silly. 'It's all right,' Olly said. 'Josh is probably drunk, or stoned – it's his birthday. It's harmless flirting, Iris. He doesn't mean anything by it. Or if he does, it's to make you jealous. Which has clearly worked.'

Olly wasn't a fan of Josh – Iris knew that – and it was like her brother was sticking up for her boyfriend. Iris wanted Olly to be firmly on her side, but his words made her think she was probably overreacting.

'Anyway, Sasha's not staying,' Olly continued. 'She's going away for the weekend. She said she was just popping in. Let's go back and you can have a good time with your friends. Come and talk to Liv and me for a bit, if you want.' Iris nodded. 'Charlie's come by car. I'll get him to take you back to Dad's if Josh is still being a dick.' That made Iris smile. 'Or we'll all leave. Liv won't mind.'

'Thanks, Bro.'

Olly was pretty cool, as brothers go. He always looked out for Iris and Margo. Millie often said she wished she wasn't an only child and she'd have liked a brother like Olly.

They didn't go back straightaway. They sat in the garden for a while and talked about other stuff. School, the holidays, music, Iris can't remember. At one point, this car pulled up at the end of the drive and the front door of Hilltop House opened at the same time. Sasha stepped outside and teetered down the gravelly driveway in high heels. Iris didn't even own a pair of high heels. Maybe Sasha didn't either and they belonged to her mum. Sasha got into the car. Iris watched the taillights until the car rounded the bend and took that as her cue to go back to the fun and games. She got to her feet and Olly followed her.

How long had they been gone? Maybe half an hour? Forty-five minutes tops. Not that long. But when they got back, no one seemed to know where Liv was.

'She was wrecked, man,' one of their classmates told Olly and Iris. He looked pretty wrecked himself. 'Like totally out of it,' he added unnecessarily.

Olly tried ringing Liv on her mobile, but she didn't answer. It took them maybe another quarter of an hour to find her – in the summerhouse in the garden. She was almost unconscious. She couldn't string two words together. Her eyes kept rolling back into her head.

'How much did she have to drink?' Iris asked Olly. 'Did she smoke any pot?'

'Same as me. A couple of beers,' he said. 'She's not drunk or stoned, Iris. I think she's been drugged. We need to get her to the hospital.'

Iris took her mobile out of her little handbag to call for an ambulance.

But Olly said, 'We'll take her. It will be much quicker. I'll get Charlie.'

It didn't occur to Iris it might have been Josh who sold the drugs. Not at first. Iris knew he sold hash, but she assumed it was just to his mates. She didn't approve, exactly, but it didn't bother her. After all, they all smoked spliffs at parties. Iris didn't buy it, but she didn't turn her nose up when someone passed her the joint. She had no idea Josh sold ecstasy and roofies and shit, too. And not just to his mates. That was, like, a whole other level.

Olly was the one who told her, actually. About the drugs. He said he'd overheard some kids talking about it at school. He came into her room one night, months after she and Josh had split up – months after her video had gone viral, for that matter – and told her Josh was selling roofies. He asked for her help.

'I think he sold the Rohypnol that was given to Liv that night. What I want to know, is who he sold the drugs to,' Olly explained. 'I need to get Josh alone.'

'What does Liv think about this?' Iris asked.

'She doesn't know. I don't want her to know. Not until I've found out more.'

'He won't tell you,' Iris said.

'He will if I threaten him. If I can get him alone, he'll talk.'

Iris didn't like the way Olly was talking or where this was going. But she got why he needed to know. And there was no other way of finding out. 'He runs in Lower Buryknoll Wood every Sunday morning. I mean, unless he's changed his routine. He calls it his LSD run – long slow distance.'

'LSD. How appropriate,' Olly commented, rolling his eyes.

'I know, right? He calls the woods *his* woods. Because of his surname?' Iris says. 'I can show you his route, if you like. I went with him a few times, ages ago, back when we were ... you know. He always runs the same loop.'

And from there, they came up with a plan. They would put it into action one Sunday. They'd wait for him in the woods.

But then Josh went missing. Olly wanted Iris to call him, but there was no way she was going to do that. Yvonne had been calling her, wanting to know if Iris knew where he might be. Iris thought about it and thought that she probably did know where he was, but she wasn't going to tell Yvonne. She told Olly, though.

'Chances are, he's in the woods,' Iris said after a couple of days. Josh had shown her a spot on one of their runs and said he'd like to camp there one weekend. With her. Luckily, he hadn't insisted. Lying on hard ground, being kept awake by strange noises, getting bitten by mosquitoes, their tent surrounded by wild nocturnal animals … it wasn't Iris's idea of fun.

Olly took a knife from the kitchen drawer. It was the one Mum and Daniel used for chopping up onions. Iris wasn't happy about the knife, but Olly said he only wanted to threaten him.

They found him. Josh. Right where Iris thought he would be. She saw the tent before she saw him. He was crouching down, making a fire. In the woods. He stood up when he saw Iris. Olly circled round and came in from behind Josh, then jumped him, holding the knife to his throat. Josh showed no fear. If anything, his hazel eyes glittered with amusement. He knew Olly wasn't violent. He didn't sense any danger. Iris was standing downwind of Josh, two or three metres away, but the familiar smell of his sweat reached her and made her feel sick.

'The night Olivia was attacked—' Olly growled; his voice was strange, not like Olly's voice at all '—who did you sell the roofies to?'

'I didn't sell them to anyone.'

'Who did you give them to, then?'

'No one.'

'For fuck's sake, Josh! Stop pissing about.' Iris thought she saw Olly push the knife harder against Josh's skin, but Josh still didn't look fazed. 'You know what I mean. Who drugged Liv at your eighteenth birthday party?'

'I did,' he said.

Iris's jaw dropped. She could see by the expression on Olly's face that he hadn't expected this either. Was Josh for real? 'You drugged Liv?' Iris could barely get the words out. 'But why?'

'She wanted it. She just needed a bit of encouragement.' He had a sort of conceited grin on his face. His words were clear despite the knife against his throat. He even sounded like he was bragging. 'Not everyone is as easy as you, babe.'

'You mean you …?' Iris couldn't bring herself to say it.

Olly managed, though. 'You raped her.'

It didn't come out like a question. But Josh replied. 'I don't know if you could call it that. She didn't put up much of a fight. She didn't say no.'

'You raped her, you bastard,' Iris hissed.

Josh gave a little chuckle. 'If you say so,' he said. He still looked so confident, totally unruffled, like he'd forgotten Olly was holding a knife to his throat, like nothing bad could ever happen to him. Iris wanted to lunge at Josh and gouge his eyes out, but she clocked Olly's face, as he looked at her over Josh's shoulder. Olly's eyes were flashing wildly and his face was all twisted. It was like he was warning her to stay put.

'No way to prove it though,' Josh continued, taunting them, his eyes locked on Iris's. 'Just like you can never prove it was me who shared your porn vid.'

It happened really fast. Josh pulled Olly's arm away, turned round and pushed him hard in the chest with both hands, knocking him to the ground. Then he broke into a run, but as he passed Iris, he tripped over her foot and flew through the air, landing with a thud on a large stone.

Olly, who had leapt to his feet, pounced on Josh and rolled him over, then sat astride him. He plunged the knife into Josh, just once. Then he paused and let go of the knife, like he realized what he'd done.

'Olly!' Iris screamed.

Iris was frozen to the spot and could only watch, helplessly, as Olly lost it. Like, completely lost it. He grabbed the knife and pulled it out of Josh's chest, then plunged it into him, again and again. It was the blood that finally galvanized her into action. She tried to hold back Olly's arm as he thrust it into Josh's body one last time. But she could see from Josh's eyes that it was already too late.

They sat next to Josh's lifeless form for what seemed like hours, but was probably only a few minutes. Olly cried. Iris put her arm round him, but shock prevented her from finding any words. She had a massive lump in her throat, but fought hard to swallow it down. Olly needed her to stay strong. She thought about the night he'd sat with her in the bathroom, his arm around her. The night she'd wanted to kill herself. And now, here they were, Iris with her arm around her brother, who had just killed Josh.

She replayed the scene in her head. So many ifs were racing around her brain. If Josh hadn't tripped, he would have outrun them. If he'd denied drugging – and raping – Liv, he'd still be alive. If Olly hadn't lost it. If Josh hadn't been so smug, so sure that Olly wouldn't hurt him. If she'd made Josh leave the knife at home. If only.

It started to rain as Iris and Olly were walking slowly home. Spitting at first, but then it poured. Iris saw Josh's blood dripping from Olly's sodden T-shirt and from the knife she'd taken from Olly and was holding between her thumb and her forefinger. It was like the rain was deliberately washing away the evidence.

Olly stopped next to the stream and washed his hands and arms. Iris took off her hoodie. It was wet and it was way too small for Olly, but he managed to squeeze into it. It had a bit of blood on the inside of the sleeve, where she'd put her arm around him. Other than that, Iris had no blood on her, but she washed her hands and face in the cold stream even so.

Finally, she found her voice. 'Olly, we can't tell anyone about this,' she said, at the same time as Olly said, 'We need to go home and get Mum to call Ian.'

Iris started crying then, tears that mixed with the rain coursing down her face. 'I'm not l-losing you because of what he d-did,' she said. 'He did something to me that I'll n-never forgive him for. And h-he has done something that's just as unforgivable to Liv.'

'Two wrongs don't make a right,' Olly said. His voice was wobbly and so quiet that Iris had to strain to hear what he was saying. 'We have to tell Mum. Or Dad. And Ian. I killed someone.'

'You killed a monster. A monster who ruined my life *and* Liv's. We're both slowly getting back on track. If ... anything happens to you, Olly, I ... won't ... be able ... Please. Promise me.'

But Olly shook his head. 'You haven't thought this through,' he said.

'What do you mean?' Iris asked.

'I mean, when they find Josh, they'll think it was you.'

Chapter 39

Carla

NOW

Iris won't say any more and we set off on our journey home from the beach in silence. But I hear her words clearly, as though she's repeating them out loud. Briefly, they transport me back to the terrasse of the Saunton Sands Hotel, where we were sitting at a table in the setting sun just a few minutes ago. *Josh supplied the drugs. I only found that out afterwards. A long time afterwards.* I glance at my daughter, sitting in the passenger's seat. She gives me a taut smile, but her expression is impassive and I have no idea what she's thinking. I hear my own words, too: *Why didn't you tell your dad and me about this at the time? Why didn't you tell us Josh had been dealing drugs?*

Another question is pinwheeling around my brain. I think it might actually be the answer to the questions that Iris ignored. But the words don't make it past my lips, although they're screaming in my head: *Did Olly know?*

Iris puts on the music. It's some sort of angry hip-hop, which

I usually hate, but right now it helps to drown out my nagging suspicions.

It's relatively flat for the first few miles, but as soon as we reach a steep hill, I realize Iris's car is still playing up. It just doesn't seem to have enough energy to make it to the top. I have my foot to the floor, in first gear, and the car slows to an alarming snail's pace. The driver in the car behind me is riding my bumper, so I flick on the hazards and he backs off.

Once we're on a downhill stretch, Iris rings Daniel with my phone to tell him we're on our way home. He says he'll have dinner ready. I describe the problem with Iris's Twingo. Without thinking, I tell him Iris was too scared to drive it home, which earns me a black look from the passenger's seat.

'Hmm. It's not tyre pressure – I checked the tyres not long ago,' Daniel says. 'Maybe the spark plugs? We'll have to take it in to the garage.'

I sigh. Daniel has a busy week ahead – he's away for three days – and I have another deadline.

Daniel seems to read my mind. 'Perhaps Olly can take it in next week, make himself useful.'

I bristle at my partner's thinly veiled criticism of my son, but he's got a point. Olly does very little to help out. And it's the October half-term next week, so the kids are off school. 'I'll ring the garage on Monday and ask when they can take a look at it,' I say.

After the phone call to Daniel, Iris leaves the music off and there's nothing to act as a buffer for my thoughts. I sift through my earlier conversation with Iris again, trying to read between the lines of what she said and work out what she didn't say. According to Ash, Olly said Liv was raped by some guy at a party. Iris has just told me it was Josh's eighteenth birthday party. When she told me that it was Josh who supplied the drugs, she hesitated, as if she was going to say something else, then thought better of it. *Josh … he … er … supplied the drugs.* Why am I so sure there's something Iris didn't tell me?

And then it hits me like a blow to the stomach.

'Iris,' I say. She grunts. 'Was it Josh who drugged Liv? Is that what happened? Did Josh—'

Iris bursts into tears. I turn towards her, alarmed. 'Oh, Iris, don't cry. I didn't mean to make you cry,' I say. 'Sweetie, I just want to help. I want to protect you.' I expect her to make a snide remark, to point out that I've failed – miserably – to protect her until now. But she doesn't. 'I think it might be time to tell me the whole story,' I say gently.

We're heading towards Holtleigh along a narrow lane with tufts of grass sprouting up in the middle. There's a car coming the other way, so I pull into a lay-by to allow it to pass. I stay in the lay-by, even after the other car has gone, and turn to Iris, looking at her questioningly.

It comes out as a whisper. 'Yes,' she admits.

'Josh drugged Liv?'

'Yes,' she repeats.

'Did he … did he …?'

'Yes, he was the one who raped her, if that's what you're asking.'

Iris is crying again. I reach out and put my arm around her shoulders. We stay there for a while, in the lay-by, until Iris is all cried out. She finds a pocket pack of tissues in the glove box and blows her nose loudly.

At home, I go through the motions. I set the table, listen to Margo babbling away, tell Daniel that dinner smells great. I sit at the dinner table, forcing myself to eat and watching as Iris does the same. I glance from Olly to Iris and back again. Iris seems to be doing the same as me. Putting on a brave face, pretending everything is fine. Inside, I'm reeling from shock.

I try to confine my suspicions to a corner of my mind for the rest of the evening, but as soon as I go to bed, they clamour for my undivided attention. My first thought when Iris told me that

Josh had been selling drugs to his classmates was that someone else might have had a motive to kill him. Now I know there's more to it than that. Josh wrecked Iris's life, then ruined Liv's. The more I think about it, the more I believe my daughter is innocent after all.

And the more I believe my son is guilty.

'Carla, Harry Tomlinson was arrested for Josh's murder,' Ash points out. I thought it would do me good to talk to Ash on the phone, but for once, his gentle, deep voice does nothing to soothe me. 'He's dead. It's over. You have to let this go. It's time to move on.'

I burst into tears. I can't help it. I've had hardly any sleep, I have a looming deadline and I've added more things to my to-do list than I've crossed off. I just don't have the bandwidth to deal with any of this. I certainly can't cope with the mental torture my brain seems hellbent on putting me through.

'Carla, I'm coming round,' Ash says. 'I'll be there in half an hour.'

I wipe my eyes in the sleeve of my cardigan, sniff loudly and then take a deep breath. 'There's no need. Really.' But I don't sound convincing, not even to myself.

Forty-five minutes later, Ash is standing on the doorstep of Crooked Oak Cottage, looking both awkward and professional in his suit, as always. I picture myself through his eyes – dishevelled, without make-up, in tracksuit trousers and a hoodie, my working clothes very different to his. He takes one look at me and folds me into a hug. The fresh marine notes of the cologne he has always worn is achingly familiar and, reluctantly, I unfold myself from his embrace. I open the front door wide to let him in. He bends down to unlace his leather shoes in the hallway and then walks ahead of me, in his socked feet, into the kitchen, where, without asking, he flicks on the kettle and makes us both a mug of tea. I've already had two cuppas and two coffees this morning in an attempt to wake myself up and I'm jittery and wired. But I take the mug and dutifully sip my tea. Ash has made it exactly the way I like it.

We're standing, side by side, gazing out of the patio window at the view. I study this same scene every day, marvelling at how different it appears, depending on the season and the weather, like a series of impressionist paintings. Today, the patchwork of green and yellow fields is dotted with white sheep. The sky is a dramatic mix of grey and dark blue, announcing imminent rain, but for the moment, stubborn bursts of sunlight pierce through the clouds, illuminating the silver surface of the river Bray as it meanders its way across the canvas, dividing it in two.

'You were so sure that Iris killed Joshua Knoll,' Ash says. 'What makes you think it was Olly? Why have you changed your mind?'

I explain about the drugs. I tell him Iris admitted that Josh drugged Liv with Rohypnol. The date-rape drug.

I can tell from the shocked expression on Ash's face that this is all news to him. But there's something else I can't quite read in his expression, as if he can now understand something that didn't make complete sense to him before.

'So, let me get this straight—' Ash begins, but he doesn't say it unkindly; I think he's just trying to understand my train of thought and fitting together the pieces I told him over the phone and what I've told him just now '—you think our son had motive because Joshua shared Iris's video and then drugged and raped Liv.'

'That's exactly what I think, yes.' Ash is the only person in the world I could ever admit that to.

'But Carla, even if Olly had something to do with Josh's death – Christ, I can't believe I've just spoken those words – it would only have been because he wanted to protect his sister and his girlfriend.'

I turn away from the window to face Ash. 'He wasn't protecting them, Ash. He was *avenging* them.'

Ash is silent for a second or two. Then he says, 'So, what do you want to do now? You wanted to cover for Iris when you thought she might have had something to do with Josh's death. Surely—'

'I didn't think she had ...' Who am I kidding? Ash knows me so well. I did suspect Iris. And Ash saw through me.

'Surely you don't want to turn our son in?'

'I didn't say that. I don't know. No!' I go and sit down at the kitchen table. Ash takes the seat opposite mine. Olly's seat. 'What? What are you thinking?' I ask.

'*If* the culprit was Olly, not Iris, does it make any difference? I mean, when you thought Iris might have killed Josh, you destroyed evidence and I tried to persuade Roly to plant some. *If* it's our son and not our daughter, we'd still protect Olly, just as we protected Iris, right?'

From Ash's face and the way he stresses the word 'if' each time, I can tell that Ash hasn't swallowed a word of my theory. He doesn't believe for an instant that Olly could be behind Josh's death. This reassures me. Perhaps I have jumped to the wrong conclusion. But that's a good question. If Olly killed Joshua, does it make any difference? Would we – Ash and I – act any differently? I try to think this through.

Iris was Joshua's victim before he became hers. Iris wanted to take her own life because of Joshua. Instead, she took his, or so I'd thought until now. It's wrong to kill someone – anyone. But I really couldn't blame her.

But Olly was a victim, too. He suffered from what Josh did – both to Iris and to Liv. Ash and I – and Daniel – paid Olly less attention. We focused on Iris. Olly was the one who found Iris in the bathroom that evening. I shudder at the thought of it, seeing it through Olly's eyes. His sister, naked on the floor, contemplating suicide. And then he lost his girlfriend because of the same kid.

Joshua was stabbed several times. It was a horrifically violent crime. There's no getting away from that. And when I imagine my daughter plunging the knife into the body of the evil young man who ruined her life, I get it. When I picture the knife in the hands of my son, it seems less justifiable somehow. I also fantasized about killing Joshua because of what he'd done to Iris – I'd never felt so murderous towards someone in my life; I wanted to strangle him with my bare hands – but there's no way I would ever have done it. And yet, Olly did. He didn't just think about it. He went through with it. Was he provoked? Did Joshua say or do something that made Olly snap? If so, would that exonerate my son in my eyes?

I try to gauge Ash's expression. Usually, I can read him like a book, but although his eyes lock on to mine, his face is blank. I took his tone to mean he didn't believe me just now, but now I find myself reassessing my assumption. He's not shocked, not ruffled in the slightest.

'Olly's not a violent person, Carla,' Ash reasons.

A memory rears its ugly head, as if to contradict what Ash has just said. Olly threw a punch at Joshua and knocked him to the floor. He was suspended for this act of violence. I push the memory aside. Just because Olly threw a punch, it doesn't make him a murderer. We're not talking about the same level of violence at all.

I'm Olly's mother. I'm programmed to protect him, no matter what. When it comes down to it, I would fight tooth and nail to defend him, even if what he did was undefendable. I would do the same for my son as I would for my daughter.

'You're right. It makes no difference,' I say, mustering a tight smile. 'Oh, Ash, I'm a terrible, terrible mother.' My eyes fill with tears that I furiously blink away. I need to get a grip. I can't cry in front of Ash again.

'You're not! What on earth makes you say that?'

'First, I was convinced my daughter had committed murder, then I convince myself it was my son instead. What sort of a mother believes their kids are capable of doing something like that? I should believe my kids are innocent, even if they aren't.'

'Carla, you're a great mum. To Olly, to Iris and to Margo. It's not always easy to be a perfect parent when circumstances challenge you. And, God knows, we've had our fair share of challenges lately.'

'Thank you.' I give him a grateful, watery smile. 'You always say the right things.'

'My work here is done,' Ash says, spreading his arms theatrically, no doubt in an attempt to ease the tension. 'I need to get back to the office, Carla, I'm afraid. I've still got work to do there.'

I follow him into the hallway, where he sits on the stairs to put on his shoes. He stands up and kisses me on the forehead.

'It's time to let this go, Carla,' Ash says. His voice is firm, as if he's issuing an order.

I open the front door for him and watch him walk away from me and get into the car. Then I close the door behind him and lean against it. I just need to keep telling myself what Ash told me earlier. *Tomlinson is dead. This is over. Time to move on.* I repeat it to myself, over and over, like a mantra, until I almost believe it.

Chapter 40

Ash

NOW

Ash gets a chance to talk to Olly a few days later. Olly is on his half-term break and Ash is taking the week off work. He knows Olly and Iris don't need babysitting, but he hopes they'll come round to Mayflower Farm if he's there. At Ash's request – well, insistence, really – Olly has come round to help him do a bit of DIY. It's about time Ash got the Mayflower looking ship-shape, so to speak. Ash was doubtful Olly would actually show up. When he asked for his son's help, he got a noncommittal grunt in reply.

Ash has decided to install a shower in the downstairs toilet. Although it's a large room for a lavatory, it's going to be cramped as a bathroom. But when Olly and Iris stay over – and, more recently, Liv, too – one bathroom simply isn't enough for all of them. The girls each spend an inordinate amount of time in there, drying their hair and putting on make-up. Olly spends nearly as long, although the transformation is less apparent when he emerges.

'I haven't got long, Dad,' Olly says, by way of a greeting as he slopes into the house, hands thrust deep into the pockets of his jeans. He has cycled over from Holtleigh. 'Liv's picking me up.'

'Sit down a sec,' Ash says, pointing at the bar stool in the kitchen. 'Do you want something to drink?'

'Nah. I'm good.'

Ash takes the stool next to Olly's and waits for his son to look at him, to establish eye contact. Then he takes a deep breath and says, 'Olly, your mum knows.'

'Knows what?'

Ash waits for the penny to drop. It only takes a second or two. Olly's eyes widen and his mouth forms a large 'O', but no sound comes out.

'Shit!' Olly says at length. 'Did you tell her? Or did Iris?' His tone is accusatory.

'Neither of us,' Ash says. 'She worked it out by herself, sort of put two and two together.' He pauses, hearing the words as they leave his mouth. Carla sometimes points out that he uses a lot of mathematics idioms. It's a stand-in joke between them. The thought makes him smile wistfully in spite of everything. 'I didn't confirm it,' Ash continues. 'In fact, I did my best to convince your mum she'd got it wrong.'

'So she doesn't really *know*, then,' Olly says.

'No, you're right,' Ash says. He should have planned what he was going to say before his son arrived today. 'She suspects you had something to do with Josh's death. Let's put it that way. I just thought I'd give you the heads-up. You know, in case she brings it up. I don't think she will, but if she does, you'll be ready. I didn't know everything either.'

'What do you mean?'

'You didn't tell me it was Josh who drugged and raped Liv. You let on it was some random guy she didn't know at a party. But it was his party, his drugs; it was him.'

'Yeah.'

'Did you know all along?'

'What? No. I found out ... it's the reason why ... he thought it was ...'

Olly clearly isn't going to finish any of his sentences, so Ash says, 'It's what made you lose it, isn't it? That day in the woods.'

'Yeah. So now you know.'

'You could have told me.'

Olly shrugs. 'Does it matter? Liv didn't want anyone to know she was raped.'

Ash ponders that question. He understands Olly's motive better now. As Carla said, he was avenging both his sister and his girlfriend. And it matters that his son didn't think he could confide in him. But he leaves the question unanswered.

Ash's mind takes him back to that evening, which kicked off with a phone call from Iris, who was clearly very distraught. He set off immediately in the car and picked up Olly and Iris from Lower Buryknoll Wood. They were soaked to the skin – it was raining heavily – and Olly's clothing was bloodstained. Iris said they hadn't meant to kill Josh; they'd wanted to threaten him, to get the truth out of him. Ash had believed her. He'd assumed she meant the truth about the video, that she'd wanted him to admit he did it. It didn't occur to him there might be more to it.

Ash's immediate instinct was to cover for Olly. It's what Iris was insisting he should do, even though they were all aware that suspicion could fall on her. Ash was ready to provide an alibi; he washed the knife on the highest setting in the dishwasher and instructed Olly to put it back where he'd found it at the earliest opportunity; he disposed of Olly's clothing – and Carla thought she was the one getting rid of evidence! Ash tells Carla everything. It's the one and only secret he hasn't shared with her, partly for her own sake, but mainly because Iris swore him to secrecy.

Ash gets down from the stool and puts on the kettle. He could do with a coffee. He has a high-end espresso maker – a present from Carla and the kids for his fiftieth – but he has run out of coffee beans, so it will have to be instant.

He has his back turned when Olly suddenly says, 'Dad, I've been thinking.'

'Uh-oh,' Ash says in a feeble attempt to lighten the mood. 'Are you feeling OK?' He winces as his joke falls flat.

'I want you to ring Uncle Ian.'

Ash stiffens. He hasn't heard Olly call Roly that for years, not since Olly was about eight years old. 'What for?' he asks, though he can hazard a guess.

'I want to hand myself in, Dad. I wanted to hand myself in then. You know I did. That's why Iris told you in the first place. So you would talk me out of it.'

Ash turns to face his son. 'Look, Olly, you killed a vile, hateful, evil person. If he'd lived, he would have gone on to cause even more trouble and hurt even more people.'

'We don't know that for sure.'

'I think we can be pretty sure.'

'Doesn't make what I did OK, though, does it? It hasn't even stopped the problems. Jordan and Jasper are pushing drugs now. It's like they've taken over the family business or something.'

'Plus, a man was arrested in connection with Josh's murder,' Ash continues, as if his son hasn't spoken. 'You don't have to do this.'

'We can't let an innocent man take the rap.'

'An innocent man? Tomlinson?' Ash scoffs. 'One: he wasn't all that innocent himself. He was a paedophile. And two: he's dead.'

He's doing it again. One and two. Carla would have said A and B. She works with letters; he works with numbers. Opposites that fit together, he and Carla. He still thinks of her as the yin to his yang, especially when it comes to the kids. Christ, he wishes she was in on this, backing him up and finding the right arguments.

'Doesn't make it OK,' Olly repeats, his voice at least an octave too high. 'And what about his loved ones?'

Ash gets that Olly has a conscience – that's all very honourable.

He also understands his son's desire to come clean and put an end to all of this. He must have felt as if he was in limbo over the past few weeks, as if the sword of Damocles was hanging over his head. But his son has no idea what will happen to him if he goes to prison. Or what it will do to Carla. 'Olly,' Ash says gently, 'I don't think he had any. Loved ones, I mean. But you do. Your mum—'

'Dad, I did something bad.' Olly's eyes are bright, too watery. Ash realizes his son is on the verge of tears. 'I should pay for it. I want you to ring Ian.'

Ash contemplates ringing his friend. Would Roly help him out here? Ash is well aware that Roly took himself off the case for Iris's sake. But would he help Ash to talk Olly out of this? Or would he want to do the right thing by the law?

Ash runs his fingers through his hair. His son is impulsive. Always has been. He acts without thinking things through and then often regrets it afterwards. 'Olly, why don't you think about it first?'

'I *have* been thinking about it, Dad!' Olly shouts. 'It's all I think about!'

Olly will come round. Ash needs to play for time. Is he wrong to want to protect his son when his son has killed someone? Does it make a difference, morally, that Olly didn't plan to kill Josh? It wasn't a premeditated crime – Olly only meant to scare Joshua into telling him the truth. Does it make a difference that the world is a better place – and the women in it better off – with Joshua Knoll six feet under?

'How about I give him a ring later and sound him out?' Ash suggests. 'We could talk through what would happen. Hypothetically.'

Olly lets out a sigh. It sounds like relief rather than frustration. Or is that just Ash's wishful thinking?

'Yeah. All right,' Olly says. 'Good idea.'

His answer gives Ash a flicker of hope. Just as he'd thought. His son has spoken rashly and he's already having second thoughts. Ash should have asked for Roly's advice months ago. His advice as a best friend, not as a police officer. Ash takes a sip of his coffee, and then sets down the mug, grimacing. It's revolting. He can't drink it. He steals a glance at Olly. He's so proud of his son. Does Olly know how proud he is of him? He's about to tell him, but Olly speaks before Ash can.

'So, you wanna make a start on the bathroom?' Olly gives him a quick smile, but it looks forced and quickly capsizes.

'You don't have to,' Ash says. 'It's not urgent.' He tries to sound upbeat, but he feels a bit like crying. He can't remember the last time he cried. Carla crying earlier nearly set him off. And now Olly's clearly upset even though he's trying to put a brave face on it. He can't bear for his family to be sad.

'I want to. But I haven't got long. Like I said.'

'OK. Well, let's do this!'

Olly fetches Ash's portable Bluetooth speaker and connects his phone to stream a playlist through it.

'What is this?' Ash asks after a while, more to make conversation than out of interest. It's awful, in Ash's opinion, loud and monotonous, worse even than Carla's opera music.

'Rap,' his son informs him. 'Drake. What do you think?'

'Yeah,' Ash says, 'groovy.'

Olly rolls his eyes and Ash feels old. He has given up trying to speak his son's language. He has given up, too, trying to convert Olly to music from the Eighties, which is all Ash ever listens to himself. By choice anyway.

They've been working for about an hour, Ash removing the tiles on one wall with a hammer and chisel and Olly sanding down the wall opposite – when a car horn sounds from outside. Ash hardly registers it over the music and the racket they're making, but Olly drops everything and rushes to the front door to greet Liv. Olly's a mess, but he doesn't seem to care. He washes his hands in the kitchen – Ash has cut off the water in the downstairs loo — and brushes down his jeans with his hands, which dirties them again without visibly improving the state of his jeans. As he says goodbye to Ash, Olly's face is still stippled grey with dust, and tufts of his blond hair, also speckled with grey, stick up like antennae.

Liv doesn't seem to mind Olly's scruffiness, so Ash doesn't say anything. In fact, she's smiling. It's the first time Ash has seen her looking genuinely happy for a while.

'Liv and I will be back before dinner,' Olly says. ''Bout five-ish.'

Ash watches from the open doorway as Liv and Olly get into her Nissan Micra — Ash learnt to drive in one of those, albeit a much older model, decades ago. Unlike Olly, who passed his test on his first go and crashed his car a month or so later, it took Ash three attempts to pass his driving test, but he has never had an accident. He thinks back to Roly's accident, years ago, when they were at uni, and wonders how Tracey is now. Does she still walk with a limp after all these years? Does Roly ask himself the same question?

He's still observing them when Olly leaps back out of the car and runs up to him.

'Don't tell Liv what we were talking about earlier,' he says, looking over his shoulder, as if to check she's well out of earshot. 'I'll tell her when we've spoken to Ian, when we know, like, what to expect if ... you know. Liv will blame herself. I haven't told her anything. Ring Ian, though, yeah? Promise?'

It's not very coherent, but Ash gets the general idea. 'Yes, I promise, if you're sure that's what you want,' he says.

'Yeah. But, like, a hypothetical convo, yeah? Like you said.'

Ash has forgotten his exact words, but he definitely didn't phrase it quite like that. 'No problem, Olly,' he says. 'Go and have some fun.'

'Oh, we're not going out for fun,' Olly says. 'We've got jobs and stuff to do.'

'Jobs?'

'Yeah, like, chores.'

'What? Who for?'

But if Olly hears him, he doesn't answer. He has already turned away and raises one hand in a wave without looking back at Ash.

Ash closes the front door and walks slowly into the kitchen, where he pours himself a glass of water and guzzles it down thirstily. He'd be very surprised if Olly had any errands to do. It's more likely an excuse to get out of doing any more DIY. Ash sighs. Then he slides his phone out of the back pocket of his jeans and, before he can change his mind and break his promise to Olly, he rings Roly.

Chapter 41

Carla

NOW

I'm sitting at the kitchen table, neck-deep in work, when my mobile rings. I hate being interrupted when I'm working and I occasionally switch off my phone altogether when I need to concentrate, but I don't like to do that if the kids are out, which is the case today. Margo's at her friend Ellie's Hallowe'en party – I've done a great job with the face paint to go with her witch's costume, though I say it myself. Iris has gone for a swim with a friend – not Mille, who comes up in a rash whenever she comes into contact with chlorine, but a boy in her English class called Tom Fischer whom Iris has mentioned a few times lately. And Olly has gone to Barnstaple.

I glance at the caller ID. It's Jo. It won't be urgent, so I decide to call her back later – I don't want to lose my train of thought – and I let the phone ring out. I went for a walk earlier with Cheddar – it did us both a lot of good – but I need to get on with my work now. But my mobile immediately starts ringing again. I look at the screen a second time. It's Jo once more. Maybe it is urgent, after all. Or maybe she just really wants a chat.

Leaning back in my office chair, which I've wheeled into the kitchen from my study, I swipe to take the call. 'Hey, Jo,' I say, careful not to let any exasperation seep into my voice. 'How are you?'

'Carla, oh my God, I don't know how to say this. I think ... unless I'm mistaken ...' Jo sounds distraught. I hear her take a deep breath. 'Do you know where Iris is?' she asks.

'Iris? Why?' I look at the clock on the kitchen wall. It stopped long ago. I pull my mobile away from my ear and check the time. Half five. 'She's probably on her way back from the pool in Barnstaple right now. What on earth's the matter, Jo?'

'Would she take the link road?'

'Probably. Why? What's going on?' I'm getting impatient now and my sense of unease is growing.

'There's a car ... overturned ... on the link road. And I saw ... I saw a car ... the car looked a lot like Yvonne's. I mean, I don't know what Yvonne's car looks like, but I'm almost certain she was at the wheel.'

'Who was at the wheel? Yvonne?' My voice comes out high-pitched. 'Jo, what are you talking about?'

'Listen, I don't want to cause you alarm unnecessarily—'

'It's a bit late for that!'

'—so I'll ring Ian and see what he can find out and then ring you back.'

'No! No! Don't hang up on me! Jo! Jo, just tell me—'

'I'll ring you straight back. I promise.'

I'm torn between keeping the phone line clear and ringing Iris. I get up and pace up and down, phone in hand, and then I call Iris. But it goes straight to voicemail.

It seems like an eternity before Jo rings me back. I answer without registering the caller ID.

'Hi, Mum.' It's not Jo. It's Iris. For a few seconds, I'm so stunned I can't say anything. 'Mum, you rang. I'm returning your call?' she says. Her intonation rises, as if she's asking me a question.

'Iris! Where are you?'

'We're on our way home.'

'You're not—'

'I'm not driving, no, Mum,' she says. 'Tom is.' I imagine her rolling her eyes at Tom Fischer.

That's not what I was going to ask, although I do warn Iris all the time not to touch her phone while she's driving. I was going to ask if she was hurt. The aborted conversation with Jo, if you can even call it a conversation, has caused all sorts of wild ideas to streak through my head. Jo said something about an overturned car and she mentioned Yvonne, but it wasn't clear to me if she meant that Yvonne had flipped her car. If so, why did she ask where Iris was?

'OK,' I say. 'Go slowly.'

'I'm not the one driving, Mum,' she reminds me. 'And we are going slowly, like really slowly. We're stuck behind a tractor.' She giggles.

'Are you on the link road?'

'No. There was a sign up to say it's closed.'

'Why's the link road closed?'

'How should I know?' she says. I need to get Iris off the phone and get hold of Jo, find out what's going on. 'Are you all right, Mum?' Her tone has softened.

'Yes, sweetie.' I force myself to sound normal. 'I'll see you when you get home.'

I end the call with my daughter and try Jo once, but it goes straight to voicemail. I resume my pacing, but some of the tension has left my shoulders. Whatever spooked Jo, it was a false alarm. Iris is fine. I try to piece together the snippets Jo gave me. An overturned car. Yvonne at the wheel. Where does Iris fit in? It doesn't make sense. What's taking Jo so long?

The ringtone doesn't even sound on my mobile when Jo finally gets back to me – I answer the phone as soon as I see her name flash up on the screen.

'I've just spoken to Iris,' I say. 'She's on her way home after a swim with a friend. They're not on the link road.' It all comes out in a gush. 'What's going on, Jo?'

'Oh, thank goodness,' she says. I hear her sigh with relief and a wave of relief breaks over me, too. 'Well, I *am* on the link road and there has been an accident.'

'A car accident?'

'Yes. The traffic is completely stationary in front of me and behind me. But seconds after we came to a standstill, this car came racing through on the other side of the road, swerving all over the place and I could have sworn it was Yvonne Knoll. It was the last car to come through from the other direction. It's all blocked in both directions now.'

'That's strange.'

'I know!'

'But I don't get it. Why did you ask about Iris?'

'Oh, well, it looked like her car, you see.'

I really don't see. 'Hang on, Jo. I'm missing an episode. So, you're saying that a driver that looked like Yvonne was driving a car that looked like Iris's?'

'No. Yvonne was driving her SUV. When I realized we weren't going anywhere any time soon, I got out of my car – loads of us did – and went to see what the problem was. There are only about ten cars in front of me and then there's the one that crashed. It has somehow ended up right in the middle of the road, upside down, with bits of it – metal and glass and rubber – all over both sides of the road. It's a really bad crash. The car has folded like an omelette. And, oh God, I thought it was Iris. There were people everywhere, trying to help, I think, and I couldn't get any closer. I was a bit scared to see any more, to be honest, so I came back to my own car to …' I can hear sirens through the phone and the last part of what Jo says is drowned out by the din. 'The police and ambulance have arrived,' Jo says then, a little unnecessarily, if you ask me.

The noise quietens, but doesn't disappear completely. 'What made you think it was Iris's car?' I ask Jo.

'It just looked like her car, that's all. A light-blue Twingo, the same car and the same colour.'

'Powder blue,' I say. 'There's quite a few of them on the road.' I've realized this since Ash bought the car for Iris.

'And it had that green "P" plate on the back.'

'What?' My legs buckle under me and I grab the worktop to stop myself from falling to the floor.

'You know, that magnetic sticker with the green "P" for drivers who have just passed their test. There was one stuck on the boot of the car.'

Blood rushes through my ears and I can hardly make out a word Jo's saying. The same make, model and colour. That could be a coincidence. But the probationary plates, too? I drop my phone to the floor as fear paralyses my whole body. It's Iris's car. It has to be.

But Olly was the one driving it. He was taking it to the garage in Barnstaple.

Chapter 42

Ash

NOW

He has made headway in the loo slash bathroom downstairs and he's feeling proud of himself – conceited, really, if he's honest – when he peels off his filthy DIY clothes and goes upstairs to take a shower. He has no idea what time it is, but he must have worked most of the afternoon. He checks the red digits of the alarm clock in his bedroom. It's nearly 6 p.m. Shouldn't Olly be home by now? Ash could have sworn Olly said he'd be home by five. Once he has pulled on some clean clothes, he goes back down to the kitchen, where he has left his mobile charging, to give Olly a ring and find out where he's got to. It would be just like his son to change his plans and forget to tell him.

He has three missed calls and a voicemail. All from Carla. He listens to the message, but it's garbled and he can't make out much of it. Something about a car accident on the link road. Carla mentions Iris, Olly, Jo and, strangely, Yvonne, and so he can't work out who – if any of them – is involved in the crash.

Carla sounds absolutely frantic, which makes him panic, although he tells himself not to get worked up until he knows what has happened. He tries to ring her, but he can't get through. Maybe she's on the phone to someone else.

He puts on his shoes, jumps into his car and drives – much faster than usual – to Crooked Oak Cottage, hoping that's where she is. On the way, he instructs Siri to call Olly. But Olly isn't answering either, which does nothing to calm Ash's nerves. He reasons with himself, aloud. Olly spends that much time on his mobile, you'd think his hands were surgically attached to the damn thing, and yet he hardly ever answers when Ash calls him. Carla's always whingeing about that, too. So if Ash can't get hold of Olly, it's not necessarily a cause for alarm.

He skids to a halt in the driveway of Crooked Oak Cottage and flings off his seatbelt. Carla opens the front door before he reaches it. She's ashen and her eyes are red-rimmed, as if she's been crying. She holds open the door for him to come inside.

'What's going on?' Ash asks, kicking the door closed behind him.

'There's been a car accident on the link road. I think it's Olly,' Carla gushes, 'in Iris's car.'

Ash frowns. Olly left his place with Liv, in her car. 'Carla, I don't think—'

'I asked him to take Iris's car to the garage. And then Jo rang to say a car, just like Iris's, had been involved in a bad crash.'

'*Like* Iris's?' Ash echoes.

'Yes. A powder blue Twingo.'

'Loads of people have—'

'With green "P" plates.'

'Oh. Oh God.' That does sounds like Iris's car. Ash tries to come up with an alternative scenario, as much for himself as for Carla. 'Are you sure Olly took the car in?'

'Yes.'

'Did you see him drive off in it? Only, he left my place with

Liv. In her car. At around lunchtime.'

But even before Carla answers, Ash remembers why Olly left. He had to run some errands. Ash thought it was an excuse, but it looks like Olly was telling the truth after all.

'Yes, to take in Iris's car.' Carla's voice is a mixture of impatience and fear. 'I asked him to do it. He had to take it in for two this afternoon. I went for a walk with Cheddar and when I got back, Olly had left with the car.'

They're still standing in the hallway. Ash leads Carla into the kitchen. He gets her seated at the table and then pours her a glass of water. He sits down next to her. She sips from the glass, holding it in one hand while she clutches her mobile in the other.

What should they do next? Ash's heart is pounding and he feels light-headed. He imagines Olly at the wheel of Iris's car, thinking about handing himself in for murdering Josh and allowing himself to be distracted while he's at the wheel. Olly is heavy-footed on the accelerator at the best of times.

He already knows Olly isn't answering his phone. 'Have you rung Liv?' he asks Carla.

'I've rung everyone I can think of,' Carla says. 'Jo rang me and she was going to ring Ian. I've rung Iris. She's on her way home. And Olly, Liv and Daniel aren't answering. Daniel went out for a bike ride. I couldn't get hold of Jo again either. She's probably on the phone to Ian.'

And with that, Carla bursts into tears. Ash puts his arm around her shoulders and pulls her in close. 'Try not to worry,' he says. He can hear the panic in his voice. He should take his own advice before he makes things worse. He clears his throat. 'I'll ring Roly.' He wants to do something useful, but it's the only thing he can think of to do.

'Ash.' Roly answers straightaway and Ash sighs with relief. He needs his best friend. And if anyone can find out what's going on, Roly can.

'I'm at Crooked Oak Cottage,' Ash manages. 'Jo rang Carla—'

'I'm on my way to Carla's right now,' Roly says. Ash has loads of questions for him, but before he can ask them, Roly adds, 'I'll be there as soon as I can. In the meantime, can you text me the registration number of Iris's car?'

'Yes, but Roly …'

'Yes?'

'Iris isn't in the car—'

'Thank God for that.'

'—Olly is.'

'Shit.' There's a long pause. 'I'm on my way,' Roly repeats at length. 'Try not to worry. It's probably not even Iris's car. Hopefully, this is all a false alarm.'

Ash manages to grunt a reply before he ends the call. Carla has to hunt out the papers for the Twingo so he can send Roly the plate number.

It's only when he has sent the message that he remembers Carla mentioning Yvonne in the voicemail message she left him. What the hell does Yvonne have to do with anything? He has no idea why this has suddenly come back to him now, but he is engulfed by a wave of intense fear.

Chapter 43

Ian

NOW

Ian swears as a tractor appears out of nowhere. He brakes hard and almost skids into it because the ground is wet from the rain. He has to reverse several metres to a lay-by to let the farmer past. Ian has lived in North Devon for most of his adult life, and he's used to navigating his way along these narrow, tortuous lanes, bounded by tall hedges that conceal any oncoming traffic, including wily tractors. He's used to the rain – sure, it rains a lot in Derry, too. But he needs to drive more slowly. Especially around these bends and especially in the pouring rain. He needs to get to Crooked Oak Cottage in one piece or he'll be of no use to the Ashfords at all. Another car crash is the last thing anyone needs today. The tractor passes, the farmer raising his hand in thanks.

Ian has already spoken to DC Ward – Gail. She's trying to find out more about the accident. Jo couldn't give him the make and model of Yvonne's car when he asked her (she only knew it was an SUV), so Ian is clinging to the hope that his wife has misidentified the car that crashed on the link road, too. It's probably not Iris's car at all, just as he told Ash. It might even turn out to be a different colour, knowing Jo. Until he has more info, he's trying to think about something else (anything else) so that he doesn't give in to paranoia. North Devon, his family, Derry. He looks out of the window, all around him, trying to distract himself. Cows in that field; two people walking their dog across another.

It's not working. He's stressed out; there's no denying that. He glances at the speedometer and eases up on the accelerator, drumming his fingers on the steering wheel. He's never needed a cigarette more in his life. Christ, even a roll-up would do. How long is it going to take Gail to ring him back?

No sooner has he had that thought than his ringtone blares out through the car speakers. The caller ID comes up on the dashboard infotainment screen. He reaches out and taps the green button, far harder than necessary.

'Hi, Ian,' Gail says. 'So, I've managed to contact an officer at the scene with the registration plate you gave me.' She's getting straight to the point, which Ian appreciates. 'It's a match for your goddaughter's car, I'm afraid.'

Ian swears.

'She wasn't driving. It was a male driver.'

'Yes,' Ian says. 'Her brother.'

'Oh. Oh, dear God. I've got bad news, I'm afraid, Ian. The driver … um … lost his life in the accident. From what I've been told, he was dead before the ambulance got there. He was probably killed instantly in the crash.'

Ian doesn't speak for several seconds. Gail says nothing for a moment either, clearly giving Ian a moment to digest that piece of information as best he can. He knows she has tried to cushion it as best she can. Olly is dead, but he didn't suffer. But it's impossible to sugar-coat something like this.

Eventually, Gail says, 'I'm terribly sorry to have to be the one to tell you, Ian. I will let you know as soon as I have more information.'

'Thank you, Gail,' he manages.

He ends the call just as he arrives at Crooked Oak Cottage and pulls into the driveway. How on earth is he going to break that news to the Ashfords? He'll have to witness them going through another ordeal, this one far worse than the previous one. He doesn't want to be the one to do it. Technically, it's not his role. But it will be better coming from him than some PC they've never met. Or worse, the PC that Iris dislikes so much.

Ian sits in the car for a minute or two, putting off the moment for as long as possible. Jo pulls into the driveway and parks behind him. He has to start up the car again and inch forwards so she has enough space. There are six vehicles parked in front of the house now – Carla's, Ash's and Daniel's cars as well as his and Jo's. And a Nissan Micra. Ian has no idea who it belongs to. Only Iris's car is missing.

He and Jo don't seem to have attracted the attention of anyone in the house, so, before they go inside, Ian tells Jo about his conversation with Gail. Jo goes white and Ian thinks her pallor must mirror his own.

When he can't put it off any longer, he knocks and goes inside without waiting for someone to come and open the door. Jo follows him.

Chapter 44

Carla

NOW

Shellshocked. I can't think of any other way to describe it when Ian tells us the news. I knew before he said it. He made us all sit down first and that's when it hit me. Someone – I think it's Jo – brings me a weak, sugary tea and encourages me to drink it, but my hands are shaking too much. I hear wailing and I'm not sure if it's me or Iris. Perhaps it's both of us in chorus.

Time seems to have stopped. I have no idea how long we all sit in the living room – Ash; Iris; her friend, Tom, who is sitting on the floor because the armchairs and sofas are taken; Jo; Ian and me. Some of us – maybe all of us – are crying. I hear Ian – or maybe Ash – ask Jo about Yvonne. I can hear voices, but muffled, as if I'm sinking underwater. My lungs feel as if they're full of water, too.

'She was there. I saw her drive away. Like a madwoman. In her SUV. I told you.'

'But you don't even know the make and model of her car.' Definitely Ian this time, although he is speaking in a whisper and what he's saying isn't really registering. I can hear the words, but they don't make any sense to me.

'I know Yvonne! I recognized her!' Jo raises her voice. She's not shouting, but until now the little that has been said has been spoken in hushed tones, and it stuns us all into silence. The wailing stops. Finally.

'D'you think Yvonne caused the crash?' Ash. He's next to me, holding me or holding on to me. I'm not sure if he's keeping me afloat or if it's the other way round. I'm clinging to him as if I'm drowning and he's my life raft.

'I don't know.'

'They'll check traffic cameras and ask for dashcam footage,' Ian says. 'Would Yvonne know Iris's car? I mean, Iris hasn't had it that long.'

'I d-drove … Iris's car when I went to Hilltop House … that d-day,' I manage to say. I'm nowhere near as coherent as Ash, although his voice is unrecognizable. No one asks why I went there.

'Could Yvonne have done this … deliberately?' Ash asks Ian.

'Perhaps she thought Iris was the one driving,' Jo adds, her voice barely a whisper. 'She may have cut her up or run her off the road or something.'

'Let's not jump to conclusions,' Ian says.

He hasn't finished, but the rest of what he says is lost to me. I'm having trouble concentrating, my mind numb to everything except the pain I'm feeling.

I'm not sure what we're waiting for, who we're waiting for. Someone to come and confirm it officially? Someone to take Ash and me to identify Olly?

I start crying again, less loudly this time, but just as uncontrollably. Ash holds me tighter. Tom leans forwards and hands me a tissue. I squeeze it up in my hand.

Karma. What goes around comes around. Olly killed Josh. And now he's … oh, God, is my son really dead? Is that why he's dead?

Is it karma? Or is it payback? Did Yvonne do this on purpose?

There's someone at the door. It must be whoever we've been waiting for. But they don't knock. I hear the front door close. Someone's inside the house now. There are voices, chatting, loudly. Two people, insouciant, unaware of the drama playing out in here. Recognizing one of voices, I whirl round, looking over my shoulder. The sudden movement makes my head spin and for a split second, I think I may pass out.

I feel the blood drain from my face. I'm sure I was pale before, but now I must look as if I've just seen a ghost. For a moment, I wonder if I have. Liv has just walked into the sitting toom, and behind her, his hands in his pockets, is Olly.

'Olly!' Iris jumps to her feet and throws herself into her brother's arms.

'Whooaa,' he says, with a little laugh, as he stumbles backwards.

'Olly?' Ash sounds as bewildered – and relieved – as I feel.

'Olly, d-d-didn't you take Iris's c-car in?' I stutter. I want to stand up, run to my son, but I can't feel my legs and don't trust them to take me the short distance to him.

'No, sorry. I completely forgot,' Olly says, looking sheepish. He clearly hasn't picked up on the funereal vibes in the room. 'We had to do shopping and stuff for Liv's gran.'

Liv is more perceptive. 'Are you OK, Carla?' she asks. 'Wh-what's wrong?'

Some of the feeling comes back into my legs and I feel less dizzy, as if the haze that had descended on my brain is lifting. As I stand up, there's a rush of tiny stars to my head, but Ash has stood, too, and stops me from falling. Together, we make our way over to Iris and Olly, who has barely stepped over the threshold into the living room. The four of us hug and I never want to let go.

'What's going on, Mum? Dad?'

Ian is the one who explains. 'There's been a car accident,' he says. 'A fatal one. We thought you … we thought you were …'

My brain kicks into gear. Was it a coincidence? Jo didn't even know the make or model of Yvonne's car. Maybe she got it wrong for Iris's car, too. But then I remember Iris's car isn't in the driveway. And didn't Ian say something about the registration number being a match? I get there at the same time as Olly spells it out for me.

'Daniel sent me a text to say he would take the car to the garage. 'Cos I'd obviously forgotten.' And then it dawns on him, too. 'Oh, shit. Oh, no.'

Iris breaks the ensuing silence. 'Where's Margo?' she asks.

I find myself flanked by Jo and Ash, who take an elbow each and sit me back down on the sofa again. I'm still so relieved that Olly is here, alive, that I haven't computed the fact I've lost Daniel yet. 'She's at Ellie's Hallowe'en party.' I pick up my mobile from the coffee table and check the time. 'I should have picked her up half an hour ago.'

'I'll go,' Olly offers.

'No!' Ash and I shout at the same time.

'I'll go. I'm parked in the road, blocking everyone in.' It's Iris's friend. Tom Fischer. His name comes back to me now.

'I'll come with you,' Iris says.

'No, you stay with your mum,' Ash says. 'I'll—'

'I'll go with Tom,' Jo says firmly. I think she must know him from school. Perhaps he was one of her pupils. 'Carla needs you both here. Brayworthy, right?'

'Coombe Farm,' Ian says.

I look up, surprised. Then I remember how he knows that. Margo was supposed to be at her friend Ellie's house when Daniel and I reported her missing. And suddenly, I feel overwhelmed. Iris's video. Joshua's murder. Margo's disappearance. My partner's ... I can't even say it in my head. I can't take any more.

Chapter 45

Ash

<u>NOW</u>

Daniel's dead. The police have been and gone. Carla will probably have to formally identify Daniel's body, of course, but Daniel had ID on him and, this time, there's no doubt. Time has trundled by and it's late now. The evening's stress and shocks have been enervating for everyone. Tom and Liv have both left, promising to check in the following morning. Jo has put a tearful Margo to bed, in Carla's bed – Margo insisted. Jo's still upstairs. She promised Margo she'd stay with her until Carla came up. Ash doesn't know whether Carla will go to bed tonight. She has barely moved from the sofa for hours. He'll stay here either way. He'll stay up with Carla if she doesn't turn in and he'll sleep on the sofa if she does.

Roly has been here all this time, except for a few minutes, when he popped to the Grove to buy a packet of cigarettes. He and Ash are standing in the porch, sheltering from the rain. Roly is on his second cigarette. Ash bums one off him, but after two or three puffs, it makes him feel sick, so he stops smoking, letting the cigarette burn down to the butt.

'I keep thinking about Yvonne's role in all of this,' Ash says. 'What if she thought Iris was driving? She's convinced Iris killed Josh. Maybe Yvonne wanted to scare Iris.' Ash pictures Yvonne driving too close to Iris's car, or overtaking and cutting in, causing Daniel to brake and swerve off the road.

'It's possible,' Roly says. 'The police will check it out. There will be witnesses, for sure – people who were on the link road and saw more than Jo did. I can call in a few favours and keep you updated. OK?'

'Thanks. I appreciate it.'

'Now's probably not the right time, mate,' Roly says, his tone indicating he's keen to change the subject, 'but you left me a message earlier. What was it you wanted to discuss?'

It takes Ash a moment to work out what Roly's referring to. Olly wanted Ash to ask Roly – hypothetically – what would happen to him if he confessed to murdering Joshua Knoll. 'Oh, it was nothing. Really.' Ash makes a dismissive gesture with his hand. 'Nothing important.'

As Roly stubs out his cigarette, he hands the packet to Ash. 'Keep that. Or throw it out. I was doing well, you know. Temporary blip. I'll carry on giving up now.'

'Good for you,' Ash says.

They've come outside without coats. Ash, who doesn't usually feel the cold, is shivering. But he's in no hurry to go back inside. The atmosphere in the house is understandably oppressive. Roly doesn't seem to be in any rush either.

'You can take off, if you like,' Ash says. 'Not much more we can do tonight.'

'I'll wait for Jo,' Roly says. 'I mean, we've come in separate cars, but I'll wait for her.'

'I never liked the bloke,' Ash says, speaking his thoughts out loud, 'but this is awful. I wouldn't have wished this on him. Not ever.'

Daniel sank further in Ash's estimation the day he rang Roly on the pretext of thanking him for his help finding Margo. Roly didn't actually do anything in the end – Margo had been located. And Ash knows the real reason for the call. Daniel was going to shop Iris. Daniel was convinced – as was Carla – that Iris had killed Joshua Knoll. Daniel's betrayal is unforgivable, but he didn't deserve to die for it.

'I wasn't fond of him either,' Roly admits.

'Poor Carla. Poor Margo,' Ash says.

'Poor wee mite,' Roly agrees. 'First her mother, then her father.'

When they go back inside, Iris tells Ash that Carla has gone to bed. Iris clears up the mugs in the living room while Olly gets an umbrella to take the dog out for a wee. Jo and Roly get ready to leave.

'We'll be back first thing tomorrow morning,' Jo says as she pushes her feet into her shoes and puts on her coat in the hallway.

Ash follows Iris from the living room into the kitchen, where she loads the mugs into the dishwasher. It strikes him as incongruous, what she's doing, as if it's too soon for life to go on after such a big shock. He admires her ability to take charge, even of such a mundane task. His daughter is more than capable of keeping the household going until Carla can cope.

'Are you all right?' Ash asks Iris.

'Yeah. I'm in shock, like everyone else, but—' she looks around her and lowers her voice '—I'm so relieved it wasn't Olly.' She lowers her head, too, almost as though she has said something wrong. Ash nods. He couldn't agree more. 'Night, Dad.' She pecks him on the cheek.

'Goodnight, darling,' Ash says, enveloping her in a big hug.

Ash is the only one left downstairs. He waits for Olly to come back in with Cheddar. He'll check everything is locked up before he tries to make himself comfortable on the sofa. There's a guest room upstairs, but he doesn't suppose the bed is made up and he doesn't want to trouble anyone.

Ash hears the front door open and close, then Cheddar comes into the kitchen, his claws click-clacking on the tiles. Cheddar turns round and round, nose to tail, several times in his bed before dropping down onto it. He looks up at Ash with large brown eyes, his head on his paws, and sighs.

'Know how you feel, Cheddar,' Ash says, bending down to stroke the dog.

'Dad?'

Ash didn't hear Olly come into the kitchen in his socks. Straightening up, Ash turns to face his son.

'About what we were discussing earlier. You know, when I asked you to call Ian?'

Ash waits, but it's apparently his turn to speak. 'I rang Roly,' he says, 'and left him a message. We haven't discussed the ... matter any further.'

What he's doing is illegal; Ash is well aware of that. He has covered for his son all this time. He has actively dissuaded him from going to the police. Olly wanted to do the right thing; Ash is preventing him from doing that. He can't really see what's right and what's wrong anymore. All he knows is, he has to hold his family together at all costs.

'Listen, Olly, your mum has just lost her partner,' Ash continues. 'She can't possibly lose her son right now. You can't give yourself in.' Ash doesn't add what he's thinking. *Especially if Daniel has died because Yvonne somehow caused the crash.*

'Yeah,' Olly says. 'That's what I thought. I did something bad, though. And I want to do something good. You know, to make up for that. Sort of ... atone.'

'I think that's ...'

Ash breaks off, catching sight of Iris, standing in the doorway. How much of the conversation has she overheard? Enough to grasp what they're talking about?

'Er ... Dad, I just came down to tell you that I'll sleep in Margo's bed and you can have mine. I've changed the sheets for you.'

'Oh. Thank you, Iris. That's very kind of you,' Ash says.

Iris comes closer to Olly and Ash. To Olly she says, 'I can't lose you either, bro. And Margo needs her big brother, too. Now more than ever.'

That night, Ash lies wide awake in Iris's bed. He's exhausted and he's comfortable, but sleep eludes him. He can't get the day's events out of his mind. The confused phone call from Carla, the fear and devastation when they thought they'd lost Olly, the shock of Daniel's death. All the emotions of the past few hours are still whirring round inside him, tangled and chaotic. Sleep, when it does come, is sporadic and turbulent.

Epilogue

Iris

NOW: NOVEMBER 2025

It's been a year to the day since Daniel died. Iris takes Margo – in her mum's car – to the florist's in South Molton to choose some flowers, then she drives to St John the Baptist's church in Brayworthy and parks right in front of it. She puts her arm around Margo, who carries the flowers with both hands, hugging them to her to protect them from the wind. They make their way to Daniel's grave, next to his father's.

Margo kneels down, beside Daniel's grave, like she doesn't care about the wet grass, and chatters away, filling her dad in on all the minutiae of her life since she last came to talk to him a few weeks ago. Iris clocks the fresh flowers in one of the permanent metal vases at the base of the headstone. Mrs Duffy, Daniel's mother, has clearly been here today or yesterday. Iris takes Margo's bouquet and arranges the flowers in the other vase. Then she takes a step back to give Margo some privacy.

Josh is buried in this churchyard somewhere, but Iris hasn't looked for his grave. She still feels a mixture of anger and sadness when she thinks about him. She tries not to think about him at all, but it's weird knowing that part of who she is today is because of him. Because of what he did to her. Perhaps Liv feels the same way. And Sasha. Iris doesn't believe Josh would ever have changed. No matter how many last chances he was given.

Iris looks at Margo, then at Daniel's headstone. *Daniel Duffy. Loving father, partner and stepfather*, it reads. *Died 1st November 2024. Aged 51 years. Gone, but not forgotten.* He wasn't the best stepdad in the world and Iris wouldn't want to speak ill of the dead, or whatever, but he was totally useless after that video of her went viral. She could have done with his support – or, at least, without his criticism – and Mum really needed him. But Iris misses Daniel even so. She misses his tuneless humming, his cooking and his dad jokes. And she can't even begin to imagine what it must be like for Margo, losing her dad as well as her mum. Mum and Jo keep going on about how resilient kids are and they're not wrong. Margo has been really strong.

For a while, they were worried they would lose Margo. Margo's aunt Paula – Daniel's sister-in-law – wanted to take Margo to live with her and her family in Loggerheads, a place Iris had never heard of, which is apparently up north somewhere – in Staffordshire, if Iris remembers correctly. In the end, though, everyone thought it best not to uproot Margo. Plus, Paula and her husband already had four kids. Her husband wasn't keen to take on anyone else's children, even if she was family. Mum and Paula are planning to get together, so that Margo can get to know her cousins. Paula herself, who didn't 'see eye to eye with Daniel' hasn't seen her niece since her sister – Margo's mother – died, but they've started FaceTiming. Mum's looking into adopting Margo officially with Paula's support.

Yvonne was charged with causing death by dangerous driving and failing to stop, or something like that. The police couldn't prove it was deliberate. She rammed into the back of Iris's car, causing Daniel to lose control of the vehicle. Yvonne claimed it was a moment of inattention. She said she hadn't recognized Iris's car. Iris doesn't believe a word of it. Nor does Mum. It took nine months for Yvonne's case to go to court. She was given a four-year prison sentence and she's been disqualified from driving for eight years. Iris guesses that means she won't be able to drive for another four years after she gets out of prison. Or maybe she'll get out early. Everyone says Yvonne got off lightly.

Olly and Iris both passed their A levels. Iris's grades were actually quite good and Olly's were excellent. Olly has gone to university – Bristol – to study medicine. He wants to become a doctor and save lives. He's really helpful around the house when he comes home during the holidays, which is totally unlike him. Mum says it won't last. Olly's also been helping Dad with a load of DIY projects. They finished the downstairs bathroom at Dad's place months ago, but they're always working on something or other at Mayflower Farm or at Crooked Oak Cottage. Olly was always kind, but since Daniel died and Dad persuaded him not to tell anyone what really happened in Buryknoll Wood, he has practically become a saint. Even though he's really busy with his studies, he does volunteer work for the Red Cross at public events and he has been talking about taking a gap year when he has graduated and applying for a medical volunteer project abroad. Olly probably feels bad about Daniel's death, too, even though it definitely wasn't his fault. Olly and Liv are still together – Liv's studying at the University of Bath, so they're not far away from each other.

Mum is doing well. It took a while for her to smile again, but lately Iris has heard her laughing. Mum has learnt to cook a few more dishes since Daniel died. She still works as a freelance editor, but she avoids taking on crime fiction – she says there has been more than enough drama in her life. She goes for long walks every single day, whatever the weather, across Exmoor with Cheddar. Iris goes with her when she can.

Dad's round at Crooked Oak Cottage a lot. As Mum says, he's always been there to catch her when she falls. Mum pitches in with the DIY stuff, too. She says it's like old times. They take it in turns to choose music to listen to while they work. Mum always chooses some awful opera stuff with lyrics no one can understand, but when Dad puts on his Eighties playlists, they both sing along, so it's only marginally better.

Dad's biggest worry is for what might happen once Yvonne gets out of prison. Iris overheard Dad discussing it with Ian. Dad fears the worst. A personal vendetta. A feud between their two families – the Ashfords and the Knolls. Iris hopes he's wrong and that it's all over now.

As for Iris, she got into the University of Nottingham to study English Literature, but she has deferred her entry. For one thing, there's no way Mum could have handled both her and Olly leaving the nest at the same time. Also, Margo needs her big sister. And Iris has been spending *a lot* of time with Dad, setting up a website for victims of cyber sexual abuse. Revenge porn. She wants to share her story and if it makes just one person think twice about sending a nude pic, then it'll be worth it. If it makes just one person think twice about sharing someone else's nudes, then it'll be *totally* worth it. She's using a pseudo and she'll encourage everyone else to do the same. For one thing, she can't use her real name, not now Josh is dead; that would just be cruel. And for another thing, Iris thinks other 'victim-survivors' – to use Melanie's term – might feel more inclined to open up if they don't have to use their true identities. Another week or so and the website should be ready to go live.

Iris has also been spending a lot of time with Tom Fischer. He's deferred his entry to university, too. He wants to gain some professional experience with an internship. He and Iris are getting on really well. Just good friends for the moment. But Iris really likes him and Tom seems to be into her, too. So, who knows? This summer, they're going backpacking together for two whole months around Europe. In the meantime, Iris is working in a supermarket in South Molton. It's boring AF, but she's saving up the money she earns for the trip.

Above all, the gap year is doing Iris a lot of good. She's happier and more confident than she was, but she feels like she needs a bit more time to take stock of everything. She still sees Melanie from time to time, but not as often. She still gets nightmares occasionally, but now she can go back to sleep afterwards, whereas before she would lie awake for the rest of the night. She still wonders every time she meets someone new if they recognize her from her video. But although she knows it's still out there, she's aware that at some point she's got to stop obsessing about it. She's making progress. She's moving forwards. Moving on.

A Letter From The Author

Dear Reader,

Firstly, I'd like to thank you for choosing *A Mother Always Knows* and for reading it. I couldn't be a published author without my readers and I'm incredibly grateful for your support.

A Mother Always Knows is my eighth psychological thriller. I sometimes think it should get easier to write each book, but this one was by far the hardest yet. I work full-time, teaching English in a school on the outskirts of Lyon in France, where I live, and because I write mainly during the weekends and school holidays, it takes me on average fourteen months to get the first draft of each novel done. This doesn't include the month or so I spend planning it, usually while I'm still working on the previous book! *A Mother Always Knows* took me considerably longer. I started writing it in January 2023, after spending two months planning it out in some detail. But 10,000 words in, I started to really struggle with it. So, I stopped, intending to scrap it altogether, and instead, I wrote a completely different book – *The Crime Writer*. I had a lot of fun creating the characters of Matt, the eponymous crime writer, who is suspected of murdering his wife, and Gabi, the journalist who befriends him to try to get the scoop that will launch her career. It was lighter in tone, I love creating unreliable narrators (Matt) and the writing flowed.

Once *The Crime Writer* was done and dusted, I reread the opening to *A Mother Always Knows*. Even though the laws concerning intimate image abuse had changed in the UK by then, I decided I had to carry on with this book. I finally handed in the first draft in May 2025.

One of the reasons it was so challenging to write, I think, is that *A Mother Always Knows* deals with very real fears of mine: on the one hand, how to prepare my teenage children for and protect them from the dangerous world we live in, and, on the other hand, the dangers of the internet. I'm sure many of you will relate to these issues. While absolutely anyone (not only teenagers) can become the victim of an internet scam or revenge porn or cyberbullying to mention just a few of the threats the internet presents, as both a mother and a teacher, I feel I have a role to play that I'm ill-equipped for. I have to warn my kids and my pupils about the dangers of the internet when I didn't grow up with it, when I could easily fall into the same traps myself and when they know far more about the internet than I do. Carla voices my opinion in chapter 37 when she says:

'Our parents warned us not to talk to strangers, to look both ways before crossing the road, to talk to an adult if we were bullied at school. They talked to us about the birds and the bees. They gave us the tools we needed to work our way through life, avoiding most of the potholes. How can we, as adults and as parents, do this in turn for our children? How can we warn them about their use of smartphones when we ourselves didn't have them growing up? Both Olly and Iris are Gen Z kids. By definition, Zoomers have grown up with social media and the internet. My children know far more about digital technology than I do. How can anything I say be credible? We didn't have the date-rape drug when I was growing up either. Yet another problem our children's generation has to deal with. It's not tools

I need to be giving my kids; it's weapons. And it's not potholes they need to avoid; it's craters.'

While my book doesn't suggest an answer to the questions that Carla and I ask ourselves, I hope you, as my readers, will relate to some of the topics I've dealt with and that you will ask yourselves what you would have done in my characters' shoes, whether it be Carla's sensible shoes or Ian's boots or Ash's brogues or Iris's Vans or even Yvonne's high heels. And if you'd like to share your thoughts with me, I'd love to hear from you. I can be contacted through my website or via social media (mainly Instagram and my Facebook author page).

And for my next book, I'm currently working on a 'triple twist serial killer thriller', so much lighter subject matter!

Take care,
Diane
xxx

Intimate Image Abuse: What the law says

In **2015,** according to the Criminal Justice and Courts Act, it became illegal to share intimate sexual images without consent in England and Wales, but the prosecution had to prove 'intent to cause distress'. The maximum penalty was 2 years' imprisonment.

The **2021** Domestic Abuse Act amended the 2015 Act to include the threat to share such images.

The new intimate image abuse laws that came into effect on **31st January 2024** via the Online Safety Act have introduced several changes:

• The prosecution is no longer required to prove intent to cause distress.

• Victims now have lifelong anonymity and can benefit from special measures during trials.

• The new law also criminalizes the sharing of intimate images for sexual gratification.

- The definition of intimate images now includes deep fakes.

- The base offence (sharing images without consent) can carry up to 6 months' imprisonment. More serious offences (sharing with intent to cause distress / for sexual gratification) can carry up to 2 years' imprisonment. In serious cases, culprits may be placed on the sex offenders register.

Unfortunately, there are limitations to the 2015 law. Firstly, the 2015 law is not retroactive, which means that it does not apply to offences committed prior to 31st January 2024. These incidents are dealt with in accordance with the previous 2015 law. Secondly, while sharing or threatening to share intimate images is illegal, the possession of such images (if shared by someone else) is still not a criminal offence under this new law.

Scotland and Northern Ireland have also updated their laws concerning the sharing of intimate images.

More information and help is available on https://revengeporn-helpline.org.uk

Acknowledgements

I'd like to start by thanking my lovely editor Kate Mills. Thank you for your insightful comments, enthusiasm and general bubbliness! This is the second novel I've worked on with you and it has been a lot of fun!

Thank you, too, to the HQ family: Lisa Milton, you are such an inspiration; Lou Nyuar, Abigail Soddy, Grace Marshall, Anna Sikorska, Donna Hillyer. Publishing a book is a team effort and you make up an incredible team of dedicated people. I'm very proud to have eight books published with HQ.

A special shout-out for all the wonderful bloggers who relentlessly spread the word about books on social media. Because of you, I spend an absolute fortune buying books, but thanks to you, I also sell a few of my own, which makes up for it! No, seriously, I'm very grateful for your hard work and unwavering support. There are far too many of you to mention, but, as ever, I do have to name Stu Cummins and Mark Fearn, who, apart from being amazing, are also good friends.

Thank you to my friend Ian Rowland, who made a donation to a charity of my choice to have a character named after him in this book. Rolly, I hope you like your namesake and that you'll forgive me for taking an 'L' out of your nickname to differentiate from 'Olly'. No one who knows me will be surprised to learn that my chosen charity was Guide Dogs UK.

Thank you to my beta readers and writing buddies: Tina Orr Munro, Orlando Murrin, Sarah Clarke and Louise Mangos. A massive thanks to all of you for your help, feedback and friendship. A big thank you to my North Devon and West Buckland School friends, for reading my books and keeping in touch. One of the reasons I write is the connection it allows me with the place I think of as home, so I do appreciate it. A particularly big thank you to Lorraine Rawle and family.

Thank you to all the supportive librarians and booksellers who stock my novels. To the teams at Waterstones Barnstaple, the Barnstaple Library, Waterstones Taunton, the Bookery in Crediton and Waterstones Yeovil, my thanks again on behalf of the *Three Faces of Crime* for hosting our book tour this year.

A massive thank you to my family: my children, Ben, Amélie and Elise; my husband, Flo; and my dog, Cookie – who all live with me and have to put up with me when I'm being creative (and also when I'm not). Thank you, too, to my mum and dad, my uncles and aunts, my cousins and my in-laws, my nephews and nieces in England, Northern Ireland, France and Australia, who read my novels in English and/or in French and who (mostly) say nice things (or, failing that, honest things) about them and who come to my book launches and events. I have the best family!

And, finally, but most importantly, thank YOU for reading this book. I usually say at this point that I hope you enjoyed reading this book as much as I enjoyed writing it, but for a number of reasons this book was really hard to write, so I'll just say that I really hope you enjoyed it, full stop.

Anyway, if you did enjoy it, please consider leaving a (short) review somewhere (Waterstones, Amazon, etc.) or recommending it to a friend or local library or, better still, reading another of my novels. There are seven more to choose from and more on the way!

I love hearing from readers, so please get in touch (via the contact form on my website) or follow me on social media. I'm on X, Bluesky and Facebook, but mainly Instagram. I also occasionally send out newsletters to which you can sign up via my website in order to be the first to know about any promos, events and new releases.

Take care,
Diane
xxx

Reading Group Questions

Warning: Contains spoilers

1. Yvonne wants justice for Josh. She's the one who says, 'A mother always knows.' What do you think of this title? Does it fit the book?

2. Throughout the book, as the evidence against Iris mounts, Carla's suspicions that her daughter has committed murder grow. She believes that anyone is capable of murder if they're pushed hard enough to commit one. Do you think that, as a mother, Carla should have automatically believed in her daughter's innocence?

3. According to Ian, Carla has unofficially diagnosed Joshua as having narcissistic personality disorder. Do you think that the author's portrayal of Josh as a manipulative narcissist is convincing?

4. Carla finds it difficult to know how to warn her Gen Z children about the dangers of the internet and their use of smartphones when she herself didn't have this technology growing up. Do you agree with Carla that teenagers have to navigate their way through more dangers in today's world?

5. Ash acknowledges that in covering for his son, he's breaking the law. He should encourage Olly to go to the police. Instead, he asks Olly not to tell the truth. How does Ash justify his position to himself? And to Olly? Is what Ash does at all justifiable?

6. Carla believes in her own form of karma – 'if you do good deeds, then good things end up happening to you, whereas if you do something bad, you eventually get what's coming to you'. Which of the characters get their comeuppance? Do any of them go unpunished?

7. Daniel calls Ian to 'shop' Iris. Ash sees this as an unforgivable betrayal. Was Daniel right to denounce Iris or do you agree with Ash?

8. Olly has killed a man, but his crime wasn't premeditated and his victim was a 'vile, hateful, evil person', according to Ash. Ash wonders if it makes a difference that 'the world is a better place – and the women in it better off – with Joshua Knoll six feet under'. Do these circumstances mitigate Olly's crime?

9. *A Mother Always Knows* is told from the perspectives of four characters: Carla, Iris, Ash and Ian. Were you invested equally in each of these characters? How did your feelings for each of the characters evolve?

10. Did you find the ending satisfying or shocking?

Gripped by *A Mother Always Knows*?

Don't miss *The Crime Writer* …

He plots perfect murders. Did he commit one?

The Crime Writer is out now!

Why not try *The Other Couple*?

Two couples. A fatal accident. And a decision that changes everything …

The Other Couple is out now!

Dear Reader,
We hope you enjoyed reading this book. If you did, we'd be so appreciative if you left a review. It really helps us and the author to bring more books like this to you.

Here at HQ Digital we are dedicated to publishing fiction that will keep you turning the pages into the early hours. Don't want to miss a thing? To find out more about our books, promotions, discover exclusive content and enter competitions you can keep in touch in the following ways:

JOIN OUR COMMUNITY:
Sign up to our new email newsletter: http://smarturl.it/SignUpHQ
Read our new blog www.hqstories.co.uk

🐦 https://twitter.com/HQStories
f www.facebook.com/HQStories

BUDDING WRITER?
We're also looking for authors to join the HQ Digital family!
Find out more here:

https://www.hqstories.co.uk/want-to-write-for-us/

Thanks for reading, from the HQ Digital team